Curses and Thunder

Sweet Briar Series Book 1

April Gaisford

Triggers and Content

This series contains sexual assault, abortion, infertility, violence, kinks and use of a safe word, homophobia, and death of a family member. This list is not all inclusive.

Your mental health matters. Please read at your own discretion.

Contents

Prologue

Once upon a time, a wealthy kingdom called Sweet Briar spread from the sea to the mountains. The King and Queen ruled the land, and the people were happy and healthy. The forests were lush, and the farmlands were fertile. The villages were well-maintained and hosted many people. The people wanted nothing. The king was kind and just and ruled with warmth and compassion. The Queen was cunning and intelligent, and she searched for ways to improve their kingdom.

After some time, the king and Queen decided they wanted an heir. They spent many years trying to have a child. They prayed to the gods to grant them an heir. They sought healers and herbs and clergymen and witches. Finally, after many, many years of trying, the Queen learned she was with child. The entire kingdom thrummed with excitement. Banquets were planned. Celebrations were had. Everyone gave gifts to the new parents and the baby.

When the baby was born, the king named her Jasmin because she was a gift from the gods. The king raised Jasmin to be kind and see the value in others. He taught her to treasure the people in their castle and kingdom equally. The Queen raised her to be sharp and clever. She taught Jasmin to strive for more and aspire to greatness. The king handled his daughter with love and warmth. The Queen regarded her more coolly, wanting her to be strong.

On her 16th birthday, the king gave Jasmin the key to his personal library. The library included many works of fiction and history. The king wanted her to treasure learning and knowledge to expand her mind. Her mother gifted her with a new white horse named Vesper. The Queen told Jasmin that appearances are important and she must always look her best. The horse came with a new stable hand. The stable hand arrived from a foreign country with his family. He had a wife, a daughter named Dahlia the same age as Jasmin, and a younger boy. Dahlia and Jasmin became quick friends. They spent many days together, exploring the castle and the grounds, reading books, and learning to entertain themselves.

Their relationship grew. They experienced great love and great tragedy. The girls lived a lifetime of joy and heartache in their short time together. Jasmin's life changed significantly with the arrival of the stable hand's family. But her luck would all change with the arrival of a witch and the curse lingering on her lips.

Part One

TRUE LOVE EDICT

Chapter 1

JASMIN

"This really is the best option, milady." Lord Thurston insists. He holds the paper in my direction again, encouraging me to read it. I take the paper, looking it over with a sigh, frustrated with this new edict.

"How will this work? How will I find my true love from 1 or 2 men from each village? How can they love me if they are forced to be here? How could I love them knowing they aren't here willingly?" I toss the paper back, anger rising.

"Princess, they will come willingly. Men will want to be here." Lord Thurston is relentless. The others sit quietly, watching this interaction. Lord Thurston governs the largest village in the kingdom. Vadried is wealthier and has more people than the other five villages. He stands to lose the most if the kingdom collapses. This is the first meeting he's attended without multiple young bachelors. His hope has always been that I would break the curse quickly.

It has been eight years since the curse began. After three years, I stopped holding regular meetings with the village lords. The villages could govern themselves. I only met with the lords to discuss taxes or an occasional problem they needed my oversight on. I hate the politics of it all. For all my mother tried to instill in me, I would love nothing more than to disband the entire royal court.

The kingdom is failing, though. The lands aren't as fertile as they used to be. There is still some life in them, but the fields will be barren within a matter of years. Our cattle aren't reproducing fast enough to keep up with the demand. The villagers are locked inside the kingdom, unable to leave or find other resources. Despite the curse, things have been going well until this past year. Nothing drastic has occurred since the curse settled, but we are seeing the effects of it now. The curse has minimally affected most of the people of my kingdom, for which I am thankful. Even I haven't seen many terrible outcomes due to it. We have reached a turning point where stagnation will worsen the quality of life.

The location of this meeting is bright and airy. The windows allow the late evening sun to shine through while a breeze cools the area. I look around the large table, taking in the ornate details of the room. This castle has been around for centuries. This room is where my father always held court. It's not the space I would have chosen to work in, but the council was already accustomed to it. The start of a curse, a sudden shift in powers, and near chaos isn't the time to insist on meeting in a new room. Since then, I've grown accustomed to the room. My father's presence can still be felt in this space.

"Have we spoken to every witch in the kingdom? Every aspiring witch? What of the scholars? Have they found anything?" If we are going to enact this new edict, I want to be sure every stone has been overturned.

"Yes, your highness." Lord David speaks. "We have spoken to everyone we know. Many are still searching for answers, but none have any. I suspect none are close, either. I know this isn't ideal, but this is the best option for now."

Lord David governs Arkaley. It is the smallest village as far as population goes but has the second largest farmlands. Most people are farmers or laborers, not having much wealth between them. The village is prosperous, with few people in poverty. While their farms are valuable, the lack of other tradable commodities has prevented the territory from increasing its wealth. The produce is great but only turns a small profit after the cost of production. Lord David is older than most of the other Lords. He worked with my father for many years before the curse, and I have known him for most of my life. He is kind and rules justly, and that is what my father valued most in him. He is my favorite of them all. I value his word more than anyone else, and he knows that.

I bristle, exhausted and overwhelmed with this whole situation. Finn, my Great Pyrenees, has his head resting on my lap. He goes everywhere with me. The Lords hate that I allow him in. They insist it isn't proper to allow a dog into the meeting. Nothing is proper anymore. I scratch behind Finn's ears mindlessly. The Lords have presented a new edict for me to send out. This would require each village to send one or two eligible bachelors to stay in the castle with me. The goal is to find true love and break the curse on my kingdom.

I stand, pacing the room, stressed about letting so many bachelors in my space. Another complaint from the advisors. "Royalty should never pace. It's a sign of weakness," they always tout. Finn whimpers as I walk away. My mind functions better when I am moving. Trying to process this edict is no simple task. I snatch the paper off the table, reading over the words again as I pace.

The edict presented to me would allow the men to leave the castle of their own accord or mine. It also requires a replacement for the bachelor if one leaves. This means 5-10 men living in my castle until I find my one true love. The men will engage in activities with me as a group to get to know each other better. It will only end when I find my true love and break the curse. Men of the Lords' choosing will live here, with me for gods' know how long. I curse under my breath. I haven't found anyone in eight years. How long will it take to find true love? I've grown quite fond of having a primarily empty castle.

After the curse began, I released every one of their duties, allowing them to return to their villages to be with their families. Since we couldn't leave the kingdom, diplomats were not needed. With the possibility of the kingdom ending, there was also no need for courtiers. Many people left. A few stayed that wanted to help or had no family to return to. Everyone was allowed to choose a new position or keep the one they had. I ensured they were paid well. Something I was astonished to learn hadn't been done before. Despite my royal title, I've spent the past eight years essentially being a moderator for the villages.

I look at the faces of the five lords around the table. One Lord from each village. Their faces are a mix of boredom and discomfort. Most of the lords have never been comfortable with the sole heir being a woman, let alone a cursed woman. I finally meet the eyes of Lord David. His wrinkled eyes meet mine, expressing warmth and urgency.

"What will they think when they realize I am damaged?" I ask him, waving to my face. Three long scars decorate my face, cutting from my temple to my cheek. Slashes from a dark period of my life. My hair has remained short since the curse began. The long, beautiful waves I had before haven't grown back, an oddity of the curse. I haven't visited any of the village centers since the curse began, staying on the outskirts of towns or remaining at the castle. My clothing is far from regal. I wear pants and loose shifts in the summer and sweaters in the winter, another complaint from the Lords.

"We can get a veil for you, Your Highness." Lord Erland suggests. I cringe at his suggestion, but it would hide my scars. At least for a bit. Covering any part of my identity chips away at my already damaged heart. I hate that I need to hide or shield who I am from other people.

Lord Erland governs Obele, the village to the south of the kingdom. He isn't a mean man, but I prefer to interact with him as little as possible. He is the oldest Lord in my kingdom, and it shows. He moves slowly and is always crotchety and angry. He tends to be more conservative with his village's money. I get the impression he is out of touch with his people, but staying locked in the castle, I am too. I probably have more in common with him than I would like to admit. Obele is a beautiful village full of culture and arts. Lord Erland isn't entirely terrible, allowing the artists of my kingdom a place to thrive.

Finn nudges up against my leg. I glance down, rubbing his sizable furry head. "Well, boy, I guess we're about to get lots of new guests in the castle." With another sigh and a frown, I grab a quill and sign my name to the edict. The Lords rise, giving words of approval and action to prepare the villages and the castle. I simply nod and walk out of the room, and I don't look back to see if they bow.

I wander through the hallways with Finn by my side. He has been loyal to me these past several years. He still has moments of puppyish charm. I'm terrified of the day I lose my best friend. Finn has a beautiful life here. He loves roaming the halls, resting by the fireplaces, and frolicking with the animals. He will be excited about all the new guests in the building. Hopefully, they are as kind to Finn as he deserves.

These can't be the same halls I ran when I was a little girl. The halls seem dimmer than I remember. As a child, my father would chase me through the halls, both of us giggling, running around servants. I was a happy child. Father ensured I never went without. I wonder what he would think of this situation now. He always encouraged me to follow my heart. I knew I would marry one day. I'm destined to be Queen. Obviously, I would need to marry. I had foolishly believed I would meet a kind prince or princess and fall madly in love. That's what happened in all of the storybooks and bedtime stories. It was always a long shot at best.

Now I roam the faded halls, reality knocking at the cusp of my mind. I don't want to let it in. I want to stay in the quiet without others trying to woo me. My life has never been peaceful, but with the curse, at least the politics and pageantry ceased these past few years. It's time to accept that part is coming back.

Finn and I walk outside, heading toward the royal gardens. My mother insisted on gardens specifically for beauty instead of production. The gardens for fruits and vegetables are further away from the castle. Many people wanted to tear out the gardens after the curse began. I allowed them to take some of the space but insisted on keeping part of the garden as it was. The gardens are peaceful. A perfect place to pace when stressed, for everyone at the castle. They are open to all, whereas my mother had them limited to people she approved of.

We saunter down the gravel path. The scent of the flowers is powerful. Peonies, roses, and begonias grow abundantly. There are fewer in bloom due to the lateness of the season. The sun has already set, and the moon is dark tonight. The autumnal equinox is in a couple of weeks. The eligible bachelors will arrive by then. There will be a grand celebration to welcome them.

Mindlessly, my feet carry me down the path, crunching on the stones, leaves occasionally brushing my legs. Finn stays by my side. I stop and stare up at the darkened night sky. The stars shine brilliantly above. A deep breath settles my mind and body. Comfort always finds me more quickly outside.

"I thought I might find you here." The woman speaks in a thick, clipped accent. Sunette is a tall, dark-skinned woman. Despite wearing whatever is in fashion in Sweet Briar, she still has small details that pay homage to her homeland. Her hair is braided close to her head and falls down her back. Tiny beads are placed in her hair. Intricate silver and gold jewelry decorates her long brown hair. She is lanky, with straps on her biceps that stand out against her skin. Sunette's deep brown eyes see everything, even things the best gossips miss.

Her husband accompanied my horse when my mother purchased him for my 16th birthday. It wasn't until the curse began and I released all courtiers that I realized they had been here as slaves. By that time, they couldn't leave the kingdom to return home. They chose to stay with the horses and me, but I paid them handsomely and gave them wages for the two years they had worked prior to that. It was the least I could do for them. Sunette has always treated me like a second daughter. I carry guilt over knowing their status within my kingdom.

Slaves were a small part of our kingdom, most working heavy labor jobs. It wasn't discussed in front of me when I was young. I was shocked to learn there were people enslaved in my kingdom. I had presumed Sweet Briar was a welcoming, affirming space, at least for the workers. The majority of the enslaved people were in Vadried and Arkaley. Tilrade, the largest trading port, had far fewer enslaved people and wasn't necessarily involved in the trade. Most enslaved people were from my own kingdom, forced into slavery through familial debts. Once a person was forced into slavery, it became difficult for their children to be freed. Free labor was valued over humanity.

Upon learning this, I passed a bill immediately to free all enslaved people, forcing the owners to pay reparations. Many farms and merchant stands are now owned by previously enslaved people due to the owners' inability to pay generations of wages. I have no guilt over bankrupting slave owners. Some chose to stay on the farm. Others relocated to a different village to start over. Many were outraged and tried to push back but ultimately were overpowered. Tensions regarding slavery have died down in the past few years, though I know some still hold anger toward me.

"I heard about the edict." Sunette's voice brings me back to reality. Word spreads like wildfire around the castle. Everyone is such a gossip. I should be surprised she already knows, but Sunette knows everything. I frown, about to say something. She steps next to me, wrapping her long fingers around mine. "Walk with me."

I hold her hand, walking next to her through the gardens. She has been the most prominent influence in maintaining my sanity for the past eight years. I grew close to her during my relationship with her daughter. She has always treated me well, despite everything that happened. I stay close to her as we walk, enjoying her warmth.

She leads me to the greenhouse. The previous gardener left when the curse began, and Sunette took over those duties. Her former job had been as a farm hand. She is exceptionally skilled at growing things. My mother denied her request to work in the Royal Gardens and forced her to work in the fields instead. Despite the curse, the Royal Gardens have thrived because of her skill and knowledge. As we enter the greenhouse, a strong smell of jasmine wafts through the space.

"Do you remember how hard Dahlia fought to get the jasmine seeds? She insisted you needed them." Sunette's question sends a slight smile across my face at the memory. Shortly after I befriended her, Dahlia, Sunette's daughter, remembered seeing jasmine plants in her home kingdom. She wanted one desperately. She wrote to her family members and even managed to enlist my father in her hunt for the plant or seeds. My father was thrilled over the possibility of growing my namesake. He learned about the flower during diplomatic trips but had never found seeds. Two months before the curse, the seeds finally arrived. Dahlia planted them in the greenhouse, ensuring they would have the climate they preferred. She instructed her mother, me, the gardener, and anyone else who might enter the greenhouse on how to care for the plant.

The plant is blooming beautifully, even nine years after she planted it. It is climbing up the trellis Dahlia built. The delicate white flowers are pure, emitting their scent in the entire room. The plant looks healthier than it has in years. I release Sunette's hand, taking one of the flowers between my fingers. The petals are silky and smooth, healthy.

"This plant has flourished this year more than any before," she speaks softly. I glance back at her. Sorrow is written across her face, but there's something else too. Sunette looks hopeful. My fingers trace the plant up the trellis. The memory of Dahlia building it flashes in my mind, leaving a bittersweet trail of heartache and longing.

"I think it's a sign. The kingdom needs the curse to break. You," Sunette's hand grazes my scarred cheek lovingly, "need to break your curse." I lean into her touch, her comfort. She speaks the truth. The curse needs to be broken.

"I don't want to love without her," I whisper. Tears build behind my eyes, threatening to escape. Sunette pulls me close to her body, wrapping me tightly in her arms. I grab her back, her long locs bumping against my arms.

"I know, child. But she isn't here. You are. She would want you to be happy." The tears escape, sliding down my cheeks. So many tears have been shed over the past eight years for her daughter. I have doubts as to whether they will ever stop. The gaping hole in my chest over the sudden loss of her, my parents, and the curse feels like it will never heal. There is a never-ending well of sorrow inside me from the pain of this life of mine. Sunette holds me like that for a long time, easing some of the ache but never coming close to repairing the damage. I am finally ushered back to my room and instructed to rest before tomorrow. I have been told we must begin preparations for the True Love Edict immediately. Even in my empty room, sitting on my bed, I roll my eyes at that thought.

Chapter 2

CLEM

This has always been my favorite time of day. As the sun is setting across Arkaley, a golden hue engulfs everything. Houses that are worn down have a vibrant sheen. People that are usually angry and yelling look less intimidating and more god-like. The land with grass that is dry and brown looks more whimsical in the fading sunlight. It makes our dying village seem happier and healthier than it has been since the curse began.

The kingdom has been cursed for eight years. There are rumors about how the curse began and how to break it. The only thing consistent in the rumors is that the Princess is involved. Some say she caused the curse; others say she'll break it. More yet believe the curse came from a scorned lover. The things I know to be true about the curse are that we cannot leave the kingdom, and our lands are suffering for it. For now, we can still farm and hunt. That won't last forever, though.

I wash up in my room, preparing to head into town. I work in the fields for a farmer, tending and harvesting land too large for him to manage alone. He gives the first pick of the harvest and pays a small wage. It's not much, but it's fair. My older sister, Bea, also works on the farm, but she tends to the animals he uses. She has a gift with the beasts. My mother helps other families in our village. She cleans and mends laundry for a small fee or barters for other items we need. Between the three of us, we do well. We're not wealthy, but we don't go without either. My younger sister is able to attend school. I can't ask for much more than that.

"Hey Ma," I greet her in the main room. She's still working on laundry from her day. "I'm going to the pub."

"Ok, sweetie. Be safe." She barely glances at me as I slip my shoes on.

"Hold on, Clem!" Bea calls from her room.

She walks out a moment later, shifting her hand to give me something. I catch a few coins she drops into my hand. I try to push them back to her.

"I don't need your money, Bea." I retort. She shrugs. She works as hard for her money as I do. I've never asked if our wages are equal, but I don't want to take her money when I have my own. Bea rarely spends her earnings on herself, but I refuse to let her spend it on me.

"Maybe, but I don't really need it either. I got extra this week because Fergus's cow gave birth, and I helped. That heifer was messy, too." I cringe at the image, still trying to hand the money back.

"You need to save it for dowry. We all know no one will take you in for cheap." I laugh, but our mother huffs from her seat, not looking up. She doesn't appreciate the jests between Bea and me. When we were younger, Ma would try to stop us from making comments to each other but has since given up. Now, Ma grunts or sighs her disapproval but doesn't say anything. Bea reaches past my outstretched hand and ruffles my hair. I try to jerk away, but she pulls it free from the leather strip I tied it back with.

"Looks like you need it to buy some love. Who's going to take a lonely man with disheveled hair?"

I step away from her, smoothing my hair back again. I decided to stop cutting it a few years ago and let it grow out. It just recently reached a length that allows me to pull it back. The thick blonde hair settles into place again. For as long as I keep mine, Bea keeps hers that short. With her stocky frame, she has a more masculine look than I ever had. She has never been interested in the things other girls were. She is a person all her own. I love her all the more for it.

"Fine, Bea. I'll take the money. Just don't touch my hair again." I'm not vain. It's too much effort to restyle it but too hot to leave it down.

On the walk to the pub, I observe Arkaley. The sun is lower now, casting orange and pink hues instead of golden rays. People are settling into their homes. Children are running around, screaming, or chasing animals into coops. Women are sweeping porches or pulling in the laundry. Men are walking the streets, heading home from the fields or shops. It is a quiet village. Routine. Static. People know their place and their role, and not many question it.

The wooden walls of the pub create a dark interior. Sconces light the room but cast as many shadows around the tables as they illuminate. The pub smells of yeast and dirt, but the ale is good. Arriving early allows me to find a table near a window, letting a draft drive away unpleasant smells. I order a mug and grab a table, waiting for my friends to arrive.

They begin to filter in shortly after I do. Most I know from our school days. They are married and working various jobs. The nights we go to the pub are the only times we still see each other. We usually meet about once a fortnight. The desire to drink was never strong for me. Some guys come every day and know everyone in the pub by name.

We chat about fields, families, and, as always, women. Being 27, I am the only one in our group still unwed. Because of the curse, my options are limited. The other guys are crass in their discussion. They share tales of their wives and their escorts. When they tire of that, they move in on me.

"So, Clem, does your dick even work at this point?" This is met with loud, raucous laughter. Shouts of more obscenities. I nod along, sipping my ale. The comments don't phase me at this point. I long since learned responding has an ill effect. Most of us have crooked noses from this exact conversation.

"Ah, he won't marry anyone from around here. He's too good for us. Only the Princess will do for him." One of them swoons, singing out the last part. I roll my eyes.

"Aye, still harboring a crush on the Princess?"

When we were 17, before the curse, the royal family rode through the village on a tour of the kingdom. The Princess passed on a large, white horse. She looked resplendent in her dress. Her long, brown hair fell softly down her back, with a small gold tiara atop her head. Unwittingly, I announced that I would marry her someday. No one has ever forgotten that.

"Well, now's your chance, Clem. She announced a new edict today, looking for her true love." I turn to him, confusion written on my face. A new edict?

"She's asking eligible bachelors to stay at the castle until they all fall in love together," my friend roars with laughter. Others join in as I consider this new information. Even if I didn't fall in love with her, I could at least get out of Arkaley for a bit because I certainly am not her true love. Before I can do anything else, Jackson walks up.

"She's not worth it, mate." He steps up behind me, clasping a hand on my shoulder. "That beast thinks she's better than anyone else. I heard she prefers the company of women."

"Just because she didn't enjoy your tiny dick doesn't mean she prefers women," I retort. It is rumored that Jackson courted the Princess before the curse. I assume he started those rumors to satisfy his own ego.

"Oy, Jackson! Don't talk ill of Clem's wife! He'll have to break your nose again!" The area erupts again in laughter. Jackson scowls at me, unimpressed with my comments about the Princess, who is not, and never will be, my wife, much to my disdain. I broke his nose a few years back when he tried to start rumors about Bea. I won't tolerate his bullshit, and everyone knows that now.

"That beast of a princess is probably all Clem will ever get close to. She's a washed-up prude with a failing kingdom to offer. Who would want her anyways?" Jackson spits as he spews his hate. There probably is something to his rumors of being with her if his hatred is that strong. I take that as my cue to leave. Violence doesn't have any appeal tonight. I'd rather be alone than with these men any longer. I've had all I can tolerate from them.

Lord David is sitting at a table, drinking with a couple of older men. I'm not as familiar with the other men. They have some role in governing our village, but I neither know nor care.

"Lord David, is it true about this edict? The Princess wants men at the castle?" If this is true, I want to be the one going. He looks up at me, a bit tired.

"Yes, it is true, Clem." He doesn't offer any other information, instead drinking from his ale. I turn back to the barmaid, tossing her a coin, indicating she should refill his ale. She walks off to grab another. I don't typically use money to sway a situation in my favor. I doubt a single ale will have a significant impact, but I can still treat him to one.

"I want to go."

He and the others looked me up and down, considering. One leans toward Lord David and speaks softly, "I assumed we should send younger men." Lord David seems to be considering the comment.

"Yes, I had, too. Perhaps the Princess would be more comfortable with a man closer to her own age. She, after all, isn't the young princess we last saw roaming through the village all those years ago." As he says the last part, he gives me a foreshadowing look. I don't know what he intends to portray, but it doesn't change my mind.

"When do you need me to leave?" I ask confidently. I have no plans of not letting this happen. Lord David strokes his chin as the barmaid finally returns with his ale. He nods thanks for the ale.

"Let me finalize the edict. Since we are close to the royal grounds, we don't need to leave immediately." I return his nod calmly, but inside, I'm ready to pack and start walking toward the castle.

As I leave the pub, Rachel comes to walk by my side. I had considered marrying her a few years ago. I couldn't go through with a proposal. I ended the relationship after realizing she was still fucking half the men in town. We move outside, passing through the town toward the road to my house.

"What do you want, Rachel?"

She looks up at me. Her sultry blue eyes meet mine, conveying her desires. She loops her arm through mine, stepping closer as we walk. I know what she wants. It is always the same thing. She wants sexual release. She wants not to be alone. Conveniently, those are the same things I want at this moment. We walk silently for a few more moments. By this point, she knows I would shove her away if I didn't want anything from her. My house is at the end of the lane. The side of the house is next to the forest, providing the perfect amount of privacy without actually being inside.

I lead her to the side, as I have many times before. Once around the corner, she shoves me against the wall, her lips crashing into mine. A thought races through my mind. This could be my last time with her. Even if I'm not the Princess's true love, I can find someone else at the castle. Or at least somewhere else to be. The thrill of this new development surges pleasure through my body. I match her kisses, grabbing the collar of her shirt. I pull the string to untie it. Sliding my fingers under the material, I squeeze her breast tightly. A moan escapes her lips.

She breaks the kiss, dropping to her knees in front of me. My cock is erect from excitement. If Rachel hadn't shown up when she did, I would be seeking release from my own hand right now. Instead, I look down to see her fingers deftly untying my pants. My dick springs free in front of her face. She licks her lips as her eyes meet mine. Her lips part, then wrap around the tip. I close my eyes, tilting my head back to rest against the side of the house. She slides her lips over my member, taking in as much as possible. I lace my fingers through her hair, holding for now.

Typically, I prefer to watch her lips sliding over my cock. The way her cheeks hollow, her lips flared over me, her eyes meeting my own, making the whole experience more intense. Tonight I lean my head back, letting my mind envision she is the Princess. The girl with the long brown hair. A woman now desperate to save her kingdom. Me, just a man willing to do anything to help her. Rachel wraps her fingers around my balls as the tip of my cock bumps into the back of her throat. Her gagging causes my fingers to tighten in her hair, driving her back down until she makes the noise again.

I glance down at Rachel. I don't usually take charge of her like that. The thought of the Princess drove me to do things I don't usually do. Tears streaked down her face. She still cups my balls, squeezing in time with her tongue lapping under my dick. I notice her free hand is under her dress, pleasuring herself. She moans over my cock, sending vibrations down her cheeks. I grunt, feeling my balls tighten with release. I pull my fingers again on her head, watching for her reaction. When she doesn't show any signs of needing me to stop, I take over again, thrusting in her once, twice, a third time before I orgasm, spilling deep down her throat. She moans against me, leaning her forehead against my stomach, pressing down with her orgasm.

She licks me clean, my eyes rolling back from bliss. As she stands, I help her with her clothes, ensuring she looks acceptable to walk home. She lives a few houses down from me and will return alone safely. This isn't the first time we have done this. After a quick goodbye, she leaves. I turn toward the back, entering through the door closest to the woods. Bea stands in the doorway with her hands on her hips.

"One of these days, the two of you will get caught by someone who cares," she touts.

"It won't happen again," I inform her.

"Yes, it will. How many times has it already happened?"

"It won't happen again," I snap through gritted teeth, my annoyance with this conversation growing, "because I won't be here." I'm exhausted, spent, and don't want to be around anyone else right now.

My statement stuns Bea. I shove past her, pushing my way into the house. She grabs my arm, spinning me around. "What do you mean, 'won't be here'?"

"I'm going to the castle." Bea likely hasn't heard about the edict, but I'm no longer in the mood to explain. I'm ready for bed and nothing else. Bea considers my words as I make my way to my bedroom.

"You're going to the castle under that new edict? To try to fall in love with the Princess?" I raise my eyebrows at her, surprised by her questions. "People spoke of it in the barn all day," she explains in a soft, irritated voice. She isn't impressed with the gossip that happens at the farm.

"Yes. I told Lord David tonight I want to go. I need to get out of here, Bea. Even if just for a bit." She nods at me, clearly understanding my desires.

"Ma won't be happy."

"Sure she will. I'll send her flowers from their gardens." I smirk with a wink, as if this is the greatest revelation of all, and walk into my room to collapse on the bed. Mother always spoke of visiting the royal gardens at the castle. She swore they were the best of any kingdom. She won't be happy that I am leaving, but I'm sure she will be fine without me. She's been pushing me to marry and move on for a while. Now, I am doing just that.

Chapter 3

CLEM

After a few days, Lord David finds me. He informs me I will be sent to the castle, along with another young man. Apparently, the other governors didn't want to send just one "old" man to the Princess. That doesn't bother me at all. Definitely not. He tells me they will take a cart with horses to carry our luggage in a week.

I pack and leave the next day. There isn't any need to wait around. The farmer's land is cleared enough without needing my presence. Ma and Bea can function without me. Maybe if I get there early, I can get extra time with the Princess. Or at least the best room available. Whatever happens, I'm ready for it.

I carry a single bag with my clothes. Arkaley is closest to the castle grounds but still several hours on foot. I take the time to appreciate the land and enjoy the changing views. Arkaley is primarily flat, built at the Beinn Mountains' foothills. The land beyond Arkaley is used for farming. The road to the castle winds through the mountains and is dangerous in several places during winter or bad weather. The path is quiet today; fair weather makes the trail easy to pass. Animals scurry in the distance. A soft breeze ruffles the trees.

I can't help the excitement over this journey. I've never considered leaving Arkaley. The other villages don't seem to offer anything different. Before the curse began, I thought about leaving the kingdom. Exploring, seeing what is out in the rest of the world. I was 18 when the curse hit. I was focused on one thing. At the time, there were plenty of willing girls. They slowly married off, leaving only a few I had nothing in common with. It didn't seem necessary to force a marriage with someone I didn't like. But the castle. It's a new opportunity. Maybe the Princess will find her true love. Maybe I can get in her good graces and be a diplomat and travel to other kingdoms. Maybe even find a cute maidservant until then.

After several hours, I can see the castle from the top of a huge hill. The stone walls are tall, with vines trailing up the sides. Farmlands are beyond the castle, and a horse stable is on one side. The castle is much larger than I had anticipated. I'm stunned for a few moments. I knew it would be large, but seeing the sheer size in person is astounding.

The walk from the top of the hill to the front door takes more than half an hour. The grounds are vast. There are no guards at the door, and I am able to walk straight inside the castle. I assumed there would be someone to stop me, but no one does. The entryway is large and open. Ornate, highly detailed rugs spread across the floor. Chandeliers hang from the ceiling; to the left, a hallway stretches with many doors along it. A set of grand stairs curves to both sides and then extends into other wings. I lower my bag, taking in the grandeur of the castle.

A massive body crashes into me, knocking me to the ground. My hands cover my face, protecting me against a threat I can't recognize. Legs are stepping on me. There is a loud sniffing sound, a wet tongue. Is this a dog?

"Finn! Stop!" A strong feminine voice calls out.

White fur is rubbing against my cheeks, between my arms. I lower my arms to look at the beast, only to be attacked with more licks. I laugh, realizing this is the largest dog I have ever seen. It stands to reason that the largest castle would house the largest dog. I rub his ears and neck as he finally moves back. I sit up, looking at the woman that called him. She's trying to pull him off me, still giving him commands. The woman is small, though, just barely larger than the dog. She has short brown hair and three scars across her face. I don't know who she is, but she has a fascinating aura. I want to know who she is.

She notices I am watching her. She manages to get the dog away from me and back by her side. Her gaze instantly shifts to uncertainty and anger. Her hand rests on the dog's head, who has decided I am a friend and looks eager to tackle me again. I quickly stand in front of her. Her spine straightens. Her eyebrows rise, clearly waiting for me to tell her why I am here.

"Oh, um. Hi. I'm Clem. I'm here as a bachelor under the new edict."

She looks me up and down appraisingly.

"You're early. No one is supposed to arrive until next week." I shrug, tucking my hands in my pockets.

"I know. I just didn't want to wait at home." I nod down to the dog. "Is that the guard?"

Her lips purse. Her fingers idly scratch his ears.

"His name is Finn. I apologize for him tackling you. He's not used to new people just waltzing in." She glances behind me at the door, wondering where the guards are. "Since he seems to like you, you can spend the next week helping me train him not to jump."

The excitement of having a job shows clearly on my face. "Yeah, I would love to do that." I pat my legs, motioning to Finn. He wags his tail but looks at the girl before moving to me. She nods to him, and he lurches at me. I'm prepared this time and don't fall when he jumps on me. I rub his sides. It's hard to tell who is more excited about this situation, Finn or me. After a minute, she calls him back.

"Not all of the rooms are ready, but I think one or two are. If you want to bring your bag, I can help you settle."

I toss my bag on my shoulder. She turns to walk down the hallway to the left. Some of the doors are open, showing various sitting and meeting rooms. Some are larger than others. A couple of the rooms are clearly intended for more intimate meetings.

"So, do you know where the Princess is?" I question. Her shoulders tense. She doesn't turn back as she responds.

"She is in her room. She prefers solace to company. You likely won't see much of her before the autumnal equinox." She glances back at me before leading me up a set of stairs. "I'm Tia, by the way."

"Pleasure to meet you, Tia." With a wink, I add, "Will I see more of you before then?"

Tia stops at the end of the hallway, assessing me again. Her look makes me uncomfortable. I refuse to cower, though. I adjust my shoulders, standing straighter, waiting to see the verdict of her gaze. She nods silently, then opens the door and leads me into a room. The room is a good size, much larger than my own at home. There is a bed and dresser with a wash table. A small desk next to an open window already has paper and ink well on it. I drop my bag next to the bed, taking in the simple decorations of the room. This room does not match the ornateness of the entryway, but it is more than enough. Tia steps toward the window.

"This is the best room, in my opinion. A privy room is down the hall. Close, but not so close as to smell anything. But this window overlooks the royal gardens." Her hand waves out the window.

I step to the window, looking down. The gardens are directly below this window. There are gravel walking paths with various plants and flowers in bloom. A dark-skinned woman is tending to the plants. The gardens are the only part of this castle that seems small. Ma always described them as large and never-ending. While the plot is still sizable, it's not nearly never-ending. My attention returns to Tia, who stares longingly out at the gardens. Something is enchanting about her, maybe her short stature or the scars across her face. I want to know more about her. As if she senses my gaze, she looks up at me.

"You can get settled in. I will let others know of your presence. I will return shortly to give you a tour of the castle." With that, she walks out of the room. The large, white dog sniffs my leg. I rub his head again before he follows her off. I collapse on the bed, dreaming of ways to seduce Tia, forgetting about the Princess.

I fell asleep on the bed unintentionally after Tia left. When I awake, the sun is setting outside the window. I sit up, rubbing my eyes, noticing how warm the bed feels. My hands drop, finding something furry on my side. I startle, not accustomed to waking with something fuzzy next to me. Finn has returned and crawled into bed with me. I wonder if he is allowed to do that but settle for rubbing his back. His tail wags appreciatively.

"How long have you been in here, boy?" I speak softly to the oversized pup.

"Finn!" Tia shouts, stomping her foot. "Get out of that bed now!" The dog whines and inches out of the bed. He slinks over my legs and down to the floor, whining as he does. I can't help but laugh at his antics. I scratch his back until he finally reaches the floor, stretching his long legs and body across my room. Tia sighs, shaking her head at the dog.

"When they told me about the edict, I knew Finn would be excited. I didn't think he would take to anyone this well, though. If he bothers you," she pauses, giving me an assessing look again, "just shove him to the side. He'll get the idea eventually." I laugh, standing to stretch. My arms reach above my head. The loose shirt I have on falls against my smooth stomach. Again, Tia looks with her calculating gaze, but her lips seem to curve up. She's clearly pleased with what she finds.

She motions for me to follow. We walk through the castle, weaving in and out of hallways. She tells me about the various rooms and areas. Finn walks obediently by her side, which is such a contrast to his other behaviors. I follow along, just behind, taking in the scenery, trying to remember some directions. While most of my skills are in farming, being in the castle over the winter will allow me to explore other activities. Tia has shown me various meeting rooms, the throne room, and the dining hall, where I will normally take my meals, but not now since I have arrived so early.

In the kitchen, another woman greets us. Tia quickly approaches her to whisper in the other woman's ear. The woman's eyes raise in surprise, but she nods before rushing off.

"She's going to get us a tray for dinner. They don't like people in the kitchen that don't belong there. We have brought in an extra cook to accommodate the men arriving. They are training now."

Once the woman returns, she hands me a tray with bowls of rice and vegetables, bread, two apples, glasses, and a jug of what looks like wine. I take the tray from her, a bit startled that it was handed directly to me. Tia grabs a jar of biscuits from the counter, then leads me through the castle again. We exit through a side door, just past the royal gardens. I glance back at the castle, trying to map out whether that door is close to the window of my room.

Tia leads up a small hill, sitting beneath a large oak tree. The sun has set, but there is enough light off the castle to see each other. We both sit on the ground, the tray between us. She pours the wine as I start eating. I realize how hungry I am from my trek. I had food along the way but I am more famished than I thought. Tia pulls a biscuit from the jar, tossing one to the side for Finn.

"The cook makes special biscuits just for Finn," she explains. The dog chomps on the treat, lying down at our feet. She turns toward me, tearing small bits of her bread. I have nearly finished the rice and vegetables.

"Why did you decide to come here?" I can't remember if I told her I asked to come instead of being chosen. It's possible I mentioned it.

"Honestly, I want a change." I take a sip of the wine. "I doubt I'm the Princess's true love, but a few months in the castle, away from my quiet, redundant village, is too good an opportunity to pass."

She tosses another biscuit to Finn, drinking her wine. She seems lost in her thoughts. She's staring back at the castle. It's beautiful from this spot. The fires around the building cast a glow around the walls. People move around the grounds, winding down their days. If Arkaley is impressive at this time, the castle is downright magical.

"Do you work for the Princess?" Tia slowly turns her attention to me. The scars are almost hidden in the low light. She's a beautiful woman. The scars and short-cut hair give her an edge I wouldn't expect from someone working with the royal family.

"Sort of." She sips her wine, keeping her answer short.

"How long have you been here?"

"My whole life."

I guess Tia isn't very talkative. I finish eating the bread, then lean back with my wine. We sit quietly while she eats her food. She occasionally tosses a biscuit to Finn. He seems content just sitting with us. I want to ask more questions and learn more about the castle. We never talked much about royalty at home, especially once the curse hit. Tia eats her food slowly, giving me time to take her in. I really want to know who she is, what she likes, and what she is thinking. And specifically, if her lips are as soft as they look. How those scars feel under my lips.

"Are you married, Tia?"

"What? Me? No," she gives a soft, awkward chuckle. She is startled by my question. Is it the question itself or breaking the silence?

"Why not?" Her eyes meet mine. Staring into her eyes drives that desire even deeper.

"Likely reasons similar to your own. No interest, not enough partners," she shrugs but grabs her wine and settles back closer to me.

"Fair enough." I sip my wine, giving pause in my words. "So, what do you like to do for fun?"

"I've been perfecting flaying recently. Though, horse quartering will always be my favorite. I don't get messy, and the crows will clean up everything else. Plus, there's a satisfying sound when things start separating."

Tia says this with a straight face, serious as she can be. My mouth drops open. I can only stare at her. She finally looks at me and bursts out laughing. Her laugh is loud and joyful, easing some of the discomfort from my chest. I nervously chuckle along with her, unsure why we're laughing.

"Oh gods, you should see your face." She shoves my chest. Her touch sends a shock through my body. "I'm kidding, Clem. I've never flayed anyone." I sip my wine, needing something to do.

"But you've quartered someone?" I ask apprehensively. Maybe the fascinating aura is that she's a murderer.

"Well, no, but I am familiar with the process," she says sadly. Her face drops, sadness taking over her look. I reach up to stroke her cheek gently. It is smooth until I reached the jagged edge of the scar. Her hand stops mine, slowly pulling it away from her face.

"I'm sorry. They tell me my humor is too dark and not actually funny. I can blame it on lack of interaction, right?" She speaks softly, embarrassed by the sudden change.

"Don't apologize to me. I can handle dark humor. But I don't know you well enough to realize it's humor." Her eyes lift to mine; hope sparks under the sadness. A smile spreads across my face. "So, let's change that."

"Alright," her lips curve upwards, "I've lived in the castle my whole life. My parents are dead." Her eyes cut to mine, "That's not a joke; that's real. I have a twisted sense of reality because of the curse and enjoy ruining the expectations of royalty. I'm trapped here at the castle, but at least I get Finn." We glance down at the dog. He's asleep near our feet, softly snoring. "As for your question, for fun, I love to insult the Lords from the villages and... I don't know. Masturbate? There are only so many things to do around here."

I laugh loudly at her statement. While I have been around several brazen women, I didn't expect to find one at the castle. She laughs along with me.

"Listen, let's get married and run off from the castle. The Princess will manage just fine without one bachelor and a handmaid."

Her laughter increases. It's the most bewitching sound I have ever heard. I could listen to that for the rest of my life and never tire of it. Her shoulder nudges mine.

"It's getting dark. We should head back inside." She starts collecting our things. A small burst of disappointment spreads through my body; despite joking about running off, the idea is appealing. I help her gather things and carry the tray. We walk silently. Finn walks behind us, even slower than we are. Once inside, she takes the tray and leaves it in the kitchen, which is already dark. She walks next to me, heading toward my room. We reach my room, and she stops.

"Do you ride horses, Clem?"

"Yes."

"Would you like to go for a ride with me tomorrow?"

"Yes."

"Good. I'll find you in the morning." She reaches out and squeezes my arm before walking off. I watch her walk away. I can't tear my eyes away from her, but her ass looks amazing in her pants. There is an extra swish that I overlooked before. I wonder if that is added for my pleasure. Either way, it will undoubtedly be part of my pleasure in a few minutes.

Chapter 4

CLEM

The next morning, I find my way back to the kitchen. I don't get lost on this trip but am positive I will at some point. This castle has many winding halls and twisting stairways. I find Tia, where we gathered a tray from the kitchen last night. She is chatting quietly with an older woman. She doesn't seem so happy about their conversation. I stop several paces back, not wanting to intrude.

Tia notices me, meeting my eyes. Her attention doesn't drop from her conversation, but mine does as I take her in. She is wearing riding pants that are tighter than the ones she had on yesterday. Her shirt is also more fitted. Her petite body hosts full hips. The only thing I can think about is kneeling in front of her, rubbing those hips as I bury my face between them. Her waist dips just enough that it would be perfect for grabbing onto while thrusting deep inside her.

A smile spreads across her face as if she could read my mind. She ends the conversation with the older woman, grabbing a bag from the kitchen and walking toward me. I meet her eyes, trying and failing to clear the thoughts of her body from my mind. She stops in front of me, and I look down at her. She has a wicked grin on her face. Her eyes drag from mine down to my feet, then back up. She licks her lips, and I'm positive she knows exactly where my mind is.

"Come on," she says, shoving the bag into my stomach. I wrap my arms around the bag, slowly coming back to reality. I glance around, looking for anyone that might have observed the interaction. I don't see anyone and rush to catch up with her.

"I have food for lunch. The horses don't get as much exercise as they used to. So we'll be gone for a while, letting them run," she speaks as she walks, which is surprisingly quick for someone with such short legs.

I follow her silently to the stables, where two horses are waiting. A solid white one is saddled and ready to go. It resembles the horse I saw the Princess on many years ago. A slightly smaller brown horse stands next to it. Tia walks up to the white one, rubbing its neck, speaking softly to it. It must be the Princess's since Tia is so familiar with him. She climbs on effortlessly, then holds a hand out toward me. Still reeling from our entire interaction, I take her hand in mine. She laughs loudly.

"Clem," she chuckles, "give me the bag and mount your horse. And at some point, please get your head out of my pants."

I jerk my hand back, laughing uncomfortably. I haven't been this consumed since I was younger. I don't try to make an excuse as I do what I am told. With a wide grin still on her face, she guides her horse beside mine. The horse I am riding is called Acer and is familiar with keeping up with Vesper, the horse Tia is riding. She gives a devilish grin, winks then takes off on her horse. I snap the reins, urging Acer to keep up.

She heads north in the opposite direction from Arkaley. The horses gallop smoothly over the terrain, clearly familiar with this path. The land is flat, with trees scattered around. It looks so different from the land I walked through to get here. Despite the beautiful area, I'm worried that I have made things awkward with Tia. She is riding fast as if trying to get away. Not only do I not want to ruin a chance with her, but I don't want to cause her discomfort. After a while, Tia slows her horse, allowing mine to fall into a trot next to it.

"Tia, I'm sorry for staring earlier. I didn't mean to be so awkward." I decide to apologize before anything else can be said. She almost looks confused by my apology.

"Do you intend to stop staring at me?" She asks curiously.

"I...well, I mean...yes?" I feel very unsure of my answer. I won't be able to stop staring at her. I don't want to stop staring at her. But if that is what she wants, I will find a way to stop. She laughs at me.

"I don't want you to stop. But an apology without change is just manipulation, Clem. Are you trying to manipulate me?" Oh, gods.

"No! No. I'm not trying to do that! Shit, I'm so sorry, Tia! I won't stop staring." What are these words coming out of my mouth? She's still laughing. That's a good sign.

"Calm down. I don't mind if you stare. I would prefer you not become so awkward. But I won't fault you for that either." She flicks her hand over her shoulder as if to flick long hair away. "I'm worth staring at."

I stay silent this time, not wanting to sound crazy. I completely agree she is worth staring at. It's even more appealing that she knows it. I'm glad for this time with her. Despite being here for the Princess, I hope the other bachelors distract her enough that I can spend as much time as I want with Tia. I didn't expect to meet such a phenomenal woman so early on in this journey, but I definitely have.

"There is a small brook ahead. We'll let the horses rest and have lunch." She nods ahead, maintaining a steady pace. She's comfortable with the horse and Finn; such an endearing trait, comfort around animals. They usually have a better perception of people. As we approach the brook, she dismounts with ease despite her animal's large size. She takes the reins of my horse while I climb off, less smoothly than her. She leads them to water, then brings the pack over. We sit in the grass, and she unpacks the food.

"I don't know much about the land beyond Arkaley. Are we still on the castle grounds?" I ask, taking a bite of an apple.

"Yes," she nods, then points behind us, "Vadried is a few miles that way. Most of the castle's farmland borders Vadried's." She sips from a water pouch, then offers it to me. "On the way back, we'll pass along the side of the royal farmlands. I like riding by them when they are producing."

It is impressive how much she knows about the area and her interest in it. I've never met a maid to a princess, but I wouldn't have thought they would be so involved in the running of the kingdom. I suppose it does make sense. If she works with the Princess closely.

We continue chatting idly during lunch. It's easy to talk with Tia. As enchanting as she is, she's also comfortable to be around. I feel so drawn to her. I simply want to be with her, doing anything, everything, nothing. It doesn't even matter what. After eating, she lies back in the grass, looking at the sky. I slide closer to her and lie next to her. Not touching, but close enough that I could.

"I love watching the clouds move. It always makes me feel small, like nothing really matters. It's kind of comforting." I give a small grunt, considering her words.

As we lie in the grass, staring at the clouds, I slide my hand over hers. My finger strokes the back of her hand softly. She doesn't move or react at all. I look at her face, but her eyes are closed. She is taking in the warmth of the sun beating down on us. I turn my face back toward the sky. Deciding to push my luck, I slip my hand under hers, lacing our fingers together. Her thumb rubs the outside of mine. The movement was so small I wouldn't notice it under normal circumstances. I don't push it any further; content just touching her hand at this point.

We lie in the grass for a while. The soft breeze blows the grass and leaves around us. Crickets chirp, and soon small animals begin to scurry in the distance. The horses are quiet by the water. It's such a peaceful moment I wonder if Tia has fallen asleep. My thumb gently traces her skin. I can feel calluses inside her palm. I wonder what she has done to earn those.

"Clem," her voice is soft. I open my eyes to see her sitting above me. I offer a sleepy smile, rubbing my eyes to wake up. She has pulled her hand away from mine. A small emptiness creeps through me at the loss, but she doesn't move away immediately. Hope flairs, driving the emptiness away.

"We need to head back." She stands, offering me her hand. I take it, pulling myself off the ground. I hope to pull her close to me, but she breaks away before

I get the chance. I help her gather our items and make our way to the horses. We are both quiet, lost in thought. We mount the horses and ride back slower than when we came out.

We follow along orchards with fruit trees. There are more options than I realized. This must be where a lot of the fruit in our village comes from. While Arkaley has a lot of farmlands, most of it is vegetables and root plants. We don't grow a lot of fruit. It's refreshing to see the fields where the fruit comes from. The orchards quickly stop and shift to vegetable fields. Corn and potatoes and squash cover the land. I notice many people out working the fields. A bit of longing hits. I enjoy having a set job to do. A task to help. It is nice to relax and experience something new. Maybe I'll find a job at the castle soon, something to keep me busy.

Tia rides just ahead of me, watching the fields and their workers. I wonder if she has any kind of relationship with them. She looks back at me, then slows her horse to ride beside me.

"In the past, these fields were almost overcrowded with plants. Because of the curse, there is less growing now than ever before." Sadness is written across her face and body. I look at the fields again and see empty spaces I didn't notice before. There will still be a good crop turnout this year. If the fields were nearly overcrowded before, this would be a smaller yield. Seeing the bare spots reminds me why I am here. I feel selfish for not wanting to help the Princess more. I shouldn't be so focused on Tia when I am here for the princess. Who knows? Maybe fate will be in my favor. Perhaps she'll be better than Tia, and I'll be happier, and the whole kingdom will prosper.

I look back at Tia and can't imagine anyone being better than her.

After returning, Tia left me alone for the evening. I wandered the castle, familiarizing myself with routes and rooms. I had dinner and eventually went to sleep. I expect to see Tia today. When I awake, Finn is in my bed again. I roll over, scratching his ears. He wags his thick tail, smacking my legs hard. There is a parchment on his collar.

Clem,

I need to stay with the princess today. We have to finalize plans for the bachelors and the autumnal equinox celebrations. I've sent Finn to keep you company. He loves to play fetch, but please keep him away from the kitchens. He is not as welcome there as he wants to be. Enjoy your time in the castle. If we finish, I will find you after dinner.

Your unreliable guide,

Tia xo

I chuckle, rubbing Finn's furry head. "Guess it's just you and me today, buddy." He wags his tail, rolling toward me. I reach over to scratch his belly. As much as yesterday made me realize I should be here for the princess, I can't shake the feeling I would rather be with Tia and Finn. I decide to get breakfast and head toward the fields today. I may not be able to do much to break the curse, but at least I can work.

After breakfast, which was surprisingly tricky with Finn, we go to the fields. I find the man in charge. His name is Mikhail. Finn is already familiar with him and seeks attention from him. Mikhail pets Finn, scratching his back while telling him he's a good boy, and Finn soaks up the attention.

"I would like to help out in the fields. I'm here as one of the bachelors for the edict but arrived early. I want to help where I can. I worked farms in Arkaley and am familiar with the work."

Mikhail nods appreciatively. "I could use the help. Is the Princess around to watch Finn?" The dog barks at his name, drawing the farmer's attention back to him.

"No, Tia left him with me today while they finalize plans for the celebrations."

"Tia?" The farmer looks confused but carries on anyways. "Sorry, but if Finn is with you today, I'll have to turn you away. Finn is a good dog," he says, looking down and scratching the dog's head, "but he causes chaos in the fields." I chuckle at the thought of Finn trying to play in the fields. This dog definitely has a reputation about him. "Come back when you don't have Finn, and I'll gladly let you work."

I nod thanks and call Finn away. I know I can have a task, but that still leaves me free today. Finn runs off, and I chase him through the grass toward the castle. He has so much energy right now. Maybe I can wear him out and let him rest while I find something else to do. So we play in the field until lunchtime. I track down food for both of us, avoiding the kitchens. After eating, we wander slowly through the castle. Eventually, I stumble into the library.

The library is massive. Arkaley had a small library, barely larger than the bedroom in my house. Seeing this library takes my breath away. There are at least two floors of books. Shelves upon shelves. The room is endless, longer than the dining hall. There are nooks and crannies with chairs and pillows. Plants and various decorations sit on some of the shelves between the books. Several large floor-to-ceiling windows allow the sunlight to shine through. There are candles, sconces, and candelabras scattered around for dark hours. It's quiet. There doesn't seem to be anyone else in the room.

I begin to peruse the shelves, taking in the different sections to familiarize myself with the layout. I could never finish all of these books. I will always have something new to read as long as I stay here. I could die in this room and still only read half of the books. The thought of returning to the fields has vanished from my mind. All I want now is to spend all my time here, reading these books. Consuming these stories. Being lost in worlds that are not my own.

I wander the entire bottom floor, then the top floor. The top floor is more reference and historical pieces. I make my way back to the main floor. I find a book about dragons and knights that seems interesting. Most of the books in Arkaley were informative. There were only a handful of storybooks. The thought of reading various storybooks excites me more than it should. After grabbing my book, I realize Finn isn't with me anymore. I find him lying between shelves in a sunny spot. There is an oversized chair behind him that looks perfect. I settle in, reading my book while Finn snoozes on the floor.

I lose track of time as I read my book. Finn continues to sleep at my feet, properly worn out from running through the grass earlier. My excitement over the book fades, and my eyes grow heavy. I doze off, unaware but in a state of pure literary bliss.

"I swear, no one in this castle sleeps as much as you two."

I crack my eye open. Tia is standing just past Finn with her hands on her hips. Finn wags his tail but makes no effort to move. If I had a tail to acknowledge pleasure, I would do the same. Instead, I stretch, scooting over in the chair. I pat the spot next to me. It's not an ample space, but enough room for Tia to fit beside me. She glances around the library before stepping over the dog and sitting with me. She grabs the book I was reading, looking at it.

"Do you read a lot?" She questions, scanning the page I last was on.

"I've never seen this many books in my life. I love to read but haven't had the opportunity." I stretch my arm behind her. She isn't impressed with my smooth move, but she doesn't push me away, either. "How was your planning? Did you finish everything?"

She sighs before answering. "Yes, the other bachelors," her eyebrows raise at me, sassing my inability to arrive with everyone else, "will arrive in two days, like they are supposed to. The plans for the celebrations are in place. Everything should go smoothly now. Did Finn give you any trouble today?" His ears perk up at his name.

"Oh yes. So much trouble. We almost didn't eat, and he got us kicked out of the fields. But I wore him out in the grass. Then he found the perfect place in the library. So I can't complain." Finn whines at my comments. He rises and walks over to Tia, placing his head in her lap. She scratches his ears, talking to him in a small voice.

"Oh no, this baby didn't do that. He is a sweet baby that doesn't cause any problems. Is Clem telling fibs about you?"

Finn barks in agreement with Tia, leading us both to laugh. She leans back, resting her head against my shoulder. It feels so natural, her here in my arms. I wrap my arm around her, resting my hand on her bicep. My thumb strokes it smoothly. I turn my head, pressing a small kiss on the top of her head. She seems to stop moving. She doesn't tense but doesn't seem quite as comfortable as she did a moment ago. Am I imagining that? Does she not feel the same way I do? I've been so consumed with how I feel for her I haven't even considered if she feels the same way. Maybe the bachelors are off limits, and she is risking her position with me.

"Tia," I speak softly.

"Clem," she rises, stepping away from me. "I need to get some books. For the Princess." She holds my book out to me, and I reach to take it.

"Wait, Tia." As soon as I have the book, she walks toward the stairs to the second floor. Finn whines but follows her. I'm left stunned, holding my book. I have probably ruined everything with her and the princess. I'm not too concerned about the princess. She has at least 5 other bachelors coming for her. But Tia. I don't want to hurt her. I don't want her to be alone.

I'm so lost in my thoughts I don't realize how long it has been. I hear Tia's footprints coming toward me. I step to the end of the aisle, catching her as she walks by.

"Tia, wait." She stops, placing the two large books she carries on the table beside her.

"If you want to take books out of the library, there is a register next to the door." She motions to a large book on a podium beside the door. "Just fill it out. Be sure to mark them as returned when you bring them back." She won't meet my eyes. Her fingers tap against her books. I step closer to her.

"Tia, I'm sorry. I didn't..." She places her hand on my forearm, squeezing lightly.

"I'll find you in the morning."

She rises on the tip of her toes, pressing her lips against my cheek. Then she grabs her books and hurries out of the room. I watch her leave, a smirk I can't control spreading across my face. After a moment, I bring myself back to reality. I sign the book out, realizing Tia didn't sign out her books. The smile stays on my face until I fall asleep that night, anticipating what the morning will bring.

Chapter 5

CLEM

The bright morning sun creeps into my room, waking me from sleep. I try not to move too eagerly as I go about my morning routine. I shave my face. A beard is starting to grow, but that's not something I want to commit to yet. I tie my hair back, pull on my cleanest clothes, and go to the dining hall. There are already servants moving around, but no sign of Tia. I grab some oats and berries and find a spot to eat.

Tia doesn't show up during breakfast. She said she would find me, but I don't want to be difficult to find. I want to spend the day with her. I imagine our time will be limited the first few days after the bachelors arrive, with me needing to be with the Princess. I hope I can let Tia know I want to spend more time with her, though.

I wander through the halls, trying to look natural. It feels awkward to peek around every corner, looking for the Princess's maid. If I keep moving around, Tia will have more difficulty finding my location. I casually walk to the library, taking up the same seat I was in last night. As I sit, I remember I didn't bring my book. I debate getting a new one, but I was enjoying the book I currently have. I don't want to start a new story.

I go back to my room to get the book. After grabbing it, I tuck it safely in my pants pocket. On my way back to the library, I notice the door to the gardens. I haven't actually seen Tia in them, but I haven't fully explored them either. This seems like a good opportunity. I make my way to the gardens, keeping an eye out for anyone watching me.

The gardens are surprisingly quiet. Ma might have been wrong about the size of the royal gardens, but she definitely understood the area's atmosphere. The hedges sway quietly in the warm summer breeze. Many of the petals are falling off, creating a sheet of color on the walkway instead of the gravel paths. I quickly forget about my goal as I enjoy the plants. The way the flowers and hedges grow in harmony creates such a peacefulness. Small insects flit around, collecting what they can before winter.

I'm so absorbed in looking at the plants I stop paying attention to where I am going. No one else has been on the path I took. Everything is quiet; I wouldn't expect another person to be here. But then I crash into someone.

"Oh, I'm sorry."

"Clem!"

I look up to see Tia standing before a giant blooming flower. A large smile spreads across my face quickly.

"Hi," I say breathlessly. "I wasn't out here looking for you." That was definitely casual. "I mean, I just wanted to explore the gardens." I can feel the blood rushing to my cheeks. There is no way she will believe a word I just said.

"It's okay, Clem. I was going to find you soon." She sighs, looking back at the flower in front of her. It's then that I notice we aren't alone. I see a tall, dark-skinned woman with long locs standing beside Tia. She has a smirk on her face that suggests she knows a secret. About this time, Tia seems to remember the woman is there. But she scowls at the look the woman is making. This entire interaction is confusing. I'm embarrassed; this woman knows a secret, and Tia is mad?

"Clem, this is Sunette. She's our Head of the Royal Gardens. Sunette, Clem is here under the edict." Tia waves halfheartedly between the two of us. I reach out my hand to shake Sunette's.

"It's nice to meet you. These gardens are beautiful. My Ma always spoke highly of them. Their reputation doesn't do them justice." She shakes my hand. Her shake is firm, but I feel she is assessing me. She isn't as obvious as Tia was when I first met her.

"Thank you, Clem." Her accent is thick, and I haven't heard it before. It's intriguing and clipping, accentuating each syllable, but before either of us has the chance to speak again, Tia speaks up.

"Okay, Clem, are you ready to go?" My eyebrows raise in surprise, but I nod yes. She says goodbye to Sunette, who kisses her cheek. It's a very familiar greeting for two servants. I wonder at their relationship as Tia leads me out of the gardens. Finn comes around a corner, walking between us. There isn't enough room for the three of us to walk side by side down the path. This doesn't discourage Finn, though. He knows his place. I fall back, walking behind the two more comfortably.

At the edge of the gardens, Tia grabs a bag I didn't notice when I walked in. I offer to carry it for her, but she puts it on, ignoring me. She glances around, then looks up at me. I smile softly at her. Her gaze softens as she stares at me. She doesn't smile, but she looks more comfortable. She finally turns and starts walking. I stay close to her, not speaking. I get the feeling she doesn't want to talk right now.

She leads us down a path to the east of the castle. She walks smoothly but is still lost in her thoughts. The route we start on is well-beaten. It's used for carts and horses. Once we reach the tree line, the path narrows a bit. It's still wide enough for supplies to be brought in. I wonder which villages are in that direction and what supplies come here. I've gathered that the castle is primarily self-sufficient. Maybe they send supplies out. There are no weeds, leading me to believe this path is still used frequently.

After a few minutes, she turns off the road onto a smaller walking path. Finn runs ahead on the trail. He is clearly familiar with wherever she is leading us. I step beside her, walking at her pace. I'm close enough that I could reach out and take her hand. Our hands brush a few times, but I decide not to try to grab her.

"Where are we going?" I ask softly, not wanting to startle her out of her thoughts. Her gaze turns to me.

"There is a pond," she points straight ahead. "It's only a few minutes away. It's quiet and secluded but a favorite place of mine." I smile and nod to her. The walking path has grown smaller again. The bottom of the forest is covered with ferns and plants with large leaves. I step behind her on the trail, not wanting to disturb or crush any plants. We walk in silence for a few more minutes. Just before I see the pond, I hear a loud splash. Tia sighs, yelling out at Finn. I laugh, realizing he is going for a swim.

We finally arrive at the pond. It is small but secluded. The trees are thick. The ferns create a carpet of green around it. The pond is surprisingly clean. Despite the late summer heat, this air is cooler here. The trees cast shade on the entire area. Tia drops the bag on the ground. Then removes her shirt, revealing a wrap around her chest. She removes her pants, tossing them down with her shirt and bag. She is left in a small undergarment covering only her ass and front. I am generally not a prude, but I don't know how to handle this situation. I'm frozen in shock, unable to move even if I could figure out what to do.

Tia chuckles. "Might as well join Finn."

She walks into the pond, taking a few steps before sinking into the water. Finn swims up to her, licking her face before making another loop around the pond. I'm still frozen in place. Tia dunks under the water. When she rises, it spills off her face. Her wet hair slicks down her neck. She looks happy and comfortable now. This spurs me into action. I remove my shirt, tossing it with hers. I untie my pants but remember there is nothing underneath them. While I would love to be naked with Tia, I'm not sure she would be comfortable with that.

"There are shorts for you in that bag."

I find the shorts she mentioned in the bag, along with lunch food. The shorts are much smaller than I would typically wear but perfect for swimming in a secluded pond. I drop my pants, exposing my ass entirely to Tia. She whistles appreciatively. I blush but quickly get the shorts on and turn to her. I show them off to her. She claps and laughs.

"Now, come on! Let's swim."

I join her in the water. It's cool and crisp, as if it were a stream. I make my way toward her. The water isn't deep, so I bend my legs, dropping my chest into the water. I shiver at the sudden change. Tia splashes me as Finn swims to lick the water off my face. We both laugh. I attempt to splash her back, but Finn bites at the water, trying to catch it. We take turns splashing Finn and each other. We shout and play in the water, enjoying the company.

After a while, Tia tips back, letting her body float in the water. I take in her body. Her smooth shoulders and rounded breasts. Her legs are strong, perfectly matching her body. There are no other scars on her body like the ones on her face. Whatever happened to her face ended there. My eyes drift over her body again. I move slowly in the water until I'm by her side. Her arms are out by her side. Her chest rises and falls lightly with her breathing, keeping her afloat. Her stomach is just below the surface.

I reach out to touch her side when I notice a large bruise across her lower abdomen. It is dark and massive, spanning from one hip to the other. It strikes me as odd that she can move so casually with such an extensive injury. When did this happen?

"What is this?" My fingers graze her side, reaching toward the damaged skin. She jerks upright, sinking her body below the surface so I can no longer see the injury.

"It's nothing. Really," she looks uncomfortable, not meeting my eyes. "It's actually an old injury, and the skin just never healed properly. It doesn't even hurt anymore."

"Tia," I say softly, gliding in front of her. Before I say anything else, she speaks.

"I assure you it's nothing. I don't want to talk about it anymore." Then she weakly adds, "Please."

My body is reeling, wanting to know what happened, who did this to her, how I can fix it. My brain knows I can't force her to let me do any of that. My body burns to do something to make it better.

"Okay," I say softly, but I wrap my arms around her body, pulling her close to my chest. I can't force her to tell me what happened, but I can let her know I will do anything for her. Her arms are held awkwardly above my shoulders, not relaxing into my touch.

"But you say the word, and whoever did that to you will be ended." I squeeze her tightly, keeping her tight against my front. Her arms finally drop around my shoulders. I hold her for a moment before releasing her and moving back. Her gaze finally meets mine.

"They have already been ended. It's a long, old story I don't want to dredge up. But I appreciate your kindness."

Before I can say anything, she pushes away from me, exiting the pond. She digs in the bag and pulls a towel out, drying her arms. She keeps her back to me but speaks over her shoulder.

"I only brought one towel since the bag is small. Give me a minute to get dressed, then you can use this one before lunch."

I swim toward Finn, splashing him a couple more times before Tia calls us both over. She's back in her shirt and pants, mostly dry.

"Finn, you go over there," she points to the side away from us. "No, Finn! Stop!" But it's too late. The sizeable furry dog has shaken his fur, attempting to dry off. He splattered us and her dry clothes in the process. He waltzes up and plops down next to Tia. He looks up at her, wagging his tail, as happy as can be. She has her hands on her hips, giving him a frustrated look. I laugh, but she just tosses the towel at me. I dry off as best I can and put my clothes back on.

I sit beside her as she hands me some food, tossing a couple of biscuits to Finn. We eat quietly for a few minutes. I want to tell her how I feel. The bruise across her stomach is burned into my mind. I want her to know she isn't alone and doesn't need to hide things from me. I open my mouth to say something, but she reaches out to silence me before I can.

"Shh, look," she whispers, pointing past the pond. Her hand hits the book in my pocket. She gives me a curious look but quickly turns back to where she was pointing. A couple of deer are grazing on the other side, and they don't seem to have noticed us. Right about that time, Finn does see them. He takes off running, barking at the deer. They spook and run off. Finn is hot on their tails. Tia sighs, making a weak attempt to call him back. I laugh, settling back to watch the dog run off. He quickly realizes he won't catch them, but instead of returning, he just frolics in the ferns, chasing insects.

"What's in your pocket?" Tia asks, turning her attention back to me.

"The book I borrowed from the library." I shift, pulling it out of my pocket to show her.

"Will you read it to me?"

She lays back on her elbow, eating more of the bread and cheese she brought for lunch. I had hoped to tell her that I want her, to be with her, but I can't deny her either.

"Sure. Want me to start at the beginning?"

"No, just fill me in on the important details."

I bring her up to speed on the book. I'm nearly halfway through since I spent so much time in the library yesterday. I try not to miss any details, but she doesn't seem too concerned. I start reading the book, leaning back to get more comfortable. There are images every few pages. After the first one, she moves closer and rests her head on my thigh, looking at the book. With the way I am already sitting, I can't place a hand on her. As much as I would like to touch her, I'm content just having her rest on me.

Finn eventually returns and lies beside Tia. She scratches him idly with one hand. She uses her other hand to help me turn the pages. We work so well together. There is a comfort with her that I have never experienced with another person. Even as much as I enjoyed Rachel, things weren't this easy with her.

We stay in this position, reading all afternoon. Tia asks questions occasionally about things I forgot to mention. We finish the book as the sun begins its final descent for the evening.

"We should get back." Tia rises, gathering things to put in the bag. I help her, and we make our way back to the trail. Finn follows us happily. Once we reach the supply trail, I walk beside her. This time I take her hand, holding hers as we walk. She doesn't say anything, but a smile is on her face. We walk quietly for several minutes. When the castle comes into view, she stops walking. She turns toward me but doesn't drop my hand.

"The bachelors will begin arriving tomorrow." I had forgotten all about them. "I won't be able to see you during the day. Do you know the stairwell behind the knight's armor with the ax? It's the only one holding an ax." I vaguely remember the stairwell, though I haven't been up it.

"Yes, I think so."

"Good. Meet me there tomorrow night after dinner."

She squeezes my hand as a thrill runs through my body at what is in store. She rises and places a lingering kiss against my cheek. She drops my hand as we walk back toward the castle. She steps to the side, creating distance between us. My instinct is to step closer, not allowing the space. Then I realize she may be doing it to protect herself. It would probably be terrible if we were caught together.

"Have you heard anything about the bachelors?" She questions.

"No," I shake my head. "Lord David mentioned sending another 'younger man' with me. A couple of the other councilors thought I would be too old for the Princess." Tia laughs loudly, catching me by surprise.

"You're what? 26, 27 years old?"

"Yes, 27." I nod in response. She rolls her eyes.

"The Princess is 26. Ugh, these old men think they know what's best."

She chuckles at her own comment, shaking her head. We walk back, chatting about the bachelors. She shares some of what she knows about them. I feel she is holding some information back, but I don't question her. I'll be meeting the others soon enough. Once we enter the castle, she stops by the library.

"I'll leave you here, Clem. I had a nice time today. Thank you for reading to me." I give her a smirk.

"Any time, Tia." I grab her hand, giving her a light squeeze.

"I'll see you tomorrow evening."

She walks off, leaving me to stare again. It's a good thing I didn't promise her I would stop staring. Her ass is impressive, especially with her pants hugging her hips so well. I keep my promise and stay focused, or rather, regain my focus after a moment of indulgent staring. I return the book and get a new one before calling it a night.

The following day, men start arriving from around the kingdom. Nine men show up; most are younger than me. I don't know any of them. Not even the other guy that came from my village. He is really young, though, about 19. They drop off their packs in their own rooms. Thankfully, the castle has more than enough rooms that none of us need to share. While I spent my life sharing a room with Bea, I've grown accustomed to having my own this past week.

We are informed the Princess will meet with us tomorrow before the equinox celebrations. There are more decorations around the castle. Garlands of colorful leaves, gourds, candles, and sun and star decorations have been placed around walls and doorways. The castle has a warm atmosphere about it. They have kept us away from the royal gardens and the nearby area. That is where most of the celebration will occur.

I keep my eyes open for signs of Tia and Finn all day but never see them. I know she said she would be busy, but I still hoped to see her during the day, even just a glimpse. I chat with some of the other bachelors, getting to know them. I'm hoping one of them will distract the Princess while I steal away Tia. A couple of the other men seem well-suited to be with a princess. Two men are tall, handsome, and well-spoken. They clearly have money and court training. I assume they will be top contenders for the Princess's hand.

The day passes slowly, much slower than I would prefer. I eat my dinner anxiously, ready to escape to the rendezvous point with Tia. I barely touch my meat and vegetables. Finally, after what feels like enough time in the dining hall, I leave, heading toward the stairway. Someone is already there. A short person in pants, a shirt, and a shawl covering their head. Apparently, Tia is trying to be inconspicuous. I walk up behind her, lean to her ear, and whisper.

"Excellent disguise." She startles, jumping around to face me. "I would have never guessed it was you."

She smirks at me, swatting at my chest playfully. She scans the area, then starts walking up the stairs.

"Come on."

I follow her up the winding staircase. There aren't any other doors; only a few windows let me know we are rising above the main building of the castle. We finally reach a smaller wooden door. She opens it and leads us through. She shuts the door behind me, placing a brick in front of it.

"We can have some privacy now." She smiles, the most brilliant thing I have ever seen.

She walks away from me. We are in a turret. This is clearly a watch tower for the castle. The landing is small, extending a few feet around the entryway from the stairs. There is enough room to walk around the entire walkway. The parapet offers cover from the area below, creating a sense of privacy. Because of the height, the views are spectacular.

Toward the south of the castle, I can see the mountains that separate Arkaley from the royal grounds. They are taller than I realized. The mountains are already snowcapped, indicating the upcoming change in seasons. As I circle to the right around the turret, I see the supply road we walked down yesterday. I cannot see the pond we swam in. The road disappears into the thick forest. Next, I can see the vast farmlands. They appear much more expansive than I anticipated. I can just make out the line of trees in the orchard.

Tia continues walking around the turret. I follow but keep my eye on the landscape beyond. I've never seen the kingdom from this vantage point. It's an amazing sight. I spot the trail we rode the horses down through the undulating hills. Beyond those hills is Greynon, the village with the most witches. Much like the royal gardens, my mother spoke highly of the village.

The scenery is beautiful. The sun is setting, casting a magical golden hue across the kingdom. Tia has stopped, watching the sunset. It is setting perfectly between the mountains. It looks as if it is settling down in Obele for the night. I step beside her, taking in the view of the snowcapped mountains with a warm glowing sun on its final descent.

"The autumnal equinox is the only time the sun sets over Greynon. It will shift in the next few months, settling over Arkaley."

I look down at her. The sunlight hits her, giving her a magical glow. I thought the kingdom looked beautiful from here, but it is nothing compared to how Tia looks now. Her scars are buried under glowing sunlight. Her hair has an array of golden-brown streaks. She looks so ethereal. She turns her head toward mine.

"Maybe you'll still be here to see it," she whispers.

I step close to her. Our bodies are inches apart. My fingers rise to her face, tracing her cheekbone, her ear, and her jaw. Her hand rises to mine, settling on top. She doesn't stop or encourage me. She simply holds my hand. My breathing is shallow. The only thoughts in my mind are how soft her lips feel in the golden light. Does the sunlight make them softer? Will she let me find out? I move closer again, pressing my body against her.

"Wait, you'll miss the final descent."

She turns her body away from mine, pressing against the parapet. There will be hundreds of more sunsets, but I only get one first kiss with her. She still holds my hand, but it's no longer on her face. Unwilling to create distance, I step behind her. My arms wrap around her waist, and I press my head against hers. She isn't wrong about the sunset. We watch as it settles between the mountains.

The sunset brings a cool breeze, another sign of the changing season. Neither of us has spoken in several minutes. The sky is darkening, but I refuse to let her go. I whisper her name in her ear, tightening my grip on her waist. My fingers search her stomach, exploring the area, even with her clothes still on.

"Tomorrow, I meet the Princess," I speak softly into her ear. "But you are the one I want. I want to steal all these moments with you. I want to steal you from the Princess. I want you to be mine, Tia. Run away with me." I press small kisses to her ear, her hair, and her neck.

"You don't mean that. You don't know me. I will hurt you." I knew she had been holding back from me. I don't understand why she says that, but it isn't true.

"You won't."

She breathlessly says my name.

"I was told my name comes from a flower, but nothing could be as sweet as my name from your lips."

I turn her to face me. Before she can say anything else, my lips find hers. I press a kiss to her gently at first. Her arms slowly snake around my neck as she settles into the kiss. Her lips are exactly as soft as I thought they would be. My arms tighten on her back, pulling her tighter against me. Her breasts crush against my chest. I slide my tongue against her lips, asking for permission. She accepts my plea, parting her lips, allowing me in. I deepen the kiss, exploring her mouth, needing to claim every inch of her. My hand tangles in her hair, holding her close. She pulls back, breaking the kiss. I press my forehead to hers, trying to catch my breath. I hold her tight, refusing to let her go. I never want this moment to end.

Chapter 6

JASMIN

Fuck.

Fuck fuck fuck.

I knew this day was coming, but I am not prepared for this. Soon, I have to meet all of the bachelors. Officially meet all of them. Clem still doesn't know who I am. After he kissed me last night, I rushed off to my room. The kiss was amazing. Easily one of the best I have ever had. I'm writing it off as so magical because of the sunset. I had planned on telling him the truth last night but couldn't bring myself to speak.

The past week of being with him, not realizing I am the princess, has been incredible. I could really be myself. He didn't care about the pants I wore or my hair being short and untamed. The politics didn't matter. There weren't duties that I needed to worry about. The past few years of my life have been almost entirely researching and curses and talking about lovers, with a startling lack of actual lovers. It was refreshing to have someone give me attention for me and not what I could do for them or the kingdom. I couldn't give that up, even for the truth. He said nothing I could do would hurt him. I hope he holds true to that.

I have been studying all the other bachelors. I have pulled family genealogies from the library. The Lords have given me detailed reports of all of the men that are present. I know far more about them than I need to. I prefer to go into situations fully prepared. Ten men are entering my home. A few seem promising. The problem is that 'true love' is such a vague term. I have searched all our magical texts, hoping to define 'true love .' This would be much easier if I could choose who my true love is. I tried in the beginning. I nearly married three different men. On the day of the wedding, something didn't feel right. Thankfully, the ceremonies were private and very few people were in attendance when I canceled. I don't believe I can force fate as much as I want to end the curse. It's the only reason I agreed to allow the bachelors to stay here.

Ten men. Two from each village. Ranging in age from 17 to 27. Five are from wealthy families. They are educated and familiar with court protocols. Two are from farming families. One is a witch. One comes from a family of previous guards. His father left the castle after the curse began. He is the first male in his family history to not be raised in the Court Guard. But there's one man I've spent the past week lying to.

Now I need to walk in and officially meet them.

My breakfast and lunch both went primarily untouched. I cannot fathom eating at this point. I did manage some of the fruit for lunch. This meeting will not go smoothly if I faint from lack of eating. Emmeline, my Lady-in-waiting, enters the room to help me dress. She is a few years older than me. Her father, Mikhail, took charge of the farmlands after the curse, previously serving as a courtier to my father. We were close as children due to Mikhail's vicinity to my father. She has been my best friend for most of my life, by my side through the good and the bad. Emmeline is a few inches taller than me, with perfectly smooth pale skin and gorgeous long blonde hair. I've begged her on many occasions to swap places with me. She looks more royal than I do. She always laughs and swats me away. I think she sees too much of the dark side of the royalty to want to be involved.

"Are you ready to get dressed, Jasmin?"

She grabs my dress from the wardrobe, ready to help me. I insisted on dropping formal titles around the time I stopped wearing dresses. I never liked dresses. They were tight and thick and never as comfortable as I wanted them to be. I sigh.

"Let me have the journal again."

Many people died during the curse. First, people were injured or killed because of the barrier forming. Then, chaos ensued. People died from mobs and riots. There was looting and fighting. It took many months to settle everyone down. Finally, people died due to a lack of medical resources from other kingdoms. We have since found replacements for most of the medicines, but not all. The journal contains the names of 143 individuals. I know them by heart and no longer need to see the list. I have reprinted the list at least three times. I keep it as a reminder of why I do things like this edict.

I glance at this journal, flip through a few pages, then nod to Emmeline. She helps me dress, ensuring everything is in place. She attempts to tame my hair, though we both know this is futile. It hasn't changed at all since the curse began. I take a deep breath as she positions my crown on my head. It is still small, meant for a princess, but I don't feel like a princess today.

The men are waiting in my preferred meeting room with the Lords from each village. I pause at the door. Finn stayed with Emmeline today. I wanted him with me, but the Lords insisted it would be distracting. Seeing how he greeted Clem the first day, they are probably correct. Thinking his name stirs unease in my gut. I turn away from the door, wondering how far I could get if I ran. At the end of the hallway is a painting of my father. He always taught me to be brave and face things that bring me discomfort. I take a deep breath, forcing it out through my mouth. I take one more, for good measure, then open the door and walk in.

A round table replaces the rectangular one that usually is here. All fifteen men rise as I walk in. The door clangs shut behind me. I keep my head high as I walk to my seat. My stomach is still in knots, but I can't let that show now. I look at each of the men around the table. When I see Clem, shock is written across his face. With everyone watching, I don't acknowledge him at all. After looking at every man, I speak.

"Please, be seated." They all sit, breaking the silence with chairs scraping. Clem sits slower than everyone else. His shock slowly fading to anger.

"Thank you all for coming." I remain standing, tapping my fingers against the table to expel some of the nerves. "This meeting is a chance for us to be formally introduced. During dinner celebrations, we will have the chance to be...less formal." I give a small smile, unsure how this group will take that comment. The Lords shift uncomfortably in their seats. Some of the men snicker, and a few men grin excitedly. Clem now glares at me.

"Before we begin, I would like to say a few things. First, you are here to help me find my true love to end the curse. This is not a competition. I have no control over who the curse will deem my partner. Because of this, I will be enacting a king consort title." Gasps spread across the room. "Whoever is my true love will be so in title but will hold no power over the kingdom." Several of the men start arguing with the Lords. I didn't inform them of this decision beforehand, but based on this reaction, I can tell it was the right decision. I can immediately pick the five men from wealthy families out.

Some of the Lords try arguing with me, but I hold up my hand to silence them. "I know this is unconventional, but my ruling stands. This is not a competition, and there will be no prize at the end. The royal family has long come from lines of families committed to the kingdom, not a village. The curse has divided us within our own lands. I must ensure whoever holds the king title is committed to all villages equally." There are some grumblings, but no one tries to argue further.

"Secondly, since you are here to get to know me, I will relax some of the formalities associated with my title. Bowing and honorifics will not be required. Respect still is." A few of the men visibly relax. These must be the lower-class men.

For all I know about the men, I do not know their faces. A few of the men still look disgruntled. A couple of the bachelors seem excited. Clem is still seething. I wish I could apologize adequately to him, but duty calls first.

I take a seat, looking around at the men. They are all attractive in their own way. The features vary greatly from one man to the next. Some I am more excited to get to know than others. Not that I have a choice. I will have to get to know them all the same. If only this stupid curse had been more specific about what true love is, but that wouldn't be much of a curse, would it?

"How about some introductions?" I state. "You know I am Princess Jasmin. I also have a Great Pyrenees named Finn. He is always with me, but you will meet him at the celebrations tonight."

Introductions are always a challenging step. My father used to skip them in some of his meetings just because of this. If this were a situation where I didn't need to know their names right now, I would probably skip them too. As it stands, I probably need to know the name of my possible true love. I look to the man sitting on the right of Lord Thurston. I don't need the Lords to introduce themselves. We all know them.

"Lord Thurston, milady," he says, standing up. "And this is Erik and Sven from Vadried. Erik's father was in the guard...."

I interrupt him. "Lord Thurston, while I appreciate your input. I would like to hear from the men. I expect all are capable of speaking for themselves." A few of them snicker. Thurston looks put off but takes his seat. Erik moves to stand. I hold my hand up again.

"Please don't feel that you need to stand. Seated is fine."

Erik nods appreciatively, sinking back into his seat. He tells me his name and finishes what Thurston was saying. His family has always been part of the royal guard. This isn't surprising. Erik is a large man with strong muscles, with short brown hair kept in the style of the guard. Sven introduces himself next. He's less muscular than Erik. He looks better suited to court than battle. He is from one of the wealthy families.

Next are the two men from Obele. Philip is the wealthier of the two, as his clothes are of higher quality. He also stands and uses honorifics despite my claim. Jonas remains seated for his introduction. His strong muscles and tanned skin remind me he is from a farming family.

Beside Jonas sits Lord David. He has not given any indication of knowing I met Clem. I learned long ago he sees more than I expect him to. Nothing in his demeanor shows he would know why one of his men is still glaring furiously at me. The young man between Lord David and Clem introduces himself. He is William and from one of the wealthier families. He is also the second youngest, at only 19 years old. I usually would not show interest in someone that young, but I didn't think to limit the age.

I meet Clem's stare. His anger feels palpable. I want to look at the others to see if they notice, but I refuse to cower from him. I take a deep breath, waiting for him to speak.

"I am Clematis," he says through gritted teeth. His face reddens with anger. I feel my shoulders drop slightly. I knew he would be angry. I had hoped it wouldn't be such a big deal. He can still have all those things he wanted with Tia. She just also comes with a crown.

Before I can break my stare with him, the next man begins to speak. I finally turn my attention to him. Oscar is a dark-skinned man with a lilting accent. His family is a wealthy merchant from Tilrade. It's a village on the coast that fished and traded with kingdoms across the sea. Many families suffered when the curse created a border, making them unable to trade with foreign lands. Oscar's family found a way to thrive. I have often questioned their business practices, but Lord Gustavo insists it is all fair. Tomas is next. It's unfair to call him a man. At only 17 years old, he is the youngest in the group. I am absolutely irritated about his age. He seems kind, though. He is soft-spoken, with golden sun-kissed skin from working in the fields. His dark hair looks wet. Perhaps he has issues taming his hair too.

The last two men are from Greynon, the land in the mountains west of the castle. Dominick is from a wealthy family. Kian belongs to a coven of witches.

My sources didn't detail how much if any, magic he could do. I am intrigued to know him better and see what he can do. I have hope for him beyond the true love search. There hasn't been an advisor for the witches in decades. My mother insisted they didn't need one. Lord Alwyn tells me the witches are fine, though I distinctly feel he is lying to me.

Once all the introductions are done, I dismiss everyone. I had planned on staying to get to know the group better, but there will be time for that later. I am exhausted from wearing this dress and crown. My heart hurts from the anger in Clem's eyes. I have little hope of finding my true love in this group. I need time to recover before the equinox celebration tonight. Recovery through tears, apparently, since the wine will be frowned upon this early in the day.

Part Two

Autumnal Equinox

Chapter 7

Jasmin

The afternoon hours pass with tears, tormented rest, and general discomfort. I cannot wrap my head around any of these men being my true love. I am also incredibly tired of the phrase true love. I allow myself a couple of hours of despair and wallowing. I'll just get it out of my system and be fine. I let Clem's anger flow through me. This isn't the time for hope and sunshine. This is my time to be sad.

Long ago, my father taught me how to handle my emotions in front of everyone and break down later. He taught me the value of taking time for myself. Time to regroup, reset, and face whatever challenge was out there. When he wasn't with me, it took me several months to learn how to manage without him. The Lords have seen me cry more often than anyone should see royalty cry. My father was always kind to me, teaching me ways to survive in the harsh world with a crown. The ache of missing him has never gone away; it's just less noticeable some days. Today is not one of those days.

Emmeline comes in before the festivities begin to help me get ready. We dry my tears, put on a clean, unwrinkled dress, and finish off with a circlet instead of the tiara. The Lords wanted me to wear a tiara, but I refused. This celebration has always been about my people in the castle. This is their time to celebrate another harvest, enjoy the last warm weather, and have a safe space to let loose. I won't spoil that with titles and crowns. I did agree to the circlet to remind the bachelors of my position.

The dress is simple for a princess. The bust is fitted with pleating across my breast. The rest of the dress falls in long panels grazing the floor. I pair it with silk slippers, taking comfort over style. The dress is a creamy ivory color, and I feel divine in it. A feeling I desperately need after the afternoon I have had. We add a matching bowtie to Finn before going down to the celebration.

The space next to the gardens has been decorated with candles, gourds, leaves, and pumpkins. This is one of my favorite celebrations. It's always a phenomenal evening with food, music, and laughter. There are tables packed with food from our fields. A hog is roasting, filling the air with a delicious smell that pairs well with the baked desserts on a table nearby. A quartet is playing in the corner. It is muted now but will pick up later in the evening. There are casks of ale and wine near the food. Lots of benches and chairs line the walls of the castle and gardens. Most festivities will happen in this area, with people dancing and chatting. Some will wander off to other parts of the castle as the night goes on.

There is an odd air of anticipation among the people. I am typically the last to arrive, but they have never waited on me before. As I exit the castle and walk into the celebration, I notice several Lords standing with the bachelors. The Lords and men from wealthy families immediately bow, followed awkwardly by the rest of the bachelors. The rest of the crowd catches on, giving cumbersome bows. A trickle of anger rises that the Lords have created this situation that we haven't used since my parents were here.

"Please," I hold my hands up to the crowd, offering a warm smile as a way of apology, "don't stop on my account. Enjoy these celebrations as your own."

I emphasize this by curtseying before passing the Lords as everyone cheers and claps. I scowl, making eye contact to emphasize my anger with them. I fill a goblet with wine and turn to watch the celebration. The music has turned to a joyful beat. People are already moving to the center to dance. I do a quick scan of the crowd. Clem is in a chair near the corner, still glaring at me. Some bachelors are scattered around; some are still with the Lords, who are now approaching me. This won't do at all. I quickly drink the rest of my wine and grab the hand of the closest person to me.

Tomas startles as I grab his hand. I drag him into the dance that has started up. It's not my favorite dance, but I know it all the same. I step in line, turning toward Tomas. He seems very nervous, rubbing his elbow and looking around at other people. He is from a farming family; he may not be familiar with some of the dances.

"Do you know this dance?"

He shakes his head, casting his eyes down.

"Okay, stand here next to me." I pull him to my side, glancing back. The Lords and their crew of eligible bachelors seem put off that I quickly jumped into the dance. Inwardly, I giggle at my small triumph. This is a party, not a courting for royalty. I turn my attention back to Tomas.

"This one is pretty simple. We step and turn, then step and turn some more. And don't worry about bumping into people. It'll happen a lot with everyone. We do this dance exactly twice a year here. Everyone is rusty," I say with a wink. I take his hand as the dance starts. He's still stiff and unsure, but we start dancing together with the other people. Someone bumps into him and apologizes with a laugh before whisking off with their partner. That seems to loosen him up.

He catches on quickly to the moves. We are stepping and turning, smiling and laughing. The music grows, as does the chatter and laughter. We dance through the whole song. It ends, and we bow to everyone, clapping our hands and congratulating each other. The next song starts immediately. A wide grin spreads across my face. This is my favorite song. This is the one I always insist we practice because I love it so much. He tries to step away, but I refuse to let him. I take both of his hands, guiding him in front of me.

"This is my favorite song. You won't deny me that dance, will you, Tomas?"

"No, ma'am."

Oh, the punch to the heart. With one single word, he has wounded my soul and placed me on my deathbed.

"Tomas, if you ever call me ma'am again, I will send you back to your family in pieces." His eyes go wide. I remember he doesn't know me, and that wasn't an appropriate joke. Damn, you would think I had learned that from Clem. I laugh to break the tension.

"I'm joking, Tomas. But please don't call me ma'am." I pull his hands, dragging his body toward mine as the dance begins. He follows along, very focused on his footing. He allows me to lead, dancing opposite every other couple in this group. The men always lead, but I love when I get the chance to. Tomas doesn't seem to be upset about following my movements. He matches mine with a wide grin on his face. While I can't see spending time with him romantically, I am glad he's willing to do whatever comes his way.

"So, Tomas, how do you like the castle so far?" I continue guiding him through the dance with my hands, pushing and driving him in the right direction, hoping to break up some tension with conversation.

"Oh, it's very big, ma.... Princess?" He is so unsure of his answer I laugh at him.

"Call me Jasmin, please. Have you seen much of it?"

"No, I don't think so. They showed us the rooms, dining hall, and meeting rooms. Beyond that, I haven't had time to see anything else." I smile at him as we separate around another couple, then come back together.

"What kind of things do you like to do?"

"Well, I mostly work on my uncle's farm. I like his horses but don't spend much time with them. I'm good at whittling."

I nod to his response. "That doesn't really answer the question. You will have a lot of time here. What would you like to do?" He looks nervous again. The dance pulls us close, but I step closer, whispering in his ear.

"I'm not going to judge you. I want to get to know you. Whatever you want to say is safe with me."

We pull apart. His eyes are on me, assessing the truth behind my statement. I offer him a soft smile. The dance draws us close again. He speaks softly this time.

"I want to learn how to use a sword."

I step back, both with the dance and in surprise. "Well, Tomas, you are in the right place for that. We have excellent swordsmen here, and I may know a thing or two I can teach you." I waggle my eyebrows at him. "Later this week, I'll show you the training area." He grins at me, ending the dance with a bow. We both bow, giggling at this situation. This time I do step away from the dance floor. As much as I want to avoid the Lords, it's probably rude to do so all night.

"Princess Jasmin," Lord Gustavo addresses me first. "I see you have spent time with Tomas. Why don't you have a chat with Oscar? He comes from a prominent family and would be an excellent dance partner."

Tomas seems to flinch and move away quickly. I assess Oscar. His dark skin and finely styled hair are attractive, but something feels wrong about him. He puts off a commanding, pompous vibe. It's relatively common among some wealthy families, but I cannot stand it. I step toward the wine.

"My Princess," Oscar says, bowing, "please take my wine." He holds his out to me. I have already learned not to trust my drinks to anyone else at events like this. I am surprised he would even offer his own. Does he assume I would trust him so soon after meeting him?

"No, I will get my own." I turn to fill my goblet but notice his scowl before I do. Once I have my wine, I take a sip turning back to him. The scowl has been replaced with an award-winning grin. I should also win an award for not rolling my eyes at him.

"Why don't we sit and get to know each other better?" His voice is melodic, with a lilting accent.

I nod and lead him toward the chairs. I sit several seats down from Clem. As soon as he sees me, Clem walks to the food table. He really isn't letting go of his anger. I don't expect him to suddenly not be angry, but his actions are starting to feel excessive.

"So, Princess, tell me about the qualities your true love should have."

"Wow, okay." I am shocked at his brazenness. "Starting off strong." I sip my wine, trying to gain my thoughts. "Well, as you know, I have no control over who my true love is." I gaze Oscar up and down. He is confident and muscular, but something about him makes me uneasy.

"Yes, you have mentioned that. What kind of man do you want to be your true love?"

"I would like someone that is just and kind. I hope my true love is equal to me and respects everyone in our kingdom." Oscar nods, considering my answer.

"Well, I am very strong." He flexes his arm, then places it behind me on the chair. His arm is wrapped around my back, bringing his body closer to me than he already was. This situation is giving me claustrophobia. My body tenses, preparing for fight or flight mode. I am uncomfortable with people, especially large men, blocking me in. My breathing quickens slightly. Oscar is oblivious to everything, but I am hyper-focused on him now.

"How long do you think it will take you to determine who your true love is?"

"Ha," a fake, uncomfortable laugh, "do you have somewhere else to be, Oscar? Is there a rush?"

"Oh, no, Princess. No rush." He speaks so smoothly, then adds, "But I have a girl I proposed to at home. I'm sure she will wait, but I would love to let her free once you realize I am your true love."

Speechless. I am honestly speechless. He's engaged. Convinced he is my true love. And has this woman waiting. The audacity to do those and tell me in our first interaction is astounding. I move to stand, but he grabs my hand, pulling me back down. My body freezes, fear kicking in. I feel unsafe. All of my surroundings have faded into a blur. It is only Oscar and me. My mind is kicking and screaming, but my body is stalls with inaction. He leans in close to my ear.

"Don't be like that, Jasmin. We can make this work."

My mind is blank. Reliving trauma from my youth. An eerily similar situation. My body is tense. My eyes sting with tears building. He's too close to me. I can't breathe. I can't escape. I know the pain that is coming. I can't do this again.

Suddenly, Oscar is jerked back from me. A hand grabs my elbow, pulling me to stand. I slam into the side of a large, somewhat familiar body. His scent engulfs me. I take a deep breath and close my eyes, letting comfort and safety wash over me.

"Ay, I think it's my turn with the princess, mate."

Clem places his hand on my lower back as he guides me toward the dance area. I move with him, my mind still foggy and unsure of what is happening, but I feel less threatened with Clem.

"You owe me," is all he whispers. He steps in front of me as the music registers in my brain. The fog is slowly lifting. Oscar is still stunned in his seat. The memories are clearing from my head. I take a deep breath and move through the dance, much less enthusiastically than everyone else. Even Clem seems to be happy in his dancing. I am missing steps and trying to get a hold of my surroundings. I crash into Clem several times, but he just laughs as if this is the best thing he has ever done. He's really convincing, too. That shouldn't hurt as much as it does.

After several minutes, I mostly return to normal. I start to enjoy dancing with Clem. He keeps his hands light on me when we touch. He is smiling, but I don't think it is because he is with me. Something about his smile feels forced. The song ends, and Clem turns to leave. There is still an ache in my chest. I grab his arm, stopping him.

"Thank you," I say sheepishly. He only nods, turning back to leave.

"Stay for another dance?" I ask, a hopeful smile on my face. He looks around the dance floor.

"No." He takes a step but turns back to me. He looks around the area, then leans in to whisper. "Stay away from Oscar. Don't go off with him alone."

I had already decided on that. I don't know whether to find comfort or alarm in Clem's warning. Regardless, he saved me from what could have been a terrible situation for me. Unbelievable gratitude flows through me, followed by guilt over how I treated him. He doesn't deserve to be lied to the way I did. I watch him walk away, getting more ale. He chats with some of the kitchen staff. Something flutters through my chest, watching him interact with people from the castle. Tonight has been a powerful miscellany of emotions.

The rest of the evening passes smoothly. There aren't any more close calls, but plenty of awkward moments. I dance and chat with the remaining bachelors. I squeeze in a dance with Emmeline and Sunette, even Zander, Sunette's son. Finn spends his whole evening next to the food table, waiting for scraps. He ate better tonight than he probably ever has. He may be a good boy, but he is indeed spoiled.

I tried to find Clem again, but he disappeared shortly after he pulled me from Oscar. I want a chance to thank him and apologize properly. At this rate, I may never get to. Emotions roil through my body when I think of this situation with him. I'll find a way to repair them soon.

The celebrations have ended, and the quartet is packing up. A few people are cleaning up. I offer to help, but they shove me away. I would genuinely help, but they seem to have it covered. Not quite ready to go to bed, I decide to roam through the gardens. The gardens at night are different than during the day. While they are peaceful during the day, there is an eerie calm over them at night. It's a different kind of quiet. Most of the animals are asleep. I truly feel alone here.

No one else is in the gardens tonight. Occasionally, there will be a couple of others, but it seems everyone is elsewhere. I find my favorite bench surrounded by lazy peonies, drooping slightly in the moonlight. I sit down, closing my eyes to reflect on my days. Really just one day, and not even a whole day. Since lunch, things have been crazier than I was prepared for. The bachelors, Clem being so angry, Oscar trapping me, Clem saving me, and still being angry is a lot to process. Not to mention traditional celebrations and the impact of my father's absence.

Clem is a constant thought in my mind. His hand on my arm earlier, his grip was so firm, so sure. The kiss from the turret fills my mind. His lips were soft, but much like his grip, he was firm and confident. He knew what he wanted. Heat fills my body. I rub my thighs together, unable to quench the growing desire. I open my eyes, looking around the gardens. No one else is here. No one will see anything I do. The thrill of getting caught drives my pleasure higher. I'm mostly positive no one will see me, but I can never really know for sure.

I settle back against the bench, grazing my fingers down my neck across my breastbone. The pleated top of the dress has a string holding the pleats together. I pull it, loosening the fabric. I slide my fingers under, grazing across my breast. I gently squeeze my nipples. My hips jerk, needing more sensation now. I spread my legs, pulling the dress up my legs. The fabric slides smoothly across my shins, brushing against my knees. The sensation is tantalizing as the dress drags my skin.

Movement in a window above the gardens draws my attention. It's the closest to the gardens on the second floor. It's far enough away that the person can see all of me but not close enough to make out the finer details. I can see their clothing and face, but not the designs or small features of their face. I pause, then realize it's Clem's room. There is a dark figure standing in the window, facing my direction. The room has no lights, so I can't be confident who it is. The person has Clem's shape, tall, with strong muscles from working in the field. While this does describe several of the men that could possibly be in that wing, only one person in the bachelor wing has shoulder-length hair. The darkened figure has his hair down, brushing his shoulders.

Knowing Clem is watching gives me courage I probably shouldn't have. I leave my dress draped across my thighs. Pulling the fabric of the bust, I slide one breast out, squeezing it tightly. I pinch and pull my nipple, throwing my head back in pleasure. The figure moves away from the window. A sudden sadness fills me but doesn't stop the ache between my legs. I rest one hand on my thigh, ready to draw the dress up the rest of the way.

A small light turns on in Clem's room. He reappears in the window and places a small candle on the window sill. It's not enough to light him properly, but I can see his currently tented pants. My mouth waters at the sight, and I can feel my core dripping. He pulls the strings of his trousers loose, sliding them to the side as his cock pops out into the open. Despite the distance between his room and the bench I am currently on, I feel like we are next to each other. He begins to slowly, so slowly, stroke himself.

My pussy pulses with need. I slide my dress the rest of the way up, gathering the fabric across my hipbone. He now has full sight of me, though he may not be able to see much in the dark. The cool breeze kisses my wet lips, driving my desire sky-high. I slide my finger over my entrance. It is instantly soaked by the wetness. I make a small circle around my clit before sliding two fingers inside me. Clem speeds up his stroking, moving faster. I match his pace, in and out, savoring the feel. I close my eyes, envisioning he is the one touching me. With my other hand, I free my other breast, pulling on my nipple again. I twist it between my fingers, groaning at the painful pleasure.

The window cracks open slowly. Clem is practically leaning over the edge while stroking himself. My fingers still match his pace, rubbing against that spot inside that drives me wild. I press the heel of my palm against my clit as my fingers move in and out. I try to keep my eyes on Clem, but soon my orgasm is too close. I tilt my head back, moaning his name as my release barrels through. My eyes close tight as my body tenses and relaxes. I press my chest out as my finger wrings the rest of my orgasm out of me.

I open my eyes in time to see Clem's release. His orgasm shoots from his body. It flies over the edge of the window and lands on the ground in front of the door leading out to the royal gardens. I sit panting, still spinning from my own orgasm. When his release stops, he tucks himself away. He closes the window and clicks the latch. It feels louder in the silence after what just happened. He leans down to blow out the candle, but a playful gleam is in his eye. He won't stay mad at me forever. I refuse to let him if just masturbating in his presence was that good. With a chuckle, I straighten my clothes and go to my room. I take care to step over his mess, not cleaning it up. I didn't put it there. In my room, Finn is already asleep in my bed. I snuggle next to him, falling asleep quickly with a smile on my face.

Chapter 8

CLEM

I can't say I have ever been to a celebration quite like that. I arrived, still fuming over the lie the Princess fed me. I feel like such an idiot. For believing her, for not knowing any better, for getting my hopes up about Tia. While technically, she is still Tia, things just got a lot more complicated. And she never said anything. Didn't hint or anything. Okay, well, maybe in hindsight, there were some clues, but she still lied, and I'm still mad.

When I saw her with Oscar, though, the anger faded to this powerful desire to protect her. I don't know what happened to her. She looked so scared and withdrawn. It was apparent to anyone but Oscar that she was frozen. I don't know how many people actually saw her. The Lords had turned their back to give them privacy. Meanwhile, their promising bachelor made her so uncomfortable she couldn't speak. If it were up to me, both Oscar and his Lord would be gone. I guess it isn't up to me, though.

Jasmin does something to me that I have never felt before. I've never felt such anger over being lied to. I've never felt such a desire to protect, not even with my siblings. Then she was touching herself. Holy gods, I thought I was going to burst when my fingers just grazed my own cock. I've fucked, given oral, and even masturbated in front of a girl before, but nothing like that. Watching her from so far away, mixed with all of my emotions, was intense. I've never desired someone as desperately as I want her.

Unfortunately, now someone is banging on all the doors in the hallways and shouting at everyone. By the time they reach my door, I'm awake and opening it for them. Oscar is standing there. He looks surprised that I opened the door but quickly scowls. He skims my body. I'm only wearing trousers at this point. His face shows disgust, but he informs me the lords have called a meeting with everyone in one hour. We need to get dressed and get to the meeting room.

I intended to find Mikhail and see if I could work the rest of the season, and I suppose I can still do that later. I dress and grab some fruit from the dining hall. People are buzzing today. There is excited chatter about last night's celebrations, along with the potential topic for this meeting. Several of the bachelors are enamored with Jasmin. She is a fascinating woman, even if she is a liar.

We finally gather in the meeting room. I had assumed we would all sit where we did yesterday, but the five Lords are already sitting side by side. Even the bachelors have started forming groups. Most wealthier men have sat near the Lords, leaving only one chair open for Jasmin. I see an empty seat next to Kian and sit there. I have chatted with him several times since he arrived. I like him so far. I notice Tomas lingering near the edge. I motion him over to sit on my other side. The poor kid is so nervous in this setting. He seems like a good guy, just really unsure.

When we're all sitting, Jasmin finally walks in. The Lords and the wealthy bachelors stand. The rest of us glance at each other, ensuring others stay sitting. I specifically remember Jasmin saying we don't need to stand. The scowl on her face almost seems permanent. If I hadn't seen her before everyone else showed up, I would be positive that is her only facial expression.

"Where is my chair?" She demands. The chair she sat in yesterday is no longer here. It wasn't an ornate chair, but it was nicer than the rest of ours. More decorative, but also more worn in.

"Here, milady." Lord Thurston points to the empty chair next to him.

"That may be the spot you want me to sit, but I will do no such thing until you return my chair."

She stands still, waiting and glaring at him. Despite my mixed feelings about her, I admire her adamancy.

"Milady, we thought you wanted everyone to be treated as equals here." Lord Thurston is clearly trying to get one over on her, and she's having none of it.

"And yet you still stood and bowed. Now, Lord Thurston, go get my chair."

When he doesn't move, she looks as if she is considering something.

"I seem to recall a request for increased funding to Vadried recently, for what? What was the purpose again?" She taps her chin, trying to remember. Lord Thurston seems terrified now, scanning the faces of the men from his village.

"Oh, yes. I remember now. You wanted...." She's quickly interrupted by Thurston.

"Ah, Princess. I will get your chair now." He waves to one of the servants standing at the door.

"No, Lord Thurston. YOU will get the chair. Not your servant."

Thurston coughs but rises to do as told. Jasmin grabs the chair she doesn't want to sit in, pushing it to the wall out of the way. It seems like a much kinder gesture than he deserves. The room is surprisingly quiet, watching the interaction.

"I do want us to be on equal footing," Jasmin speaks to all of us, "but this chair belonged to my father. I have sat in it since the day he left, and I will not stop that. If you happen to find a chair in one of the meeting rooms that will fit at this table, I will happily consider swapping the chair around for you." She smiles as Thurston places the chair in her spot. He sits in his chair, then she sits in hers. She looks to the Lords expectantly.

Lord Erland stands, placing his fingers down on the table. When he speaks, his words are slow and labored due to his age. "It has come to our attention that someone got a little too excited at the celebrations last night." He clears his throat. Several of the men look at each other, confused and somewhat frightened. Jasmin just looks bored.

"There was a certain mess left on the entryway to the castle last night, and this will not be tolerated."

Oh. That. Yeah, I was definitely a little excited after the celebration. Most of the men look confused. I try to match their look, not wanting to be noticeable. Jasmin sighs, but I can see the undeniable twitch at the corners of her mouth.

"What type of mess, Lord Erland?" Jasmin questions.

The regret of inviting her instantly covers his entire face. He is undoubtedly uncomfortable with this line of questions. It is because Jasmin is present, but I also suspect he would be uncomfortable without her here too.

"Well, um..." he stutters through his thoughts. "A certain, ahem, bodily fluid."

"Someone urinated near the gardens!!" Her outrage is impressive, yelling and slamming her hands on the table. A few of the men snicker. All of the Lords are scowling at us.

"Oh, um, no, milady." Lord Erland is beet red. His voice is hoarse.

"Defecated?" Her confusion is astounding. I snicker at her antics this time. She knows what mess he is referring to. She's just being difficult. Lord Erland is still stuttering.

"Please, Lord Erland. We need to know what bodily fluid it was. Please be concise in your directions." She pauses, then adds before he can speak, "Not that anyone should be urinating or defecating anywhere on the castle grounds." She looks at each of us. The twinkle in her eye causes me to nearly laugh. I try to cover it with a cough, but it's ineffective. Several of the men are laughing now.

Lord Gustavo finally stands.

"Someone pleasured himself in the gardens and left the mess for the poor kitchen maids to find this morning." He is practically shouting. I do feel bad about the kitchen maids finding the mess this morning. I hadn't thought through that when I leaned over the window last night. I just wanted Jasmin to see it. It was meant for her, not anyone else.

The room has gone silent. All of the bachelors are looking down at the table. The Lords look angry. Jasmin has returned to her look of boredom, staring at the Lords. It's silent for a moment. I can hear Finn whimpering beyond the door. He must not be accustomed to waiting for meetings like this.

The Lords remind us of expected behaviors, a few housekeeping rules, and demands to be respectful. A few of the men eat up the rules. The rest of us, including Jasmin, just look bored. The Lords finally dismiss us, instructing us to stay close to gather for dinner. They ask Jasmin to remain behind. Several of the men groan. I just make my way toward the door. I plan to go to the fields to see if I can work.

At the door, I see Finn sitting. He tries to look in, then notices me. His tail starts wagging. He stands, taking a few steps toward me. I reach down and pet him, scratching his ears the way he likes. The other men walk around us as I speak to Finn.

"Jasmin will be in there for a while, buddy." He seems sad at my words. "Wanna go play with me?" I offer to cheer him up. I don't want to see the large pup sad. He's my buddy now, too. He barks at me. I stand, ready to go out to the grass with him. As we walk away, Oscar comes up behind me, clapping his hand on my shoulder.

"Oh, good. I'm glad you've decided to be the dog's keeper, Tim. Someone needs to keep him out of the way while I persuade the Princess to make me king."

I scrunch my nose up in disgust at him. I grab his hand, picking it off my shoulder like it is repulsive.

"It's Clem. You can convince yourself you're her true love, but I can guarantee you, if Finn doesn't like you, she won't either, O'Brien. So, try out some of that respect they were talking about. Okay?"

I walk down the hall, tapping my leg. Finn follows along closely, totally uninterested in the rest of the guys. We make it through the door as Oscar yells his reply. I let the door swing close, cutting off his words. I laugh and start running, Finn following quickly at my heels.

All of the other men broke off into other wings of the castle. I can tell immediately that Oscar won't get along well with Jasmin. I assume most of what she told me is actually true. I suppose if she was lying about all that stuff, I don't know her any better than Oscar does. I don't believe she was lying about everything, though. I hope she just wanted a chance to get to know me without the title and edict between us.

I know I should give her a break. Maybe she will apologize. I feel she has been trying to do that since the meeting yesterday. So much has happened since then; it's hard to believe it has only been one day. I've known this woman for a week now, and she's already consuming so much of my thought.

Finn and I run around for a while. I track down some lunch for us, taking him back outside instead of trying to settle him in the dining hall. After a quick bite, we go back out to play fetch in the grass. As I'm standing there, I see Tomas walk out, looking lost.

"Hey, Tomas. How's it going?"

"Oh, fine, I guess." He looks nervous. His hand is wrapped across his body, rubbing his other arm.

"What are you doing?"

"Nothing." His response is timid, but he meets my gaze. Finn runs up with the stick.

"Want to play with us?"

The kid seems unsure of himself. I would probably be the same way if I were in his shoes. While this is likely most of the men's first time away from home, Tomas is younger than all of us. He takes the stick and throws it. Finn doesn't even hesitate; he runs after the stick. Tomas throws it a few more times without either of us saying anything.

"Have you been to the castle before?" I question.

"No. First time away from home at all."

"Me too," I offer.

"Do you know your way around yet?"

"Not well, but what are you looking for? I know where a few things are."

"Well," he pauses, looking around to see who might be listening. "I would like to go see the stables."

"Oh, yeah. They're over there." I point behind my shoulder where we can just see the edge of the stables around the corner of the castle. "There are probably lots of horses there now. Do you ride?"

"Not well," he shakes his head, looking that way.

"Me either." I offer with a laugh. "Finn isn't allowed near the stables. He's too playful for some of the horses. I can take over fetch with him if you want to go." A wide grin stretches across his face. He thanks me and runs off towards the stables. He seems like a good kid. He'll be fun to get to know. I'm curious to see how the Princess handles him if she is turned off because he is so young.

When Finn starts to slow down, we go inside with the intent of going to the library. I stop by my room to grab the library books, then we saunter slowly, taking in the art and decorations of the castle. There are many large paintings on the walls, but also smaller pieces. I recognize some of the work from a sculptor in Arkaley. He doesn't make as many art pieces as he did in the past. Now he mainly creates functional dishes and pots, but he still has a distinct style that is easily recognizable. I didn't realize the art was from local sources. It gives me a sense of pride to recognize work from an artist I know. In the library, Finn quickly settles into his favorite spot. I grab some new books and settle in too. A lazy afternoon in a sunny spot sounds like the perfect escape after the past day.

Chapter 9

JASMIN

The Lords dismiss the men from our meeting, asking me to stay back. I knew there would be meetings where the men would be present and others where they were excused. I want whoever will be staying with me to be accustomed to this. At the same time, I don't want a lot of strangers involved that don't need to be.

"We should discuss a schedule, Princess." Lord Thurston says as soon as the door closes. I sigh heavily, intent on displaying my displeasure at this meeting. I heard Clem greeting Finn in the hallway. I'm glad he is taking Finn. I'm thankful they get along so well. I was worried about how Finn would take to all the new people. He is very social, but not everyone likes dogs. I don't understand that, but at least Finn has Clem.

"Yes, milady." Lord Gustavo adds, "You should plan time alone with each man to get to know them better." The hair on the back of my neck raises.

"No," my voice is just below a shout, and all the Lords jump. "Under no circumstances will I be scheduling time alone with the men at this point. It is insulting you would even suggest that."

They know some of my history with arranged courting. I have learned to be more comfortable in the presence of men, but this is not a situation I am ready for. Just having them here in the castle is overwhelming.

"We understand, Princess." Lord David speaks softly. I take a deep breath. I look up to the ceiling, trying to quickly reset my feelings. This castle is several hundred years old, possibly older. It is redecorated every few years. This room, though, hasn't actually been redecorated. The painting is touched up as needed, but it is still the original design. The ceiling is painted a dark blue with golden-yellow stars across the sky. I don't particularly like having meetings here because it spoils the beauty of the ceiling. In moments like these, though, I am thankful for their presence. It's a good reminder that this problem is smaller than it seems.

"I will spend time getting to know them," I agree in a gentler tone, bringing my attention back to the Lords. "I will not do so in one-on-one settings until I am ready. I will accept a schedule of activities for several of us."

We spend the rest of the morning creating a schedule of activities. They want to prepare the bachelors for a royal position. Since half of the men come from lower-class families, I understand their point. I would rather spend our time doing fun things, like riding horses, sword practice, jousting; something violent would be wonderful. We spend a couple of hours arguing over what is appropriate for royalty. I agree with their plans, only to get the Lords to shut up. I'm not opposed to their suggestions, but they are a bore. Painting? Court protocol? Dinners in the garden? Pass. I manage to only roll my eyes at them eight times. This took considerable restraint, and I am very proud of myself.

After the meeting, I go in search of Finn. I need some cuddles from my buddy. Where would Clem take him? They likely went outside to run first. If he did the same thing he did last time, they might be in the library.

I find them in the same spot as before; Finn sleeping and Clem reading. I collapse next to Finn, rubbing his back and sides. His tail wags violently as he rolls over for more scratches. I lean into him, kissing and whispering to him. I love Finn so much. He's my favorite being ever. Finn brings me so much comfort when my mind starts spinning. I sit back to talk to Clem. I am finally going to thank him and apologize. When I look up, he is already gone. I sigh but keep petting Finn. At least he isn't mad at me. He's my good boy.

Fuck, I hope my true love is in this batch of bachelors. I don't think I can keep socializing for an extended period. I've been making small talk for what feels like 84 years. It's barely been one day. After I found Finn in the library, I chatted with a few of the men. I do look forward to getting to know several of them. But fuck, I wish I could just skip to the part where we all know each other. How many times can I answer the question, "What do you think your true love will be like?" I don't know. A fucking turtle would be ideal.

I'm not angry. I'm not. I just need to break the curse and not have ten men fawning over me. The Lords have settled on all of us taking breakfast in the meeting room while discussing petty politics. We discuss crop output, village trading, and minor disciplinary actions. The most boring stuff of all. Today, the Lords want us all to go to the gardens for a dance lesson. They insist this will be a good learning opportunity for everyone. They even brought in one of the dance instructors that taught at the castle under my parents' reign.

We line up, listening to the instructions. Since I have been through this so many times, I focus more on the men. Watching how they behave. Tomas and Jonas soak it up. They are new to this but seem to enjoy it. Their excitement is almost contagious. Meanwhile, Oscar, Sven, and Philip are close together and sneering at everyone. They already know the steps and have no qualms about pointing out mistakes. It ruins the entire experience. I am ready to send Oscar packing at this point. He is the reason I decided to implement a king consort title.

After an hour, I notice Clem is missing. I assume he took a break, but he didn't return. This frustrates me for two reasons. One, I'm tired of him avoiding me.

I know I lied, but it doesn't deserve the silent treatment for days! Two, I'm so fucking jealous. I can't slip away from this, and it's entirely unfair to me.

The Lords have been so kind as to give us free time in the afternoon. Cue eye-rolling. I sneak off through hidden passages and spend the afternoon in my room. I don't want the bachelors to learn where my room is. I desperately need a break from them. Finn and I lounge, reading books, snoozing, and generally being lazy and antisocial. Those are my two favorite things.

Late in the afternoon, I see Clem walking back with the field hands. He is dirty but seems happy, laughing and chatting with the people he is walking with. He left our dance lessons to work in the fields. That lucky bastard. He doesn't come to dinner with the rest of us. He probably ate with the other workers and went to his room. The dining hall is packed with the new men. It is a large room, but it feels far too small with the nine men trying to crowd around me. I sit in the middle of a long table. I am next to Erik, with Oscar quickly filling the seat next to me. Kian and Tomas sit in front of me. Oscar begins to brag about some extraordinary event where he stopped a robber on the main road in Tilrade. I know what he is speaking about; Lord Gustavo informed me after it happened. I also know that Oscar wasn't actually present. I debate calling him out, but I am not in the mood for that. Instead, I settle for interrupting and changing the topic.

"Erik, you lived in the castle before the curse, correct?" He seems stunned that I am speaking to him during Oscar's monologue, but he still answers me with a smirk.

"Yes, in the guards' section. I didn't venture into the main castle often. It feels different than I remember."

"Yes, there have been some changes made to the castle," Oscar tries to interject.

"It does feel different, Erik," I turn my body away from Oscar. He loudly huffs but doesn't leave. "We only changed decorations and staffing. I let many people leave but haven't changed any of the rooms. Even the one we met in this morning is the one my father always used."

"Long live the king," Oscar shouts, raising his mug. Philip and Sven follow along in his salute, but everyone else looks uncomfortable. I slam my hands against the table as I turn to Oscar.

"If you are going to continue to interrupt and be rude, please leave." I scowl at him, and he matches my scowl but stays quiet. Maybe all hope isn't lost for him. Only time will tell how horrible he really is. I turn back to Erik.

"How are you enjoying being back?"

"I quite like it, Princess. I hope to revisit the training grounds soon." Tomas perks up at this comment. I offer him a smile.

"Ah, yes. I tried to convince the Lords to allow us time there. I failed in this round, but we will find time to get in some training." I wink at Tomas, who responds with a grin and a blush. The conversation continues, with Oscar remaining quiet. The evening isn't entirely uncomfortable. The small talk is tolerable. Maybe I can survive the rest of this period until I find my true love.

This hasn't been the worst week of my life, but it definitely ranks in the top five. Clem has managed to slip out of our regularly scheduled fun times earlier and earlier. Today, he didn't even show up for the breakfast meeting. No one has commented on it, either. I can't help but wonder how long I could get away with a similar feat. I'm sure my absence would be noticed immediately, and I would be found within minutes. I'm still jealous of Clem.

This week has allowed me to get to know some of the men better. I look forward to building relationships with Kian and Erik. Kian told me he is quite experienced with magic. I want to know more about that. Aside from the curse, I haven't actually seen much magic upfront. With the number of covens and witches in my kingdom, I question the reasoning for this. There is a stark divide in

Greynon with the witches, but I haven't put forth the effort to understand or end it. Erik is kind, which surprised me, given his family's history with the guard. He is gentle and sweet. His large stature is very deceiving. I believe he will be valuable, regardless of what fate may hold.

While Kian and Erik have distinguished themselves in the best way, Oscar, Sven, and Philip have discerned themselves in the worst possible way. To this point, I haven't come to blows with them, but I don't think that will last. Oscar asked if I had a veil to wear. Sven has commented on my lack of dresses. He questioned whether the castle needed more money for proper attire. Philip made a remark about wigs. I told the Lords I want them sent back to their villages. This led to the dark side of the edict I knew would come. They refused because they didn't want to create a rift with their families. They insisted the men just need more time. They have it for now, but my patience will not last.

Currently, the Lords are droning on about something utterly dull. Everyone in the room is bored except for the two speaking. I notice Tomas is barely staying awake. I recall him telling me he wanted to learn to fight with swords. Erik has mentioned wanting to explore the training grounds. As the plan formulates, I glance at the schedule prepared for us. Today is court protocol instruction. Nope, can't handle that. I stand abruptly, startling everyone as my chair scrapes against the floor.

"Tomas, Erik," I exclaim. They both look a little scared at my sudden outburst. Better get used to that, boys. "Let's go to the training grounds."

I walk away from the table without looking back. The Lords are barking at me to return and stick to the schedule. Chairs are scraping, and feet are shuffling behind me.

"Kian, Jonas, come along!" I wave my hands for them to follow. I don't really care if the rest come. Soon, they are all behind me. Finn joins us, bouncing around excitedly. Once we arrive at the training grounds, I tell them to help me look for the practice swords. Erik finds them quickly. He definitely remembers his way around this area. He hands a wooden sword to each man but hesitates when he gets to me. I hold my hand out, giving him an expectant look. His grin is electrifying. I instantly feel so much better.

I step back, allowing him to take the lead. I never had the chance to train with him while he was here. My father allowed me to take lessons, but my mother insisted they remain private behind closed doors. It was the best compromise for the situation. Erik tells us how to line up as the Lords burst into the area. They are shouting that this is unacceptable and not proper action for royalty. I spin, stabbing my wooden sword at Lord Gustavo's chest.

"Unless you are here for a lesson from the son of the prestigious family of guards, I suggest you quietly leave this area. We are training."

Lord Gustavo sneers at me but holds his hands up, backing away. Oscar is already complaining about the quality of this sword and how his personal weapon is much better. I spin around, whacking my sword on his back. His wide eyes focus on me, anger rising behind them.

"Shut it or leave." I seethe but turn to Erik. "Hope you're okay with a large class."

He gives me a quick smile and then shows us the basic stance with the swords. Oscar and his cronies soon break off to practice fighting in a corner. I assist Erik, helping the men without experience. Erik focuses on different stances and a couple of motions as the afternoon wears on. Oscar and his friends soon leave. The difference in everyone's attitude after they go is astounding. I vow to get more time away from them.

Tomas takes to the sword easily. He needs very few corrections. Kian is absolute shit with the sword. We wind up in many laughing fits at his expense. He laughs with us, too. Due to his awkwardness, I spend a lot of time correcting him, touching his hips, arms, and legs. He is much skinnier than Erik, even Clem. His olive skin is gorgeous all the same. I can't help the growing heat in my core. Kian is a beautiful man, inside and out.

Erik tells us we should break for the day. The remaining men are in good spirits as we clean up the training grounds. They begin to wander off to different parts of the castle. I find Erik wanting to check in with him after the class.

"How did you like training everyone?" He turns to face me, leaning against the wall. He folds his arms over his chest, thrusting out his impressive biceps. I won't admit how much wetness spreads through me at the sight.

"I enjoyed it. I spent all of my time in training. It was easy to apply everything I've been told to other people."

"Are you willing to continue?"

"Anything for you, Princess." He smirks at me, and warmth jolts through my core.

"Oh, I could get used to that."

I grab his arm, pulling him away from the wall, using any excuse to touch his large arms. I wonder if other parts of him are equally as significant. We walk to the dining hall, chatting casually with my hand on his arm. We discuss his father and more of his training. His warmth seeps off him, keeping me close to him. It isn't entirely cold yet, but his warmth is still welcome. He comes to life when he speaks about his family and training. I can hear the joy in his words, his love for these things that excite him.

During dinner, the men from the training are much happier than at previous meals. It's actually enjoyable. We discuss their families and villages and what the guards are like in their own towns. Kian explains how most guards near the covens are witches and don't carry many visible weapons. Tomas tells about his request to train being denied because of his age and family's status. I make a mental note to look into the selection process soon. Oscar and his cronies come late and mostly ignore us. They sit at a different table, huddled together, occasionally laughing so loud everyone stops to look. Clem doesn't come to dinner, though. Not that I'm paying attention to his movements or anything. Because I'm not worried about where Clem is. I'm not even thinking about him.

Erik continues his lessons all week. Tomas has taken to them very well. He is a natural with a sword. Kian still needs lots of repositioning, which means lots of touching. I've willingly taken on the task of helping him with his body position. His hips are always in the wrong place. I frequently have to stand behind him, with my body pressed against his, to show him how to use the wooden sword.

Maybe he's pretending to be terrible. Maybe I'm pretending he's worse than he is. I just know he needs so many adjustments. In the form of my body against his.

After practice, I walk out with Kian. I've tried to split my time with most of the men, but I haven't been entirely alone with any of them since this started. We either stayed in public areas or in groups around the castle's common areas.

"Jasmin, I hear you have a large collection of magical texts here at the castle." I loop my hand through his arm as we walk. This is my preferred move to touch them more. No one has complained, and I get to caress the bicep of whomever I'm walking with.

"Yes, we do! Have you not been to the library?"

"No, I haven't. Clem is particularly fond of the library and told me he would show me where it is, but he has since disappeared. I rarely see him."

"Ah," I'm not sure how I should react to the mention of Clem. "Well, I can show you after dinner."

"Perfect. I look forward to it, Jasmin." My name on his lips sounds like a promise. A secret that sends warmth flooding through my entire body.

After dinner, I grab Kian and lead him toward the library. He is much taller than me. His olive skin is creamy and smooth. His hair has a slight curl to it. I would love to run my fingers through it. I would honestly love to rub my fingers over his entire body. To see how his skin contrasts against mine, the warmth of his flesh as his body is above me, sinking deep inside my core, filling me to the brim. His lips graze my skin, biting my nipple, then gently kissing away the pain. His fingers...

"Princess," he says softly in my ear. It takes every bit of consciousness I have left not to moan. Holy hell, I need an orgasm bad.

"What?" My cheeks are burning. He stops walking, turning to face me.

"I believe we passed the library." He winks, nodding his head behind us. I turn to look slowly but already know he's correct.

"I, um. Yes, you found it all on your own. Nice job, Kian." His name comes out breathier than I intend. Based on the wicked grin on his face, he knows where my mind is. "Wow, yes. They must have turned the fires up. It is very warm in here. I lost track of things."

"Oh, Princess," he croons, "I don't think it was the fires in the castle."

If he keeps talking like that, I'm going to orgasm just from his voice. He steps closer to me, guiding me back against the wall. My arms wrap around his back, clenching his tunic in my fingers. My breathing picks up, shallow and needy. Kian places one arm on the wall behind my head. The other hand goes to the wall near my hip, trapping me between him and the wall. My brain instantly switches from arousal to fear. I don't like being trapped in this way. I release his shirt, and my eyes dart around the hallway.

Kian notices my change. He moves his hand from the wall behind my hip into his pocket. He takes half a step to the side, giving me complete access to escape. The fear settles in my body. I glance down the hall, then back up at Kian. He is watching me intently, his dark eyes taking in every breath of mine. He leans down to my ear, whispering against it. His breath sends warmth to mix with the fear that has lessened.

"Tell me what you were thinking, Jasmin."

Just as I am about to speak, the door to the library opens. Kian steps back, taking a less assuming position near me. Finn steps out of the library, sees us, and comes bounding toward us. I greet him, dropping down to the floor. Clem walks out behind him. He eyes us but turns and walks in the opposite direction. I would like to stop him, but I am entirely too flustered. Kian scratches Finn's ears. After a minute, I regain my composure.

"Why don't I show you the magical texts now?"

He follows me into the library, up the stairs, and toward the magical text section. I grab a couple of books as he starts looking around the shelves.

"Your grandmother is the matriarch of your coven, correct?" I lean against the table, letting him peruse the books he is interested in.

"She is. How did you know?" He raises an eyebrow at me, pulling a large book off the shelf.

"When the Lords decided who they were bringing in under the edict, I insisted each one offer information about the family of the men. Then I did further research through our census records." I motion over my shoulder to where those texts are.

"So, you were very prepared when we arrived?"

"I had no choice but to be. I needed to know who was coming into my home to try to tempt fate." At this point, I can no longer say that without an eye roll.

"It's almost unfair, Princess. We received no such information about you. Only the rumor mill has been churning about the royal family for several years." I sigh.

"I know. That's because little has happened." I wrap my arms around myself, not wanting to elaborate. Nothing has happened in the last few years, but the years prior to that were vicious. I have heard some of the rumors that are out there. I have no interest in stopping or changing them. People need something to talk about. It might as well be me. "Tell me about your grandmother. I don't think I ever met her."

"No, you likely wouldn't have met her. Her coven is the second largest in Greynon, but Lord Alwyn doesn't recognize our importance. We guard our own people and our borders. Alwyn has a separate guard he uses for the rest of the village. The witches and non-witches are almost entirely segregated. There is some crossover around the borders, but we all mostly stick to ourselves."

"I've always thought Alwyn was underselling the importance of the witches. After the curse started, we had one, Byron, I think that was his name. He came out to try to assess the curse and understand it better. He didn't seem very confident in what he was doing. He gave us very little to go on." Kian huffs a laugh.

"If they wanted a true assessment, they wouldn't have sent a man. While there are many powerful men, women are typically stronger. No coven leader would send a man on such an important job." He opens a book, flipping through several pages. I suspected the witch that showed up wasn't suitable for the job. It irritates me that is what happened. I suppose it isn't too late to look into it again.

"What do you know about the curse?" He shrugs but doesn't look up from the page he has settled on.

"Not much. Whoever created the curse is incredibly powerful. It's ironclad. Our coven tried many spells to break through the barrier. We were never even close to successful." His eyes scan the room, lifting away from the text to look at me. "Did you ever find the magical object? All spells have a physical item that holds the magic."

"No. That was what the other witch said. We searched. Gods, we searched for so long. We could never find anything, though. With the curse being as large and vast as it is, we couldn't even narrow down what we were looking for." I spent years thinking about what kind of item would be linked to the curse. At first, I was terrified of touching things, worried I would mess with the magic attached to the item. As more time passed, I gave up on finding the item, and my ability to touch things returned to normal. It became too frustrating, fruitlessly searching for an item while dealing with a potentially dying kingdom.

Kian steps in front of me, lifting my chin with his fingers. His touch is soft and delicate, sending flutters through my chest. "We'll figure it out, Princess." He wraps his arms around me, holding me close to his chest. I breathe in his spicy scent, allowing his touch to comfort my stressed body.

We spend a few hours in the library, reviewing different texts. We graze each other several times, but nothing as hot and bothering as the hallway. He gives me a lingering kiss on my cheek when we leave the hallway. Back in my room, the hallway plays out in my mind. Kian is gorgeous. The way he shifted when he noticed I was uncomfortable gives me all the feelings. Aside from Clem, I haven't felt this attracted to any of the bachelors yet. I like Erik, but I don't know how much of a romantic relationship I want with him. It is uncertain how much the physical connection will play in my true love breaking the curse. I can only hope whoever helps me break the curse will be great all around and not just meet one facet of my needs.

I decide to send Clem a note. I thoroughly enjoyed the week with him before everyone else showed up. No one else has made me feel entirely comfortable the way he has. Even though Kian changed his position when he noticed I was uncomfortable, it still happened. I didn't have that with Clem. Since he hasn't given me a chance to speak with him, I can at least try this way. I settle on writing him a note and sending it with Finn. I need to let him know I am sorry and would still like him here. I think there is something worth exploring with him. And who am I to let a gorgeous man slip through my grasp?

Clem,

I have noticed your absence from our meetings the past several days. I have heard from Mikhail you have been an excellent help in the fields. While I do miss your presence at our gods' awful meetings, I want you to know I am not mad at you for leaving. I am simply incredibly jealous. Also thankful but mostly jealous.

I want to apologize for pretending to be Tia when you first arrived. There is no excuse for my actions. I am very sorry for the pain I have caused you. Everything I said to you is still who I am. If you can forgive my actions, I would love for you to join us again when the harvest is complete.

I also want to thank you for spending time with Finn. He really enjoys your attention.

Oh, and thank you for ... dancing with me at the celebration. Please come back to our group and speak with me, Clem. Otherwise, I will be forced to send more letters.

Your apologetic and thankful Princess,

Jasmin xo

Chapter 10

CLEM

Jasmin's letter arrives attached to Finn's collar. I pull it off, and he promptly hops into my bed, settling in for the night. I can't fault him for that. I've spent time with him for several days since I arrived. He isn't allowed at the fields, but we still get some play time together before he runs off to find everyone else. We're comfortable around each other, and he obviously likes sleeping in my bed.

I've been content working in the fields. The harvest has been great. The crops have been producing more than expected. When I first arrived, the fields were on track to produce about three-quarters of what they should have put out. In the last couple of weeks, the plants have flourished, though. It was unexpected. We've been working longer hours than average to accommodate the extra growth. I'm glad to see so much has been produced.

The harvest is winding down, and I plan to return to the bachelor group. I hadn't meant to ignore Jasmin. The days are so long that I am exhausted by the evening. I am glad that my absence has been noted. She has been getting closer to some of the men. She's very comfortable around Erik and Tomas. Clearly, there is something between her and Kian, too. Seeing them in the hallway sent an unexpected surge of jealousy through me. All I could do was grit my teeth and walk away.

It probably could have been me in the hallway with her. I know it could have been. Instead, I went all angry caveman and insisted on working in the fields, missing a couple of weeks with her. I have used that time to daydream of nothing but her. I need to spend more time with her.

Finn keeps me warm all night. Winter will be arriving soon. The evenings are cool, but the afternoons are still warm. Finn runs to the castle after we wake, and I go to the fields. I spend the day harvesting pumpkins. I make up my mind to get back in time for dinner tonight. I can sit closer to Jasmin and chat with her. Maybe even get her alone in the hallway outside the library.

On the way back from the fields, I'm distracted, thinking of ways to get Jasmin to myself. The library is becoming a less reliable source of privacy. There are several meeting rooms near the front, but those are close to the bachelors' rooms. It's possible to have privacy, but it's not guaranteed. Even the gardens don't offer complete privacy. Maybe I can hint to Jasmin that we should spend time alone together. As I consider asking her, I'm surprised to see her run up to me, franticly trying to get my attention.

"Clem! I need your help! Please." She grabs my arm, pulling me toward the stables. She's panicked, barely even acknowledging me as she tugs my arm in her hands.

"What? What happened?" She looks scared; something isn't right.

"Tomas is having a fit. We need to get him out of the stables. I can't move him. Zander is trying to calm the horses. I need you to help me get Tomas out." Jasmin sputters while walking away. I'm still confused, but I follow her. Her eyes are wide, and her body is tense.

"Tomas, the young bachelor?"

"Yes, come on!"

We rush into the stables, where a dark-skinned man younger than me tries to calm the horses. That must be Zander. The horses are spooked but thankfully not bucking or running toward the doors. They are stomping and huffing at Zander, who is speaking quietly, trying to guide them into a different stall. Jasmin turns the corner. Tomas is sitting in the corner with his hands over his ears. He is shaking and crying with his legs pulled up to his chest. He looks small and frightened. I've never seen an adult act like this. My little sister had episodes like this when she was younger, but she outgrew them as she got older. I have heard of adults having them, but not often, and certainly not someone that would be allowed at the castle. Jasmin crouches beside him, saying something I can't hear. With a glance back toward the horses, I move closer.

"What's going on?"

"He's having a fit, but I can't get through to him. We need to get him out." She gives me a pleading look. I assess Tomas, pretty sure I can just carry him. He isn't large. I glance back at the horses again, checking that they won't try to charge. Without asking, I grab Tomas, lifting him off the ground. I nod to Jasmin.

"Lead the way."

She guides us out quickly, directing me to the tree line behind the stables. I place Tomas down at the base of the tree. He is breathing heavily, tears streaking his face. I step back as Jasmin moves in front of him. She is being delicate with him. I'm not sure how to handle this situation. I've never seen an adult behave this way. Jasmin seems confident. I stand back, not wanting to be in the way but not leaving in case she needs more help. She is speaking in a soothing voice, rubbing his back. Tomas's cries calm, but his body doesn't relax.

Jasmin sits back against the tree, pulling Tomas against her chest. Her arms wrap around him tightly, stroking his back. I'm ashamed of how jealous I feel at this moment. I want to be wrapped in her arms, resting my face against her chest. Tomas isn't aware of the position he is in. He is still breathing heavily. Jasmin begins speaking quietly to him.

"Tomas, we're here with you. You are safe." He sobs at her words. His breathing is short and choppy.

"You need to take deep breaths, okay? This will pass. Deep breaths, Tomas." He tries to take a deep breath, but it leads to more sobs and more stuttered breathing. She is swaying side to side with him in her arms. It seems very relaxing, even though he isn't calming down.

"Can I tell you a story, Tomas? I think you might like it." He nods against her chest. I sink down on the ground, on the side of the tree, listening to her words. I'm out of sight but close enough to hear. She takes several deep breaths, still stroking Tomas's back smoothly.

"Once upon a time," her words are soft, just above a whisper, "in a beautiful castle, there was a lovely knight. He was smart and kind but also unsure of himself. When he felt nervous, he took a walk through the castle grounds. He could hear the leaves rustling in the breeze." She pauses long enough for the wind to rustle the leaves above us, sending a few flying to the ground. "He could feel the grass on the ground." She places his hand in the grass. Slowly, his fingers move through the blades. My own itch to touch the blades, to feel the sharp edge, but rub the soft flat side between my thumb and index finger.

"He could see the vines climbing the walls. They were always there, growing, defying rules by growing on the building. Much like ours." She points to the vines on the side of the wall nearest. Tomas looks up slowly. His cheeks are streaked with tears that wash away the dirt on his face. His eyes are red and puffy. His breathing has returned to normal, but he is still sniffling and tense.

"He could smell the pie the baker was making." Jasmin takes a deep breath, sniffing the air. From the place we are sitting, a breeze wafts the scents from the kitchen, warm and inviting. "Pumpkin," she sighs. "The knight could taste the cinnamon and spices in the pie. The warm slice of pie would melt on his tongue. The crust so crumbly, even it melted."

She strokes his back soothingly. Tomas has calmed down completely. His fingers are still caressing the blades of grass beneath his fingers. There must be some magic in her story. Even I feel calmer. The Princess has a way about her. She knew how to handle this situation with such delicacy and grace.

"I'm sorry," Tomas says gently.

"You don't need to be sorry."

"I shouldn't have reacted that way." Neither of them speaks for several moments, Jasmin still rubbing him soothingly.

"How long have you had the fits?" He looks up at her, startled.

"A couple of years," he responds sheepishly. He sits back, rubbing his hands together. "My mother insisted I not tell anyone. She thought by sending me here, I would outgrow them." He won't look up at Jasmin, but she has a patient, knowing look on her face.

"I was probably about your age the first time I had a fit." Tomas and I both give her a shocked look. Many people are sent away for fits like that, and no one willingly admits they had them.

"No one knew how to help me. I eventually learned a few tricks to calm down from a fit. I haven't had a full-blown fit in a couple of years, but I feel them coming on every now and then."

"The story, is that one of your tricks?" Tomas asks.

"Yes. It helps me connect with my surroundings. I try to tie in things that are actually happening." She plucks a blade of grass and hands it to Tomas. He takes it from her, twirling it in his fingers. He notices me for the first time. His cheeks stain red.

"Thank you," he mumbles. Unsure if he's speaking to Jasmin or me, I don't reply. "I should go apologize to Zander." He rises to leave, but Jasmin grabs his hand.

"I'm always here if things get bad again. I won't judge you or send you away." She pats his hand, and he smiles at her. He nods before walking off to the stables. She doesn't move, just stares off in his direction. I slide closer to her. She looks tired. She offers a small smile as I scoot next to her. I wrap my arm around her shoulders, pulling her close.

Jasmin sighs, settling against my chest. I don't need to say anything right now. She gave a lot to Tomas. The least I can do is offer her support. I hold her body against mine, rubbing her arms. I rest my cheek against the top of her head, her hair tickling my chin. After a few moments, she looks up at me.

"Thank you, Clem."

There are many things I should say to her. Explain my actions of avoiding her. Explain that it wasn't my intention. I should tell her I have no intentions of leaving or abandoning her. I don't say any of that, though. Instead, I look down at her and place my hand on her cheek, stroking her scar with my thumb. I press my lips against her forehead in a long kiss.

"You're safe with me," I whisper against her skin. She shivers in my arms. My lips spread into a smile against her forehead, holding her tightly. The sky begins to darken as the breeze turns chilly. I squeeze her tightly and tell her we should probably go back in. She nods and rises, but before she can walk away, I pull her closer. My hands grab either side of her face, holding her close. Her hands land on my wrists.

"I'm not avoiding you. I genuinely enjoy being in the fields. I'm glad I have Finn, and you, here." I add softly, pressing my lips against her forehead again. I love offering this small bit of comfort to her. Jasmin allowing me to give her this small affection means the world to me. Her arms wrap around my body tightly. She doesn't say anything, just remains flat against my chest. She releases me and walks toward the castle, huddled against the chill. I catch up with her, wrapping my arm around her for warmth. We separate inside as she moves to the dining hall to get her dinner.

I join the other bachelors for dinner. Jasmin and Tomas are more subdued than normal. I chat with Kian and Erik, enjoying their company. Halfway through dinner, Jasmin leans against Erik, closing her eyes. She wraps her arm around his, propping her head against his shoulder as she rests. Jealousy courses through my body again. I do what I can to quench it with ale. Kian clenches his teeth but doesn't show any other signs of jealousy. The other men have left by this point. I wonder what their reactions to this would be. We all chat for a while before Jasmin wakes, leaving for the evening. We all offer to escort her, but she insists on going alone. Finn joined us during dinner and is walking by her side. At least she isn't entirely alone.

Sitting alone in the library is one of my favorite downtime activities. Some evenings, Finn joins me, but he isn't here tonight. I am reading a book about sea creatures. It has been more interesting than the cover suggested. Despite being interested in the book, I see Kian walk through the library. He doesn't notice me and goes to the reference section upstairs.

I stay focused on my book, but after several minutes, I hear a noise coming from upstairs. It sounds like a cat is dying or being flayed. It's loud and awful. Is it possible Finn found some stray animal in here? Just before I decide to search out the source, I recognize words in the sound. It's Kian singing. He absolutely does not have a natural talent for that. My nose crinkles. I debate yelling at him, but despite the excruciating noise, it does sound joyful. I try to ignore it and return to my book. When he stops singing, if you can call it that, I say a silent thanks to the heavens. I rub my ears, trying to stop the ringing.

He starts walking down the stairs, humming the tune he was singing earlier. Even his humming is terrible. Gods, he must be cursed with that singing voice.

"Hey, Kian!" He startles as he walks by my alcove. He drops his books, leaning against the table next to him for support.

"Good gods, Clem. I didn't know you were there!" His eyes grow suspicious. "How long have you been there?"

"Since before you." I raise my eyebrows at him, giving him a pointed look.

"Ah. Well," Kian seems to debate whether to apologize or not. "Sorry you had to hear that. I was blessed with magic and a desire to sing, but no voice." I chuckle as he grabs his books. There are several large reference books.

"A little light reading before bed?" I inquire. He places them back on the table.

"The castle has different magical texts than we have in Greynon. I want to learn more about the magic but also see if there is anything I might find about the curse that has been overlooked."

"Are you good with magic?" He shrugs.

"Depends on who you ask." I pause, considering his answer. It's not a direct response, and I get the impression he doesn't give many straightforward answers.

"What do you think of the other bachelors?" I question. I have gathered some insights about them, but working in the fields means I have missed a lot. I don't know several of the men at all. I have no clue how Jasmin is interacting with them. I imagine she enjoys some of them but probably "goes to bed early," too. Kian grabs a stool, moving into my alcove to sit with me. I sit up, putting my book aside.

"I think there are several idiots in the group. A couple of the men have some potential. Tomas is too young, but Jasmin is friendly with him. I think she's fond of Erik. She seems indifferent to Dominick and William." He pauses, giving me a curious look. "Then there is you."

"Me? What about me?"

"You've been absent from most of our meetings and activities. Jasmin has noticed. She hasn't said anything, which is interesting. She's also accepted your sudden presence at dinners without question. Rumor has it you've been working in the fields. What advantage do you gain from that?"

I stare at him, considering his words. My interactions with Kian have been amicable, but maybe things are changing now. He was standing close to Jasmin in the hallway recently. If this were a competition, and I did gain an advantage working in the fields, would I tell Kian? But this isn't that situation, is it? Is there an advantage to be gained by working on a farm instead of being with Jasmin?

"No advantage. I worked farmland in Arkaley, which seemed a better use of my time before winter." I shrug, trying to appear nonchalant. Despite that being the truth, I still feel awkward in this situation. "What about you? How close are you to the Princess?"

"Close enough." I sigh. The secrecy and competition are not what I wanted. I hadn't considered this aspect of this arrangement when I asked to come.

"Honestly, this is why I avoided the meetings and activities. I don't want to be in competition. I don't want to see what the other men are doing and how I need to show them up to get attention. I..." my thoughts are running wild. I'm unsure how much to share with him, but what do I have to lose? "I want to spend time with her. Just not with nine other men also doing the same thing."

Kian leans back, assessing me fully now. I have nothing else to add.

"I agree. It's good talking with you, but I'll let you get back to your book." I nod, grabbing my book to start reading. He stands and places his stool back on the table. He grabs his books but turns around to me.

"For what it's worth, I think that's all Jasmin wants too. You've certainly made an impression on her. If you find your way back into the meetings, I'll keep a seat open for you." I stare as he walks off. I wasn't expecting that interaction to go that way, but I am glad it did. It almost makes up for his terrible singing. Almost.

Chapter 11

CLEM

The harvest has come to an end. The fields are prepped for winter, and everything is settled. Mikhail has been very grateful for my help over the last few weeks. He said he is putting in a good word with the Princess. I'm thankful for his support, but I have met with Jasmin a few times since our interaction with Tomas. We don't get much time together, but it's something.

Now that the harvest is done, I am back to the regularly scheduled fun, as Jasmin calls it, the Lords have planned for us. I'm not looking forward to the cold months in the castle. I hope to get better clothes so I can spend some time outdoors. I daydream about snow and icy lakes as my tea grows cold. I wonder how Finn handles the snow. I can almost see him frolicking in a snow pile and blending in completely. Jasmin probably loses her mind as he disappears in a heap, yelling at him to come back. A smile spreads across my face as the image plays in my head.

I snap out of my daydream, looking around at the others in the room. The Lords are chatting about preparations for winter. Jasmin is absentmindedly scratching Finn's ears. Keeping him out of these meetings didn't last very long. The other men are a mixture of boredom and interest.

"We have some exciting news." Lord David speaks up. His hair looks grayer than it did the last time I saw him. Perhaps this situation has been stressful on the Lords too. I don't find myself bothered by that.

"Now that the harvest is complete, we can officially announce the output has increased from last year. As you all know, we have seen diminishing output from our fields across the kingdom. This is the first year we have seen any kind of increase, let alone such a large one. We," he waves between the other Lords, "believe this is due to the curse lifting." He pauses, letting what he has said sink in for everyone. "Of course, this would indicate there won't be a sudden shift with the curse but a gradual change back to what we had. We believe one of you may help break the curse." He is skirting around calling someone her true love.

Jasmin's gaze is fixed on Lord David. The other men are looking and whispering to each other, trying to figure out who it may be.

"Without more information about the curse, we will not change this group at this time, but there may be some soon."

"Did any of the villages see an increase in crop production?" Jasmin asks, still glaring.

"Unfortunately not. But we have split our output between the villages."

"Then we also need to acknowledge Clem. He played an important role in helping with the production. Mikhail was very pleased with his work." Jasmin offers a tight smile, but several men sneer at me. Kian claps me on the back. I nod to Jasmin, willing the blood not to rush to my cheeks. The chatter continues, but no one stops it or dismisses us.

"Milady," Erik speaks up, "I have a suggestion."

"Yes, Erik." She offers him a kind smile, different from the one she gave after acknowledging my work.

"I would like to host a sparring contest. Many of the men are coming along nicely in their training. It was a tradition that the new batch of guardsmen would perform for the sitting royalty. I suggest we stick with our wooden swords to prevent injury and establish that this isn't official guardsmen training." She is tapping her chin, considering his idea.

"I like this idea, Erik. You have all been working hard. I would love to see you spar together. Will you be organizing it?"

"Yes, Princess. I can. I also have another suggestion, if you don't mind." Jasmin gives him a cautionary stare.

"What is it?"

"Traditionally, the winner of the sparring contest wins a prize. In some years, it would be knighthood or marriage to a prominent maiden of the court. Obviously, these are not options." Jasmin's glare has turned to ice. Even I shiver, and she's not looking at me. Erik is braver than I am in continuing his request. "I thought, perhaps, the winner could earn a private dinner with you." His voice is very sheepish by the end. This seems to lessen the blow to Jasmin. She looks as if she might actually be considering it.

A couple of the men are cheering, clapping, or slapping the table. Several look incredulous. Lords Thurston and Gustavo are impressed. Jasmin releases a sharp breath, holding her hand out to silence everyone.

"Will everyone be participating?"

"Yes. Well, everyone who wants to." Erik responds as more cheers sound. Jasmin's eyes meet mine. I realize I have no training with a sword. I don't even know where the training grounds are. Even if I wanted a private dinner with her, I wouldn't stand a chance against any of the men that have been training for weeks.

"Will there be a host?" she inquired.

"Typically, there is one."

"I will do it." I unintentionally shout. I'm met with looks of confusion. Returning my voice to normal, "The host will need to be a neutral party. I have no training with the sword and would likely embarrass myself anyway."

Lord David speaks, "That means you would forfeit your chance at a private dinner."

"I'll find another way." I shoot a wink at Jasmin. There will be other chances for alone time with the Princess. I'll find a way to get her alone soon.

On my way to the library, I spot Jasmin walking with Finn. I don't see any of the men around and decide to follow her to see where she goes. She walks absentmindedly as if lost in thought. Her hips sway with her steps. She still wears leggings instead of dresses. She has switched from tunics to sweaters, though. The sweaters land perfectly across her ass. My fingers itch to touch.

She makes her way out to the gardens. I didn't think anything would be in bloom this late in autumn, but I follow her anyways. I didn't bring a coat, and the cool of the night is more than I am prepared for. Jasmin isn't wearing a jacket, either. I'll warm her with my body. Maybe my tongue. Definitely my fingers.

Just before I call out to stop her, I see the greenhouse. I walk in behind her and am overwhelmed with the scent of a flower I've never seen before. It's climbing up the walls. The petals are white and delicate. The plant looks to be taking over the entire space in the building. I stare at all the blooms across the walls, forgetting why I am here in the first place.

"Sunette's daughter planted them about nine years ago." I startle at the sound of her voice. I assumed she hadn't noticed me. Moving closer to her, I look at the flower she is staring at. It's one of the larger blooms in the room.

"What is it called?"

"Jasmine."

I smirk, observing the plant. Of course, there would be a plant named jasmine. I notice a bloom has fallen on the floor. I bend to pick it up. It must have just dropped, as it's still in good condition. Ma constantly berated us for picking flowers. She insisted they were there for us to look at, not take. It's not harmful if we pick one off the ground. I slide the flower behind the Princess's ear.

"A beautiful name for flowers and princesses." Her smile warms my soul. Who needs a coat when I have her? My hand lingers on her neck, stroking her chin with my thumb. I press my body against hers, wrapping my other arm around her back. She leans into my chest. Her hands rise along my sides but slip under my shirt. Her fingers brush against my skin, but they are ice cold. I gasp at her touch.

She spreads her hands flat against my back, trying to soak up my warmth. I lean down to her and press my lips against hers. She hesitates at first, then melts under my touch. My fingers wrap around the back of her neck, keeping her close. Her fingers caress my back, moving higher, touching more skin. I deepen our kiss, exploring her mouth with my tongue. It's exactly how I remember it from before. She's perfect and soft. My thumb strokes her cheek, grazing the scars on her face. Even with all her rough edges, she's all I want. My dick comes to life as her tongue tangles with mine.

Finn lets out a whine, but I ignore him. I slide my hand down her back, grabbing her ass. Her ass is just how I imagined it. Thick, squishy, fits perfectly in my palm. Her fingers are on my ribs now, no longer cold. Her lips match mine perfectly. I could stand here forever with her pressed against me.

Someone tuts near the door.

We both jump back, separating from our kiss. I realize my pants are tented over my erection. I look up quick enough to realize it is Sunette. I spin around, trying to hide my erection. I adjust myself under my pants, wishing it to go away quickly. Jasmin laughs, leaning against me.

"You're lucky it was only me that caught you." Sunette has a knowing smirk on her face. Her accent is deep and rich, making each syllable pop.

"Sorry, Sunette," Jasmin says. "We'll get out of your way."

"Ach," Sunette waves her hands at us. "I just came to see who was in here. It's not often I get visitors at night." Sunette walks around some of the plants, checking for something. Finn scoots to sit next to me, so I scratch his ears.

"You know that young boy has been spending a lot of time with Zander," Sunette states with a pointed gaze at Jasmin. There is more conversation happening between the two of them. Jasmin raises her eyebrows in a question.

"Tomas?" Sunette gives a slight nod. Jasmin seems to consider, then smiles approvingly. "Has Zander said anything?"

"Ach, no. He just talks about the boy all day." I listen to the conversation but don't have anything to add. I've had limited interaction with Tomas and have only seen Zander from a distance. I don't know anything about the two of them. I'm still scratching Finn's ears when he walks to Sunette, his nose nudging her dress.

"Yes, I have a biscuit for you, boy." She laughs, handing him a biscuit from her pocket, and he chomps happily.

"We'll get out of your way, Sunette." Jasmin takes my hand, leading me back through the gardens to the castle. Finn walks just behind us. Once inside, she kisses my cheek, wishing me good night. It may not be a private dinner, but I'm hoping most of the other men don't get time with her like I do.

Chapter 12

JASMIN

Clem has the most amazing lips. His skin is soft and warm. I push the thoughts from my mind quickly. I really need to get fucked. This ever-present ache is going to drive me insane before anything else does. Between Clem's lips and Kian's body, I'm going to die from not being sated. They won't even bury me in the royal cemetery because the headstone would read, "Here lies Princess Jasmin, death from abstinence."

I've spent enough time alone to know how to please myself, but it's barely taken the edge off. Every time I turn around, there is a new jolt to my pussy. This feeling is even worse now that Clem is back. He just enters the room, and my pussy is soaked. If he and Kian sit next to each other, I start squirming like a damn fish out of water. Even Erik and Tomas have caused arousal lately. Tomas winked at me, and my legs rubbed together involuntarily. Tomas is too young for me to react like that. Erik has such large, strong arms. He's so skilled with weapons. I bet his fingers are calloused. Oh, that rough skin...

A knock at the door breaks my thoughts. I'm in trouble. Every other thought is of one of these men sticking a dick so far in me that I meet Mother Earth.

Emmeline walks in carrying a pile of dresses. "I thought we could try out a few dresses for the sparring contest, Jasmin."

"Yes, yes. That is fine." I sigh, rising from my chair. My thoughts don't clear from the perversion. It just takes a back burner to allow me to mostly function. I look at several of the dresses she has brought in. They range from modest to elaborate. One catches my eye. It's a dark dress with extensive beadwork. The collar is high around the back but low in the front. I would recognize this dress anywhere but haven't seen it in ages. Emmeline notices me staring at it.

"Since you don't have as many formal dresses, I thought we could try some of your mother's." I meet her gaze, emotions warring inside my body. "We can have new ones made instead. There should be enough time." Emmeline adds sheepishly. I trust her judgment, but this dress sparks memories I don't want to face.

My fingers move to the long lace sleeves. My mother loved all things intricate and hard to replicate. The seamstress spent months on this dress alone. My heart squeezes in my chest. Anger, hurt, loss, fear, confusion, longing. It is too much.

"You have a good point. But not this dress." I release the sleeve, turning away before the tears fall. "Not this one."

Emmeline carries the dress away while I sort through the others. My mother's dress drove away that growing ache in my core. Maybe I can function better now. A yellow dress catches my eye as Emmeline returns to the room. I spin toward her, holding the dress up.

"That one is perfect for you." She walks over to help me try it on. There are multiple layers to it with several different types of fabric. It's not a traditional sparring contest dress, but nothing about this is traditional. Once we have the skirt layered correctly, she moves behind me to tighten the corset. Looking in the full-length mirror, I feel beautiful in this dress. It matches my skin tone perfectly. I almost look like I'm glowing.

"Oh, Jasmin. This one is beautiful." She turns around, looking in a pile for something else. As much as I love this dress, it may be too much for the sparring contest. It's so gorgeous but more formal than it needs to be. Emmeline returns, placing a small tiara in my hair. It's silver but has amber gems in it. The combination of the dress and tiara is exquisite. As she fiddles with my hair, the realization hits me.

"What the fuck?" I approach the mirror as Emmeline makes a disapproving noise at my language. She knows me better than that, but I don't respond to her. Instead, my fingers are running through my hair. Pulling it out.

"Emmeline, is my hair longer?" I ask, startled at the realization.

"My gods, it is!" She stands behind me, pulling my hair in the same manner I am. We stare at it in the mirror. It isn't significantly longer, only an inch at most. Probably not even noticeable to anyone else, but it's starting to grow back. My hair was chopped off roughly before the curse began. It hasn't grown back since. It's been awkward and untidy for the past eight years. To see it growing out now fills me with such joy.

Neither of us says anything about the reason it's growing out. We both know the curse is slowly lifting, meaning my true love is close. As stupid as I thought the edict was, it has done what it was supposed to do. I won't admit that the Lords were right. I don't like to give them that power. I am also very concerned about who is actually destined to be with me. It could be any of the ten men, not necessarily the ones I like. Gods, I'll be devastated if it's Oscar or Tomas.

Snapping out of my thoughts, I look back at the dress. I love it so much, but I don't think it's right for the contest.

"Maybe we should save this one," I suggest. Emmeline nods.

"This would be perfect for the winter solstice. Or perhaps your coronation."

"What? Is there talk of that?" I'm stunned. I haven't heard anything of my coronation. We decided not to do it when the curse began. The kingdom was in chaos. We didn't need that on top of everything else. After things settled, it just didn't make sense to have the coronation. I was trying to give more power to the villages. The Lords also didn't want to crown a young unwed woman.

"Maybe," Emmeline wiggles her eyebrows at me as she digs through the pile of dresses. She pulls one out and turns to me. "This dress is perfect for the sparring contest." It's a yellow dress, similar in color to the one I am wearing, but more casual. There aren't as many layers; it's perfect.

"Yes. Will you be joining me at the contest?" I ask as we remove the gown I am wearing, moving on from talk of the coronation.

"Of course, milady. I have always enjoyed sparring contests. It's one of the things I miss most from before the curse."

"Really? I don't particularly remember them."

"No, you wouldn't," she says with a chuckle. "You were always antsy and wanted to be anywhere else." I laugh at her statement because it's true. "I love them. Seeing the men don their armor and battle. Oh, that was exciting!" She squeals as we remove the gown and slip on the new dress. We spend the next hour or so reminiscing about past events. Her excitement is contagious. I feel much better when I leave my room.

I wander through the halls with no real goal in mind. I debate the library. Finding a good book could help distract me. I was kicked out of the training area until after the sparring contest. Erik claims it will add to the overall effect of the event. I'm sad to miss out on hands-on time with the men, but it's probably better that I'm not there. One wrong look and I'd turn into a puddle of need and arousal. No one needs to see a princess like that. Finn is still joining them in the training area. He has enough sticks to play with; he is content without me.

All this means I am alone for a few more hours until dinner time. I could wander the gardens again. Maybe I'll go to the stables and visit Zander, see what he thinks of the youngest bachelor here. As I decide to go to the stables, I hear music coming from one of the empty rooms in the hallway. I didn't know we had any musicians staying with us now. I investigate, pressing the door open slowly.

Kian is whirling around the room in a waltz. His lithe form glides through the steps with ease. His arms are in front of his body as if he has a partner. He appears to be alone. The music is coming from thin air. I watch him float around for a few more minutes. His clothes sway with each step. His long legs extend as he steps, arms swaying into the motion. As mesmerizing as he is to watch, my curiosity about the music grows.

I close the door softly behind me. I sneak along the edge of the room, staying behind Kian. I don't want to disturb him, but I need to know where the music is coming from. It sounds like a full quartet is playing. I look around for any signs of violins or violas. How could a cello be in here without me seeing it? I peer around stacks of tables and chairs but find nothing. Suddenly, there are arms around my waist, pulling me toward the center of the room. Kian spins me to face him with a warm smile on his face.

"Hello, Princess." His voice is so smooth. That ache is instantly back.

On instinct, I settle in his arms, matching the steps of his waltz. I have done this dance so many times. It's second nature now. I can't help matching his steps and movements. It takes a moment for my brain to process everything that is happening.

"Kian. What are you doing?"

"I'm dancing with you, love." I try not to blush at his pet name for me.

"But where is the music?" He leans in close to me, tightening his arms around my body.

"Don't spoil it yet," he whispers seductively. "The grand finale is coming."

The music is rising to a crescendo. Despite wanting answers, I wait. He glides around the area he is using as a dance floor. He is fantastic at dancing. His moves are natural and give him an ethereal presence. Just before the music reaches its peak, he stops and spins me away from him. He guides me through several spins on a path around him. As the music falls, he brings me close, then dips me to the side. My arms land around his shoulders. His face is happy and warm. He lifts me upright as my breathing slows. I notice the music has stopped and look around again.

"It's here." He points to a small box on one of the tables. It looks like a box for a couple of rings, something that could fit in his pocket. I didn't even notice it when I first came in. He guides me over to the table to show me the box. It's wooden with roses carved on the lid. But there is nothing inside. Nothing that would make the music. I look back at him, confusion written on my face.

"It's magic." I turn back to the box, inching my fingers toward it. I'm unsure if I can touch it. What I know about magic is more from a practical standpoint. I don't know about the nuances and delicacies of spelled objects. He picks up on my interests. Instead of telling me I can touch it, he steps behind me. His chest presses against my back as my breath catches. His hands slip over my arms, guiding my hands to the box. I take it in my hands, lifting it to look at it. It just feels like a regular wooden box. There isn't anything special about it.

"It's a spell I learned several years ago. The spell is easy enough but time-consuming and expensive to create, and it is only good for one use."

I turn my head enough to see his face. He offers me a smile, lifting the box higher.

"When musicians are performing, we enchant the box just before they begin. We place it close and leave it as long as they play or until we have what we want. The longer the set, the more powerful the spell needs to be. A song or two doesn't need anything excessive. Most young witches can capture the sound. The music stays inside until you open the box. Then it will play, and the enchantment ends."

He shrugs slightly, twisting to lean against the table. He drops his hands to his sides. I'm still examining the box. The music was so loud and lifelike. I'm astounded that it was magic and not an actual quartet.

"How many of these do you have?"

"That was my only one."

"And you used it in here? Alone?"

"I wasn't alone the whole time." He winks as his fingers raise to stroke my cheek. I struggle against swooning at his touch. I place the box down and step in front of him. With him leaning against the table, he is at my eye level. I gently place my fingers on his hips. I've touched him enough in the training area I don't feel uncomfortable touching him this way. I don't think he is uncomfortable, either. I trace a seam on his shirt.

"Could you make another?" I ask coyly. He smirks at me.

"I suppose. If there were musicians. And a space without other people. But the price is high for one." I look up to meet his gaze. There is a twinkle of playfulness in his eyes.

"Oh? how much, Kian?" He licks his bottom lip as I say his name. It's moments like this that I am thankful I have a pussy and not a cock. At least he doesn't know how wet I am.

"Tell me, Princess, what would you give for your own music box?" He leans in close, whispering the last few words against my ear. His fingers squeeze my waist. Mine trail across his stomach, landing on his chest. My breathing is shallow against his neck. I run my nose along his skin, stopping at his ear. My brain is too fogged over to think of an appropriate response.

"Is a bag of gold enough?" I manage breathily.

"No, Princess." His lips are against the top of my ear.

"The castle?"

"No, Princess." I slide my hands back down to his hips, toying with the band of his trousers.

"What about a princess?"

"Ah, that's something I could accept." He purrs in my ear. My hips press into his. He presses small kisses along my jaw until he reaches my lips. My eyes close as he kisses me deeply. His lips are full, covering mine completely. I melt against him as he tightens his arms around me. My tongue slips out, caressing the crease of his lips. He opens his mouth. I explore his mouth with my tongue. I can feel his cock growing between us. I lean back enough to get my hand between us. I place my hand over his cock, trying to palm it.

"Jasmin," he breathes.

He spins me around, adjusting his dick so I can't feel it pressed between us. One hand snakes under my sweater, squeezing my breast. The other cups my pussy over my leggings. I arch back, my head landing against his shoulder. He instantly places kisses along my neck. I moan under his touch. His fingers slide from my pussy to the waistband of my leggings.

"Can I touch you, Princess?" His breath is hot against my neck.

"Yes, gods. Please, yes!"

He smiles against my skin as his fingers slide beneath my leggings. My hands palm his thighs, scratching against his trousers. His fingers are moving lower at an agonizingly slow pace. This will be the moment I die from denied pleasure. I can feel it building. A few touches, and I will explode. Or a few more minutes, and I will die from need. Either way, something is happening very soon.

His fingers finally reach my apex. Despite the tight fit of my leggings, he still makes room for his fingers to skim my core very lightly. I wiggle in his arms, needing more contact. He chuckles, his chest rumbling against my back. He nips at my neck and ear.

"Mmm, Kian, please." I moan, trying to grind into his hand.

"So needy, Princess."

He finally slips a finger inside me. I gasp at the sensation. My eyes close with pleasure. I turn my face into his neck, kissing him. My hand goes to the other side of his neck, holding him close. I place my other hand on his forearm, using my fingers to help him set pace inside me. His fingers plunge in and out, scratching that itch that has been building. His fingers are exploring me but still increasing my pleasure.

My core begins to tighten around his fingers. He presses his palm into my clit as his fingers plunge in and out faster. I moan against his neck. My fingers tighten around his forearm. My breathing is quick as my orgasm builds. He turns his face against mine, finding my ear again.

"Come for me, Princess."

He bites my ear lobe hard enough to send me over the edge. I cry out as his arms tighten around me, supporting my soaring body. His fingers thrust ruthlessly inside me, wringing out every last bit of my orgasm. My body tenses with pleasure, enjoying the warmth from his chest as I arch back against him. I settle into his body as my soul returns. I feel calmer than I have in weeks. He removes his hand from my pants slowly. I watch as he brings his fingers to his mouth, licking my taste off them.

I turn to face him, lust filling my body again despite my orgasm. I lick my lips as his eyes stay focused on mine. My hands go to his trousers, working on untying them.

"Not now, Princess," he grabs my wrist, pulling them away. "There will be time for that later."

He pulls me against his body, wrapping my arms around his back. His lips crash against mine desperately. The faint taste of my arousal is on his lips. His fingers twist in my hair, pulling it down tightly. The movement forces me to open my mouth, and his tongue is instantly in mine. He kisses me for several minutes before pulling away.

He stands, forcing me to step back away from him. I am still floating from my orgasm, but I also want more. There is a slight sting because he is stopping this. I could stand to do more with him, especially since we are actually alone. This must be written on my face. He grabs his box with one hand, and the other touches my face.

"There will be time for more, Princess." His lips press against my cheek. "Now, you should get to dinner before the others question your absence."

I sigh, knowing he's right. The sun is almost set outside. Someone will notice I haven't been around all afternoon. He motions for me to walk to the door. It's probably not a good idea for us to leave together. Especially if he has tented pants. As I make my way back to the door, I turn back to get a look at him. He is facing the opposite direction, standing over the table. I turn around, disappointed about not seeing more of him. I readjust my clothes before leaving the room for dinner, sated but still desperate.

Chapter 13

CLEM

Fifteen books.

That's how many I have read in the past two weeks. I enjoy reading, but I really need something else to do. I have attended some of the training sessions Erik leads. They gave me a sword a couple of times, but it's not something I am interested in. I watched to get insights for the sparring contest next week. At least that gives me something to look forward to. Mostly, I wander the halls like a sad, undead ghost.

Jasmin doesn't attend the training sessions, which makes them even more boring. I haven't figured out where she's been off to during the day. Kian occasionally disappears from the training, only to show up at dinner with a shit-eating grin. I have a hunch he has found Jasmin on a couple of occasions. I haven't asked him about it. More evenings than not, he and I can be found in the library. Not always together, but we have developed a camaraderie. Sometimes I help him find texts. Sometimes we discuss the curse. Sometimes we just reminisce about our homes. If Jasmin is going to spend time with anyone else here, I'd rather it be him.

He isn't in the library tonight. It's just me. Several of the other men are soaking up the last of the warmth outside. I moved a chaise lounge from another spot in the library to my favorite alcove. A small fire is going on. Despite my perpetual boredom, I can't deny how nice this is. I stretch out on the lounge, reading my current book. This one is about witches. It's been fascinating to read.

Finn wanders in and plops down in front of me. I greet him, reaching out to scratch his ears. Jasmin walks in, and without hesitating, she climbs over me into the lounge, resting on my side. Her brazenness startles me, but I'm not going to deny her. I wrap my arm around her, holding her close.

"Oh, hello, Jasmin. Please make yourself comfortable," I tease.

"I will. Thank you."

She settles in, her head resting on my chest. I kiss the top of her hair. Her floral soap smells divine on her. I've never cared much for the floral scents, but I do love the way she smells. Her hand stretches across my chest. She wraps one of her legs over mine. The position is so familiar and comfortable; this is all new to me. I'm so swept up in her touch I have forgotten the book I was reading. My arm is still raised, holding it so I can read.

"Read to me?" She pleads softly, turning her head to look at me.

"Of course. Want me to fill you in?"

"No, just read."

She settles her head against my chest as I find the spot I am reading. It takes me a moment to locate it, as I was in the middle of a paragraph. I decide to just start the section over. Jasmin usually prefers a quick synopsis of what I have read so far. Maybe she has already read this book. I speak softly, reading the story of a witch on a journey away from their coven. She idly traces circles on my chest. Her breathing becomes slow and even.

After a couple of pages, I realize she has fallen asleep on me. An overwhelming sense of pride fills me, realizing she is comfortable enough to sleep on me. It would be better if there weren't clothes, but we'll get there soon enough. I decide to keep reading out loud. It's a bit slower than not speaking, but I don't want to wake her with any changes I make.

Kian walks through the library at one point. He stops when he sees me. He contemplates the position I am in with her. Thus far, no one else has seen me alone with her. I have been lucky enough to have actual alone time with Jasmin. I'm pretty sure Kian has too, but I don't know how many others are getting alone time. I worry Kian might say something, but he simply nods and walks to his preferred area in the library.

After interacting with Kian, I decide not to read aloud anymore. I don't want to disturb him, and Jasmin hasn't noticed the quiet. I lose track of time, reading several chapters. Kian passes back through, a book tucked under his arm. He smirks at me, still in the same position as before. He shakes his head as he leaves the library. I debate staying here all night with Jasmin, but both of us would be sore tomorrow from this position. My shoulders are already starting to ache. I begrudgingly wake her. Sleepily, she kisses my cheek before leaving the library. I really should have just dealt with sore muscles tomorrow. It would've been worth it.

Here I am, aimlessly wandering the halls again. I seriously need to find another task to stay busy with. I notice Oscar and his brood snickering down the hall. I debate engaging with them but decide it's not worth it. Occasionally, riling them up is fun, but I'm just not feeling that today. I continue down the hall in my sad, undead ghost manner.

I find Jasmin kneeling on the ground, with Finn lying under her. I rush over to her and ask what's going on. Tears streak down her face. I look at Finn. Spots of blood are around his mouth. He's still breathing, but something is wrong.

"Shit, where is your animal healer?"

She wipes her eyes, "We don't have one. After the curse, we only kept horses and some fowl here. All the other animals were traded off to other villages. Sabeko takes care of the horses."

About that time, Kian and Tomas round the corner quickly with a stocky dark-skinned man. I have seen him around the stables before. He kneels next to Finn, rubbing his fingers across his side. I wrap my arm around Jasmin, holding her out of the way. The man touches Finn's body, looking for any sign of ailment. When he reaches his neck, Finn whines and gags, his whole body convulsing.

The man looks up at Jasmin with sad eyes. When he speaks, his accent is thick. It sounds like Sunette's, but his voice is hoarse and hard to hear.

"I'm sorry, Princess. I don't know about dogs. I can help make him comfortable, but I fear anything I do will only make him worse."

A sob escapes from Jasmin. I tighten my arms around her, holding her up. A sudden need to fix this spreads through my body. I look around at the others in the room. Sabeko has returned to petting Finn, possibly still assessing him. Kian looks worried, glancing between the Princess and Finn. Tomas is fidgeting, searching around the area like something in here might help.

"Where's the closest animal healer?" I ask. The others look at me but don't answer.

"Um," Jasmin speaks, still sniffling. "Obele is the easiest, but I think it's half a day's ride from here." I shake my head. That won't do; it's too far. My mind is racing through ideas. It might be our best option, though. I don't know how to get to Obele from the castle. I've only been to Obele from Arkaley. That would have to be out of the way since my house takes a different trail than the one for Obele. Wait! My house.

"Bea," I say, standing up. "Bea can do it!"

Everyone looks at me like I'm crazy except for Jasmin. She looks confused.

"Your sister?"

"Yes! She doesn't have the training, but she's worked with all the farm animals. She worked on the same farm I did. They had several dogs, and I know at some point, she helped them. I could get her back by," I glance around, trying to figure out the time, "possibly by dinner if I can leave fast enough." Jasmin jumps up.

"Sabeko, can you and Zander prepare Vesper and Acer? Clem, you can take those two. They can make the trip quickly." I stand next to her, trying to decide if I need anything. Erik has walked up at some point.

"Take Shena instead of Acer. She is better with women she doesn't know. She'll be as fast as Vesper and able to keep up for the whole journey." Jasmin nods to Sabeko. He and Zander leave together, quickly going to the stables. Kian steps up beside Jasmin, grabbing her arm gently.

"Let's get Finn out of the hallway. Erik and I will help you while Clem readies for his journey." She nods, turning away from me without another word. I head to the kitchen to grab food, then to my room for warmer clothes. When packed, I walk toward the front door, spotting Jasmin, Kian, and Erik in a meeting room near the front. They are discussing preparations as I step inside. When she notices me, Jasmin runs over, wrapping her arms around me.

"Thank you for doing this, Clem."

"Finn is my buddy, too. I don't want to see him hurt," I say, deflecting the real reason I'm doing this. She nods, pressing a quick kiss to my cheek. I wave to the others and head to the stables.

After a few parting words from Sabeko, I mount Vesper and take the lead for Shena. She's a beautiful horse. She's grey and nearly as tall as Vesper. With the little I know about horses, I assume she is the same breed as Vesper. The two look resplendent together, him being nearly all white and her a complimentary grey. We ride off at a quick pace, taking the trail toward Arkaley.

I'm lucky that it is still autumn. In the next month or so, these hills will be covered with snow and nearly impassable. Vesper and Shena make great time, having no issues running along these trails. At this rate, we can make the journey there without stopping. I'll need to give them a good break at the house, but that will provide Bea time to pack and gather what she needs.

A deep longing fills my chest, realizing I haven't seen my family in months. Excitement and nervousness course through my body at the same time. I want to see them all again. To hug my mother and sisters. I wish I had more time to visit with them, tell them all about the castle, about the Princess. There will be time for that later.

We approach the house, and I slow them to a trot as we enter the yard. I lead them to our watering bucket and make my way inside. The house is warm and smells like my mother is baking a pie.

"Bea!" I call out for her but instead am attacked by my younger sister, Claire, latching onto my legs. She shouts my name between cheers and laughter. I can't help my own laughter at seeing her face. I swear she has grown so much in the months since I saw her last. I try to pry her off me, but she won't budge. Instead, I kneel down, wrapping my arms around her body and lifting her up. She is heavy, and I know I won't be able to do this for much longer, but I can still do it now. She wraps her arms around my neck tightly. Even though I can't really breathe, I'm overwhelmed with the emotions of holding her close.

I snuggle into her hug, taking in her scents of dirt, grass, and a hint of candied apples. I press quick kisses to her forehead and ask where Bea is. My mother enters the room, tears threatening to spill from her eyes. She uses the small cloth in her hands to dab her eyes and tells me Bea is in her room. I place my sister down on the floor. Without acknowledging Ma's words, I rush to her, wrapping her in a tight hug.

I lift her off the ground, holding her petite body to my chest. My own tears are threatening to spill over. I hadn't realized how much I missed her. With her warm embrace and loving attitude, I have taken everything she has done for us for granted. She finally pushes me back.

"What are you doing here? Did you marry the Princess yet? Are you going to be King?" I laugh at her, both of us wiping our eyes.

"No, Ma. Nothing like that." We chuckle for a moment, then I remember the reason I came here. "I need Bea!"

I rush down the hallway as she finally emerges from her room. I hug her, too. My younger sister is wrapped around my legs again. Ma is standing in the hallway, waiting for my explanation.

"Bea, I need you to come back to the castle with me tonight." Her eyebrows shoot up in surprise. "The Princess has this big dog, Finn. He's sick. Something's wrong with him, but no animal healers are at the castle anymore. They all left, and there are only horses and birds there now. The stable master isn't comfortable working on Finn, and he needs help." I am babbling, and everyone is stunned when I stop talking. They take a minute to process everything.

"So, you're close to the Princess then?" Bea questions suggestively.

"Well, Finn. I spend a lot of time with him." I toy with the hem of my shirt, uncomfortable admitting my feelings about Jasmin to my family. "I play with him while she's in meetings. Jasmin doesn't mind."

"Jasmin, the Princess? You're on such informal terms with her already?" My mother wiggles her eyebrows at me. I groan as Bea laughs at me.

"Come on, Bea. Will you come with me?"

"Yes, let me just pack."

While she gets ready, I take Claire out to see the horses. We don't own a horse anymore. Bea and I would borrow someone else's if we needed one. It just made more sense to us. I let Claire sit on Vesper, telling her it's the Princess's horse. She was only a year old when the Princess first rode Vesper through our village. She doesn't remember seeing the two together the way I do. The horses are surprisingly calm around my younger sister. I help her down and give her carrots and apples to feed the horses.

Back inside, Bea is gathering what she needs. Ma comes out of her room with a small stack of parchment. She hands them over to me, all neatly wrapped in twine.

"Lord David said he would come back at some point to give me an update and could take a package to you. He hasn't come back, though. So I have all of these letters for you. There's nothing important in them. Just little updates and things I wanted you to know."

Love tugs at my chest as I take the stack from her. I kiss her cheek. "I'll find a way to get you out to visit the castle before this is over, Ma. I promise." She waves me off, walking into the kitchen to work with some dough she has laid out. As

I finish placing the letters in my bag, Bea finally comes out of the room. We say goodbye to Ma and our sister. Bea promises to be back in a day or two.

We ride off from the house at a slower pace than I came in on. I don't want to injure the horses by pushing them too hard. As we ride, I tell her about Jasmin and Finn and all the others around the castle. She asks some questions about Finn to get a better idea of his condition, but we spend the rest of the ride chatting about other things that have been happening the past couple of months.

When the castle is finally in sight, we rush to the doors. Tomas sees us coming in and goes to fetch Sabeko and Zander. They take the horses from us, leaving us to enter the castle. I lead her to the room where Finn was set up before I left. He is lying on the floor, Jasmin sitting behind him. Kian is leaning next to the fireplace, lost in his thoughts. Erik is standing guard next to the door as we walk in. Jasmin sees us and rushes over.

"Oh, I'm so glad you came, Bea. I've been so worried. Come over and see Finn, please." Jasmin pulls her to Finn, leaving space for Bea to sit in front of him.

"That's Princess Jasmin, by the way," I add as I guide Bea over. She seems very nervous now that we are here. "That's Kian and Erik." I motion to the other men in the room. I've already told her about them and don't feel the need to elaborate. When Bea looks at Erik, something flashes across her face. I look at Erik, and he blushes, looking away quickly. Before I can give it any thought, Bea kneels down as Jasmin rambles about Finn's condition. I step over to Kian to whisper quietly.

"How's she doing?" He shrugs.

"She's upset and nervous. I haven't seen her this hopeful since you left, though." I nod, glad that Bea could bring her some hope. Jasmin stops speaking as Bea rubs her hands over Finn. He whines when she reaches his head and neck. When Bea tries to look into his mouth, he snaps and growls, but it turns into a painful whimper. We all wince at his sounds. Jasmin has tears running down her face again.

"He's never violent. He's the sweetest dog." Bea nods her head in response.

"Do you have anything to sedate him?" Jasmin shakes her head no, more tears falling. Bea looks up to Kian.

"You're a witch, right? Can you sedate him?"

"I can," he says nervously. "I've never done it to an animal. He may be uncon-scious longer than he needs to be. Or come out of it sooner." Jasmin snaps her head up.

"Unconscious??"

"Yes, Princess." Kian's voice is soothing as he steps closer to Jasmin. "He'll wake up eventually. I just can't be sure when."

"Ok, we need to do that. I think I know what's wrong, but I can't check with Finn awake." Bea states as Jasmin sobs, sinking down over Finn's body. She rubs him, pressing several kisses to his back and shoulders. I walk over and grab her shoulders.

"Come with me. We'll stay out of the way. Just come find us when you're done."

Jasmin sniffles several times but follows me out of the room. I don't know what Bea needs to do, but having Jasmin there in her current state would not be helpful. Erik still stands by the door, saying he'll ensure no one else enters. We close the door behind us and make our way down the hallway. I should have thought this out more because I don't have a plan. Thankfully Jasmin walks toward another room just a few doors down and enters it.

We are in a smaller sitting room. A few chairs, a couple of tables, and a piano are in the corner. She moves to a loveseat, collapsing into it with her face in her hands. I sit next to her, wrapping my arms around her shoulders. I try to comfort her by telling her how confident I am in Bea's abilities. I don't actually know how good Bea is with dogs. I know she has lots of experience with cattle and fowl. She has helped with the dogs before, but I think it was only a broken leg or maybe a litter being born. She would have said something if she wasn't confident, though.

I pull Jasmin back against my chest, leaning back on the sofa. She follows me, settling onto my body so comfortably. I'm still astounded by how easy it is to be around Jasmin. Even in this challenging situation, it still feels right.

"Tell me about when you got Finn."

Jasmin looks up at me a bit sadly. "I got him a few years ago. I was out riding Vesper around the fields. I noticed this tiny white ball of fluff on the ground. I brought him back to the castle. He was dirty and hungry. I washed and fed him, and he followed me around everywhere. I sent word to Lord Thurston to try to find his owner. Turns out, Finn had wandered off from a family of breeders and wound up at our fields. He had wandered so far. So I bought him from them, and he's been mine ever since."

"Just being a rascal and annoying everyone but you, huh?" She chuckles.

"Yeah, they tolerate him around here. But there are so many places he can't go anymore." We both laugh at that. I tell her about the day he got me kicked out of the fields and all the times we had to get creative with meals. It occurs to me I haven't eaten since this morning. I've been so busy collecting Bea I completely forgot.

"Have you had dinner, Jasmin?" She shakes her head no. "Do you think Erik or Kian have?" Another head shake. "Why don't we go collect some dinner for everyone? We can check up on Finn and drop their food off."

We leave the small room, making our way to the kitchen. Jasmin is still on edge, but she seems a bit more settled. I'm glad Bea could come and hope she can help Finn. Despite my uncertainties, I still have full confidence in her. We gather food for everyone. I carry a tray stacked high with multiple dishes. Jasmin brings a wine decanter with several glasses for everyone. Once we get to the room, Jasmin is able to knock. Erik sticks his head out before moving aside to let us in. Bea looks over her shoulder, wiping her hands on a rag.

"We were just about to come find you. He's all better now. Just sleeping off the spell Kian put on him." Bea smiles up at us, relief washed over her face. Jasmin rushes to put the wine down, then over to Finn's side. She rubs his body as she lies next to him, wrapping her petite body around his, which is nearly equal in size.

I head to the table, putting down the tray as Bea, Kian, and Erik walk toward me. I notice Erik stand closer to Bea than he needs to, but I don't acknowledge it now. Bea speaks to me, but loudly enough that Jasmin can hear too.

"He had a stick caught in his throat. It turned sideways and was stabbing him. It did cut his throat. That's why there was blood. I was able to get it out with minimal damage, but he needs to stick to broth for a few days while it heals. Have him rest for the next couple of days."

"Oh, he is not going to like that." I joke.

"I don't know how long he'll sleep," Kian explains. " The spell I used is light, but I extended the time because I didn't want him to wake up while Bea was in the middle of something. It could be later tonight or tomorrow." He looks hurt over his statement. I clap his shoulder, thanking him for his work. I motion to the food and drink. We all sit, eating quietly. Kian takes his food and some for Jasmin and sits next to her. Bea and I sit at the table, and Erik pulls up a chair next to Bea. She blushes when she realizes how close he is to her. I've never seen her blush in my life!

Erik compliments Bea's work on Finn. They fall into quiet conversation. I eat my food, realizing I have no one to talk to. After eating, I offer to stay with Finn so everyone can rest.

"You're crazy if you think I'm leaving Finn tonight," Jasmin sasses.

"Ok, well, I'm not letting you stay here alone. You're too close to the other men, and I don't exactly trust them," I sass back.

"Fine."

"I'll stay in case Finn has a weird reaction waking up from my magic," Kian asserts.

"I'll stay and stand guard again," Erik adds.

The three of us stare at each other, knowing we didn't necessarily want the others to stay but unwilling to admit that.

"Okay," Bea starts slowly, unsure how to handle this awkward pissing contest we've conjured up. "Well, I would like to sleep in an actual bed. Is there a room close I could stay in? You can come wake me if you need anything."

"I'll take you to mine." I grab the dirty dishes and lead her out of the room. Dropping them by the kitchen, I take her to my room. I show her where things are and how to lock the door. I reiterate that the door needs to stay locked. She rolls her eyes at me.

"I wouldn't want Erik sneaking in here tonight." I tease. She punches me in the arm harder than I expect. "Damn. Bea. I was teasing."

"Well, don't." She states, "He's a good man and doesn't need you teasing him." I hold my hands up in surrender. There is definitely something between them.

"Alright. Thank you for coming, though. Seriously. It means a lot you would help me out that way." She just nods, moving into the room to settle down. I wish her good night and step out, waiting until she locks the door before I leave. I remember a closet with extra mattress pads, pillows, and blankets. So I grab a mattress pad for Jasmin and all the blankets and pillows I can for everyone else.

Back in the room, I realize someone has brought more wine in. Jasmin is sitting on the floor next to Finn, still rubbing his back with one hand while holding wine in the other. I tell her I brought the mattress pad so she can sleep next to him. Kian helps me get it all arranged for her. For the next couple of hours, we take turns sitting next to her, chatting idly, just offering company and support. As she starts to doze off, Erik says he will stand outside the room. Ever the gentleman. I have no intention of leaving her alone in this room. Kian has the same idea, apparently.

Jasmin lies down next to Finn, falling asleep quickly. Kian wraps a blanket around her before he moves to a chair. We continue to drink our wine for a bit in silence. My mind swims around Jasmin. I would do anything for her. I just rode half a day to get my sister to save Jasmin's dog. I'm wondering now if there is anything I wouldn't do for her. As my mind runs through scenarios of all the things I would do for her, Kian shifts in his chair, drawing my attention to him. I wonder how he feels about her. He is here and put a spell on Finn to help. Clearly, he has some feelings.

"Have you spent any time alone with Jasmin?" I speak quietly, curious about his response.

"Yes, some. You?"

"Yeah," I nod, not wanting to give too much away.

"You were here before anyone else, right?"

"I showed up around a week before the others."

"Did you spend time with her then?" I look at him, debating how I should answer. I don't particularly like lying, but I'm unsure if I should tell the truth. I think I can trust Kian since we're sort of friends. We are both after the same girl, regardless of how much control any of us have in this situation.

"Yeah, I got to spend a few days with her and Finn."

"Lucky." He stares off, looking both jealous and thoughtful.

"She actually didn't tell me who she was. I didn't know she was the Princess. I thought she was a handmaid or something." He chuckles, then realization dawns on his face.

"That's why you were so pissed those first few days?" I nod, laughing. I decide to trust him and share more with him.

"I was also pretty embarrassed. The night everyone showed up, I met her to spend more time with her. I asked her to run away with me, insisting the Princess wouldn't miss one handmaid." We both start laughing over my confession.

"What did she say to you then?" Kian asks between breaths and laughter.

"Nothing, really. She said she needed to get to bed." I roll my eyes, realizing how stupid I have been. We laugh for a couple of more minutes, our fits reigniting when we look at each other. Finally, we calm down enough to continue our conversation. He asks who I think her true love is.

"Honestly, I don't know. I hope it's not Oscar or his crew. But I think the rest of the men are good choices." Kian eyes me as he takes a sip of his wine. I can't tell what he is thinking.

"What about yourself?" He inquires.

"Oh, I don't think it's me. That wouldn't make any sense."

"Why not?"

"I'm a farmer from Arkaley. I'm not fit to be a princess's true love. Let alone a king. I just wanted to get out of Arkaley." He finishes his glass of wine, setting it on the table. He doesn't say anything else. I don't, either. My mind is running through all the reasons it is definitely not me. I couldn't be destined to love Jasmin, to save her. She's amazing, and I would do anything for her, but I don't get to choose who I am for her. I'm certainly not her true love. Kian, possibly. Maybe even Erik. Not me. No.

I stand up. "I'm gonna go check on Erik." I need to move around a bit to clear my mind. He nods at me.

"For what it's worth, I think you could be the one to break the curse."

Chapter 14

CLEM

Kian doesn't know what he is talking about. I give Erik a break, contemplating how ridiculous Kian's claim is. If anyone, it's probably him. He's a witch. He would be a better candidate for breaking the curse than I would. He may even know how to change it in his favor.

When I return to the room, he is lying next to Jasmin. He mouths that she had a bad dream. I nod, unsure of what else to do. I settle in the chair, trying to get a couple hours of sleep. It's a fitful sleep at best. Eventually, Bea and Erik enter the room, chatting happily. I don't know why they are so happy right now. It just rubs me the wrong way, and now I'm irritated. My whole day is starting off terribly. At least Kian moved away at some point and isn't still cuddling with Jasmin.

She wakes when Bea comes in, sliding over so Bea can inspect Finn. He's starting to wake up but is still drowsy. Bea suggests getting him some warm broth and letting him rest. Kian offers, striding out of the room. Finn has flopped over, and his head rests on Bea's lap while his tail smacks Jasmin. She laughs at him, forcing a smile onto my face despite my irritation.

I leave to get washed up and find clean clothes. Unfortunately, this does nothing for my mood. Half of the other bachelors are in the hallway. Tomas stops me to ask about Finn, which results in a barrage of questions from everyone else. I eventually snap at them, sulking off to my room. Bea comes in later, telling me Finn's doing well. She says Erik is going to take her to the stables, and she plans to head back in the morning. I give a snarky reply, but she just ignores me and leaves. I don't know why my mood is so sullen, but I can't shake it now. I decide to rest for a bit. It doesn't seem like I'll be needed anywhere else.

I wake feeling better. Not happy, but less grumpy. I realize I slept nearly the whole day because it is almost dinner time. I start walking toward the dining hall and come across Tomas. I apologize to him for my earlier behavior. It was rude of me to snap at him like that. In the dining hall, Jasmin is sitting at the table with Finn beside her. Both look happy and healthy. She is wearing a red sweater that highlights the color of her cheeks. Despite being told to only drink fluids, Finn is begging for bites under the table. Apparently, not even Bea can keep him in line.

Bea is sitting at the end of the table with Erik. He usually sits closer to the middle, nearer to Jasmin. He is on the far end tonight, whispering and giggling with my sister. Anger rolls through my body at the sight of him. Who does he think he is? Flirting with her in front of me. Making her giggle and blush like some schoolgirl. Wait. Bea is giggling and blushing. Why am I so angry? I should be happy.

Trying to clear my head, I grab some food and walk toward the table. Kian, Tomas, and a few other bachelors are sitting around Jasmin. I decide not to sit near her and plop down at the opposite end of the long table from Erik and Bea. I'm still grumpy and trying to sort out my emotions. I don't want to deal with other people too. I eat my food with my head hung over my bowls, contemplating everything I know. Why I'm here, why Bea is here, what I actually feel for the Princess. I don't notice everyone else clearing out of the hall until someone sits down next to me.

"Hi," Jasmin mumbles. I offer a soft smile, not really feeling it.

"Hey." Finn slowly walks over, lying down beneath our feet. He seems more worn out than usual.

"You've been awfully quiet today."

"Yeah, I didn't sleep much last night." Her hand strokes my back as she nods along. Her touch is more comforting than it should be.

"Want to talk about it?" The way she understands my mood isn't just about my sleep habits ripples through my already warring emotions.

"No," I answer too quickly, and it sounds rude. I make a face on my own. "Sorry. I'm pretty grumpy and snapping at everyone today." She snorts at my response, trying to suppress a giggle. I didn't say anything funny. Her response rubs me the wrong way. She stands next to me, running her fingers through my long hair. I close my eyes. I don't want to give away how good that feels.

"That's my entire life, Clem." She chuckles, lifting my face up to look at her. "Thank you for getting your sister for Finn. I don't know what I would do without him. Your willingness to help me didn't go unnoticed." Her hand slides over my neck as she leans in. Her lips press against mine. All the anger and irritation settle in my body. My shoulders relax as her thumb strokes my cheek. Before it goes any further, she pulls away, a chill running across my skin. She motions to Finn as they turn to leave.

As she's walking away, my mind is racing. I don't want her to leave. I know Finn needs rest, but I need her.

"Wait," I call out to her. She turns to me. Shit, I really have to start thinking these things through. "Um, oh! Could we send some flowers from the greenhouse to my mother? It would mean a lot to her." I hope we can go out there now, but don't expect her to agree to that.

"Of course, Clem! That's a great idea. Meet me at the door in the morning. I'll have Sunette there to help us arrange some for her." It's not what I hoped for, but it's better than nothing.

Bea is sitting on my bed with a smitten look on her face. My mind is finally calmer than it was earlier. I walk into the room, remove my sweater and place it on the chair.

"Oh," Bea says, rising from the bed. "I didn't know where you were going to sleep. I can find somewhere else." I roll my eyes at her.

"Bea, we shared a room until two months ago. I'll go grab a mattress pad and sleep on the floor." I peer back at her with a wide smirk on my face. "Unless you wanna share a bed with Erik." She steps over, punching me in the arm again.

"Fuck," I groan. "The same spot again? Are you trying to maim me?"

"Keep up with those comments, and I will!" She threatens with a snarl. I roll my eyes, leaving the room for the mattress pad, assuming my arm still works well enough to carry it. I chuckle to myself about her reaction. She did get pretty angry over the accusation that she had feelings for Erik. I know how she feels. That's how I've felt since Kian said something to me about Jasmin.

Fuck. I stop in my tracks as realization dawns on me. I've been angry for the past day because someone else told me about my feelings for her. I was angry because I couldn't admit what others could see. I do have feelings for the Princess. But so do several of the other men. Or at least they want her. We are all here for the same purpose. I sigh, not wanting to linger on that train of thought anymore. I don't press Bea about Erik anymore. I just curl up and sleep on the floor.

Jasmin and Finn are waiting at the door for me the next morning. I still feel exhausted, especially knowing I have a long day ahead of me, riding home and back. The thought of staying home has crossed my mind several times, but I'm not ready to give up on Jasmin. I would miss Finn too much. She wouldn't appreciate it if I took him with me.

Noticing my forlorn demeanor, she doesn't say anything, just offers a smile as she loops her arm through mine and leads me into the gardens. Nothing is in bloom this late in the season, but the greenhouse still has several plants. The scent of jasmine is powerful as we enter. Sunette is already here, humming as she prunes some of the plants. She greets us, and Jasmin explains what we want.

"Ma always spoke highly of the royal gardens. She would love a bouquet of whatever you can spare." I add as an explanation. Sunette agrees and explains what we should get and how to cut it. She tells us how much to gather, then hands a pair of shears to Jasmin and walks off. I wasn't expecting her to leave us alone.

I follow Jasmin around like a lost puppy, much like Finn does. After a couple of minutes of touching flowers, she sighs.

"Clem, what is going on with you? You haven't been like this before."

"It's nothing. I'm just tired." I wave her off. Pointing to a flower, "What about this one?"

"No, that one won't last long. It's at its peak now. We need some that aren't quite there yet." We walk in silence for a few more minutes. She gathers a few flowers, then goes over to a workbench. She places down the items she has and turns back to me. She wraps her arms around me as I settle against her.

"Why don't you let Erik take Bea back, and you can stay here with me? I...I..." She struggles to think of what to say next. Then her face lights up. "I need help rearranging the library. Someone," she pokes my side teasingly, "has been moving all of my furniture around, and none of it is in the right place anymore." I chuckle, pulling my arms free to wrap around her.

"I can't imagine why anyone would move all the furniture around. It's not like certain chairs work better in certain alcoves than other chairs. It's all just chairs," I tease. She smiles up at me.

"There you are." She rises on her toes and presses a kiss to my jaw. "Will you stay with me?"

"Of course, Jasmin." I kiss her forehead, breathing her scent in deeply. She tightens her arms around me. I wouldn't say no to anything she asked. I'm sad about not seeing Ma and my sister again, but they'll be fine without me. I ask about sending books back with Bea for Claire. She says she has the perfect ones. We finish with the bouquet, wrapping it in parchment to protect it during their journey back. She leaves to grab the books, and then we meet at the stables.

Bea and Erik are already there, prepping the horses for their trip. It'll be easier on them this time since there isn't such a rush. Finn prances up to Bea when he sees her. She greets him with pets and demands to behave. He snorts at her, and we all laugh. He frolics off into the field, chasing some invisible creature.

"Bea, is it ok if Erik escorts you home? I need Clem to help me with a task here." Erik's cheeks redden as he looks down at the ground. A grin spreads across his face that he is trying to hide. Bea looks at him, but at seeing his response, she straightens her shoulders.

"Yes, that would be perfectly fine." I smile at her, handing her the items we send to my family. She tucks them away in her bag as Jasmin steps closer to Erik, speaking to him quietly. I hug Bea, holding her tight, realizing I don't know when I'll see her again.

"Tell Ma I love her, please."

"Ok. Just let us know when the wedding is." She teases.

I nod in Erik's direction. "I'll be sure to plan it after yours. Don't want your little brother getting married before you and all." She punches me in the arm again. I should have seen that coming, though.

"Fuck, Bea. I need that arm."

"You can learn to masturbate with the other one."

As she says this, Jasmin walks up to my side. Her eyes go wide, glancing between Bea and me. Bea turns a dark shade of red. I grin amusedly. Jasmin has said and done far worse things, but Bea doesn't know that. She drops her head.

"I'm so sorry, Princess. That was inappropriate." Jasmin takes my arm, looking disappointed in my sister.

"You're right, Bea. That was inappropriate. Surely, we can find a better way to relieve Clem when you break his arm." I snicker at her comment as Erik howls with laughter. Bea looks petrified, glancing between all of us. Her face is bright red. A nervous smile creeps onto her face, unsure how to take Jasmin. Before anything else can be said, Jasmin releases me and pulls Bea into a hug. She whispers something that I don't quite catch but has to do with "pleasing her brother." I didn't think it was possible, but Bea turns an even darker shade of red. Another comment from Jasmin, and she might break out in hives.

I help Bea mount Vesper, not that she needs any help. I thank her again and walk to the side. Jasmin hands her a bag of coins. Bea tries to refuse it, but Jasmin just tucks it into one of her bags. They are both so stubborn. Jasmin instructs Erik to let her know of his return. He promises, and they head off. We watch as they ride down the lane, both in awkward positions.

Jasmin pulls me inside, heading toward the library. We come across a woman named Emmeline. I've seen her a few times but don't know her well. Jasmin asks her to take Finn back to her room, letting him rest. She tells Emmeline we'll be in the library, rearranging, and asks not to be disturbed. I don't think distractions will be a problem, but getting some alone time with Jasmin will be nice. After the last couple of days, I could use some alone time with her to settle my emotions.

I plop down in the library on the chaise lounge I moved into my favorite alcove. The sun shines through the window, casting a warm spot on the chair. This alcove is hidden from the main view. No one can see inside unless they walk directly in front of it. It's one of the reasons I chose this spot. The privacy is perfect. I can still see through the books, but it's harder to see in because of the angle.

"I don't know who has been rearranging all of the furniture, but I think he must be a genius. I mean, just look at this spot." I stretch back, closing my eyes as the sun warms my face. My arms are stretched behind my head, a perfectly relaxed pose. I feel Jasmin sitting on the lounge between my legs. Her fingers grab my hips, slipping under my shirt to touch my stomach. I gasp, opening my eyes and dropping my arms.

"Maybe he is a genius." Her sultry eyes meet mine as her fingers spread across my stomach and chest. Her thumbs hook the hem of my shirt, lifting it up to expose my skin. She finally breaks her stare and leans down, pressing her lips below my navel. I groan as she places several more feather-light kisses across my abdomen. I whisper her name, sliding my hands over her arms. She sits up slightly, pushing my shirt higher.

"Take it off," she whispers.

I lean up, ripping the shirt over my head. Now I understand why she asked for the library not to be disturbed. She presses several kisses to my chest before licking my nipple and sucking the nub between her lips. The sensation causes my hips to grind into her. My cock is rock hard, aching for touch. She rubs her hips against mine, my member directly underneath her center. There are too many clothes between us. I try to slide my hands along her clothes to remove them, but she shifts first, lowering herself from my body. Her fingers glide over my stomach to the strings of my pants. She loosens them, my dick straining against the fabric. As she works on the ties, she rubs her forearm along my member and presses several kisses over it. She's teasing me so much; I may come before she even gets my pants off.

"If you keep that up," I hiss between my teeth, "there won't be anything left to do once you get the pants undone."

She chuckles but finally springs my dick free from my trousers. I wonder why men don't just wear dresses all the time for easier access. My thoughts fray as her hands wrap around the base of my cock. Her tongue swirls the tip, her hot breath causing my eyes to roll back in my head. I force myself to open my eyes and watch her. I don't want to miss any of this. As I open my eyes, her mouth wraps around the tip. I groan loudly, doing everything to keep my eyes on her. I wrap my fingers around her head, holding her there. Her tongue swirls again as her grip tightens.

"Take me, Jasmin. Make me come for you."

She removes one hand as she drops down over my cock, taking me deep in her throat. She keeps one hand on the base, squeezing and twisting. She slides her mouth back to the tip, swirling her tongue around briefly before taking more into her mouth. She presses down as far as she can, and my tip hits the back of her throat, causing her to gag. The sound is glorious, her gagging on my cock.

"Yes, gag on me, Jasmin. Do it again."

She slides down, her tongue gliding along the underside of my dick. Her fingers release the base as she takes all of me in. She gags again as I hit the back of her throat. It takes a lot of effort not to grab her and thrust in repeatedly. She begins to bob up and down, causing my balls to tighten in ecstasy. Her fingers graze lightly across them as I feel my orgasm rising through my body.

"I'm about to come," I warn, not wanting to release in her mouth if she doesn't want that. To my surprise, she takes me as deep as she can, sucking around my whole shaft. She lightly squeezes my balls as I erupt inside her mouth. I groan, unable to keep my eyes open. My warm fluids shoot inside her. She pulls back just enough to swallow, increasing the pleasure of my orgasm. A loud moan leaves my mouth as she bobs slowly. She pulls off, licking me clean. My breathing is hard and quick, but my body is calm and relaxed. She slides next to me, lying on my side.

Her head rests on my chest, fingers drawing lazy circles while I slowly return to life. Her fingers reach over to my arm, stroking my bicep where a bruise forms.

"She did actually bruise you, huh?"

"Well, she punched me in the same spot three different times."

"You probably deserved it."

"Oh, did I?" I tease, flipping us so she is on her back and I'm hovering over her. "I guess I better ensure you don't want to punch me too."

I drop my face to her neck, peppering her with kisses. She stretches her neck, giving me better access. Her arm reaches around my back, digging into my skin. I place my hand on her stomach, sliding my hands up her chest. I cup her breast, flicking my thumb across her nipple. She moans as I squeeze it between my thumb and forefinger, swirling it around. I pull my hand back, grabbing the hem of her shirt.

"I think it's time for your shirt to come off now."

"No." She jerks her hands down, holding her shirt against her body. I lean back, startled at her response. My hand is trapped against her stomach under her shirt.

"Do you want me to stop?"

"No, but I don't want to remove my clothes." She bites her lip, looking nervous. I shrug.

"Okay."

I slide my hand to the waist of her pants, slipping just the tips under the edge.

"Can I touch you under your clothes?" I whisper against her neck, licking the trail I kissed earlier. She just shakes her head yes at me. I slip my fingers further, feeling the soft patch of hair above her entrance.

"You have control here," I whisper in a deep voice. "Tell me if I should stop." Her hips thrust up toward my hand.

"Oh, gods. Clem, please don't stop."

My fingers slide lower, caressing her wet pussy. I knew she was aroused by our activities, but I had no idea how much. I press the tip of my middle finger between her folds, feeling the soft, wet skin. She moans, stretching her head further to the side. I tease her by flicking my finger inside her, not going more than knuckle deep. She groans, trying to wiggle her hips for more friction.

"Now, who's desperate for release?"

"Me, Clem, me!"

Hearing my name from her pushes me and drives me crazy. I plunge two fingers deep inside of her. Her back arches at the intrusion, and I capture her mouth with mine, not wanting her to make too much noise. As her body settles down, I slide them in and out, feeling her skin, searching for the spots she likes best. She groans, telling me I have found that sweet spot. I swirl my fingers around it, then flick it, rubbing it quickly. Her muscles clench around my fingers. I shift my weight to lean on my legs instead of my arm. I wrap my free hand around her throat, not squeezing, just holding it. Her eyes meet mine, wide and blown with lust.

"I'm going to make you come, little flower. And when I do, I want to hear you crying my name."

She shakes her head against my hand. I give her a wicked smile. My fingers increase speed, rubbing over that spot she likes so much. I slip my thumb down, flicking against her clit. She explodes around me. Her cunt contracts over my fingers. Her body arches against mine while her hands grab my back, pulling me closer to her. I release her neck, dropping my hand to support my weight again. She is chanting my name as her body convulses beneath me. I press my lips against her neck, kissing her on the other side as she rides her orgasm.

She settles down, relaxing in the lounge. I slowly remove my fingers from her, bringing them straight to my mouth. She bites her bottom lip as I suck her taste off my fingers. She curses under her breath, then pulls me into a searing kiss. After we break, I lift her gently, lying back on the lounge, pulling her into my side again. I press a kiss on her forehead.

"I can still work with an injured arm." She giggles softly, sending warmth through my body.

"Yeah, maybe you'll be better when you aren't injured." I stare at her with my mouth agape, both insulted and impressed.

"Maybe I'll find someone else to chant my name next time." I feign being hurt. She just laughs, wrapping around my chest tightly. I hold her close, very glad that she brought me here. I feel much better being with her, not just because of the orgasm. Jasmin brings me a sense of calm and security like I have never felt before. It's both invigorating and daunting.

Chapter 15

JASMIN

Today is the day of the sparring contest. Finn healed wonderfully and is back to his typical menacing ways. I haven't seen any of the men spar in several weeks since Erik refused to let me attend the training. I am excited to see how far they have progressed. Emmeline is particularly keen, practically bouncing around my room. While she is helping me get ready, I am also helping her. She will sit at my side in the Queen's chair while I occupy the King's chair.

We decided to wear formal gowns today to make it more fun. Mine is a navy blue, with beadwork on the chest, long sleeves that extend past my wrists, and a full skirt. Emmeline is wearing a light blue gown. The skirt is smaller but still stunning on her. We giggle and chat as we get ready, excited to have an event like this to get ready for. It's been so long since we have done something of this nature.

"Who do you think will win, Emmeline?" I question. She has been allowed to attend some of the training.

"Honestly, I think Tomas could win. He's such a natural." I groan. Tomas is sweet, but at only 17, he is so young. "The real question, Jasmin, is who do you want to win?" I toss her a sly smile.

"Oh, I don't know."

"Yes, you do. Spill it." She nudges my shoulder, reaching over to grab a brush.

"Ok. Fine. I know Kian is terrible, but I wouldn't be upset if he won. Clem isn't competing, so he can't. I wouldn't be opposed to spending more time with Erik." She gives a small huff, accepting my answer.

"It's interesting that your first two options don't even stand a chance today." I roll my eyes at her.

She grins, twisting my hair up to style. It has been growing longer in the last few weeks. Even the Lords have noticed the change now. It's finally long enough to style in an updo with many extra pins. Emmeline's fingers work through my hair, twisting and pinning it around my head. The style is elegant when she is done. I pull her into the chair as I rise, starting to work on her hair. I'm not as skilled as her. She gets a braid that I twist around at the base of her neck. It still looks lovely, but it's not as stunning as mine. I let the task distract me from thinking about this event. I don't want to focus on the winner. I just want to enjoy the event today.

"Has anything else been said about a coronation, Jasmin?"

"No." I sigh. "I haven't brought it up yet. I want to do it without the bachelors in the room, but we haven't done that in a while. I'm also ready for the Lords to leave."

"They need to go soon to beat the snow." She adds. The weather has turned chilly. The first snow isn't far off. "I always wish for snow before the winter solstice, but it so rarely comes." She sighs, staring out the window with a dreamy look.

"You're such a romantic. Let's go to the sparring contest. It's time."

We enter the arena, taking our seats on the platform. The Lords are all seated off to my left. Everyone else in the castle has joined us on the right and behind us. I smile, waving to everyone. Finn is down in the arena, running around with a small chest piece of armor, barking at everyone. I don't know whose idea it was to include him, but I love it so much.

Clem walks out wearing fitted pants and a jacket with the kingdom's emblem on the chest. He either got lucky in finding one that fit him or had a tailor fit it to him. It looks regal on him. He calms the crowd, welcoming everyone to the contest. Clem chatted with some of the old guards, writing a script to recreate what a traditional match would sound like. Royalty is meant to be stoic at this event, but I can't hide my amusement at all the details the men put into this.

Kian and Tomas battle first. They are still using the wooden swords we trained with. Tomas could obviously work with a real sword at this point. His movements are smooth and precise. He really does have natural talent and has significantly improved in the weeks he has been training. Kian, however, did not retain anything I helped him with. I had assumed at one point he was pretending to be terrible to get extra assistance from me. I see now my assumption was wrong. He is genuinely awful.

The two battle for several minutes. It is almost comical how different their skills are. Tomas makes a killing blow as Kian drops to the ground, calling out for his princess. We erupt in laughter and applause. Clem steps up to announce Tomas as the winner of the battle, but he can't be heard over the cheers. Kian and Tomas bow and Tomas exits back to the training rooms. Kian hops up on the stage, taking my hand and bowing in front of me. The crowd swoons, leading me to glare at them quickly. Kian kisses my hand, then sits to the left in front of the Lords to watch the rest of the matches.

Next to battle are Oscar and one of his buddies, Sven. The battle is even shorter than Kian and Tomas's. Sven has thrown the match. He looks skilled with his sword, but when Oscar takes a stab at his chest, Sven doesn't move or attempt to block the blow. He drops to his knee, indicating the match is over. Oscar raises his hand in triumph. The crowd claps apathetically, and Oscar scowls at the lack of enthusiasm. Clem names him the winner as Sven follows Kian's move, jumping to me. He takes my hand, apologizing for not winning for my honor.

"There is no honor in throwing a match." I snatch my hand back, nodding toward Kian. "Please take your seat." I don't look at Sven again, disappointed in his actions. I notice a playful smirk on Kian's face before turning back toward Clem for the next battle.

The morning continues on. The number of bachelors on the bench to my left grows. Tomas has won every match he has been in, as has Oscar. It seems as if those two will face off in the end. Oscar battled against his other buddy, Philip, and barely won. It was the longest battle. Oscar was panting and covered in sweat when he got lucky. Philip had let his guard down, glancing at the crowd, and Oscar took the opportunity. I thanked Philip for not throwing his contest but was sad when Oscar won again.

Tomas is now fighting Erik, the last bachelor left. After this battle, the winner and Oscar will square off in the final fight to see who is crowned victor and wins a private dinner with me. Erik has received training his entire life from his family, but Tomas's natural ability equally matches Erik's training. This battle will come down to a technicality. Part of me actually hopes Tomas will win. While I would love to have Erik win the whole championship and spend time with him, Tomas certainly has the underdog story on his side. Oscar is standing in the corner, glaring as he watches the battle. They swing and clash. The sounds of their weapons are met with gasps and cheers from the crowd. The crowd is also split in who they want to win. Many people know Erik's family and are therefore rooting for him. I do notice Zander sitting with Sunette. They seem to be cheering for Tomas. I have managed to maintain my stoic demeanor during this fight, unsure of who I truly want to root for.

I notice Oscar growing increasingly agitated out of the corner of my eye. It has been clear he is less skilled than Tomas or Erik. While losing to Erik may not be a massive blow to his pride, losing to Tomas certainly would be. He takes a couple of steps toward the two fighting. Then I notice the rack of steel swords he sneaks past. All of the battles have used wooden training swords, which is what Erik and Tomas still have. Both wear a mail chest piece, but those won't protect other areas.

I stand, my eyes trained on Oscar. Only Emmeline notices my stance changing. Everyone else, including the few guardsmen supervising the contest, are all focused on Tomas and Erik. The sounds of the wood clashing are mixed with cheers and taunts from the crowd. It's so noisy nothing else can be heard. Oscar takes several quick steps, breaking into a run. I scream no, leaping from the platform to intervene. Not that I would be any better against Oscar's sword than Erik's or Tomas's wooden ones, but my mind is in fight mode. I cannot let Oscar attack them while I stand by.

As I land in the sandy arena, Erik and Tomas turn their attention toward me. Oscar is closer to them than I am now. Erik registers my face as I try to point beyond. The sounds of the crowd have faded behind me, but they are shouting. Erik spins as Oscar reaches them. Tomas is still staring at me as Oscar's blade strikes his arm. He screams, falling to the ground. Erik wraps around Oscar's waist and grabs his arms, holding them behind his back.

Everything starts moving at a fast pace again. Tomas is screaming in agony. The guards are rushing in to detain Oscar. The Lords are standing in shock while some bachelors run after Tomas or me. Oscar still holds his sword, waving it at anyone near him. He is fighting against Erik's hold, shouting angry words about cheating and unfair treatment. His words don't actually register in my brain. Several guardsmen try to convince Oscar to drop the sword, but he won't do it. He has backed away enough that I have access to the weapons rack. My father insisted on enough training when I was younger that I am comfortable with them.

Walking toward the weapons, I grab a long mace. I don't want to remove any body parts from Oscar with a sword, but maiming him wouldn't ruin my day. While the guards and Oscar are distracted in the heat of the moment, I make eye contact with Erik. His eyes go wide as he realizes what I am about to do. He braces his grip around Oscar's arms as I swing the mace out past my side. I sling it out as hard as possible on Oscar's hand on the sword. His screams wrench all attention to him. Everyone looks up to see what happened.

Erik kicks his sword away, and I pick it up. The guards move in, cuffing Oscar. He is sobbing and screaming, trying to grab his hand. I pass the sword and the mace to Erik, letting him clean them and put them away. With everyone stunned, I take advantage of the silence.

"Guards, please take Oscar to the dungeons. Healers, when you are done with Tomas, someone needs to see Oscar. There needs to be a guard with him at all times. Lords," I turn to them. They have a mix of horror and anger across their faces. "I want a meeting with all of you in one hour. Henry and Erik, I would like you at the meeting." Henry, my Captain of Guards, is standing near Erik now. Both nod in acknowledgment.

I approach Tomas, who is lying on the ground as the medics look over him. I kneel to his side, taking his uninjured hand. He starts apologizing to me. I silence him with a kiss on his forehead. I look up to Kian, asking if he can help the healers. He nods as a couple of other men arrive with a stretcher. They load Tomas up and all leave together. I find Emmeline, letting her know I would like a change of clothes shortly. She takes off, rushing to my room to get things ready. I address the remaining crowd, apologizing for the turn of events and reminding them of the feast and wine that was prepared for later. I implore them to start that now, and the rest of us will join soon.

Without waiting to see what everyone else does, I exit down a long hallway off the training grounds. I quickly step into an empty room, planning to take a few deep breaths to recenter myself. My blood is thrumming through my body, and my head feels like it might explode. I take a deep inhale but hear the door shut behind me. I turn to see who followed me and slam into Clem's chest. His arms wrap around me, holding me tightly. I relax against him. I try to take my deep breaths, but sobs escape instead. He tightens his arms, supporting my weight as tears roll down my face.

We stand like that for several moments before I regain my composure. He loosens his arms, removing one to hand me a handkerchief. I thank him, patting my face dry. I look up at him with a sad smile.

"What the fuck," is all I can say.

He chuckles lightly, taking the handkerchief from me and rubbing my face. He doesn't say anything else, just offers his comfort and warmth.

"Shit! Where's Finn?"

"Don't worry, Jasmin. He's waiting in the hallway. He followed you back here."

Clem opens the door and lets Finn enter. I spend several minutes comforting him before walking to my room to change. I need to check on Tomas before meeting with the Lords. Clem offers to check on him and update me before the meeting. I agree; it would spare me a few minutes.

Finn and I change quickly, removing his armor before entering the meeting room. Clem is waiting in the hallway for me. He informs me Tomas is still out, thanks to Kian's spell, but the wound isn't deep. He'll likely have a scar and possibly limited use, but he won't lose his arm.

"Will you come into the meeting with me?" I ask on impulse. Clem's presence is very comforting, and I could use that right about now. I haven't taken a stand against the Lords since I came into power, but today feels like a good day to change that. We walk into the room with Finn just behind us. The Lords have the decency to rise as I enter, treating me with the respect my position deserves. It feels odd, but not wrong, to walk in with Clem like this. We head to our seats, and I wave for them to sit down. Finn is positioned between Clem and me, with Clem stroking his ears. I take a deep breath before speaking, then stand to look at everyone.

"I am outraged at this turn of events." I pause, gathering my thoughts. "Oscar is officially a prisoner of the castle. His trial will be held in seven days, though it is a formality. Lord Gustavo, you have four days to notify his family and invite them to attend his trial if they wish. I want a response of their plans." He nods sullenly but has the good sense not to argue with me.

"I want Sven and Philip sent to their homes. Their behavior with Oscar has been long overlooked because of their families, and I will not tolerate it anymore. If we find the changes in the curse reversal due to their presence, we will bring them back." No one else argues. I turn to Henry, my Captain of the Guard.

"Will you be able to have someone guard the dungeons at all times?"

"Yes, milady."

"Good. We will still treat Oscar respectfully, allowing him three meals daily. No visitors at this time. Erik," I turn to him, "Thank you for your efforts today, both in the contest and dealing with Oscar. I want you to know I greatly appreciate what you have done." He nods to me but doesn't speak.

"Now that those items are out of the way. Winter solstice is in a few weeks. Preparations have already begun for that. After the celebration, I want you to return to your homes." I speak to the Lords. It's long past time for them to leave. A couple of them begin to argue, but I hold my hand, silencing them. "You were never meant to remain here at the castle. You are also well aware the paths to Greynon and Arkaley will become impassable once the snow starts. Your villages need you more than I do. If you suspect the men you brought are incapable of respectable behavior without your presence, take them with you.

"On that note, I want all bachelors to be allowed the option to return home for the winters without replacements. We know one of them is my true love, but without removing some, we cannot narrow down who it is. Give them a choice to leave." Erik and Clem both look terrified by the suggestion.

"My final point, I want to be appointed Queen in the spring. Once the paths are clear of snow and passable for everyone, we will have the coronation. There is no reason to put this off any longer. I will collaborate with people within the castle over the winter to plan it. If you have suggestions, make them before Winter Solstice or when you return in the spring." With that, I fold my hands in front of my waist and sit down, allowing them to speak up if they have anything to say. No one does for several moments, then Erik addresses me.

"Princess Jasmin, what about those of us who are not your true love but would like to remain in the castle?" I choose not to address the point that he thinks he isn't my true love.

"There are several men I would like to offer a position to within the castle, regardless of fate. I haven't decided when I will do that, but I would like to talk with you more on this topic later." He nods, not adding anything else.

There is some chatter about the suddenness of everything, which I shut down promptly. Everything is long overdue at this point, and nothing is sudden. We discuss a few minor details before I dismiss everyone. I visit Tomas, ensuring he is doing well. He is barely awake but assures me he is fine. Then I retire to my room for a fitful night's sleep. I never expected this turn of events.

Chapter 16

JASMIN

Tomas awoke in good spirits when Kian's spell wore off. He spent a few days in the infirmary while he was healing. Once he was released, he spent a lot of time in the stables with Zander. At first, we were worried he would further injure his arm. Turns out, he was being near Zander. I didn't mind this so much, even encouraged it. The two have a special bond I didn't want to interfere with.

Since the contest didn't go according to plan, I decided to have a private dinner with Erik. He tried to insist it should go to someone else, but I argued it should be him due to his efforts. We now sit in the small room, eating our food quietly. He was never one to talk much, always being content just being around the rest of us. We sit in silence until we finish our food. I lean back, sipping my wine.

"Erik, would you like to stay on and work with Henry to train more guardsmen?" His eyes light up.

"I would love that, milady."

We chat about training and guard duty for the rest of the evening. Erik is so animated when he speaks about training. While I don't think he fits the bill of my true love, I do enjoy his company. We end the evening in good spirits, laughing as we wander the halls.

The next day, some especially chatty kitchen maids say that the tailor is working on fitting Kian for a new jacket for the winter solstice. This is something I should check in on. After learning where they would be, I make my way to the room, sneaking in quietly. Kian is standing in the middle of the room without a shirt on. I lick my lips as they are suddenly dry, unlike other parts of my body.

He is gorgeous. His muscles are perfectly defined. His olive skin is smooth and unmarked, except for a small tattoo on his left chest, just a couple of inches above his nipple. My fingers twitch, wanting to run down his ribs, feeling each before sliding over the v that leads beneath his trousers.

"Hello, Princess." His smug expression shows he knows exactly where my mind is. He is always more aware of my presence than I give him credit for.

"Oh, milady! I didn't hear you come in." The older man is our preferred tailor because of his exquisite work. "Did you need me? I am just finishing up here."

"Oh, no. I came to see what Kian wanted. I heard he has requested a jacket for the winter solstice."

"Yes, milady. That's what I am making for him." The tailor looks between us, trying to hide his grin. "Well, let me get out of your way." He gathers his things quickly and leaves, closing the door behind him. I approach Kian, reaching out to run my fingers along his stomach. He watches me as I explore his tanned skin.

The tattoo is the symbol of his coven. I haven't seen one up close before, but I know the image. The crescent moon with flowers around it has been used by his coven for generations. My fingers continue their crusade across his chest, down his stomach, and to the waist of his pants. I step closer, placing my lips on his chest, kissing, nipping, sucking. When I look up at him, he is watching intently. As I hold his stare, my fingers begin to unlace his pants. His hands catch my wrists, stilling my hands.

"What's wrong, Kian?"

"I don't want to disappoint you, Princess." I give him a confused look.

"You won't." He gives a small grunt.

"I can't satisfy you like this." This catches me off guard, unsure what he could mean. I look down to see a bulge in his pants, but it's not prominent. His statement makes more sense now.

"Oh." He releases my hands, thinking I have stopped for him. Once he does, I rip his pants away, pulling them down as I drop to my knees in front of him. He looks startled but doesn't try to stop me. I pull his clothes away, exposing his cock. It is smaller than any I've seen before. I wrap my fist around it, only the tip hanging past my hand. I look up at Kian's face. He seems nervous and unsure of what to do now that I am in this position with him.

I lick my lips, maintaining eye contact with him, and swirl my tongue against the tip. He groans at the touch. I slide my hand back, taking more in my mouth. I keep my eyes locked on his. My hands grab his hips as I take his length in entirely. It doesn't go far in my throat, and I can slide my tongue around it. I bob up and down, careful not to pull back too far. His hands slide into my hair as my fingers dig into his hips. His breathing becomes more erratic. One hand glides from his hips to caress his balls as they tighten with his orgasm.

"Please don't stop; I'm so close," he begs. I hum against him, letting him know I'm not stopping. His hand tightens in my hair as I continue my pace. I squeeze his balls again, pushing him over the edge. His release spills into my mouth. I swallow, swirling my tongue around him as his orgasm courses through his body. I suck every last drop from him, licking to ensure nothing is left behind. As he goes limp, I release him from my mouth, standing in front of him, my hands still on his body.

"Fuck, Princess." He mutters before crashing into my lips. I return his kiss, thrusting my tongue into his mouth so he can taste himself on me. He breaks the kiss, pulling his pants up from his thighs. His gaze returns to me, intense and lust-filled.

"Now, it's my turn."

He walks me back to a chair, then drops to his knees. He goes to lift my shirt, but I hold it down. I don't want him to see the marks across my stomach. Thankfully, he understands my intent and doesn't push the issue. He grabs the waist of my leggings, pulling them down to my ankles. His arms wrap around my hips, pressing several kisses into the hair above my core. I make sure my shirt stays down. When he leans back, he instructs me to sit as he digs in his pocket.

"Do you trust me, Princess?" His voice is deep and sultry and sends a wave of moisture through my core. I nod, biting my lip. After everything he has done, how could I not trust him? He pulls a small marble-sized ball from his pocket. He presses the inside of my knees, spreading me further apart. I am completely exposed to him. He taps the ball with his finger, and it starts vibrating. My eyebrows rise in surprise and wonder.

"Magic," he whispers.

He leans in, pressing his lips softly against my core. He rolls the ball to my pussy. He slides it up my slit, then pushes it against my clit. I have never felt anything so unique. So overwhelming. My breath increases instantly as pleasure pulses through my body. My orgasm builds quickly and intensely. I force myself to look back at him. He is just watching me, enjoying this almost as much as I am.

He shifts his arm on top of my hips, keeping the vibrating ball pressed against me. He licks me from my ass to my pussy before his tongue dives deep inside me. My entire body is clenching in pleasure. I may actually break apart with this orgasm. My body will literally be in pieces on the floor by the time this is over. He thrusts his tongue in and out several times as I pant his name.

He removes his lips, leaning back to stare at me. The loss of his warm mouth exposes me to the cool air, which surprisingly causes my pussy to clench. He smirks, noticing the reaction. Again, he taps the ball with his fingers. I didn't think it was possible, but the vibrations increase. Now, I am squirming in this chair, so close to orgasm. My functional brain isn't working. The only thing coursing through me is a pleasure like I have never experienced before. My eyes roll back in my head, on the cusp of exploding. Kian slides one finger inside me, pushing me over the edge. I arch off the back of the chair. My pussy clenches tightly around his finger, releasing more fluids than I have ever experienced in my life. I cry out as my body jerks with the orgasm. It is intense. Stars fill my vision as my body twists, unsure how to move with this much unadulterated pleasure.

He stops the vibrations of the ball but doesn't remove it yet. I lean back against the chair as his finger slips out of me. My mind doesn't even register him tasting his finger. As my heavy breathing slowly returns to normal, he tugs my pants back up, assisting me before pulling me into his lap. My pants have wet spots from the extra fluid in my orgasm. I curl against his chest as his arms wrap around me. I want to say something but don't even know what to say.

"Thank you for letting me try that," he whispers. I shoot upright in his lap.

"Try that?? You've never done that before." He grins sheepishly.

"No. I understood the concept but never found anyone to test it on."

"Holy fuck." I mutter. "Can I have that ball?" I tease, but also actually want. He chuckles at me.

"I need to make some adjustments. But I'll give you one when I refine it." I shiver with excitement at the prospect. He chuckles at my reaction, the sound resonating through his chest. His arms are warm, and his spicy scent is more pungent now. I can't quite decide if I am happier here or with Clem, but one thing is certain. I need that ball for masturbation and more time with these men.

The problem with such a mind-blowing orgasm is the rest of the week has nowhere to go but down. My spirits dampen as Oscar's trial arrives. His family traveled in. I am not looking forward to having them here. I have never gotten along with them. They were always entitled, believing they should be treated differently because of their position in the kingdom. Lord Gustavo stayed with Lord Thurston to attend the trial, but the rest of the Lords left.

Today is my first time using the throne room for a trial. Any other disciplinary actions were dealt with more remotely. The Lords would explain the situation, and I would make a ruling. That was that. Since Oscar committed this assault on royal grounds, I have decided to hold an actual trial to make it fair and appease his family. I enter the throne room, heading toward the dais. Everyone stands as I walk down the center aisle. A very small portion of the seats is filled due to the lack of people at the castle.

Oscar's family sits on one side of the aisle. Everyone else, including the bachelors, is on the other side. Only Clem is missing. He offered to entertain Finn while Emmeline attended the trial. Erik and another guard bring Oscar to the front after I take my position on the throne. Sitting up here is awkward, but I hold my position, refusing to show any discomfort. Oscar looks terrible. His hand is wrapped in bandages. While he was allowed to bathe and wear fresh clothes, being in the dungeons has not done anything for him. He is paler; his dark skin is ashy in places. His dark hair is knotted and unkempt. Erik informed me he refuses to bathe. He believes Oscar skipped it to gain pity, but he won't find any here.

"Oscar Morrin, you are brought before this court on charges of assault, illegal use of a weapon, and attempted robbery of royal property. How do you plead?" I ask loudly so everyone can hear. He stares at the ground, not responding. Erik nudges him, but he doesn't respond.

"Very well. No response shall be taken as a plea of guilty. For your sentence...."

"Wait, Jasmin!" Oscar's father stands from his seat, walking around to stand next to his son. He has been a member of the court for far too long to act like this. I am stunned by his brazen disregard for titles. His tall, thick body towers over Oscar. Oscar's paleness and ashy skin is more striking when his father stands next to him. His father's skin is a rich brown color, smooth and healthy. "Surely we can work something out."

"I will say this only once, Sir Morrin. You are to respect court protocols." I glare at him, and he has the decency to give a shallow bow in response. "Are you offering counsel on behalf of your son?"

"Well, yes. Jasmin. I cannot believe Oscar committed any of these acts."

"Erik, please cuff this man for contempt of court." Sir Morrin looks appalled, but I'm more surprised he chose to address me so casually immediately after being told not to. Erik pulls Sir Morrin's hands behind his back as another guard hands him cuffs. Oscar has kept his head down the entire time. I turn toward Tomas, who is sitting in front of the group closest to me. "Tomas, please explain what happened at the sparring contest."

Tomas stands, his arm still wrapped in gauze around his body to allow it to heal properly. He gives a quick recount of what happened at the sparring contest.

"Thank you. Lady Emmeline, can you please explain what you saw?" She stands from her seat behind Tomas and gives a similar account, only more vividly describing the pain Tomas experienced. I ask Henry and Erik the same question. As I address Kian, Sir Morrin speaks up.

"That's enough."

"Good. Oscar Morrin, you are hereby found guilty of assault, illegal use of weapons, and attempted robbery. You shall serve no less than four years in the dungeons, at which time you shall be released to a work program in the fields that will have you. You will serve as a field hand until such a time as I, Lord Gustavo, and the field owners feel you have been succinctly reformed at least four years. Your punishment will last a minimum of eight years." There is some chatter around the ruling. I decided on this sentence a few days ago. I believe it is fair, though somewhat unconventional from the rulings my parents dealt. They never included reformation clauses, but I like the idea of ensuring that justice includes change.

"Sir Morrin, you are charged with contempt of court. How do you plead?" He looks up at me, confused. Realization dawns on him. He glances at Lord Gustavo, who just shakes his head, encouraging him not to argue.

"Guilty, Your Majesty."

"Good; you are hereby sentenced to pay a fine of 1000 gold coins to the castle." Outrage stretches across his face. I know this is a small price for him, but it will make enough of a dent that they won't forget. It is excessive, but I don't care at this point.

"Furthermore, since I have sentenced both father and son on the same day for crimes occurring in the castle, I am placing your family on probation. If anyone from your family steps out of line before Oscar's sentence is completed, your family will be stripped of title, land, and two-thirds of your wealth. Do I make myself clear?" The entire family pales and blanches but manages to nod.

"Henry, allow Oscar and his family a brief goodbye in the small corridor, then escort him back to the dungeon. Erik, see to it Sir Morrin pays the court accountant, then he is free to go." I dismiss them with a wave. The rest of the crowd cheers as Oscar and his family are escorted away from the throne room. I remain in my seat, watching everyone leave. No one approaches me on the throne. I am left alone with my thoughts.

I am not disappointed in my first judgment. I had hoped to avoid it for longer, at least until I was officially crowned. Things could have been worse all around. Tomas will heal soon. Hopefully, Oscar will have an attitude adjustment and will be free within a decade. I won't be upset if I need to strip his family of their position, but I don't particularly want to do that. Now, I get to focus on the upcoming winter solstice celebration, my coronation, and figuring out who my true love is. And hopefully, get more of the fun balls from Kian.

Part Three

WINTER SOLSTICE

Chapter 17

CLEM

The foyer of the castle is exhilarating. It's empty, save for me. Decorations for the winter solstice are scattered beautifully throughout. Wreaths and boughs of evergreens, candles, and holly with red berries and pointed leaves hang with bows. Colored sashes and banners are strung on walls and around windows. The entire castle is exquisitely decorated to celebrate the year's longest night.

The seating has been removed in the throne room, leaving ample open space for dancing and mingling and later meditating or just being with the people you choose. Kian asked to incorporate a reading from his coven's favorite stories. It's a tradition his family has done for generations. Jasmin requested we all share our own traditions. The only other tradition anyone had was gift-giving. Jasmin hesitantly agreed to that. She didn't want many gifts. Apparently, she has an aversion to people treating her well. Tomas argued that we have all been receiving a stipend while here but didn't need to use it. She allowed us to go into the villages to buy gifts and send some back home. We get to give her gifts later this evening before the sunrises.

Now, the music is playing loudly behind the closed doors of the throne room. Everyone is waiting on Jasmin to enter and start the celebration. This event is more formal than the autumn celebration. While that was to celebrate hard work, this is to mark an end to the darkness. The throne room is dim, only lit by smaller candles scattered around the room instead of the regular sconces and torches. The foyer is still brightly lit in case anyone needs to leave the throne room.

For the past few years, Jasmin has entered the celebration alone or with one of the Lords. Since the Lords aren't here, we decided a bachelor should escort her in. There are only four of us left. With Oscar in the dungeons and Philip and Sven forced to return, Dominick, Jonas, and William decided to leave, also. This left Kian, Tomas, Erik, and me here with the Princess. We drew sticks to see who would escort her. I won that contest. Now I stand in the foyer at the bottom of the stairs, waiting for Jasmin to arrive.

A sound draws my attention up the stairs. I turn to look, and my breath catches. Even if I wanted to breathe, I couldn't. Jasmin is walking down one side of the stairs, holding onto the rail. Her head is turned back, laughing at something. I can only see her. Her hair is shoulder-length now. It has been softly curled with a silver crown placed atop her head. It has amber-colored gems in the metalwork. Her dress has a full skirt of yellow with layers of soft flowing material. She looks stunning.

That isn't what caught my breath, though. While she appears to be glowing, seeing Jasmin walk down the stairs, my heart sings for her. I love her. This woman holds every bit of my heart, body, and soul, and she doesn't even realize it. I want nothing more in life than to spend every day until my dying breath worshipping her. My heart beats rapidly in my chest as she continues down the stairs.

Jasmin turns her attention to me as I am finally able to breathe in. My eyes find hers, and my soul feels complete. A warmth spreads through my body as her lips spread into a smile across her face. We didn't tell her who would be escorting her. She is genuinely happy to see me. My quick beating heart explodes in my chest. I can hear it. A loud beat sounds like thunder. It sounds as powerful as a summer storm. Jasmin hears the sound too. She looks around, confused about what she heard, but I can't take my eyes off her. I am soaking in every inch of her, committing her to my memory lest I forget a single detail.

"Was that thunder? Why is there thunder this late in the year?" She asks as she reaches the bottom step.

I need to hold her. I need to tell her I love her. I need her to know. This need is more powerful than anything I have ever felt before. But...I may not be her true love. I finally look away from her face, taking her hand in mine. I can't put my feelings on her if we're not meant to be together. My fingers wrap around hers, bringing her small hand to my lips. I press a soft kiss to the back of her hand as my eyes close. My heart is shattering and rebuilding in this instant. I love her but can't share that with her now. Her hand is soft and delicate, and even though it is all I want in life, I can't take it as mine.

I lower her hand, lifting my eyes to her. The inquisitive look on her face is searching mine. It's as if she knows what I am thinking but can't admit it, either. She is standing on the bottom step, placing her at my height. I need to touch her, to hold her. I can't deny that powerful sensation any longer. I wrap my arms around her waist in a sudden move, tugging her against my chest. I bury my face in her hair, breathing deeply. She takes a moment to process what I am doing before her arms settle around my shoulders.

I remember the first time I kissed her on the turret when I still thought she was Tia. I've loved her since the beginning; it just took me a long time to realize it. I want her to be mine. I need her.

"I want to steal you away from the kingdom," I whisper against her neck. "I want to take you away, just you and me. Run away with me." I pour my heart into my words, meaning every one of them. We could run out the front door and build a home somewhere else. The kingdom will find a way to survive as it has the past eight years. We can be happy together.

She laughs gently, pressing a kiss to my cheek. Jasmin whispers my name as I lean back to look at her. Her fingers rub against my cheek, rubbing where she just kissed. I know she can't run away with me. I know that. But my heart hoped. It shatters again, falling in chunks in my chest. I lean in to kiss her, needing her to calm the swelling in my chest. She sways back as I lean in.

"You can't kiss me," she explains quickly, "because you'll ruin my lip stain. Then Emmeline," she motions over her shoulders to the top of the stairs, where Emmeline must have been when Jasmin first walked down, "will kill you. Then Mikhail will be devastated that you led his daughter to murder and will probably curse your name. I'm already dealing with enough curses, Clem. So no kisses right now."

I laugh at her description. While I would prefer a kiss, she still has a way of settling me. I concede my efforts but still press my lips against her neck several times. I place a final kiss against her forehead. I rest my forehead against hers, fighting the urge to kiss her anyway.

"Sorry," I whisper, "I probably shouldn't have had that glass of wine." There was no wine, but she doesn't know that. I pull back, offering her a smile. I step to the side, holding my arm out for her. She takes my elbow, willing to overlook my outburst of emotion. I remind myself of my task. Lead her into the center of the room. Bow and walk away. She gives a small speech, leads a few dances, then we relax for the rest of the evening. I can do that. Lead her in, bow, and walk away. It's manageable.

The doors to the throne room are opened by guards in royal colors. I can't fight off the feeling of how right this all feels. I lead her into the room, and the crowd bows as we walk by. She is standing tall at my side. I take in the prestige from the people in the castle. They love her, not in the way I do, but in their own way. Jasmin is a strong woman and will be a powerful ruler when she comes into her position.

As we reach the center of the room, I stretch my hand out, taking hers in mine as I bow. I place a final kiss on her hand. She looks at me with warmth and desire in her eyes. I long to stay with her but know my place is no longer on her side. I rise from my bow and back away, inching toward the food as people swarm her. Everyone is doting on her, wishing her a happy solstice, complimenting her. I can't deny her that attention.

I grab a goblet of wine, downing it at once, then getting a refill. My newfound emotions need to be subdued for a while. Kian walks up next to me, watching me curiously.

"Quite an entrance you made." I nod, taking another long drink of wine. "Some might even say you looked entirely enamored with the Princess." I choke on my drink. I didn't realize my feelings were written on my face for everyone to see. It doesn't surprise me; I've never been good at hiding my feelings. That doesn't mean I want everyone to know. Kian slaps my back as I cough through gasping breaths. Jasmin looks my way, alarmed. I offer a smile to indicate I'm fine, but it's a weak attempt.

"Was it that obvious?" I ask in a scratchy voice. Kian shrugs.

"Only if someone looked at you." He winks at me before slinking off into the crowd. Kian just loves to make some revelatory proclamation and then waltz away while someone's world shatters. He really is suited for politics.

I finish off my goblet of wine and refill it again. This is going to be a long night, both literally and figuratively. Before the wine sets in, I make my way to the food table. My head is swimming with thoughts of Jasmin, wondering if anyone else noticed. Kian is more perceptive than others, particularly when it comes to Jasmin. Does he realize my feelings for her? I wonder what he is thinking about this situation.

"Hungry?" Erik asks, motioning at my hand. I look down, realizing I grabbed an entire loaf of bread instead of breaking some off. I just nod. This is my bread now.

"Did you hear that thunder earlier?" I give him a confused look. "Surely you heard it. It was loud in here; I bet it was even louder in the foyer without everyone around." I glance around at the people in the room, racking my brain for any occurrence of thunder. It's winter now; we don't get thunder this late in the season.

"Was it a canon?" I ask.

"No. Everyone is here." He waves his hand around the room. I scan again, this time landing on Jasmin. She is still making her way through the crowd. Soon she will reach the dance floor and begin the dances for the evening. That's exactly what I want to watch; the woman I love dancing with other men that may also love her. Or she them. I shake my head, pushing that thought away. Then I remember Jasmin saying something about thunder.

"Oh, Jasmin mentioned the thunder as she came down the stairs. I didn't notice."

Erik looks shocked. Was it really that loud? "You should probably visit the healer if you didn't hear that. Was your head in the ground?" I angrily tear off a bite of the bread with my teeth as he laughs at me.

The music changes as Jasmin reaches the dance area. The section before her dais has been cleared of all the decorations. She steps into the middle of the area, curtseying low. She appears to be glowing even more in the low light from the candles than she did in the foyer. She looks like an angel or fairy. Like any moment, wings will appear, and she will fly out of the room, leaving us all behind. My heart squeezes at the sight.

A classic waltz starts as Kian glides across the floor toward her. I was aware he was dancing with her. I underestimated how perfectly matched they are. He is a head taller than her, but his lithe body glides around the floor with her. If she were going to sprout wings, he would walk on the clouds and join her. The smile between them is intimate. This isn't the first time they have done this dance. They are comfortable with each other as they spin and step across the dance floor. She holds his shoulders, he her hand. They sway with the grace of royalty. They belong together. He is the King this kingdom needs. He is the man she needs.

I can feel my heart shattering again. Tonight, I am destined to be in a whirlwind of emotions. Love and heartbreak, desire and jealousy. I tear off another angry bite of my bread. Finn walks up, sitting next to my leg. I scratch his head. He is watching Jasmin dance with Kian. He looks up at me. I probably imagine it, but he looks sad too. I tear off a chunk of bread, handing it over to him. He doesn't look so sad anymore. I chuckle at him, tearing off another bite. I still feel sad, though. This bread isn't making me happy.

The song ends with Kian and Jasmin bowing together. I can't get the image of them on thrones together out of my mind. They are so perfect for each other. The band starts with a more upbeat dance, and everyone else joins in, twirling and stepping. They laugh and chat throughout the dance, having a grand time. Jasmin stays in the mix, cycling through several other partners, including Erik and Tomas. She looks so merry. This is clearly the best night she has had in a long time. Things have been tense since the sparring contest. I vow to not ruin the night with my grumpy demeanor. I can be sad tomorrow.

I toss the rest of the loaf to Finn, then head out to the dance floor. She grins as she sees me approach. My heart swells with the look in her eyes. At least she is happy to see me. Her hands extend toward mine, and I unwittingly reach for her. I'm swept away with her, grinning and laughing as we whirl through the other couples. She stays with me through another song. Her cheeks are red from the movement. When the song ends, I dip her low. She laughs, throwing her arms around my shoulders.

"Am I still banned from kissing you?" I ask with a wink.

"Yes!" She laughs as I lift her up, but she hugs me tight, and I feel her lips against my neck.

"I'm going to get a drink." I start to go with her, but Emmeline steps in front and asks me to dance. I oblige. I don't need to follow Jasmin around all night, despite wanting to. Emmeline and I twirl through the dance. This one doesn't have us close or touching constantly. We step and jump around each other and others in our group. She's a delightful partner. Her smile is bright and genuine. The song ends, and we bow to each other, then everyone else in our group.

"Thank you for dancing with me, Clem." She seems to want to say more, but Kian speaks up from the dais.

"Princess Jasmin has given me permission to share one of the traditions of my coven. I will be starting that in a few moments." He waves his hand in front of the dais, where people bring over rugs, pillows, and blankets. I didn't realize we would be sitting on the floor. I turn back to Emmeline, but she is already making her way to the drink table. I decide not to get another glass. The bread and dancing helped, but any more would undo any efforts made. I bump into the kitchen maids and chat with them for several minutes. Finally, Kian calls out to everyone to gather around.

I search for Jasmin. I finally spot her sitting with Erik. She is leaning against his shoulder, letting him support her weight. I take a deep breath, pressing down the jealousy. I want to sit next to her, but her dress is so full it takes up the length of her legs around her. I settle for sitting to the side of her. She doesn't notice me at first but does when she turns to look at someone else calling her. She smiles at me, drawing her dress up so I can scoot closer to her. It's still not as close as I would like, but it is better than before. I take her hand and kiss it, needing contact with her.

Kian begins speaking, telling a tale of this kingdom when it was young. I haven't heard this story before, not that I am familiar with witch folklore. While he is speaking, a few people are walking around, blowing out some of the candles. The room dims as they move around. Kian's voice is smooth as he speaks of a witch approaching a king, asking for sovereignty for the witches. Suddenly, a burst of light flares from a lantern on the dais. The blaze is orange but fades to purple. Tiny twinkling lights depict a witch standing on the dais. She is kneeling, begging silently. Jasmin sits up, watching the conjuration. Several people in the crowd gasp.

Kian continues his story, the king unwilling to lose the power of the witches. He refuses their sovereignty but allows them to create their own village. The image of the witch takes to the sky, flying over what appears to be the kingdom. Kian has stopped speaking as his conjuration shows the story. The witch flies away from the castle, over the coast of Tilrade, through the small rolling hills of Obele. Fingers stretch across mine as the purple witch glides over the mountains behind Arkaley. Jasmin has my hand, squeezing it without looking back at me.

The witch turns back toward the castle, then soars over the flat farmland of Vadried. The color of the witch changes subtly to blue. She zooms faster, then higher over the kingdom. She stops in the air, high enough to seem from Vadried to Arkaley. She hasn't settled in a village. Despite no sound, the room is tense, waiting to see what will happen. The witch finally looks northwest to the mountain range between Arkaley and Vadried. From her vantage, we can see the mountain range is crescent-shaped, with the thickest bulge closest to the castle. The witch zooms in, riding through trees, mountains, and streams. She settles on the side of a mountain that juts out over the valley between.

"This is how Greynon came to be," Kian announces with a bang. The conjuration disappears, but the candles blown out earlier suddenly burn again. The crowd gasps but immediately begins cheering. Jasmin pulls her hand away from mine to clap loudly. I follow suit. I knew Kian was skilled with magic; I just had no idea how talented he is. He takes several bows, then makes his way over to us.

"Thank you for allowing me to share that story, Princess." He croons. Even I have to admit his voice is smooth.

"That was wonderful, Kian! I've never seen anything like it!"

"For a cursed princess, you seem to have a severe lack of experience with magic." She huffs a laugh while several people walk over, congratulating or thanking Kian. Interestingly, there is such a lack of magic outside of Greynon. Do the witches harbor resentment over not being granted sovereignty all those years ago? Or are the people of Sweet Briar scared of what they don't know since the witches are so isolated? As I ponder this, Erik leaves to get more wine. Jasmin shifts like she would stay closer to Kian, then settles against me. I position myself to support her weight and mine on the floor.

"Kian can have this moment. He's earned it," she explains. With her this close, I kiss the side of her head. She sighs contentedly, relaxing against my body. I don't particularly care what her reasoning is; if she wants to lean against me, she can. I suppose I can steal these moments of happiness with her and be content for a while, at least until we confirm who her true love is. Then I can deal with the emotional fallout of being in love with a cursed princess. Until then, I whisper how beautiful she is, wrap my arm around her waist, and kiss her ear gently.

Tomas walks over, looking nervous. He fiddles with his fingers but squares his shoulders before speaking.

"Princess Jasmin, would you like to open your gift now?"

A smile spreads over her face as she nods to him. She shifts away from me, using my shoulder to stand up. I watch her walk away, feeling lonely and cold without her beside me. I don't have any right to be this upset by her walking away, but I can't control my feelings when it comes to her. The two walk toward a small room where we left all the gifts. Jasmin looks happy, chatting animatedly with Tomas.

I saunter over to the wine table, needing something to do instead. Emmeline walks over, getting a drink herself.

"What do you think everyone got her?" She asks.

"Tomas had some candy made from the kitchen. He wanted to make it, but they immediately kicked him out." Emmeline laughs at that. Tomas is a sweet kid, but he is still young. "I think Erik said he had a figurine made for her, but I don't know much about it. I don't know what Kian got her."

"I'm curious to see what he got her. He is the one that insisted on exchanging gifts privately." Her comment strikes me. What could Kian have gotten for her that needed to be given privately? Is he fucking her? She's fooled around with me some, but we haven't fucked yet. Has she been fucking him? Is she fucking others? As my mind spirals, Erik enters the room as Tomas leaves. Shit. I want to get in there with her before Kian. I don't want to walk in after he fucks her. I want to fuck her first, so he can't get any.

As my outrage builds, something wet and warm presses against my hand. Finn is nudging me for more treats. I sigh, pushing the frustrations from my mind for the moment. I grab some bread to give him a bite. He is acting playful, so I toss some in the air for him, letting him jump to catch them. We play longer than I realize because soon, Erik walks over, asking if he can toss one too. I glance at the closed door, but Erik tells me Kian entered right after him.

My vision turns red as my jaw clenches several times. I take a deep breath. This is fine. I can take the last spot, giving me more time with her since no one else is waiting. It's fine; I can wait. Erik takes over the game with Finn, and the two eventually wander off. I stand, staring at the door.

After what feels like an eternity, the door opens, and Kian walks out. He has this shit-eating grin on his face. His cheeks are flushed, and he looks too satisfied with himself for my liking. He saunters over in a way someone who just fucked my girl would.

"She's all yours," he says with a wink. I'm going to kill him.

Chapter 18

JASMIN

The door slams behind me. I turn to see Clem standing there, seething. My cheeks are still flushed from Kian's gift. Clem is breathing hard, trying to calm down whatever thoughts are raging through his mind. He isn't very successful, though. I take several deep breaths, trying to steady my own state. The gifts I have received have been more meaningful than I anticipated. These men are absolutely incredible. They are sweet and care for me deeply. It thrills me to have men be kind without expecting to gain anything from my position. I don't feel used with Tomas, Erik, Kian, and Clem. That alone is a more precious gift than any of them gave me, but I enjoy the other presents, too. Especially Kian's, which now has Clem furious. Does he know what it is?

"I didn't know sex was an appropriate gift. I would have saved my coin and fucked you myself."

"It's always on the table, Clem." I walk over, stopping in front of him. "Are you jealous?"

"No." He answers far too quickly. I wrap my arms around his shoulders, lacing my fingers through his hair. His hair is thick and soft. It's probably my favorite thing to play with right now. That could easily change based on how this night goes.

"Are you angry? Because you think he fucked me?"

"Did he?"

"No." An incredulous laugh escapes his lips.

"He comes out grinning like he won a prize, making lewd comments. And here you are, flushed and looking dazed." I chuckle softly at him.

"Oh, Clem, you are jealous." I stroke his cheek, letting my hands glide down his chest, then grab his wrist. "Come here."

He hesitates at first but gives in quickly, walking behind me, never willing to outright tell me no. I pull him to the bench Kian and I were just on. I sit, tugging him down next to me. He plops down heavily. His jaw clenches several times as he fights off his emotions. I grab a small device and hold it up for Clem to see. He looks between me and the smooth wooden cylinder, clearly confused.

"This is the gift he gave me. He wanted to watch me use it. Alone."

Clem raises an eyebrow, unsure of what I mean. I hold the device out for him, placing it in his hand then I tap it. It springs to life, vibrating across his palm. Both eyebrows shoot high in surprise. I explain what it is used for and how I use it.

"So, he watched?" I nod.

"And you used this?" I nod again.

"He didn't touch you?" I shake my head, smiling as he realizes he is jealous over nothing. He gets a wicked gleam in his eyes.

"Can I watch?" I bite my bottom lip, unsure I want to be watched again.

"Don't you want to exchange gifts?"

"I want nothing more than you, my little flower." My heart skips a beat at his words. I stare at him for a moment longer, my brain unable to fully process what he is saying.

I lean in, pressing my lips against his. He hesitates, then returns the kiss. His hand reaches the side of my face, pressing the still-vibrating item between his hand and my cheek. We both laugh at the foreign feeling but keep kissing each other. Nothing feels so intrinsic in my life as being with him. Even his jealousy and anger are easy to deal with. Not that I would ever justify his behavior, but I understand it. He feels things deeply. It's one of my favorite things about him. He breaks the kiss, holding his hand between us.

"Show me how to use it."

Without thinking, I shift back against him. He spreads his legs, pulling me against his chest. Together, we pull the layers of fabric up against my stomach. The ache has already returned. He uses one hand to hold the material out of the way. I pluck the device from his hand, lowering it to my clit. I sink my head back on his shoulder as the vibrating sends pulses through my body. I glance up at him. His eyes are focused on my hand, desire written all over his face. Seeing his emotions spears pleasure through my body.

"There are three speeds," I say breathlessly. "A tap increases them."

Before I finish the last bit, his hand reaches down to tap the device. It buzzes faster as my hips jerk against it. I can already tell this orgasm will be more intense. The tips of his fingers stroke down my soaking wet core, teasing me. I moan his name, his lips kissing and nipping my neck.

"Give it to me," he whispers.

His hand glides over mine, cupping the device. I release it into his hand, wrapping my fingers around his arm. He holds the device in place as his fingers dip inside me. They are longer than mine and hit that tender little spot perfectly. I groan against him, my hips undulating in his hand.

"Can it go inside you?" I shrug. Kian never said anything about that.

Clem decides to test this out anyway. He slips it inside with his finger, pressing it directly against the sensitive area inside. I moan his name, cursing the skies and heavens, then sending prayers to those same people. If I thought my orgasm was good with Kian, I knew nothing. My brain has stopped functioning. There is only the growing pleasure pulsing through my body. His fingers throb inside me as the device vibrates faster against that spot. My body is tensing, tightening, convulsing. I cry out his name over and over; his hand pulls away from my dress, wrapping his fingers lightly over my neck. My hips are involuntarily thrusting against his hand while he still pounds his fingers in and out.

"Come apart for me, my little flower." He whispers in my ear, breathing against my tender skin. I'm so close to release. One of the thin layers of the dress slips down and brushes against my aching clit. I yell out, arching back into him more. He tightens his hand on my neck slightly. Not enough to cut off circulation, but enough to bring me right to the edge. He presses the heel of his palm into my clit, and my orgasm barrels through me. My body convulses under his grip. My vision goes black, and nothing exists around my floating body.

Pleasure like I have never known courses through my veins. Every heartbeat sends another wave of ecstasy crashing through me. In some distant part of my brain, I hear Clem praising me. I am beautiful. I am perfect. I should see how lovely I look right now. My soul begins to sink back into the sensations around me. Clem's fingers are stroking my cheek. His other arm is draped across my middle. He removed the device earlier, but it is still vibrating somewhere. I open my eyes, but stars are dancing around the room, so I close them again. My breathing is labored and fast. I can feel moisture on my forehead as I press against Clem's cheek.

He holds me tightly as my body returns to normal. It takes longer than I have ever experienced before to return to normal. I want nothing more than to roll over and sleep against him. This is my safe place. His arms hold me tightly as I slowly blink open my eyes. I look up at him, and we both giggle over what just happened. He kisses my forehead. His hand rises to cradle my cheek, his thumb stroking the scars on my face. I sigh against him, wrapping my arms around him. I have no intentions of moving at this moment. One does not experience a life-shattering orgasm and simply move on with life.

He inhales deeply, keeping a tight grip on my body. His hold feels desperate like he doesn't want to let me go. He has been acting strange all night. He didn't hear the thunder, which was absurd. The thunder was unexpected and unnatural; how could he not hear it? He's been close and unwilling to leave my side, but in the next moment, he would be far away from me, not even glancing at me. Here he is, back to holding me close. Perhaps he can't make up his mind on whether or not to get close to me. I'm glad to have these men here with me now, but the uncertainty of this situation is frustrating. If only I could make everyone happy at once...

Speaking of making everyone happy, Clem didn't get off with me. I slide my hand down his chest, inching toward his cock. Just before I reach the hem of his trousers, he catches my wrists, stopping my descent. He doesn't say anything, just holds my wrist in place. I twist to look up at him.

"Why did you stop me?"

"You don't need to do that." His lazy grin doesn't explain any more than his words. Confusion spreads on my face, scrunching my eyebrows together. I push my hand against him, trying to grab his cock. It isn't a matter of "need to do it," but I'm not going to leave him hanging after I received such a fantastic orgasm. His fingers tighten on my wrist, but I break away. The jerk away from his hand sends my hand flying directly over his soft penis. Confusion and hurt slam into my chest, nearly knocking the air from my chest. Why is he soft? Was he not aroused too? Does he not want to fuck me?

Clem chuckles at my expression. At this point in the evening, or early morning, actually, I can no longer control my face. Exhaustion is preventing me from hiding my emotions over his soft dick. He kisses my forehead, wraps his fingers around my wrist, and draws them to a spot on his pants just above his penis. The location is damp, and I am unsure what I am feeling. His pants are moist in this small area, with something beneath the material. Realization dawns on me at a much slower rate than I would prefer. This is his release. He came when I did while I was undulating against his chest.

A laugh breaks through, then another, then I fall into hysterics. He finished with me as I rubbed against him. I don't need to worry about him because he already came. He keeps me pressed against his chest, chuckling along with me. Perhaps his actions this evening aren't as unjustified as I suspected a moment ago. Maybe the thunder has thrown us all off. I twist in his arms, finding his lips with my own. My hand slides up his chest, settling on his neck. Unable to help myself, I tangle my fingers in his hair. I deepen the kiss, swirling my tongue against his.

It's a lazy, sensual kiss, not meant to arouse but to learn, enjoy, and experience. I could love him.

Thunder booms outside, rattling the windows. Screams from the next room break my focus, and I pull away from Clem. An almost insignificant pang of guilt rolls through me, realizing how long I have been away from my people for this gift exchange. While they won't comment, I don't want to give the impression I am avoiding celebrating with them. I sit up, putting some distance between us. If I didn't have obligations, I would stay there all night.

"Let's trade gifts." I smile sweetly, grabbing the two remaining gifts on the table. He removes his hand from my body for the first time since we sat down to take his gift. He opens it slowly, enjoying the thrill of unwrapping the present. He once lamented my library contains thousands of books but not his favorite. I was surprised. My father was a curator of books; how could Clem have read a book we didn't have?

After he told me the title and author, I began a search of the castle, something about the name was familiar. The investigation led me into my father's chambers. Despite my temporary distraction in reminiscing, I found the book I sought. There were two in his bedroom, left on his bedside table. Both copies were well-worn from frequent readings. I had no idea it was my father's favorite. I placed one copy in the library but saved the other.

"Jasmin," he gasps, "is this the author's copy?" He paused on one page with notes in the corner.

"Yes. After you mentioned it, I recalled the author had visited the castle many years ago. I didn't remember outright because I was young when he came. I found details of the visit in my father's chambers. The author visited, spent several weeks at the castle, and wrote in various places, drawing inspiration from our kingdom." Clem's eyes go wide with astonishment. He flips through several more pages in stunned silence. "The author left this copy, taking a cleaner version with him to be published. He later sent a completed version, which was also in my father's chambers. It must have been his favorite, too." Warmth spreads in my chest at the thought of my father. He would have liked Clem.

Clem hugs me tightly, nearly knocking the breath out of me. He chuckles, pulling back to look at the book again. "No one has ever given me such a meaningful gift." I grin brightly at him. I was unsure what to get him for a long time. I debated an expensive gift but didn't think that was what he would like. Pleasure fills me because I was able to give him this. I just hope I haven't set the bar too high now.

"My turn," I exclaim, taking the gift from his lap. The box is long and thin, wrapped in brown paper with holly tied on with twine. It's beautiful and simple, absolutely perfect. It's so lovely I almost don't want to rip it open, but I do anyway. The box is wooden with a single latch on one side. I open the box, gasping at the necklace inside. Silver posts hang from the thin silver chain. Between the posts, more chains link them together, but what is secured between them is the most impressive. There are seven studs with a stamped emblem between each, one for each village and a sixth for the kingdom. Beneath each stamped coin are gems in the corresponding colors. I own nothing as eloquent and representative of my kingdom as this. Even my own crowns don't represent the entire kingdom.

"I have a friend in Arkaley that makes things. Before the curse, she made jewelry but hasn't in a while, focusing on more practical things. I requested this necklace from her. The design was her idea," he pauses, watching my fingers touch each of the pendants and gems.

"Put it on me," I whisper, voice cracking.

He lifts the necklace while I turn. Once it is secured around my neck, I glance down at it, feeling tears build in my eyes. He commissioned a necklace to represent my kingdom, something I don't own. It had to cost quite a bit. My heart swells more than it has in years over what this means to me. He may not realize the significance. Maybe he assumes I have many pieces like this, but I don't. No one has ever thought to make something to represent my entire kingdom.

I twist quickly, crashing into his chest before the tears spill. His arms wrap around me, and I inhale deeply. He smells of sunshine and dirt. I couldn't describe what sunshine smells like, but it's him. He is warm and safe and may burn me if I get too close, but gods, I want to. Slap wings on me and call me Icarus because

I want whatever makes Clem feel like sunshine. I want him to be that for me. I need him to be that for me, but he can't. I can't fly too close to the sun. I don't get to fly at all. I have a kingdom to save, and that may not include Clem. I can't risk getting this close to him yet. He may not be my true love. I can't risk falling for him now. But oh, how hard I could fall.

Chapter 19

CLEM

She belongs in my arms. The fucking magic needs to catch up and realize she is mine. There is no way she isn't. Four other bachelors may still be in the castle, but I want her. I need her.

She quickly rises, turning away from me, but I see her wipe her eyes. She is crying but won't let me see. If she is happy with the necklace, and those are happy tears, why would she hide them from me? I've seen her cry before. She doesn't need to hide that from me.

"Will you go find Emmeline, please?" She requests softly. "I need her to help me change out of this dress."

"Jasmin…" I'm not going to leave her alone while she's crying.

"I'm fine, Clem. I love the necklace. So much. Please get Emmeline."

"What's wrong? I can help."

"No, please just go."

"Jasmin, I'm not leaving you like this."

"Please," she whimpers, sniffling and wiping her cheek again.

I concede, giving her what she wants this time. I don't like leaving her like this, but it's not my place to force her to let me help. Shit, what if she doesn't want me to help? Did I upset her somehow? Is she upset that I gave her that gift? She said she liked it, but why would she cry over that? I stop at the door, looking back at her.

"Jasmin?" I speak softly.

She just sniffles, waving her hand at me. I'm obviously not the person she wants here. I don't know what happened; she doesn't want me to console her. She has let me at other times; why not now? My hurt grows, shifting from sadness to anger as I leave. I let Emmeline know Jasmin needs her before going to my room to change pants. My anger and confusion grow over this situation. This night has been a long twisty emotional experience.

I change my pants but don't get fully dressed again. My shirttail is hanging out, and I left the jacket off. I'm not going back to the celebration. The only thing left to do is watch the sunrise. I can do that any day. There's nothing extraordinary about today's, other than the sentimental meaning we have placed behind it. I'm not feeling very sentimental anyway. I'll just go to bed early.

I fall back on my bed, uncaring about my clothes or the sheets. None of this matters. I should just go back to Arkaley. Jasmin and Kian can break the curse, and I can settle in to care for Ma and my siblings, tending to my broken heart. I grab my pillow to adjust it and find a letter I left yesterday. It's one of my favorites Ma wrote. She talks about Claire going back to school. Bea was working long hours at the farm, and Ma was alone all day. My heart pulled for her. She said she enjoyed the silence for a few minutes, then it became deafening. That is a feeling I can relate to. Just as I reach the end of the letter, there is a soft knock at my door.

"The Princess is waiting for you to join her again." Emmeline stands in the doorway, watching me. I sit up, placing the letter aside.

"She doesn't need me. She has a room full of people to celebrate with her. I'm going to sleep." I rise, walking around the room to get ready for bed half-heartedly.

"And yet, she's requested you by name." Emmeline rubs her chin. Her face is confused, but her eyes hint that she knows why.

"I made her cry. Why would she want me there?" She huffs a laugh, walking into the room to stand by the window. These women sure do love the view from my room.

"It's not the first time you've made her cry, and it won't be the last. Why is tonight different?" She turns to face me.

"It's different because I didn't do anything wrong." A realization dawns on me. "Wait, what do you mean 'this isn't the first time I made her cry?'" Disbelief floods her face.

"She cried for hours after the first meeting when you were so angry at her. You were justified that day, but in the following weeks, she hurt over your absence. She won't admit it, but she fell asleep with tears many nights during your days in the fields." My shoulders slump as I collapse down on the bed.

I knew she wouldn't enjoy my decision to work the fields, but she had nine other men to get to know. I didn't honestly think she would notice my absence. Kian hinted at it a couple of times. That damn perceptive man. I should have listened to him and stayed with the group. I can't undo that now. Things have been better since then. Until I gave her the necklace

"Why was she crying tonight? She wouldn't tell me." Emmeline turns toward the window with her back to me.

"A little bit of this, a little bit of that. It wasn't anything you did. But it's not my place to tell you. That necklace, Clem, it is amazing. It is absolutely perfect for her. You really nailed the quintessential gift. In fact, I'm pretty mad that she still hasn't opened mine. Because it will look like junk after your gift." She turns back with a hint of humor in her eyes. "Just come finish the celebration with her. Then, in a day or two, after everyone has slept, you can talk with her."

I sigh heavily. I know Emmeline's right. That is the smart thing to do. I don't know if I'd consider myself a smart man, but what else am I going to do? Sit here and pout until I fall asleep? I would like to see the sunrise. I'll also sleep better knowing Jasmin is okay. If she is upset over something I did, she wouldn't have sent Emmeline to get me. I stand to grab my clothes, but Emmeline intercepts first, heading toward my wardrobe. She shuffles through my things while I watch with exhausted curiosity. I didn't realize she was my lady-in-waiting, too.

"Here, you should wear this." She hands me a worn-out blue sweater. It once belonged to my father. He gave it to me shortly before the curse began. I don't wear it often, worried I'll tear it or wear it out. I have other things of his, but this one has always held sentimental value to me.

"I have nicer things to wear," I say, reluctant to take the sweater.

"I know," she shrugs. "Just trust me, okay?" I take the sweater, tuck in my shirt, and pull it on. I don't know if I should trust her, but I have no reason not to. Mikhail mentioned several times that she has an excellent sense of these things. We walk down the hallway together silently, then she speaks up.

"We had an outfit planned for Jasmin to change into. We knew she would likely change at some point in the evening. She's not keen on formal wear." She turns a corner, speaking as if I'm not really there. I know she's talking to me, but she might as well be speaking to the portraits on the wall. "When I went to her after you called for me, she insisted I select a whole new outfit for her." I nod, even though she can't see me. I'm not sure why she is telling me this information. Is it essential for me?

As we round the next corner, Jasmin is waiting in the foyer at the bottom of the stairs. The same place I waited for her before the celebration began. She has a navy blue dress, nearly the same color as my sweater. The bodice is fitted with gold trim around the seams. The gold contrasts with her dress the same way my light brown pants contrast my sweater. The neckline of her dress is scooped low, exposing some of her cleavage. Draped across her chest, almost as if on display, is the necklace I bought. Her face has been washed and looks more natural than earlier in the night. Her formal crown from earlier has been replaced with a silver circlet that pairs perfectly with the necklace. It has a few chains running from one side of her head to the other in a similar fashion as the necklace. Her hair has been pulled back to a single point at the nape of her neck. Even in more casual clothing, she is still as breathtaking as she was earlier.

She thanks Emmeline as she walks by. They kiss each other's cheek, then Emmeline continues on. As Jasmin turns her attention back to me, I freeze in place. I feel like I should bow or kneel in front of her. Ideally, the latter, but preferably with less clothing. As my mind tries to catch up with real-time, she walks up to me, holding out her arms. The sleeves on her dress fall low. Without conscious thought, I step into her arms, lowering my body to match hers. This is the place I want to be. That doesn't require any thought. She kisses my cheek, wrapping her arms around my shoulders.

"I'm sorry for sending you away like that. I just really needed Emmeline's help." I squeeze her tight. I don't understand the difference between Emmeline and me, but I can respect her wishes. She pulls away from me, running her hands over my chest.

"Did Emmeline tell you to wear this?" Her fingers stroke over the stitches, taking in the finer details of the handiwork. I just nod. She laughs, cursing her friend under her breath. "Well, come on. We're going to miss the sunrise. It's the best part."

I hold my arm out as she wraps her hand around my bicep. I love that I need so few words with her. I don't normally feel the need to talk much. Not needing to with her gives me more happiness than I ever thought something like that could offer. We walk toward the cathedral room linked together. The cathedral room has large glass windows along one side of the wall. It faces the east as if it were planned to enjoy the sunrise. Benches have been brought in so people can sit while they watch. As we enter the doors, she points toward the center of the windows. The row closest has two spots open between Kian and Eric. I lead her over, and she sits next to Kian. I take the spot next to Eric.

The cathedral room has a few candles burning for lighting but is mostly dark. A few guards are walking around with torches to light the way for anyone still coming in. In a few moments, they will leave the room, and the candles will be blown out, allowing us to enjoy the full effects of the rising winter sun. Most people are quiet or whispering to their neighbors. Jasmin is whispering to Kian about the necklace she is wearing. She is very impressed with it, going into specific details about its emblems. Erik is sitting next to me, falling asleep. I debate leaving him alone but figure some chatter will help keep him awake. We whisper softly about how the night has gone for each of us. He yawns several times but stays engaged in the conversation.

Soon the torches are removed, and all the candles are blown out. The room falls eerily silent. It's a calm I haven't experienced before. Everyone is waiting on the same thing. Anticipation and excitement course through the room. Jasmin links her fingers with mine. I wrap my hands around hers, tightly holding her hand between mine.

The first light of day breaks over the trees leading to Tilrade. It's a slow shift from darkness to light. The sun slowly chases back the light as gasps fill the room. Bright, piercing light enters the room as the sun breaks over the horizon. The tree line becomes hard to see as the sun darkens everything beneath it. Rays shoot through the sky, fighting back night, welcoming in the morning. The sky changes from dark to blue to orange, with some soft pinks mixed in too. Jasmin's hand squeezes mine.

"I haven't seen it look so brilliant before," she whispers. She also holds Kian's hand but releases both of us as she leans forward, staring into the sky.

"Princess," Kian speaks softly. Jasmin tears her view from the sunrise to look at him. He points at her chest, "Look at your necklace."

We look down as she presses her chest forward to get a better look. The sunlight is glinting off the gems, lighting the necklace in an array of colors. The colors glint off the gems, giving a variety of colored lights. She shifts her shoulders one way, then the other, letting the light bounce off the necklace. Each direction provides new colors based on which gems the light hits. It's an impressive display of light playing off the jewelry.

Jasmin is enamored with the necklace, forgetting about the sunrise altogether. People around the room begin to whisper. I can't hear them, but I can tell they are talking about Jasmin. I'm not sure whether I should be concerned about that or not. I haven't gotten the impression anyone would speak ill of her, certainly not within earshot. She settles back into the bench, resting her head on my shoulder.

"You must give me the name of the artist. I need him to make more pieces for me. Has he ever done a crown?" She asks in muted tones.

"I doubt she has made a crown before. Though I'm sure she would love the opportunity. She mostly makes bracelets and necklaces."

"She?" Jasmin jolts up, stunned. "Well, I must have her out here before my coronation!"

"Yes, my Queen," I whisper teasingly. She slaps my arm before resting her head against me. I hope she commissions my friend. It would be an excellent opportunity for Ingrid. She's talked about making pieces for the royal family before. She was delighted when I asked her to make the piece for me to give to Jasmin. I can only imagine how she would react to having Jasmin request more.

The sun continues its ascent into the sky, bringing daylight and mild warmth against the cold winter night. Once the sun is firmly above the horizon, Jasmin rises, faces the crowd, and thanks everyone for joining her. She walks toward the end of the row to shake hands with everyone else. I stand back, intending to let her have her time with them. Kian steps up behind me, grabbing my arm.

"You should go stand with her."

"What? Why?" I question incredulously. Why would he suggest that?

"She's going to tell everyone about the necklace, and I have a feeling." What does that mean? "Just trust me." I eye him suspiciously, but he pushes me toward her. I stumble at first but am soon by her side.

Sure enough, she is already talking about the necklace. She grabs my arm, pulling me close as she explains the gift to someone. I smile, dropping my arm to her back. Her hand settles on my shoulder, her body nestled into my side. If Kian is playing some sort of game, I don't particularly care. I enjoy standing by the Princess. He got the pleasure of dancing with her and being in the spotlight with his story earlier. I can take the chance to hold her while she greets the people in her castle.

She has such grace about her while she speaks with everyone. She knows all their names, every servant, family member, and child. She speaks with them as if she knows every single detail like they are all her closest friends. There must be plenty of time for her to get to know everyone, with them being stuck in the castle, but there isn't any unwillingness from her. No anxiousness, no detachment. She is comfortable with everyone. She knows so many details about them. I try to remember some of the points she mentions. I don't know how she remembers everything, though. By the time the crowd is gone, my brain feels like mush. I gave up trying to remember details and just focused on names. When that became overwhelming, I tried to focus on people I knew. Now I just need rest.

"Want me to escort you to your room?" She looks around the room, realizing everyone else, save a couple of guards, is gone. She nods, calling good night to the guards. I follow suit, trying to at least commit their names to my memory. One of her hands loops around my arm while the other hand rises to fidget with the necklace. Neither of us speaks, walking in companionable silence.

I soon realize I haven't been to this part of the castle before. While the décor looks similar, guards have more positions to take up. They are currently empty. This must be where the royal family normally stays when there are more. The portraits are of kings and queens of the past. I recognize a few from my days in school. There are also several of these paintings in the city center of Arkaley. The ornate doors are closed, preventing me from seeing what is behind them. We arrive at the only set of doors that are open. A hall is behind them, but no portraits are on the walls. The walls are dark, with only a few small paintings of flowers hung. The most astonishing part of the doorway is the two guards standing on either side. Both are in royal uniform with swords attached to their belts. Their tunics have the kingdom's emblem on the chest. Both have a spear and several other weapons I can't see, I'm sure. Jasmin must be serious about keeping unwanted guests out of her room. I wonder how many of the bachelors know where her rooms are.

She steps in front of me, looking up at me with dazed eyes. Her fingers are still toying with the necklace.

"Kiss me goodnight, Clem."

I glance over to the guards, but they mind their own business or at least putting on a show of it. I wrap my fingers around her neck, pulling her in as I kiss her. It's a soft, gentle kiss. A perfect ending for the long night. As I pull away, her eyes are still closed, enjoying the sensation of the kiss. Unable to help myself, I press another quick kiss to her cheek before stepping back. She has a dreamy look in her eyes when she turns and walks down her hallway. I take half a step towards her when one of the guards holds his hand out to stop me. I jump back, throwing my hands up. I didn't mean to raise any alarm. Jasmin has already disappeared into one of the rooms. I nod to the guards, turning to walk back to my own room.

When I was young, my father told us how we spent winter solstice would determine how our year would go. We always celebrated with each other, spending time together, swapping gifts, eating good food, reading, playing, and doing whatever hobby we were into at the time. I always believed him, trying to make the most of my night. I always believed him until the curse happened. Nothing on our winter solstice could have prepared me for the tragedy to come. If he was right, though, if there was any truth to his belief, while I may be in for an emotional year, maybe I can get a happily ever after of my own.

Chapter 20

JASMIN

"Princess," Emmeline calls to me as I finish styling my hair. "You'll need to go to the meeting room to get your shawl. That was the last place I saw it."

"I don't even remember having it in there." She shrugs as she leaves the room, not offering any further comment on how my shawl wound up in the meeting room. I swear if I didn't love her, I would probably consider getting rid of her. Well, not really. She keeps me functioning at an acceptable level. I couldn't do anything without her, but she's getting on my last nerve right now. I'm cold and now have to walk across the castle to get my favorite shawl.

I slept for a few hours after sunrise. In an attempt to not become a night owl, as I have done in the past, I plan to stay awake for a few more hours and go to bed at a regular time. That's the goal. I am so exhausted, though. I make my way through the chilly halls, angry my shawl ended up in the meeting room. Why is it even in there? After the Lords left, the remaining bachelors agreed we would only meet when needed, which isn't that often. I haven't been in the meeting room in at least a week, and I know I have had my shawl since then.

Finn is walking along next to me. He left the party early last night to go to bed and is perfectly happy this morning. The halls are quiet; everyone sleeping in their own rooms. I love the calm of the castle after long nights. The air is still; there isn't much noise. It's eerie in a comforting way. Wandering through the halls on quiet mornings is my favorite pastime.

Finn bounds ahead of me into the meeting room when we get closer. I roll my eyes at the dog. Maybe if I had slept half the night, I would feel like running through the halls, too. Now, all I want is my shawl. The winter chill is setting in, and the sweater Emmeline gave me to wear today is not nearly thick enough on its own. I enter the meeting room, getting several steps in before I realize what is happening. Clem, Kian, Tomas, and Erik are all standing around the table.

"What are you....Oh gods."

Simultaneously, they all bow in front of me. I groan loudly, walking over to my chair. My shawl is folded on the table, not in a way that I would have left it. It's obvious Emmeline is in on whatever this is. The men are standing next to their chairs, Kian and Clem on either side of me, while Tomas and Erik are on the other side of the circle. Kian and Clem are smirking at each other. One of the two is clearly the ringleader.

"The thing I have always found interesting about court protocol is the amount of time one must bow in the presence of royalty." I wrap my shawl around my shoulders, slowly walking toward the men. I step behind Kian, running my hand along his back, then pushing his shoulders lower. When satisfied with his new position, I amble toward Tomas.

"When passing royalty in the hallway, you only need to bow until they pass or dismiss you, whichever comes first." I approach Tomas, making a few adjustments to his position. He doesn't have as much experience with protocol as Kian and Erik. "But," I emphasize as I step behind Erik. He doesn't need any corrections, so I just stroke my hand across his back teasingly. "When a royal member enters a room, specifically for a meeting, whether they are aware of it or not, one must remain in the bowed position until the highest-ranking member releases them."

I walk around to Clem, who is starting to look uncomfortable. Surely, he knows I can play games just as well as they can. Did he think I would just wave them away quickly? Before I get to Clem, I notice Finn on the ground. His front legs are stretched out with his snout near the ground. His back legs are high; his tail wags when I walk near him.

"Et tu, Finn?" I place my hand over my heart as if I've been wounded. He barks when I say his name, jumping up from his position. The men snicker but remain bowing. Finn prances to my side. I give in, petting his head while he nuzzles into my hand. I can't stay mad at him. I step behind Clem, running my hand along his spine. I push his shoulders lower, too, feeling a slight tremor in his muscles. I stroke down his back again, pausing just above his ass. He does have a nice ass. It's not huge, but round. I could sink my teeth into it. Instead, I pinch it, causing him to yelp. The others look up to see what happened, but I cast them a glare. They quickly drop their eyes again.

I stand behind my chair, watching them, making them wait. They are all shifting, clearly questioning their decision. I let them squirm for another moment. I'm in no rush. I have my shawl and am perfectly warm now.

"You may rise."

They sigh and stand up, half-hearted smiles on their faces.

"Since you are all here, I do have something I wanted to ask of you. But this is too formal. Let's settle over here by the fire."

We walk over to the hearth, where a small fire is burning. Only a few chairs are here since the main space is around the table. A few fluffy pillows are nearby. I grab one and plop down on the floor. Finn settles into my side. Tomas quickly darts around the others to sit next to me. He isn't normally one to rush next to me. I enjoy spending time with Tomas, but I usually wind up with one of the other three men next to me. It's a welcome surprise to see him next to me. I squeeze his hand while the others settle in near us.

"Thanks for settling in over here. Much more comfortable. I hope you all enjoyed the winter solstice." They nod affirmations of enjoyment. "Good. I know the four of you wished to remain here, whether for yourself or for me. I want to let you know I appreciate having you here and have found value in each of you. This is why I want to offer positions to you. You are under no obligation to accept them. If you want to stay here under the edict and not take any further responsibility, that is entirely acceptable. I feel like I know you all well enough to know you would appreciate the duties." They all nod, wanting to do more. I knew they would, but I didn't want to pressure them into accepting something they didn't want.

"Erik, I want you to work under Henry to develop a new training routine for our guards. You did phenomenally with the sparring contest. If we are as close to ending the curse as people believe, we will need to fortify our borders, which means new recruits. I would like you to help with that." He offers a kind, excited smile.

"I would be honored, Princess."

"Thank you." I turn to the side. "Tomas, I would like you to be the Guard Liaison to the Stables. I assume you want to be in the guard, yes?" The excitement on his face is contagious. I can't help smiling at him.

"Yes! I want to be in the guard."

"Excellent. I know you already have a good relationship with Sabeko and Zander. I would like you to help them adjust to the training schedule Henry and Erik create, assisting with the horses as needed for guards."

"Yes, Princess. I would love to do that." I can't think of a better job for him. I don't know that we have ever had a position like that before. I don't think there was a designated person to serve between both stables and guards, but Tomas will be perfect for it.

"Kian, I would like you to be my Coven Advisor." He tilts his head in intrigue. This is definitely a new position. "In the past, the Lord of Greynon has always served as the communicator between the castle and the covens. However, I do not have the greatest faith in Lord Alwyn. I would like you to take on this position separately from him. You will need to work with him since you are still in his village. But I would like separate communication with the witch community. Is this something you are interested in? It could create some issues with the Lords, but I believe you are cunning enough to handle them."

He seems to consider for a moment. We all have eyes on him, anxious to hear his response. "I believe this is a good position. My first concern, however, is some of the coven leaders may not be happy with another man filling this type of position." That's a good point.

"I see." A woman would make the coven leaders more comfortable, but I don't know any women. I certainly don't trust any of them the way I do Kian.

"Perhaps," he starts slowly, bringing my attention from problem-solving back to him, "I could start in the position to get a feel for how it will go. I do believe the covens will feel better having a more direct link to you. If they don't like me in that spot, I can foster introductions to select a new person."

"I like that, Kian. Let's start with you and see how it goes." I match his smile. I love his genuine smiles. A hint of magic always gleams in his eyes when it's genuine. "I want you to arrange a meeting with them this spring. I want to establish communication with them soon." He offers a single nod, accepting the role. I hadn't planned on any issues due to these positions, but I'm glad Kian isn't worried about bringing up potential problems. It's one of the reasons I wanted him for this spot.

Finally, I turn to Clem. He is looking down at his hands, fiddling with some string hanging from the hem of his tunic. His eyes lift up to mine, looking sad and defeated. He speaks before I get a chance.

"You don't have to offer me a position. I'm just glad to be here. I know I don't have any skills like them." He motions toward the other before turning back to the string. It's surprising that he doesn't think he has any skills.

"Clem," I shake my head, trying to clear the disbelief over his lack of self-awareness. "You...I want you to be the Master of Gardens for the kingdom." He looks stunned, forgetting the string.

"Master of Gardens?"

"Yes. I want you to assist the head gardeners of each village and the castle. Foster communication and trade between them. When the borders are open again, I also want you to facilitate trade and communication between other kingdoms."

He stares with his mouth open, entirely in disbelief. He tries to speak, but nothing comes out of his mouth.

"You spent several weeks with Mikhail at the end of the harvest season. A time in which you were supposed to be wooing a certain Princess." His cheeks flair a deep red color. He closes his mouth, trying not to say anything else. "While you were there, you showed him a new way to harvest that would be easier and more efficient, did you not?" He just nods, still not speaking. "You clearly understand farming well and have the skills to assist farmers in new techniques. We have been secluded for eight years. There could be many new techniques we don't know about in other lands. I would like you to be the person to learn the best ways and convey it to the rest of the kingdom."

He stares at me, trying to process everything I told him. He has so many valuable skills; it's hard to believe he isn't aware of them. He starts to shake his head no, but I reach out and grab his hand.

"I know I said you all have the choice here, but I've changed my mind," I smirk at him, trying to lessen the mood. I wouldn't take this choice away from him, but I know this position is good for him. "You will take this position. Try it out for this season. If you hate it, you can drop it. Besides, what else are you going to do?"

He shrugs, giving a feeble laugh. "Okay," he mumbles. I squeeze his hand.

"Good. Now that all that is settled, I'm starving. Some fop decided to arrange this meeting without any breakfast." I push off Tomas's shoulder to stand, then offer him my hand. He stands with me as the others rise. After adjusting my shawl, I wrap my hand around Tomas's arm.

"Lead the way to breakfast, Sir Tomas." We both giggle as he makes his way toward breakfast. I feel much better knowing all the men accepted their new positions. I wasn't worried they wouldn't, but these are new positions in the kingdom. I intend to foster energy to prepare our kingdom for the end of the curse. I hope I am right that it is ending. I can't fathom seeing so many changes, the increased harvest, my longer hair, the brilliant winter sun rising, the thunder in winter, and not having the curse lifted.

Chapter 21

CLEM

Trees sway calmly in the chilly breeze. All the leaves are gone. Eaten by animals or decaying on the soft, mushy ground. Winter is in full effect, leaving the air cold and dry. I pull my coat around my shoulders tighter. The winter air is not clearing my head the way I wanted it to. It's dried out my skin, but my doubts and fears seem to be festering in the quiet cold.

I crunch along the path, unsure how I got here. Both literally and figuratively. The trail behind me is soft, my feet leaving prints from everywhere I step. Only a few months ago, I walked the streets of Arkaley, dispirited and alone. Now I walk the paths of the castle grounds. I thought being here would raise my spirits. It did for a moment, but I am still morose many days. Being with Jasmin raises my spirits, but her time is still split between the remaining three men, with Kian taking a larger block of time than the others. I love her more than any other person I have loved before. She isn't mine, though; that thought never leaves my desolate emotions. It's always there to remind me of what I can't have.

Jasmin tasked me as Master of Gardeners. She believes in my ability to work with the land. My concern is in my ability to interact with other gardeners. I get along well with Mikhail because he is a great man. I also came to him at a vital time and offered what he needed. That won't always be the case in this position. I'll need to learn how to deal with people, an act I am not looking forward to.

My feet crunch the leaves and sticks that are still on the ground. The sky turns a slight shade of grey. Snow is about to fall. I turn and head back to the edge of the forest. I sit beneath a tree, overlooking the castle. Just before my regular melancholy sinks in, Jasmin walks out of the side door, Finn zooming past her into the grass. She curses at him but steps to the side, sitting on a bench. Just as the thought of joining her crosses my mind, Kian walks out and sits beside her. Of course, he does. They sit close, cuddled together for warmth and nothing else. No other reason for them to sit that close. My heart doesn't buy the lie.

Finn grabs a stick, dropping it in Jasmin's lap. She throws it, and Finn takes off running but stops before he can get to the stick. Giant white clumps are falling through the sky. Finn abandons the stick, instead trying to catch the snowflakes by snapping in the air. I can't stop the smile as I watch him. I keep my eyes on the sky, on Finn, on the snowflakes in front of my face, anywhere but the bench near the door. The snowfall feels magical. The first snow always does. There's something special about the first flakes breaking through the sky, dropping to the ground in quiet confidence. They belong here. They know their role.

In my attempt not to watch the bench, I didn't notice Jasmin leave. When she sits down by my side, squeezing into my arms, I'm startled by her sudden appearance.

"Oh, hi." My words are sheepish, trying to hide the surprise. She snuggles in closer, trying to steal my warmth.

"What are you doing out here by yourself?"

"I was walking to clear my head. Realized it was about to snow and sat to watch." I wave one hand toward the castle, wrapping my other around her to pull her close. Finn is running around with Kian now. Jasmin nods, wrapping her arms around my body. Neither of us says anything; we just watch as the snow falls, melting into the dying grass below. There likely won't be much snow accumulating from this storm.

Suddenly, Jasmin stands, holding her hand out for mine. I was prepared to stay outside for a while, not yet ready to go back in. "Do you remember the pond?"

"Yes." My face scrunches in confusion. Of course, I remember, but it's too cold for swimming now.

"Good, let's go." She flicks her hand at me, encouraging me to take it to stand.

"Jasmin," I admonish, "it's freezing out here." She sighs, grabbing my hand.

"Come on, you large oaf. Trust me."

I snort at her but take her hand and stand anyways. There is no way I am swimming in this weather. I don't wish to turn into an icicle, but the alternative is sitting here under a tree alone. She leads the way through the grounds to the other side of the castle, where the service road is. Along the way, Kian catches up with us, asking where we are going. Jasmin gives me a questioning look. I don't respond to her, though; I just wait to see what she says. She tells Kian we're going to her favorite spot. He insists on tagging along, walking on her other side. It's not ideal, but I'm not going to speak up, either. Jasmin is still wrapped around my arm. That's good enough.

Jasmin tells Kian about the pond, describing what it looks like in summer. I ask if she's ever been in winter.

"Only once, shortly after the curse began. I needed to get away and went to that spot. The water was surprisingly warm. I didn't get in, just lay on a rock with my hand in the water. Something about that area is so peaceful. It always helps me relax. Have you been back?"

"No. I never considered it."

"Back?" Kian asks, quizzically looking between us.

"Uh, yeah," I say nervously, scratching the back of my head. "She took me that week I was here before anyone else." Jasmin glances between the two of us, unsure what else to say.

"When you thought she was a handmaid?" He laughs teasingly. Jasmin and I laugh with him, nodding in agreement. Jasmin and Kian fall into friendly banter as we walk, teasing each other about this whole situation. Things seem so easy for the two of them. Kian hasn't shown any signs of jealousy, even going as far as forcing the rest of us to be with Jasmin. She has had moments of doubts around us all but pushes through flawlessly. She's such a strong woman.

We are walking along the service road. It has already narrowed, wide grooves from wagons dug into the dirt, creating the path's edges. Jasmin and Kian stop talking as she watches the side of the road for the trail. I don't remember exactly where she turned off, but I know we have to be getting close. Soon she stops, looking back along the road, searching for something.

"Huh, that's weird."

"What?" Kian asks.

"There was always a flower that bloomed along the side, so I would know where to turn. Even in the winter, it was always there." She looks up and down, but no flowers can be seen.

"Could it be further down?" Kian questions.

"No, it wasn't that far." The three of us are looking along the edge for any signs of a flower. Finn has joined us but wanders around, looking for branches or something tasty.

"Do you think we will arrive at it if we just start walking in that direction?" I suggest pointing toward the spot where the pond should be. She shrugs but steps off the road, walking toward the pond. We stay side by side. Unlike the time she brought me, there is no path. The ground is bare; only dead leaves and twigs from the trees are beneath our feet. There are no ferns. No signs of the pond.

We walk for several minutes, much longer than we should have needed to before Jasmin stops. She looks around the area, knowing we should be standing in the pond at this point. Her gaze turns to mine, tears building in her eyes.

"Where is it?" she whimpers.

I rush to her at the same time as Kian. My arms wrap around her waist. He reaches her back and rubs her shoulders. We stand there with her body between ours. Her face presses against my chest, a soft sob escaping. Kian and I both start talking to her at the same time.

"You're probably just tired...."

"Maybe this isn't the right spot...."

"...and it doesn't look the same in the winter."

"...you probably missed the turn with us distracting you."

She nods her head between us, taking slow deep breaths. It feels odd to have her smashed this close between both of us. I haven't been this close to Kian before. I want to stroke Jasmin's hair, but doing so would cause me to also stroke Kian's hand. My desire not to stroke him is stronger than the one to stroke Jasmin's hair. I settle for kissing the side of her head. He kisses the top of her head; being taller than me, that spot is easier for him to reach without making this any more awkward. Jasmin shifts slightly, and we both back off, giving her space.

"Thanks," she offers softly. "I guess I just missed the turn. Let's go back inside, though. This snow is making me too chilly." She tries to laugh, but it feels insincere. Kian wraps his arm around her shoulders, leading her back to the path. I turn and yell for Finn, not wanting to leave him out this far alone. He zooms past me, then Kian and Jasmin, running toward the castle. I stay a few steps behind them. The hug was awkward enough, and I don't really want to get into another situation with Kian too.

"How did you find the pond?" Kian asks Jasmin.

"My friend showed it to me a long time ago. She told me it was enchanted; it would always be my private space." She turns back to look at me. "Sunette's daughter found it." She holds her hand out for me to take again. Despite her still being in Kian's arms, something in my soul prevents me from denying her. I step up and take her hand, lacing my fingers with hers. I still stay a step away from her, but not so much as to pull her away from Kian.

"Sunette, the gardener?" Kian asks.

"Yes."

"I didn't realize she had a daughter. I know Zander, but no one has ever mentioned any other children." Jasmin nods, her eyes glazing over again. I squeeze her hand. I have heard Jasmin mention her friend once or twice, but it's always brief. She never shares much about herself.

"She died before the curse. It was very traumatic. We don't talk about it now." Her voice drops to just above a whisper as she finishes. Kian squeezes her arm, pulling her tighter against him. I keep my fingers laced with hers, not wanting to let her go. I don't know much of her history. After the curse, everyone stopped speaking about the royal family. No news came out of the castle; we all just did our own thing. Jasmin has a whole life I know nothing about.

She leads us inside, wandering through the halls as she removes her coat. Kian offers to grab some mead for us. She suggests a sitting room on the second floor that overlooks the front of the castle. Kian walks one way to head to the kitchen while I follow Jasmin. We reach the sitting room, removing our jackets. She sighs, stepping toward me. I hold out my arms, allowing her to wrap her arms around me. I hold her tight, wanting to comfort her, keep her close, and make her happy. I may be melancholic most days, but I would do anything to keep her from feeling that way.

"Why couldn't we find the pond, Clem?" she whispers.

"I don't know, Jas. Maybe it looks different in the winter." She looks up at me, propping her chin on my chest. Her eyes knit together with curiosity.

"What did you call me?"

"Jas? Sorry. Do you not want me to call you that?" A soft smile stretches across her lips. Her hands flatten on my back, fingers stroking against my shoulder blades. She turns her head, pressing her cheek against my chest.

"She called me that." Her voice is dreamy and soft.

"Sunette's daughter?"

"Yes. She's the only one that ever did."

"Oh," I pause, unsure how to respond. Jasmin turns her head to look up at me, loosening her grip. Her face is soft. The warm light from the fireplace cast a soft glow on her skin.

"You can call me that too." She whispers, rising slowly on her toes. I don't need an invitation. I lean down, meeting her lips in a tender kiss. My arms caress her back tenderly. These are the moments that drive my misery away. These are the moments I live for. A feeling of belonging flares in my chest as her lips press firmly against mine. My tongue slides against her, asking for permission, wanting to deepen this moment.

A loud crackle sounds in the room. We break the kiss, tightening our grip on each other. My shoulders slump around her, trying to protect her. Her hands tighten around my back, pulling me closer to her. We both look around but don't see anything strange. I glance at the fire, but no logs shift. She is looking around the room, trying to find the source of the noise.

"Guess who's here!" Kian announces as he walks into the room with a tray of snacks and drinks. Jasmin steps toward him to help. As they set up the food on the table, a thought occurs to me. They work so seamlessly together; what if the noise was related to him breaking the curse? He would have been close to the room when the crackle sounded. Perhaps it's magic's way of telling me to back off. That seems logical enough, given my limited knowledge of magic. Instead of acknowledging that thought, I help them get things set up. The three of us settle onto the floor, drinking mead, eating the snacks Kian brought, and chatting about winter and other unimportant things.

After a while, Jasmin lies down and places her head on Kian's lap. My teeth grind in agitation, but she stretches her legs out slightly. I grab her ankle, sliding her feet toward me. It's not the same as having her head, but it's something. She relaxes as I rub her calves through her leggings. Kian strokes her hair, telling her a story about the first time he went on a walk through the snow-covered forest as a young child. Finn walks in, slumping over next to Jasmin. She wraps her arms around the fluffy animal, sighing contentedly. I can't deny that this is enjoyable. I would rather have her head in my lap, but I'm not terribly upset over this, either.

"Why can't this be my happily ever after?" Her eyes are closed, fingers idly brushing through Finn's thick fur. "This is perfect." She sighs again. Kian chuckles.

"You want a triad, Princess?" I fight to hide the cringe at his question.

"I've never done anything like that before, but I probably wouldn't say no. Would you want to be in a triad?" She looks up at Kian, twisting enough to see his face. His fingers are still caressing her hair. I realize my own hands have stopped moving. In an attempt to seem unaffected, I start rubbing her leg again, but it feels unnatural now. Did I use this much pressure before? How big were the circles I was making? Should I create a new pattern now?

"With the right people, I would consider it." He winks at her. Involuntarily, my grip tightens on her leg. She shifts her leg slightly under my hand. I lift my hand away quickly, worried I've hurt her. She doesn't show any signs of being hurt, though. I need to get a grip on my anger. They aren't suggesting sharing; they are just talking about a hypothetical situation. Why am I reacting so strongly to this?

"Would you be in a triad, Clem?" I meet her eyes, trying to hide the hurt over the thought of having to share her.

"I don't think so." Kian eyes me suspiciously. I don't like whatever he is thinking.

"What if it was someone else? Two other people, not the Princess?" I try to consider the question, but confusion overpowers my thought process.

"Not Jasmin, just two other people?"

"Yes. If you aren't her true love, could you be in a triad with other people?" I consider this question. I ended the engagement with Rachel because she was still sleeping with other men. Although, that wasn't because I was jealous. I was more concerned about getting some disease or being stuck raising another man's child. I suppose if I had known ahead of time it was only the three of us in a relationship, it wouldn't be so bad. I've never considered that an option. We don't get to have multiple people in relationships. Concubines are common among royalty, but it's never a true triad. There are rumors of triads, but no one ever admits to wanting to be in one or being willing to accept one.

"Maybe. I don't know. I guess it would depend."

"So you wouldn't share the Princess? You would deny her pleasure at the hands of another man?" He asks coyly. I laugh at his antics. I see what he is getting at now.

"If she were mine, she wouldn't need pleasure at the hands of another man." He laughs loudly, throwing his head back. She laughs along, rubbing her feet against my thigh.

"Touché," he finally responds.

"That's a response I can live with." I squeeze her calf, rubbing her leg sooth-ingly, finding the comfortable pressure and pattern I used before. All this talk is hypothetical, anyway. Jasmin has *a* true love, not several true loves.

Chapter 22

JASMIN

Snow has accumulated on the ground. There are several inches worth, covering everything in a blanket of shimmering white. I love seeing the fresh snowfall on the ground. It's serene, shimmery, and absolutely magical. Usually, I like to bundle up in the chair in my room. I place it between the hearth and the window, staring at the ground beyond. Despite my wishes, Finn needs to be taken out. My room is so warm and cozy, though. I'd just send him on if I wasn't so worried about Finn peeing on everything between here and the door. Instead, I get up and slip into some lined leggings, a thick knit sweater, long knit socks, and a pair of boots. We make our way to the door. It won't keep me warm for long, just long enough to get him out.

As soon as the door opens, Finn leaps into the air, forgetting his needs. He prances in the snow for a solid minute before I yell at him. I'm freezing my tits off, and he's playing. He trots joyfully over to a bush, finally taking care of his business. I wrap my arms around my waist, cool air slipping through my sweater and chilling my body. I should have grabbed my coat. Finn finishes up and starts to walk toward me but pauses.

"Oh, come on, Finn!" I yell. "You don't need to catch that poor little mouse or whatever. Let's go back inside." Finn starts barking excitedly, wagging his tail quickly through the air. I see it coming in but don't have time to process it or duck out of the way. A snowball flies through the air, crashing into my chest. I scream, trying to knock the snow off my sweater, but small flakes slip through, freezing my already chilled chest. I look around to see who threw it. Another ball is flying toward me. I try to jump to the side, but it still slams into my hip. I yell again, trying to figure out who is throwing snowballs at me.

"Finn!!" I scream at him, but he's disappeared, chasing whoever is throwing the snowballs. "Finn, save me!" Another snowball is careening through the air in my direction. Before I can jump out of the way, Erik dives in front of me.

"No!" He screams dramatically as the ball hits him in the chest, then lands on the ground with a thud at my feet. I drop by his side, feigning concern. I dust his chest off, looking over his body.

"Erik! No!" I cry out, shaking a fist at the sky, equally dramatic. He grabs my hand, drawing my attention back to him.

"Avenge me, Princess," he says choppily, as if breathless. He clutches his chest, gasping for breath.

"I will, Erik. I will avenge you!" He sighs a heavy breath, pretending it's his last. I wail at the pretend loss of him. After my long wail ends, I climb over him, straddling him as I press a kiss to his lips. While kissing him, I realize I haven't actually kissed him before. He seems to also realize this, and the kiss becomes awkward. I pull away, kiss his forehead, and climb off him. No harm done in an awkward kiss, right? Now, I need to avenge him. I run off in the direction of the snowballs. I still don't know who is throwing them or where they are.

I definitely regret not putting on more clothes. My shoes are wet, and the socks aren't great at keeping my feet dry. The looser knit of the sweater allows air to stream straight through. My nipples may literally fall off before I head inside. I charge forward, hand held high, yelling words of avenging Erik's death, cheeks stinging from the cold and grins. I don't see the snowball flying toward me. It slams into my chest, directly on my frozen breast. I cry out in actual pain, wrapping my arms around my chest as I drop to my knees.

"Ow, you fuck face. That was my godsdammed breast. Holy shit, my nipple!" I groan, rubbing my hands against my breast to knock away the snow. Tomas comes running from behind a tree.

"I'm so sorry, Princess." His face is stricken with terror. " I didn't mean to do that. I wasn't aiming for your..." he gulps, clearly nervous. He is reaching out, trying to help knock the snow off my sweater. Despite his attempt to help, he is just caressing my breasts at this point. I drop my hands, looking up at him with a pointed gaze. He meets my eyes, and the terror on his face intensifies. His face is now a deep red. He throws his hands in the air, about shoulder height. He flinches when his previously injured arm moves that quickly, but he forces himself to hold it up. He isn't completely healed yet, but the healers think he will regain full use of his arm with enough exercise.

"I'm so so sorry, Princess. I'm an idiot."

Behind me, Clem and Erik are rolling on the ground laughing at this situation. Kian is not far behind, with a massive grin on his face. Finn runs up, licking my face. I shove him out of the way, grabbing Tomas's uninjured arm and pulling him up with me.

"It's fine, Tomas. I didn't think you were intentionally aiming for my breast." I consider my next thought, "Though, good job if you were. The groping felt a bit more intentional." I laugh, knocking the rest of the snow off my shirt.

"It wasn't intentional, Princess. I swear."

"Tomas, I'm teasing. I know it wasn't intentional."

He relaxes minimally, clearly convinced he did something wrong. From the corner of my eye, I notice Kian and Clem moving closer.

"Have you been out here..."

Two snowballs simultaneously hit me, one in the chest, one in the ass. Immediately after the snow makes contact, Kian and Clem are on me, apologizing for their "mistake," swearing over their clumsiness and groping me. Kian is fondling my breasts, despite hitting me in the back while Clem is stroking my ass. I drop my arms in defeat, looking at Tomas.

"Look what you started." He gives a small laugh, relaxing a bit more. "Erik!" I shout, looking around for him. "Erik, come save me!"

Finn jumps on Clem, trying to knock him away. Finn is barking loudly; everyone is laughing again. Suddenly, large arms scoop me up and take off, running toward the door.

"Erik! My savior! I'm so glad you aren't dead." I giggle as he carries me inside the castle.

The warmth coats my cold body, causing me to shiver more. My clothes are wet, soaked from snowballs, and hands groping all over. Erik's grip tightens on me.

"Where to, milady?"

"T-t-t-t-oo..." My teeth are chattering too hard now to even speak. I want to change out of my clothes, but Erik hasn't been to my room. There is no way for me to guide him there without being able to talk.

"How about a fire?" I nod at his suggestion. That will at least warm me up enough that I can make it to my room on my own. He ducks into the first room he can find with a fire going. He sets me down on the hearth, grabbing a blanket off the couch nearby to wrap around me. He settles in behind me, pulling me into his lap. I'm grateful for him. His large body is always warm and comfortable to relax against. I snuggle against his chest as my body shivers from the cold. He rubs his hands over my arms, trying to warm me up quickly.

"S-sorry, I didn't avenge you b-better." The shivering has calmed down but isn't completely gone. He chuckles, his chest rumbling against my side.

"Thank you for trying."

He keeps one arm wrapped around my back, holding me close. His other hand slides up to my neck, caressing his thumb against my jaw. I look up at him. I haven't really considered whether he could be my true love in a while. It's entirely possible, though. I've been caught up with Kian and Clem and not wanting it to be Tomas because of his age. I enjoy being with Erik. I don't feel the same attraction to him as I do with Kian and Clem, but I can't deny that he can arouse desire in me too. His thumb pushes my face toward his as he leans in. Our lips meet again, gently brushing together. Something about the touch doesn't feel right. I try to ignore it, assuming it's just nerves or awkwardness again.

I adjust, turning to face him more. His thumb strokes my cheek, brushing against my scars. An electrifying shock courses through my scar at his touch. I flinch, trying not to jerk away, but Erik notices anyway. He pulls back, confusion on his face.

"What was that?"

"Your fingers shocked me." I touch my cheek, where his fingers have just shifted away from.

"This doesn't feel natural, does it?" He questions. I give a soft chuckle, shaking my head. I settle against his chest again, giving up on kissing him. "I don't think I'm your true love."

"Why not?" I ask; even if the physical stuff isn't natural, he could technically still be my true love.

"It doesn't feel right. True love should feel right." I nod against his chest. He isn't wrong. While there are stories of fated couples that don't actually get along, there are far more that encompass all aspects of being in love.

"Is there someone else, Erik?" I glance at him, wiggling my eyebrows. "Perhaps a sibling of another bachelor?" His cheeks blush at the mention of Clem's sister. Erik was enamored with Bea when she came to help Finn. If he isn't my true love, I can at least foster this relationship.

"I'm pretty sure Clem would kill me before he let me near her again." We both laugh because I can clearly see Clem trying to fight Erik over Bea. I don't think he would unless he thought Erik would hurt her, though. Clem is protective of his sister, but he wouldn't get in the way of her happiness, I don't think.

"Meh, I don't think so. Besides, I'm pretty sure he would hate being stuck in the dungeon with Oscar more than you being with Bea." His body shakes with laughter, jostling me around in his lap. I giggle at the motion, which makes him laugh even more. He squeezes me tightly, trying to hold me still, but we both devolve into a fit of giggles. I love seeing this side of Erik. He can be so serious and resolute most of the time. It's fun to see his lighter side.

We sigh together, settling in as the fire crackles. My mind settles into a rare calm as I watch the logs burn. My head rests against his chest, the steady beat of his heart thudding against my ear. It's relaxing, sending me into a state of calmness I rarely find. My gaze is fixed on the fire but unseeing. We sit for several minutes, both just staring off.

As I doze off, my hand drops against my sweater, grazing a wet spot from the snow. It's warm now but still moist. I shift, trying to sit up. Erik blinks sleepily as if he were falling asleep too.

"I need to go change. My clothes are still wet from the snow." He nods lazily, helping me up. "Thank you for bringing me in. And saving me from those damned fools." We chuckle quietly. He bows halfway.

"Anything for a princess willing to avenge my fake snowball death." I give him a quick hug, kissing his cheek. I walk toward the door but stop before I enter the hallway. I look back to Erik, who is folding the blanket to put away.

"You know, if we bring in more guards, there will be more animals at the castle, both pets and cattle. Sabeko isn't experienced enough to tend to them. I would need to bring in an animal healer to oversee their care." I pause, offering a mischievous smile. "If you know any good animal healers, I'm open to suggestions."

He smiles appreciatively, looking down at the blanket in his hands. "Thank you, Jasmin." The moment is more meaningful because he used my name. He so rarely uses my name instead of my title.

I slowly make my way back to my room. The hallways are quiet. I can't help but wonder where the others went. I expected them to follow us, continuing the chase indoors. I'm glad they didn't. I enjoy time alone with Erik. A brief flash of worry crosses my mind about where Finn might be, but Clem wouldn't leave him outside. Clem loves Finn as much as I do. I'm sure Tomas and Kian would also bring in Finn, but they likely wouldn't remember him the way Clem would.

Emmeline is already in my room, lounging on my bed. She rises when I enter.

"Today's the day, Jasmin." She holds two bottles of wine in her hands. I clap, bouncing over to her. We have a tradition; every year, on the first good snow day, we spend the evening drinking ourselves silly and talking about all the bullshit we deal with. Some years we cry. Some years we laugh. But every year, we consume far too much wine and have a grand time. I step to my wardrobe, pulling out dry clothes as she pops the corks out of the bottles. We don't even bother with glasses. We drink straight from the bottles.

After I change, she hands me my bottle, raising hers in the air. She always gives a toast to start us off, and it's never a good one. The smirk is already spreading across my face, waiting to see what she says. She shuffles her shoulders, standing straighter, pushing a piece of blonde hair out of her face. She lifts her bottle, finally looking at me. I do my best to stifle my laughter, raising my bottle beside hers.

"No," she swears at me. "It's a good one this year! I promise." She takes a deep breath. I do the same so I don't burst out laughing prematurely.

"To good friends." Okay, strong start. "Never above you, never below you, always inside you." She clinks her bottle against mine, but I'm already roaring with laughter. I double over, laughing so hard I can't even stand straight.

"What?" She asks innocently.

"I don't...I don't think good *friends* are meant to be *inside* you." I gasp between fits of laughter. She thinks for a minute, then her eyes go wide.

"Oh, my gods!" She bursts into giggles, both of us collapse on the couch together. I haven't laughed this much in a long time. My cheeks ache, and my sides are sore, but it's such a good ache. When our giggling finally subsides, we start drinking. We don't take our drinking lightly. Within a short period, we finish half of our own bottles. When we first started drinking like this, we would share one bottle, passing it back and forth. We realized it's more efficient if we just have our own bottles. Then we don't have to figure out how to remove a cork when we are both drunk. I take a quick trip to the privy. When I return, she has pulled over one of the chaise lounges and is lying across it. I settle on the smaller couch, stretching out by the fire.

"So, who is your true love, Jasmin?" Unfortunately, I'm taking a drink as she asks, and I choke as I try to swallow too quickly. I sit up, coughing, fighting to breathe, while she sits there laughing at me. As I gasp for breath, I throw a pillow at her, smacking her in the face. I sneer at her as I calm down. I take another drink, clearing my throat.

"Oh, I don't know." I sigh. "Probably Clem or Kian. Maybe Tomas. I don't think it's Erik." I glance at her, pointing my bottle at her. "Knowing my luck, it's probably fucking Oscar."

"Oh, I keep forgetting he's here." She scowls, taking a sip. "I think it's Kian." Curious.

"Why do you think that?"

"Oh gods, he's gorgeous. And you two are so enchanting when you're together. He towers over you. Plus, he would be a great choice to mend relations with the witches." These are all great points.

"True, but I don't know that the relationship with the witches is a factor in my true love." She shrugs. We both take a drink. These bottles won't last much longer.

"The real question, though," she shifts in her seat to face me better, "who do you *want* it to be?" I sigh. That's the question I've been asking for months. "Come on," she drags out, "tell me! Please!"

I huff. I haven't actually spoken of my feelings on this topic in quite some time. Emmeline knows many of my feelings because she is observant and knows me so well. I haven't said anything, but she sees my reactions. I know she does.

"I really like Kian. He is gorgeous and smart, and cunning, and decent with court protocols." I pause, taking a long pull from my bottle. "Something is off when I'm with him, though. He's a great kisser, but something feels...not right." She laughs at my response.

"Yes, yes. Things are frequently not right," she mocks.

"Hey, give me that pillow, please." She hands the pillow to me. I take it and throw it at her face. She jumps, nearly dropping her bottle.

"Jasmin!" she admonishes. I love when she uses my name. Similar to the feeling I got with Erik, Emmeline uses honorifics around me a lot. I've asked her not to, but she insists. It does make moments like this sweeter, knowing she is being more personal.

"What about Clem?"

I bite my lip, not sure what to say about Clem. "Clem is handsome, too."

She nods, waiting for me to say more. "Yes, and?"

I shrug. "And what?"

"I swear to all the holy gods if you don't spill more about Clem this instant,"

"What, Emmeline?" I interrupt. "What are you going to do?"

"I...I..." she stumbles, never one to actually threaten anything. "I'll take your wine!" I gasp, clutching my wine to my chest. I take several large gulps.

"Never!"

"Then tell me more."

"Fine," I groan. "Clem is...amazing. He is tender and caring. He's so moody but always willing to do anything for me. He rode all the way to Arkaley to get his sister to save Finn!" I state as if she wasn't there when he did that.

"He did. You know what I think, Jasmin?"

"Hmm?"

"I think he loves you." I sit straight up.

"What?" She nods, oblivious to my shock.

"Yeah. Oh, you should have seen how devastated he was when you sent him away at the winter solstice. He didn't even want to come back to watch the sunrise. He only did because you requested him."

I didn't know that. She never told me. My mind is racing with the possibility that he loves me. That can't be right. Certainly, he doesn't. He would have said so. He's been too jealous to not tell me something like that.

"Oh, my gods," I say out loud without realizing it. He does love me! That is why he is so jealous. But why hasn't he told me?

"What?" Emmeline asks, taking the last drink from her bottle.

"He's jealous of the other men."

"Of course he is. He loves you." She says this like it's the most obvious thing in the world. I lean back against my couch, taking another sip of my wine. I completely missed his feelings. To be fair, I've been trying to court other men. And run a cursed kingdom. I've been a little busy.

"Do any of the others?" She shrugs.

"Maybe Kian. He's more guarded than Clem, though. So it's hard to tell. I think Erik loves you in a friendlier, more respectful way." She chuckles, finally meeting my gaze. I know my eyes are still wide with surprise. "You had no clue any of them loved you?" She sounds as shocked as I feel. I shake my head.

"You are so clueless." She laughs, reaching out for my wine. I take a sip, handing it to her.

"Cut me some slack. I've been a little preoccupied."

"Yeah, with getting a bunch of dicks." I snort at her. I love blunt Emmeline. She rarely relaxes like this, but it's so entertaining to watch.

"Well, Tomas doesn't love me. I know that. But he may love Zander."

"Oh," she croons, sitting up. "Do you think so?" She passes me the bottle. I drink, nodding in response.

"Definitely. He is always in the stables with him. Even Sunette noticed!"

"Well, if Sunette said something, it must be serious." I chuckle at the thought of Tomas coming to the castle to fall in love with a princess but finding love with the stableman. I sigh, finishing off my bottle and dropping it on the floor.

"We need to plan your coronation. I know you just wore yellow to the winter solstice, but gods, you look stunning in that color." I mutter a noise in agreement.

"Hand me that pillow, please." She passes it over absentmindedly.

"A yellow gown would make that necklace Clem gave you stand out. Unless you have another one made. I think you should wear...." I throw the pillow at her again, hitting her in the face. Her inability to recognize the pattern makes me laugh harder than the pillow hitting her.

"We can talk about that tomorrow," I whine.

"Well, why don't you send for one of those dicks to bring us more wine. And maybe some bread. Or pie? Is there any pie?" She looks very excited over the thought of pie. I rise from the couch, stretching my hands above my head, swaying as the alcohol courses through my veins.

"What are you doing?" she asks, confused about why I'm standing. It is too early to call it a night, but we need more wine. And snacks, apparently.

"Who do you think I normally send to fetch one of those dicks?" She thinks for a minute, then points to her chest.

"Me?" She looks so innocent. I just love her. I kiss her on her forehead.

"Yes, you fop. I'll go myself. I would hate to disturb your evening." I curtsey in front of her before ungracefully walking around the furniture.

"Well, thank you." She calls out as I reach the door, "Don't forget the pie!"

I wander through the halls slowly, making my way to the kitchen. The alcohol is keeping most thoughts away in my search for more. I'm not currently concerned about who loves me or who I love. Though, if I'm being totally honest, it's Clem and Kian. That thought slams through my body, causing me to stumble. Maybe the alcohol isn't keeping away my thoughts as well as I want it to. I just need more. Trying to push all that gibberish to the side, I plunder into the kitchen. As I dig through the small wine cellar we keep up here, a pair of hands slip around my waist.

"Can I help..."

"Kian!" I jolt back, crashing into him, startled by his sudden appearance. I thought I was alone in here. "Fuck, oh shit. I'm sorry!" I turn to make sure I didn't hurt him. I crashed into him pretty hard. He laughs, grabbing my arms to settle me down.

"I'm fine," his lilting accent is so soothing. "What are you doing in here?"

"Emmeline and I are out of wine. And pie, apparently." He laughs at my response.

"Let me help," he bows, grabbing a couple bottles from the shelf. I grab two more and turn to leave the kitchen.

"Wait. I need food. Emmeline will have my head if I return without any." He places his bottles on the counter, moving through the space, grabbing bread, cheese, and fruits.

"No pie around."

"Fuck. Well, you'll just have to come with me. She won't believe me." We grab all the items and make our way back to my room. I bump into him several times. Some of it is playful, and some of it is the alcohol.

"Are you two just up there drinking?" I nod in response.

"It's tradition. After the first good snowfall, we drink." He smiles, watching me as I sway through the steps.

"How much have you already had?"

"Just one."

"One glass?" he looks incredulously at me.

"No, one bottle! I'm not that easily drunk."

"And you need two more?" He gives me a judgmental look, but I'm not bothered.

"No. One for me. One for Emmeline. Two for you. You have to catch up." His grin grows wide, mine involuntarily matching his. I love his smile. It's so encompassing, like I could bask in the glory that is his smile.

"I'm invited?"

"Yes. You have the snacks." This is obvious, right? I lead him passed the guards, who eye him suspiciously but don't say anything. My room is quiet. I look around for Emmeline.

"She must have gone to the privy." I shrug, setting the bottles down and reaching for the corkscrew. I try to put it in the cork but miss, bouncing it off the bottle. He takes it from me, insisting he opens them. Not a problem for me. I grab a piece of bread, settling back on the couch. I tell him to open three, reaching for the first one.

"So you two just drink and eat food?"

"And gossip." I take a large gulp of wine, glad he grabbed this bottle. It's one of my favorites. I moan, savoring the smooth, rich taste. He uncorks the third bottle.

"Who do you gossip about?"

"You," I say bluntly, no longer caring what comes out of my mouth. "And Clem. And Erik." I nod, taking a small sip. "Oh, and Tomas. Oh, let me sit up so you can sit here. That is Emmeline's spot." I move on the couch, making room for him to join me. He sits, drinking from his own bottle. He wraps his arm around my shoulder.

"What did you say about me?" I relax into his side, feeling calm and happy from the wine.

"Emmeline thinks you're my true love." I wave my hands in the air dramatically. It's the reaction I always have to suppress when talking about true love, but I have an excuse to make it now. Plus, no one is judging me as the Princess. I get to be who I would be without the crown and title on these nights. Most nights, I remain somewhat restrained. Not on the nights we are drinking, though.

"What do you think?" Kian whispers in my ear. A chill runs through my body, sending jolts through my pussy. I resist the urge to moan at him.

"I think," I tap my chin, "you're pretty handsome, and that magic fun ball is pretty great." He chuckles, leaning back to drink from his bottle.

"You do enjoy the magic fun balls." I nod enthusiastically.

"Who do you think is my true love, Kian?" My breath catches, realizing I want him to honestly answer the question. There is no right answer, though. No response would make everything instantly better. No matter who it is, there will be a fallout with the other men. He shrugs nonchalantly.

"It could be Clem. It could be me. Maybe Erik."

"It's not Erik." I shake my head, drinking more. Where is Emmeline? She should be back by now.

"Ah, you kissed him earlier. No magic, then?" I shake my head, not adding anything else. I don't need to kiss and tell. We sit silently for a few minutes. I stare at the fire, my mind mostly quiet. Kian shifts, wrapping his other arm around my waist. He presses his lips against my ear. My eyes close, soaking in his closeness.

"What if I told you," he whispers, his breath warm against the shell of my ear, "I am falling for you?" I twist sharply, looking him in the eyes. He is so good at hiding his emotions. I rarely know exactly what he's thinking. Since we've gotten closer, it seems as if he's gotten better at hiding them.

"Are you?" I whisper. He doesn't say anything, just pulls me closer to his body. His lips meet mine, kissing me deeply. I wrap my arms around his shoulders, hearing the bottle thud against his back. I forgot that it was still in my hand. He doesn't seem to mind. I slip my tongue into his mouth, wanting more of him. My entire core is heating at the thought of this man loving me. I twist my body, ready to straddle him. Before I get the chance, Emmeline walks into the room.

"I'm back! Oh! Shit. Sorry. I'll be back later." She turns to walk away, but Kian calls her back with a chuckle. I silently curse him, but it's probably better. Who knows what I would have done tonight? He tells her how he brought food and more wine. Emmeline grabs her bottle and takes a long swig. We settle in, discussing more drama Kian knows about. He shows us a couple of simple spells. Spells he claims are safe while drinking. Nothing burns down, so I guess he's right. My mind is filled with the thought of him falling for me. That, combined with my own earlier realization that I also have feelings for him, consumes my thoughts for the evening.

We have a wonderful time, not mentioning true love again. We finish off the wine and the snacks, passing out on the couches. Kian leaves at some point after we pass out. He covers both of us, stoking the fire and removing the wine bottles from the room. He doesn't stay in the room with me. It's a little disappointing to wake alone with a splitting headache, but things could have been worse.

Chapter 23

JASMIN

Snow is life now. The ground has been covered for two solid weeks. There is no more fresh snow. It's gross and dirty and filled with leaves. This is the part of winter I can do without. It's never going to end. Call me dramatic, but I'm ready for either a good pile of fresh snow, so I can justify hiding in my room or for it to all be gone and the heat to come back. That's all I really want. All this gross stuff makes me restless.

I'm going to the stables today. My hope is that Vesper is also restless, and I can take him out for a bit. Finn is lounging with Clem in the library. I'm glad they like doing that, but I need a break. I need to do something else. I trudge through the slush toward the stables. I realize this may not be ideal riding conditions, but I'm getting out of the castle regardless.

An odd moaning sound comes from one of the stalls in the stable. I'm worried one of the horses is injured, so I rush toward the sound. I find the stall the noise is coming from, pushing through the door in a rush. I'm stunned by what I see. Tomas and Zander are lying on a pile of hay. Tomas is on top with his hand under Zander's pants. Zander's hands are under Tomas's shirt. Their lips are red and swollen. I stop where I am, unsure how to react to this situation. Zander and

Tomas look back at me at the same time. Tomas jumps up, moving away quickly. Zander jerks in reaction to Tomas's quick movements like he's hurt.

Tomas's eyes are wide, darting around the stall, looking for an exit. I hold my hands up to him, trying to relay that I'm not a threat to him. He's not in a good emotional state to react safely right now. I want to stop him from having another fit, but I'm unsure how to address this situation. He's gone from one emotional extreme to the next. Zander finally rolls over, sitting up in the hay.

"It's not what you think, Princess." Tomas is nearly shouting, nervous about being caught. For many people, it could be a severe situation to be caught in. I reach out to Zander, offering a hand to help him up. He stands next to me. I ask if he's okay. He says he is, dusting his pants off and adjusting them to fit correctly again. Tomas watches us, still alert and aware of everything around him. I sidestep toward the stall door, wanting to block Tomas in the stall but not wanting him to realize that. I don't want him to run and spook the horses. I eye Zander, who is watching Tomas. He is concerned, but it's more than just worry about the horses.

"How long has this been going on?" I nod toward Tomas. Maybe if I don't make a big deal of it, Tomas will calm down. Zander rubs the back of his neck, looking over at me.

"Oh, um, a month or two." I suppress the urge to swoon over this.

"There are better places to do this, you know?" I chuckle, waving my hand at the hay. Tomas is only watching us now. He isn't searching for some other threat. This is a good sign, but we aren't totally in the clear.

"Does Sabeko know?"

"No. Well, probably. You know how Papa is." I snort at his response. I've had my own fair share of run-ins with Sabeko. "Wait," Zander turns to me more fully. "Does Mama know, too?" I roll my eyes at him.

"Of course, she knows, Zander. She's suspected for a long time. Probably since before you two even thought about doing anything. Surely, you know her better than that."

"Damn," Zander curses. "I was just telling her I wanted to find a girlfriend to throw her off the trail." I laugh loudly at him. There are people he could fool in the castle. I'm probably one of them. Sunette is absolutely not.

"Did you know?" Tomas asks weakly, looking at me. My face sobers, not wanting to upset him.

"I've suspected for a while, Tomas." He wraps his arms around his body, looking embarrassed. "It's not a big deal here. Not everyone is accepting of this," I wave my hands between the two of them. "But I will do everything I can to ensure your safety. I can't make any promises if you return to Tilrade, but here, you will be safe." He looks between Zander and me in disbelief.

"Really?"

"Of course, Tomas." Zander is watching him curiously. Tomas is still glancing between the two of us. I reach over to nudge Zander's arm, getting his attention. When he looks at me, I nod toward Tomas. Zander's eyes raise in understanding. He walks over and takes Tomas's hand, pressing a kiss to it. I can see Tomas trying to recoil in my presence. It's hard to adjust to being accepted when you haven't been for so long.

"I hope you know you can trust me, Tomas. I mean what I say." Zander squeezes Tomas's hand in his to drive home my words. Tomas looks at Zander. As their eyes meet, his shoulders begin to relax. He isn't comfortable, but he is starting to see that he can be.

"I just stopped by to see if I could take Vesper out for a bit."

Zander shakes his head at me, not letting go of Tomas's hand. "No, Jasmin. The roads are too bad, and a storm is coming soon. The roads will likely be impassable for several days." I curse. That is not what I wanted to hear. I turn to leave but stop myself. Instead, I step over to the two men standing side by side. I throw one arm over each of their necks, pulling them into a tight hug. I feel Zander's hand on my back, then Tomas's.

"I love you two." I step back, rubbing their cheeks. "Be safe, okay? The stables in the middle of the day are probably not the best idea. The castle has one hundred and forty-two rooms, many with locks. Pick better locations!" We laugh together as I turn to leave. They promise to pick somewhere better next time. As I walk out of the stable, I notice they are hugging. I'm so happy they have each other. They are closer in age than Tomas and me. I hadn't realized Zander liked boys, but it doesn't surprise me either.

I wander through the castle, unsure of what to do now. I could find Emmeline and plan the coronation. Honestly, that sounds terrible. I would rather visit Oscar in the dungeon. I shudder at the thought. I get regular updates on him from Henry. Oscar is eating but still insufferable. Alright, maybe planning the coronation wouldn't be that terrible, but it's still not something I'm interested in doing.

A draft sweeps through the hallway. I pull my sweater tighter, feeling caged in. When I was a child, my mother would load us up, and we would travel during the winter. Sometimes Father went, but not always. At the time, I didn't enjoy being away for so long, but I always enjoyed traveling. Visiting other kingdoms and seeing how the people lived. We always came home with extravagant gifts. As I got older, my father insisted I stay in the kingdom over winter. One day I would be in charge, he always said. I don't think he envisioned this reality for me, though.

I find myself in the library. I don't remember walking here, but this is where my feet took me. It sounds quiet, but I don't think it's empty. I decide to walk around slowly, checking things out before I search for who might be in here. I check the logbook and peruse the closest shelves. As I near the alcove Clem is in, I hear a distinct thudding noise. A tail is thumping quickly against the floor. A smile spreads across my face. Finn is definitely in here. Nails scratch against the floor, then a whining sound follows. Clem shushes Finn. I can't be positive, but I don't think he realizes I am in here. Finn whines again at Clem, who shushes louder.

"Oh, I'm just so lonely. I have no one to pet. And I have this biscuit and no good boy to give it to." I speak softly, but Finn hears every word. He quickly runs out of the alcove, jumping at me when he sees me. I hand him the biscuit I found on the table, probably one Clem brought. Finn wags his tail as I pet him more. After a few minutes, he walks into the alcove, nudging Clem with his nose. Absentmindedly, Clem grabs another biscuit from his pocket, handing it to Finn. He is completely engrossed in his book, not giving any attention to Finn or me. I debate just leaving him, but that doesn't sound like something I would normally do. Instead, I climb onto the lounger with Clem, snuggling into his side.

"Hello, Jas."

He adjusts his position to accommodate me but doesn't stop reading. I turn the cover to see what he is reading. I recognize the book, having read it several times. The author of this book wrote some very detailed scenes between the main characters. It's one of my favorite books for that reason. Clem is enthralled in the book, mostly ignoring my presence in favor of reading. Well, that's just unacceptable.

"Read to me?"

He has to read slower when he reads out loud. The sound of his voice is comforting. The deep timbre of his voice enriches the story in a way reading the words myself doesn't. The way his chest vibrates with the words brings me solace, even on the worst of days.

"Want me to start over?"

He's already more than halfway through the story. As much as I love listening to him, I don't need him to start over. Plus, I happen to know he's getting to the good parts.

"No. I've read this one before. Have you?"

"No. First time."

A smile spreads across my face as he starts reading. I snuggle tighter against his chest, closing my eyes to take in his voice and vibrating chest. In the story, the man is visiting the woman in her home. They are sitting on a couch together. At first, others are in the house, but soon they leave, and the couple is alone. This is the best part of the book. This is the first time in the book the couple gets intimate. In most books, the scene changes to the next, implying what the couple did. This author described every last detail, though. I can't wait for Clem to get to the really good stuff. I wonder how he will react to it.

I trace circles across his chest as he reads. The anticipation of what's coming in the book makes my entire body tingle. I fight the urge to grind against him, my clit needing more pressure. He reads about the couple moving close to each other and growing more intimate. Clem hasn't shown any signs of reacting to what is happening. Meanwhile, my body is on fire, and I'm focusing all my energy on not humping his leg. I bite my lip, hoping the pain will distract me from the insatiable need in my gut. It doesn't. Somehow, it seems to make it worse. I should probably consider why pain makes my desire more intense.

My hand trails down his chest, resting just over his navel. I can't help but touch him. His stomach is smooth beneath his shirt. Slipping my hand under his shirt and caressing his warm skin would be easy. Let my fingers drop lower beneath his pants. His breath hitches, but he doesn't stop reading. I open my eyes, shifting to look up at him. His face is flushed now, his pupils growing larger. In the story, the man is cupping the woman's breasts. Clem's arm is wrapped around my body, holding the book above my head as he reads. The other is tucked on his side, resting on the lounger. He may not be in a great position to grab my breasts as much as I want him to. I am in a good position to cradle him, though. I slide my hand up, resting against his pec. I use my thumb to rub circles around his nipple through his shirt. It buds under my touch. His breathing becomes more erratic. Now he is struggling to read the words. I grin, shifting enough to wrap my lips around his nipple my cheek was resting against.

I tongue his nipple through the shirt, leaving a wet spot. He moans, whispering my name, trying to abandon the book. This scene is too good for him to stop now.

"Keep reading."

He groans but starts again. The man is hovering over the woman, pressing his erection into her. I tug Clem's nipple back into my mouth, scraping my teeth against it as his chest vibrates. My other hand drifts lower, over his stomach, down to his almost erect member. I palm in through his pants, wishing they weren't there. He moans, pressing his lips against my forehead, but continues reading. The scene in the book is led by the man, but I have no intention of letting Clem not finish this scene.

I pull my hand back, tugging his shirt away from his pants. My fingers finally brush against his warm skin. He thrusts his waist into my hand, but I hold him down. I teasingly drag my fingers along the skin just beneath his waistband. His words are choppy, inconsistent with his own arousal. I slip my hand further beneath his trousers, finding the leaking tip of his dick. I circle my fingers lightly around the tip as he groans, tipping his head back. Knowing I have this effect on him sends a spasm through my pussy. He moans my name again. I shift my body over him, wrapping my fingers around the head of his cock. I squeeze it gently between my fingers as I press my lips against his jaw.

"You haven't finished reading the scene, Clem."

"Fuck the scene, Jas. I want you." Oh, my heart burns at that comment. I press my lips against his but pull back quickly. He leans forward, trying to kiss me again. I slip my hand out of his trousers, and he gasps as his cock jerks.

"I'm going to stop every time you do." I tease. He grinds his teeth in anger, frustrated at the situation I have created. He shifts his position, holding the book higher, and begins reading again. Now the man has his cock deep inside the woman, and both cry out in pleasure. I kiss down his chest as my fingers work on the laces of his pants. Once they are loosened, I drag his shirt up, exposing his smooth stomach. Unable to resist, I lick from his belly button to just below his nipple. I latch onto the bud, nipping it slightly with my teeth. He whines but doesn't stop reading. I press his pants back, with him shifting his hips to help and pull his cock out. I wrap my fingers around it, stroking up and down as I continue to lick his stomach. The scene is almost over. The man is describing the growing ache he is feeling. I kiss down Clem's stomach, teasing him, kissing, and licking near the base of his cock without ever touching it.

Clem is reading the last few sentences of the man's orgasm. Unfortunately, the author doesn't describe the woman's. Typical. Doesn't matter now, though. My lips hover over the side of his penis, blowing hot air along the length, never quite touching. Once Clem says the man releases inside the woman, I wrap my lips around his cock, taking in as much as I can. I swirl my tongue around, getting it wet enough to slide in and out easily. He groans loudly but reads the next few sentences as I bob up and down.

"There, they fucking came. Can I please stop reading now?" It's more a demand than a question. I slip off him, kneeling on the floor in front of him.

"Stand up."

He tosses the book down, standing in front of me. I grab his hips, pulling him closer as I wrap my lips around his cock again. His hips jerk, trying to get further inside me.

"Fuck, you look amazing like this, Jasmin."

My pussy twitches at his words. I press my tongue against the bottom of his cock as I slide back. I grab his hands, pulling them to my head. He tangles his fingers in my hair, tugging on it slightly. I suck hard, pulling his cock with me as I glide back. He jerks again. I can tell he is holding back, probably worried about hurting me. I look up at him, meeting his eyes. They are burning with desire for me. He bites his lip. He is holding back, wanting more from this. I pop my lips off his cock, wrapping my fingers around his wrists near my head.

"Fuck me," I whisper.

"What?" He looks confused.

I lean in, swirling my tongue around his cock, coating it in spit. Then I open my mouth wide, holding my tongue out for him. I meet his gaze again. He looks uncertain but also very desperate. I wait, watching him as he slowly presses forward. His cock enters my mouth, sliding deep until it hits the back of my throat. I close my eyes, fighting off the urge to gag. He pulls back but doesn't take his cock out. He slowly slides back in. I drop my hands from him, letting him set the pace for this. It takes him a moment to realize I am giving him control. His thrusts grow deeper but still slow and gentle. I slide my hands up the back of his legs until I reach his ass. He pulls out, but before he can move back in, I tug his ass. His cock slams into the back of my throat. I gag at the rough intrusion. He groans loudly, clearly enjoying the roughness. I press his hips back, then slam him in again. My eyes water, but I look up at him, hoping to convey that I want him to take over.

"You want me to fuck your throat, huh?"

I groan around his cock. His fingers tighten in my hair, alternating between massaging and pulling. The shifting sensations cause my entire core to tingle.

"Do you want me to go easy on you?" His voice is deep and demanding. I shake my head around his cock, buried deep in my throat. My tongue swirls around it, tasting the beads of pre-cum leaking from the tip.

"Good. Tap my hands if it's too much." I suck his cock hard to let him know I understand.

His fingers tighten around the back of my head. I drop my hands to my thighs, releasing the tension in my mouth around his cock. He edges back before slamming into my throat. My eyes water as I gag around the brutal intrusion. He thrusts deep several times, causing me to gag repeatedly.

"That's it. Choke around my cock, like a good little princess."

I moan at his words. Something about him being in control sends shock waves through my body. My own hips grind in search of their release. His words are harsh, but hearing them in this context feels good. I know how he feels about me. I know that I am making him feel as good as I do. He picks up the pace, slamming into my throat. I wrap my hands around his thighs, needing to touch him more. He hesitates for a moment, then resumes his brutal pace. I am gagging around his cock. Tears are streaming down my cheeks as my nose begins to run too. I can't do anything about that, but he doesn't seem to mind. I slide one hand up the inside of his thigh, reaching to cup his balls. It's hard to hold them at the pace he is thrusting, but I do my best.

"Yes, Jasmin. Worship me on your knees like the slut you are."

I give a small snort at that comment but caress his balls between my fingers. He thrusts into me several more times before his balls tighten. He mumbles that he is about to come but continues pumping in and out of my throat. I feel the first jets of warm liquid hit the back of my throat. He pulls back, stroking his cock into my mouth. I hold my mouth open, letting him finish on my tongue. He groans, shooting several more strands of his cum into my open mouth. Some land on my lips, most on my tongue. He takes his hand off his cock, grabbing my jaw. His thumb and fingertips press into my cheeks, holding my mouth open. His seed tastes salty and bitter, but I keep it on my tongue for him.

"Such a good girl for me. Now swallow."

My insides twist at his words as I follow his directions. I lick my lips, removing the last of his semen from my mouth. He pulls me up to stand, crashing his lips into mine. He wraps one arm around my shoulders. The other is instantly down my pants, his fingers circling my clit. I moan against his mouth, sinking down onto his hand. He slips two fingers inside me, pressing his palm against my clit instead. His fingers stroke up and down, rubbing that spot inside that feels so amazing. I'm wiggling against him, writhing as my own orgasm grows.

"Come for me, Jas. Come over my fingers."

He presses his palm into my clit more. Then shifts his hand so his thumb is on my clit, providing more direct pressure to my most sensitive spot. I moan against his chest, pussy clenching around his fingers.

"That's it. Show me how much you like to be fucked by a farm hand."

My body tenses in pleasure, but he slows his fingers. He doesn't remove them, just slows down, drawing me back from the edge. I whimper at the change, then he starts up again. I'm already tense.

"You're so wet, Jasmin. Did you enjoy having your throat fucked?"

I groan, biting my lip. His thumb flicks against my clit as his fingers relentlessly thrust inside. My legs buckle, causing him to tighten his arm around me to support my weight. My arms wrap around his back, grabbing his shoulders for support.

"Of course you did. That's what you're good at. Taking dick like a harlot."

My face is pressed against his chest, breathing in his scent as my body flares with the heat from my impending orgasm. His words are so demeaning yet have such an impact on me. His thumb hits just the right angle on my clit, and my body explodes. Stars dance around my vision as my body tenses, clenching and spasming with delight.

"Good girl. You come so beautifully."

My pussy clenches again at his words. He chuckles, noticing the movement, too. My legs shake as my body rolls through the orgasm. He slides his hand out of my leggings slowly, causing me to groan at the loss. He scoops his arm under my legs, lifting me briefly before lowering me back onto the lounger. My eyes are still closed, allowing my body to accept my soul again. He is really good at drawing these soul-defying orgasms out of me. I have never had such experiences as I do with him. We lie together for several minutes, breathing roughly, eyes closed, savoring the bliss.

"Did I hurt you?"

His finger is stroking my cheeks, rubbing the tear streaks away. I open my mouth to answer him but flinch at the soreness at the back of my throat.

"I did!"

He looks panicked, trying to get up to do something. I don't know how he thinks he's going to fix a bruised throat. I press my hand on his chest, forcing him back. I'm not ready to move around yet, out of his arms or in general. I just want to lie here in his warmth.

"I'm fine," I croak. "Just a little sore. I'll get some tea later. It's fine."

He settles back, a skeptical look on his face. His hands are rubbing my shoulders, arms, back, all over, trying to reassure himself that I am, in fact, okay. I sigh against his chest, slowly running my fingers across his body. I'm not concerned about what hurts. I'm just content being close to him. The ache in my throat and on my clit only serves to remind me of how glorious this moment feels. My fingers wrap around his neck, tangling in his hair. Most days, he has his shoulder-length blonde hair tied back. I wish he would wear it loose more. His hair is thick and beautiful, and maybe I want to play with his hair as much as he does mine.

"Have you done that before?" I ask, turning my head up to look at him. My voice is quiet, hoarse from the soreness. He shakes his head, wrapping his arms around me tight like I might drift away from him.

"No. I've always wanted to but never trusted anyone enough to ask." My first thought is that he trusted me, but then I realize he didn't ask me. I had to tell him. Does he not trust me? I try to push back to look at him, but his arms tighten, keeping me in place. I chew on my lip, debating whether I should say anything. That was my intent when I pulled away, but he stopped me. Does he understand how his comment affected me? His body is tense, his fingers still but firm.

"I do...trust you." I listen calmly, feeling some relief that he caught onto my confusion. "I didn't want to ask you for something like that, though. It's not... normal, and I didn't want you to feel uncomfortable." I tangle my fingers in his hair again, tugging at the leather strip he has it tied back with to loosen some strands. His words settle in my mind, understanding coursing through. Some leaders will jail or commit peasants to the hospital for sexual deviancy. Even though most leaders are partaking in similar, sometimes worse, situations themselves. I've never been of that mindset, but since it isn't a topic we openly discuss, he wouldn't know that. The same with Tomas not understanding earlier. While processing his comments, I unintentionally pull the strip out of his hair. I offer a weak apology, leaving the string on his shoulder for later. He presses a kiss on my forehead. His grip loosens, but he doesn't let go.

"Do you mind the things I say to you?"

"No," I say bashfully. "I really like that." I can feel my cheeks flush under his fingers. His fingers have resumed stroking my cheek, rubbing along the scars, drawing circles on my jaw, just caressing my face. He tips my chin up toward his face and whispers. A thought breezes by casually that his touch on my scars doesn't elicit any uncomfortable feelings.

"Hm, my Princess is a sexual deviant. I'll remember that." He gently kisses my lips as butterflies flutter around my stomach. His kiss is soft and gentle, completely contrasting with how he just treated me. I love every bit of it. Clem can pull off both being harsh and controlling and gentle and tender. I realize I need both sides. I need someone to tear me down, make me feel things I don't want to feel, but put me back together again. That is why Clem feels so right to me. He is giving me something I didn't know I needed or wanted.

I close my eyes, not wanting to think about those things anymore. My fingers twist in his thick hair, basking under his warm touch. Finn walks back over, nails clanking on the floor. I didn't realize he left, but that's probably for the best. He shouldn't be exposed to our sexual deviancy. Clem moves his arm, pulling out a biscuit for Finn. He munches the biscuit, settling back on the floor beneath us. I smile at how comfortable this feels. Being in Clem's arms, Finn napping on the floor. If only I had been Tia and run away with him, we could have lived a life like this every day.

Chapter 24

JASMIN

Breakfast is honestly my least favorite meal of the day. Most days, I skip it; I would rather sleep for an extra hour than sit at the table trying to make idle chat when I can barely keep my eyes open. However, my throat is aching, and I need tea to soothe it. I haven't found anyone who willingly brings tea to my room so I can avoid everyone else, yet, not even Emmeline will do it without complaints. I don't particularly feel like explaining why I need the tea. So here I am, in the dining hall with everyone else. Several people are surprised to see me. My focus is torn between not scowling at them and just finding some fucking tea and honey.

Kian walks up, holding out an empty mug to me. A thankful smile flashes across my face before I realize it's empty. Then the scowl returns. This fool has the audacity to laugh at me. I've never been told I have the glare that could kill, but that doesn't stop me from trying to kill this man with my eyes.

"I didn't know what you would want to drink, Princess." His voice is teasing, and I don't think I like it. "I thought you might appreciate some help. There are drinks over here." His arm waves toward another table, then he leans close to me. "I can help you get to that table without interruption, assuming you don't try to kill me first." There is humor in his whisper. The sun may already be shining on this winter day, but this is still too early for this bullshit. I simply nod to him, relaxing my face so my glare doesn't kill him. Yet.

Kian escorts me to the table with the drinks, keeping his promise to keep others away while I get my beverage. I fill my mug with hot tea and pour in some honey. He asks if I want anything else. I shake my head at him; my throat is bruised to the point I don't want to talk or eat right now. I had no idea Clem's actions would have such painful consequences, but that won't stop me from doing that again. My throat may hurt, but it was completely worth it.

We go to a table, sitting down with Erik and Clem. I meet Clem's eyes as I sip the hot beverage. It is the perfect temperature to soothe my aching throat. My eyes close as the warmth engulfs the pain, releasing the tension. I sigh into the mug; the only reason I don't moan is that my throat isn't fully functioning yet. When I open my eyes, Clem looks down at his food, a slight blush on his cheeks. Kian looks inquisitive as he searches my face.

"Is your tea good, Princes?" Kian inquires.

"Very." I croak. It's a terrible sound, like a frog sitting at the table instead of an actual princess. I cough several times, trying to clear my throat. Kian is smirking knowingly. Clem blushes harder, a few strands of his hair barely concealing the bright red on his cheeks. Erik reaches over to pat my back, trying to help. After a moment, I take another sip of my tea, feeling better.

"Sorry. Yes. My tea is perfect today. I should thank the kitchen maid. I think I'll go do that now."

I stand to leave as quickly as I can. That was fairly embarrassing, and I'm still not mentally awake enough to be around people yet. Kian grabs my hand, preventing me from leaving the table.

"No, stay. You can tell her later. You aren't around for the early meal anymore since the Lords left. We miss you." He waves a hand between the three men seated with me. I spend several hours daily with these men; I doubt they miss me. Erik is grinning and nodding, encouraging me to stay. Clem has a bashful but hopeful look in his eyes. He is trying not to give anything away as to the reason my throat is sore, but I am almost positive Kian already knows. I sit back down on the bench, nodding that I'll stay. Instead of talking, I sip my tea, watching them eat. Instantly, Kian and Erik start a conversation about whether a witch could beat an armed warrior. I get a distinct feeling that this is something they have discussed multiple times before. I listen to their arguments, both making logical points and equally passionate about why their choice would win over the other. They create rules for the hypothetical fight, change them, and adapt their character to fit that battle. It's interesting without needing too much brain power to consume. It's not a terrible way to start the day.

"Clem, you've been awfully quiet," Kian quips. Of course, he comments on that. "Don't you think the witch would be better in a mountainous region than a trained warrior?"

"Oh, sure." Clem offers unenthusiastically, clearly distracted with other thoughts. I reach across the table to steal some of his bread he isn't eating. He meets my gaze, but I can't decipher his thoughts. He's closed off, lost in his own mind. He offers me the last of his bread, then rises from the bench.

"I'm meeting with Mikhail to discuss the upcoming season." He takes the rest of his food and leaves. I watch him go. He doesn't rush but doesn't dawdle, either. He was trying to get away quickly without actually doing that. I can't help the sting I feel in my chest. I wish he would tell me what he is thinking. I know things are bothering him, things concerning me. With the other men still around and the curse still unbroken, I can understand him not wanting to share everything with me. It could potentially lead to heartache, but is that not worth it?

"Isn't the season still three months away?" Kian asks.

"About two at this point. They will start prepping the fields after the final snow, but they will work on plans for where to plant and what chores to assign everyone when it is time," I explain. I have spoken with Mikhail several times over the years about what he does during the winter seasons. "But it isn't urgent," I add quietly. Clem didn't need to rush off like he did. He is really giving me whiplash, in addition to the sore throat.

"Do you have plans today, Princess?" Kian turns to me as I stuff another bite of bread in my mouth. I shake my head no. At this point, I am openly avoiding the coronation planning. Emmeline will handle all of that for me, right? She loves that stuff and is paid well for it.

"Perfect!" He claps his hands together in delight. "Then I have a surprise for you."

My eyes light up with excitement. I do love surprises, especially from Kian. He always has the best surprises. I don't think I need any more magic fun balls, but I will absolutely not say no. My clit throbs, both with ecstasy and pain, a gentle reminder of Clem's fingers. Over the rest of breakfast, Erik tells me about the training plan he and Henry have devised and started working on with Tomas and a few other men. It sounds like a wonderful strategy and could be very beneficial when we can recruit new members in the spring. It gives me hope for the future once we break the curse.

Kian leads me to his room, informing me he needs to collect an item before he gives me the surprise. I try to quell the growing ache between my legs, but it's hard to do when my mind only focuses on a certain vibrating ball. The bachelors' wing is much quieter than it used to be. I mostly avoided the area when they arrived, but I could always hear it from several rooms away. Now, with only the four men left, men who are involved in other activities around the castle, it is calm and quiet down the hall. Kian opens his door, and my mouth pops open in shock. His bed, table, chair, bench, and every other surface he has is covered in books and loose parchments. I step toward the desk, lifting a few papers to look at them.

"I didn't know you created such a mess in here, Kian." I tease, reading over the pages. It appears to be notes on spells.

"Ah, yes. Well, magic isn't simple and sometimes requires complex solutions, which are better written down to fine-tune. Don't want to utter the wrong phrase and turn Finn into a frog." We both laugh, smirking at his joke. Finn went outside this morning, and I haven't seen him since. I didn't wait for him, knowing someone would let him in eventually. He loves prancing in the snow, and I love not freezing my nipples off before I'm fully awake. I glance at a few other pages, unable to make sense of anything.

"Got it!" Kian calls from his wardrobe, stuffing something in his pocket. I leave the papers in their place, walking back to the door to exit his incredibly messy room. He pulls the door shut, offering his arm to me. I wrap my hand around his elbow as we walk away from the wing. He hasn't told me his plan, nor have I asked. At this point, I'm just content with having something else to do.

"Do you think you'll have any major issues dealing with the covens?" I inquire. We haven't discussed the positions I assigned everyone officially. I've chatted with Erik and Tomas on a few occasions. Clem hasn't said anything about it to me. I am worried he may be overwhelmed or unsure how to go about the position. It isn't like they have anyone to guide them in these roles. Knowing Clem is speaking to Mikhail today gives some relief. Kian has mentioned excitement and nervousness over his position but not many specifics.

"I don't foresee many if I can get my grandmother onboard. I think she will be helpful but reserved. She will need time to trust what you want with her. Lord Alwyn isn't the best, and your father appointed him. The coven doesn't have much faith in the crown now." I nod, knowing he is speaking the truth, but hearing my father was doing less than he should have hurts. I always saw my father as a good man, and learning about his downfalls isn't easy. "No offense intended," Kian adds quickly.

I pat his arm. "No, I understand. My father was a great man but did many things he should have never done. I hope your grandmother will be willing to see me as a different leader, unwilling to allow injustices of the past any longer."

He leads me into an empty room. It is the room I found him in when I first discovered his music box. The room is untouched from the last time we were here. The room was previously used when other royal families visited to celebrate without opening the throne room. Kian whisks away from me, leaving me in the middle of the dance area. As he makes his way to the table, I take a moment to observe the room's décor. Much is still covered with sheets to protect intricate frames from dust. The walls are covered in a deep red, creating a dark, warm atmosphere. Sconces are mounted between windows with matching molding. The room was richly embellished with the intent of showing wealth. Now it sits unused, covered, empty. Maybe soon I can host the coven matrons. Perhaps the garden hands from each village can meet here with Clem.

Music fills the room as Kian turns to me, bowing with his hand out to me. He made a music box during the solstice celebrations. My heart warms at the thought of his effort into this surprise. His willingness to make these devices and share them with me gives me a sense of comfort and belonging. I take his hand, allowing him to whisk me around the room to the music. We spin through steps, twisting and turning through crescendos and the steady beat of the drums. His arm wraps around my back while the other holds my hand. It's such an easy task to dance with him like this. He's a natural, easily giving me a run for my money.

We dance through several songs before my favorite dance comes on. It's not a traditional waltz or ballroom dance. It feels more like a folk dance, which is part of the reason I love it. It is still a dance all royalty is required to know, but it is typically done to make lower class attending our events feel more welcome. My mother always despised this dance. I sway gleefully through the movements, dipping to one side, stepping, then leaping in the air, laughing excitedly.

Kian matches my movements and excitement. I'm thrilled he is enjoying this dance as much as I am. We dance through the rest of the song, then the music ends completely. We bow, bursting into a fit of laughter as the room is engulfed in silence. He leads me to a sofa and pulls me down next to him. We are both out of breath with rosy cheeks, and grins stretched across our faces.

"I almost didn't get that last song." He speaks between deep breaths, just beginning to calm down from our vigorous activity. "I only spelled the box for three songs. When they started playing that one, I rushed over to add a touch more magic and hoped it would last. I didn't actually know if the song made it in." A smile spreads across my cheeks as I rest my head on his shoulders.

"Thank you for doing that, Kian. I absolutely love those music boxes." He presses a kiss to my temple before relaxing back on the sofa. I settle against him, closing my eyes as I relax. He has a spicy scent to him, like ginger. Warm and inviting with an edge not always appreciated.

"How do you feel about finally breaking the curse?" His voice is soft in the silence but cuts through my thoughts like a sharp knife.

"I'm nervous." I give a weak chuckle, explaining my response. "I'm nervous about what will happen when the border is gone. What I will have to deal with from other kingdoms. What I will have to deal with from people in my own villages. How people will see me as the ruler of the kingdom; how they will see my true love." I pause, considering my next words carefully. "But most of all, I'm nervous about who it is." My voice is barely above a whisper when I stop speaking.

"Do you have any thoughts on who it is?"

"Some. Things are too uncertain, though. I plan to send some of you back for a few weeks until I can narrow it down once the roads are safe to travel." Kian shifts, wrapping his arm over my shoulder. I nuzzle against his chest, resting my hand against him. It would be so much easier if I just knew who it was. It would also be a lot easier if I didn't have feelings for Kian and Clem. "The hardest part is that I have no control over it. If I could decide, it might be easier. But I don't really get that choice."

"Who would you choose?" He whispers coyly in my ear. I slap his chest.

"I'm not answering that."

He brings his hand to his chest as if hurt. "Oh, Princess, you wound me."

"Shut up," I tease. "You know it might be you."

"Or it might be Clem." I stay silent at his comment, despite its truth. Kian knows how I feel for both of them and how they both feel for me. None of us have said anything more than hinting, too scared of what may not be. We are all skating around the truth, scared of getting hurt. It will burst eventually, and we will have to face these feelings we've been trying to sequester. Things won't be easy for the next few months, but I am hopeful by the next solstice, things will be easier. Or at least not so cursed.

"I would like it to be me," Kian adds softly. We don't speak about it again.

"How is planning the coronation going?" he asks after several moments. I groan loudly.

"I suppose it's going. I would love to not be involved with it at all. Apparently, I have to be, though." I roll my eyes hard over my distaste for planning. Kian laughs at me, his whole body shaking against mine.

"Do you have a date selected?"

"No. We know it will be spring, but not sure when exactly."

"What about the spring equinox? The witches would be impressed with the symbology behind that date. The equal time between light and darkness could set a good tone for the start of your reign." I consider his words. It is a good point. The shift away from the traditional religious past is something I want. For too long, our kingdom has been ruled by oppressive religions with no real meaning behind them. People go through the motions of faith, but it means little. Being cursed for eight years has a way of breaking your spirits about gods protecting you.

"Yes," I nod in response. "I like that." I tap my chin, considering this topic. I like the idea of having the coronation on the spring equinox. It will also allow the villagers time to travel if they wish to participate. I'm sure Emmeline would love decorating for spring. She could come up with several ideas for that. I will tell her about this idea next time I see her. I'm sure she will love it.

"Kian," I question slowly as the thought forms in my mind. I sit up to look at his face. He is waiting patiently, which is just one of the many qualities I absolutely admire in this man. "What if you performed the ceremony for me?" He tilts his head in bewilderment, contemplating the idea.

"Instead of the archbishop? Will he be angry?" I snort at his question.

"I have seen the archbishop once a year since the curse began. He never liked me. The only reason he stayed was that he was fond of my mother. She had him under her thumb. I want to move away from religion, though, and who better to do that than you?" I refrain from bouncing with excitement, more reasons popping into my head as I think about it.

"You are already an excellent speaker and wonderful orator. You could embellish the tradition into something more fitting for my reign. Plus, if you turn out to be my true love, do you know how romantic that would be?" I swoon teasingly, tucking my hands under my chin. "All the old biddies would keel over with jealousy." We both laugh at the thought.

"I like that idea, Princess. I'll do it for you." I clap my hands, excited over Kian overseeing the ceremony. He will be perfect for it. Now, I think I can stand to do some planning for my coronation.

Part Four

DAHLIA

Chapter 25

CLEM

Dark clouds are growing outside. A large storm will come in soon. We have already seen more snowfall in the past several days. The snow is nearly as deep as my knees. I've taken Finn outside a couple of times. He always sinks down so his belly rests on the snow's top. We have shoveled an area near the door for him to use, but he insists on plowing through the deeper snow. Jasmin doesn't like to take him down because of the cold, she claims. I think she also worries about him getting hurt or freezing in the snow, but he's always fine.

She hasn't come back to breakfast since she came down for tea. I felt miserable over hurting her but left because I was pretty sure Kian knew why she needed the tea. I may be willing to explore sexual acts with her, but I am not ready to discuss them with others, especially not over the meal table. I would love to fuck her throat again if she lets me. Maybe we can explore other facets of our sexuality. I've never had anyone I was fully comfortable discussing these topics with, but I want to do that with Jasmin.

It occurs to me I haven't actually seen Jasmin in a day or two. Finn wandered to the door on his own yesterday. I didn't see anyone else with him, not Jasmin or Emmeline. Usually, one of them is with her.

"Have you seen Jasmin lately?" I ask Erik, Tomas, Zander, and Kian, who are all sitting at the table. I've clearly interrupted whatever conversation they were having based on how they stare at me. I don't offer an apology; I simply wait for their answer. Tomas and Zander both shake their head no. Erik says he doesn't see much of her with his training schedule.

"I haven't seen her since the day she joined us for breakfast. When was the last time you saw her?" Kian asks, looking at me. Tomas and Zander begin chatting again. It's been odd seeing them together. I assume there is more than just a platonic relationship between them, but it's not an accusation I will make.

"I haven't seen her since that morning either." I stare at my plate, recounting the past few days to be sure I haven't seen her in passing. Kian shrugs.

"She is probably just busy planning the coronation. I suggested she set a date for the spring equinox." A pang of hurt tears through my chest. Why wouldn't she tell me she had selected a date for the coronation? Not that she is obligated to tell me, but I thought we might be in a place to share those details with each other. I grab my dishes, rising from the table.

"I'm going to find her," I announce to no one in particular. Kian asks that I send her to the dining hall during a meal when I find her. I agree, dropping off my dirty dishes and working my way through the castle. I don't actually know where to start, perhaps the meeting rooms. Maybe she is just planning and has lost track of time. I check every meeting room I have ever seen her in. Then the library, but that is empty too. I decide to go to her room. I don't know if the guards will let me in, but I'm going to try.

As I near her hallway, the guards move into position to stop me. I stand in front of them, desperate for answers.

"I would like to see Princess Jasmin," I state calmly, trying not to convey my concerns.

"You can't go through here." The older guard speaks, holding his hand out to stop me. I'm not trying to break through, not that I would since they have swords.

"Is she in her room?" I question; at least an answer would help.

"We can't tell you where she is." My heart sinks. That isn't helpful.

"Please, I just want to know where she is."

The younger guard steps toward me. "You need to leave, mate. We don't want to apprehend you." I throw my hands up in defeat. I didn't realize they took these duties so seriously. Jasmin hasn't let me into her room before, but surely, I've garnered enough trust to be allowed that privilege. I turn and leave, not wanting to get risk getting apprehended. I have a feeling Jasmin wouldn't visit me in the dungeons, especially if I can't even visit her rooms.

Unsure where to go next, I ponder the rooms she might be in or the people who might help. I don't know where Emmeline would be. Mikhail might know, but I don't want to bother him with this situation. He is getting some much-needed rest in his off-season. The other bachelors didn't know. Oh! Sunette would probably know. She seems to be the eyes and ears of the castle, learning all the secrets before anyone else does. I rush to the greenhouse, not wanting to waste any time.

I find Sunette walking between the plants, humming, and pruning some leaves. Her humming is very soothing. If I weren't already on a mission, I would be content to sit and listen, taking in the strong scent of the still-blooming jasmine plants. It attests to Sunette's abilities that the plant is still in bloom.

"Don't dawdle, boy. What do you want?" She doesn't even turn to acknowledge me, speaking as if it were the plants she is regarding.

"I want to know where she is." My voice is weak and uncertain. I know I don't need to elaborate for Sunette. She already knows what I want. She turns to look at me, searching my face for whatever secrets she knows how to harvest. "Please." I offer softly.

"She is indisposed now. You can see her in a few days."

"Indisposed? Is she sick? What is wrong with her?" My mind is racing with concern. She was fine a couple of days ago. How sick is she? Have they called the healer? Who is taking care of her? Why a few days?

"It's nothing to concern yourself with. She'll find you when she is better." I move next to Sunette, taking her hand in mine.

"Please, I can't wait a few days. I need to see her now." Her eyes are full of pity, but there is understanding too.

"Clem, it isn't serious. She won't be happy if you try to see her now. She will recover soon." Her thick sing-song accent does nothing to lessen my fear. I'm about two minutes from dropping to my knees and begging to see Jasmin. Now that I know she is sick, I can't possibly give up my pursuit. "Please," I whisper again.

Sunette heaves a deep breath, placing her tools down on the workbench. She turns back to me, eyeing me suspiciously. "I will take you to her, but don't blame me when she gets angry."

"I won't. I just need to see her." Sunette wraps a scarf around her neck, leading the way back to the castle. She stops in the hallway, asking if I have been to her rooms before. I explain that I haven't, that I have only been outside the hallway, but the guards wouldn't let me in. She sighs deeply before carrying on down the hall. She doesn't speak again. My concern grows over Jasmin's condition. Why wouldn't anyone tell us she is sick? We have been here for several months. It is common knowledge one of us is her true love. It's also common knowledge Kian and I both have strong feelings for her. Why is she suffering alone without us even knowing?

Sunette stops in front of the guards. The younger one watches with curiosity; the older guard has a certain wariness in his eyes as he looks between Sunette and me. She releases a sharp breath, motioning to me. She announces I am with her before walking through the hallway without warning. Neither of the guards does anything to stop her, so I follow behind quickly. She clearly has a reputation not to be messed with around here.

She stops at the door to Jasmin's room, raising her eyes to the skies with a silent prayer on her lips. I want to push past her and enter, but I get a feeling that I should follow her lead. With as serious as she can be, I get a distinct impression that I have no idea what I am about to walk in on. Sunette glances at me, her hand on the door. She hesitates again, shakes her head, then pushes inside.

The room is warm, smelling of alcohol and a metallic coppery scent I can't quite place. I have smelled it before but can't identify it right now. The room is large, with solid grey walls. A couple of chairs and a sofa are in front of the fireplace, a well-used sitting area. Several doors to the left of the sitting area lead to a closet and bathing area and possibly another hall for an alternate escape. Large windows have thick curtains pulled tight. The sunlight would be astounding when they are open. To the right of the door is a large four-poster bed. The posts are connected at the top, but there aren't any curtains or covers on the top of the bed. A desk and chair with a shelf of books are to the side against the wall. Paintings of flowers and the night sky decorate the room. It feels very much like a space Jasmin has carefully curated for her own tastes.

Emmeline is working in front of the fireplace, tending to some laundry. I had no idea she did laundry in Jasmin's room. She smiles when she sees Sunette, but her eyes go wide when she sees me. She is only wearing a thin shift, likely due to the heat in the room. She gasps, pulling a blanket over her body. The blanket is stained with brown spots. Sunette sighs next to me.

Emmeline looks down, realizing what she is holding up. She drops it in the basket, glancing toward the bed, then rushing over to us. She speaks in a hushed voice to Sunette, giving up entirely on hiding her light clothing at this point.

"What is he doing in here? She isn't going to like this." Sunette shakes her head, eying me warily.

"I know. I told him that. He insisted he needed to see her." Emmeline groans, turning toward me.

"I assure you, she is fine. She won't be happy you are here." Her voice is still hushed, leading me to believe Jasmin is likely sleeping.

"If she is fine, let me see for myself, and I will leave." I may very well be in the presence of three of the most stubborn women in the castle. I will not back down, though. I am already here. I just need to see her. Emmeline looks to Sunette. They have some silent conversation I am not privy to.

"I'll tell her I came in here on my own. She won't even know you two were involved." Sunette grunts a laugh as Emmeline rolls her eyes.

"Oh, she'll know we were involved," Emmeline says. "We will wait just outside. We'll come in when she starts yelling." I laugh softly at her comment but stop when I realize I'm the only one laughing. Emmeline didn't mean that as a joke.

Nonetheless, I can handle a bit of yelling if it means I know Jasmin will be alright. The two women step out into the hallway, allowing a cool gust of air to blow through before they shut the door.

I walk through the room, over to the bed with a rumpled pile of pillows and blankets and Jasmin in the middle. Her hair is slicked to her head with sweat; she looks paler than expected, the edges of the scar on her cheek more visible due to her lack of color. Her eyes are closed, but her eyebrows are knit together in discomfort. She doesn't look well at all, but I can't be sure what is actually wrong with her. I kneel on the floor beside the bed, reaching for her hand. Her skin is clammy, damp with sweat. She groans, rolling onto her side and then curling into the fetal position. There is a cloth soaked in the water next to her bed. I dip it in the basin, wring it out, then tap it against her forehead. A small noise comes from her throat, not quite comfort, not quite pain.

I sit on the bed as I continue to stroke her forehead with the cloth. She shifts again, pressing her forehead into my hip. Her hands slide up, touching my body, unsure of what she is feeling. Her fingers glide around my waist, settling on my opposite hip. Her other hand wraps around my wrist, holding the cloth against her forehead. She is still for a moment, then takes a breath in. She jerks back, looking up at me with red, swollen eyes. She looks so unwell.

"Clem!" She screeches, leaping out of bed on the other side. "What the fuck!" They were not kidding about her yelling. It's an ear-piercing noise filled with horror, terror, and pain. Before I can respond, I notice the lower half of her shift is covered in blood.

"Jasmin! You're bleeding!" I rush around the bed, trying to help her. I don't know what I should do in this situation. I'm not a healer; I know nothing about helping someone who is bleeding other than to stop it. She holds her hands out to stop me as I round the corner of the bed.

"Why are you here?" Her voice is almost a cry, squeezing my heart.

"I didn't know where you were. They said you were sick, and I want to help." She shakes her head, tears falling from her eyes now. She is hunched over at the waist, not standing up straight.

"You shouldn't be here. This isn't something you can fix." Little droplets of blood are hitting the floor around her feet. Wherever the blood is coming from is still actively bleeding. She needs to get back in bed and be bandaged up. It may not be something I can fix, but I can help.

"You are bleeding. You should lie back down. I can get bandages for you." I take another step toward her, wanting to get her in bed. She retreats to another degree.

"No, Clem." Her hands stretch further toward me. The fear of her pushing me away like she did at the winter solstice seizes my brain. I cannot let that happen again. I refuse to leave her in this state. Just before I can argue again, she cries out in pain, crumpling to the ground. I rush over to catch her, lifting her back to the bed. I yell out for Emmeline, who rushes in with Sunette. I tell them how badly she is bleeding. Sunette comes to the bed, grabs Jasmin's gown, and lifts it up. Jasmin is moaning in my arms, twisting around, unable to settle. Emmeline rushes over with more dry cloths.

"We need to get her changed. These cloths are too soiled," Sunette tells Emmeline. She nods but looks up at me. "You really shouldn't be here," Emmeline tells me softly.

"I'm not leaving," I state firmly. Jasmin wails in my arms, burying her face against my stomach. Her arms wrap around my waist, holding me tightly as she cries. Sunette and Emmeline share a look, then start getting the new cloths ready.

"Jasmin," Sunette says softly but sternly. "We're going to change these cloths. Clem is going to hold you. We'll be quick." Jasmin cries out again, squeezing me. Sunette nods to Emmeline. They start by loosening the top of the sleeveless shift, pulling it down her body so she doesn't have to release her hold on me. I keep one hand on her back, the other along her arm as they remove the stained shift. I understand she is bleeding badly, but I was entirely unprepared for what was under the shift.

Several cloths are tied around her waist and between her legs, soaked with blood. Sunette begins undoing the knots on the bloody cloths as Emmeline prepares some fresh ones. The deep purple bruise on her stomach that I noticed when she took me swimming in the pond months ago looks angrier than the last time I saw it. It looks swollen and inflamed, streaks of red coursing through the deep purples and browns. Sunette removes the bloody cloths around her waist as Emmeline hands her a clean one.

"We should add an extra cloth or two. Has she been bleeding this heavily the whole time?" Emmeline shakes her head, telling her it hasn't been this bad. Women have a monthly cycle that involves bleeding, but it isn't normally this bad, is it? Jasmin hasn't been missing this long before. I've never seen my mother or Bea have bleeding cycles like this. I may not be the best brother or son in the world, but certainly, I would have noticed this.

They secure the new bandages around Jasmin's waist. Her grip has relaxed around my waist, but she hasn't let go. Her face is still buried against my side, leaving me unable to see her face. I have many questions running through my mind, but I am too stunned to actually say anything.

"We should probably change these sheets. Since Clem is still here, he can hold her while we swap them out." Sunette and Emmeline work together as if Jasmin and I aren't here. We are just objects they are dealing with. They both agree, insisting I lift her off the bed momentarily. I want to say something to prepare her like Sunette did before they changed her clothes. My mind is misfiring, and I can't get any words to come out. Instead, she crawls into my lap, burying her face against my neck, not allowing me to see her face.

I stand up, cradling her close to my body. She stays wrapped in my arms, hiding her face from me. She sniffles several times, crying softly against my neck. I squeeze her tightly, wanting to make all of this disappear, but miserably unable to help in this situation. Once they have changed the sheets, I lay her down, sitting on the bed beside her. Emmeline takes the soiled clothes to the other side of the room. Sunette brings the water basin to the side of the bed I am now sitting on. Jasmin curls away from me; into a pillow she huddles around. Sunette places the basin on the stand next to the bed. She puts a couple of small cloths in the cool water, wringing one out and handing it to me.

"She might sleep soon. I know you have questions, but let her rest. The questions can be answered later." I take the cool cloth from her, watching her and

Emmeline exit the room again. For a moment, I'm frozen in shock over what just happened. Trying to process and understand something I cannot comprehend yet is impossible. I shake my thoughts clear and slide closer to Jasmin, wrapping my body around her exposed back. She doesn't push me away but doesn't accept me, either. I place the cloth against her head, rubbing soft circles around her face, wiping away sweat and tears.

We lie together, her back to my front, quietly for several minutes. I keep wiping the cloth across her forehead, wiping away new beads of sweat and tears that fall. Her breathing becomes steady and deep. When she is asleep, I sit up, swapping the cloth for a clean one. I drape it across her face, feeling weak and tired myself. They didn't put another shift on her, leaving her exposed except for the cloths tied around her waist. I remove my own shirt, the warmth of the room and the stress of the situation leaving it uncomfortable. Unsure what else to do, I crawl back onto the bed, wrapping myself around her. I place my hand on her thigh, not really sure where else to touch at this point. I kiss her shoulder several times, wanting to connect without disturbing her. I settle in around her, soon drifting off into a restless sleep.

Jasmin doesn't sleep well, grunting and groaning through a pain I can't see. Emmeline and Sunette come in a couple of times before leaving for the night. I stay by her side the whole time. When the sun begins to rise again, Sunette comes into the room with a tray of food. She offers me some of the food but has a mug of broth for Jasmin. She likely won't drink much but needs something to keep her energy up. Sunette leaves us alone again. Emmeline pops in, dropping off fresh cloths, and taking more with her. She whispers to Jasmin that Finn is doing fine, playing with Mikhail, being a general menace like always. Jasmin doesn't react, but I thank Emmeline. Jasmin is awake but still facing away from me, unwilling to acknowledge my presence. That's fine; I've got nowhere else to be.

I grab the mug of broth, holding it out for her. She takes it without looking at me and places it down against the bed. I rub her back as I eat the food brought in for me. The bread and potatoes are delicious and filling, if bland. The usual spices and seasonings have a strong smell and might affect Jasmin. When I finish, she still hasn't touched her mug. I'm unsure how to help her; I still don't entirely understand what is wrong. I ask if she needs new cloths, but she still ignores me. At this point, I'm feeling more defeated. I don't know what I am supposed to do. My body hurts with inaction.

I notice a book on the stand beside her bed. I didn't see it there before, but grab it to read from it. She always enjoys it when I read to her. I savor the time I spend reading with Jasmin. It's a good way for us to be together doing something entertaining. I settle back against the headboard of the bed, flip to a marked page and start reading. This is an informative book on witch traditions and ceremonies. It's relatively dry, but the words don't matter at this point. I read nearly a page before Jasmin moves. She holds the mug out to me, and I take it. She pulls a blanket around her body, which seems excessive to me after a night without any coverings. She slides against my body, settling in against my chest. She still doesn't speak or look at me, but she accepts the now cold mug of broth, sipping as I start reading again.

She finishes the mug quickly, handing it to me to place on the bedside table. I offer her the leftover bread, and she nibbles while I continue reading. Soon she dozes off, unable to stay awake any longer. She looks better today; some color has returned to her face. I know she isn't back to normal, but she seems to be in less pain than before. Her sleep is less disturbed this time. She doesn't moan or grunt. She is still folded at the waist, a relaxed version of her earlier fetal position.

Sunette and Emmeline return later to change the cloths again. Jasmin holds tightly to my waist, again not looking, as the two women work. They leave the bedsheets alone, for now, delivering more food for us before bidding us good night. I find another book in the room, a storybook with multiple stories. I read that one to her instead, enjoying the more robust storytelling. She drifts into a quiet slumber for the night, sleeping without moving for several hours. I get a couple hours of sleep with her in my arms. Holding her brings me some comfort. While she may still be in pain, at least I can help in that manner.

By the first sunlight, my body aches from staying in bed with her for so long. She is still sleeping, so I take a short walk to stretch my body. I walk out of her room, instantly regretting not finding a sweater. I had grown accustomed to how warm her room was. I forgot the rest of the castle is much cooler with the winter weather. I duck into the next room, hoping there may be a blanket I can grab. The room is mostly dark, save for three candles burning on a shelf on one side. There is an odd sense of abandonment in this space. My curiosity gets the best of me; I want to see what is in here. I make my way across the open area to the window with curtains pulled tight. I crack them open, allowing light into the room.

The room is covered in bright pink flowers and lace. It doesn't seem like something Jasmin would like at all. Scanning around the area, I notice a crib, rocking chair, and a few dolls. Maybe this is Jasmin's old nursery. I don't know how the royal rooms work in the castle. Perhaps they moved her to a different room when she was old enough. I leave the curtains cracked, allowing in the light as I walk back to the shelf with the candles. The three candles are still burning and have been burning for a while. They were fairly tall candles based on the melted wax pooling around the base.

In a vase next to the candles is a single, large flower. The stem is tall, with many petals forming a large round head. The petals are a dark, rich purple, slightly curved at the end, and surprisingly short for the size of the bloom. There seems to be an ethereal glow around the flower. I have never seen this flower before. I lean in to smell it, but it has no scent. I've never come across a flower with no scent at all.

In front of the three candles is a leather-bound journal. There are no details on the front or spine about what it contains. I flip the first page open, noticing Jasmin's faded handwriting. There is a name I don't recognize, age, cause of death, and remaining family members. There are several pages with the same layout and different information. This book is surprisingly thick to be full of obituaries. Why would Jasmin write this information? Aren't there historians that keep track of that information? I continue flipping through the pages until one catches my eye.

William Byrne

Age: 39

Crushed by barrier

Wife: Ada – 37. Children: Beatrice – 21. Clematis– 19. Claire – 3.

Seeing my father's name in this journal is like a punch to the soul. It's so cold, technical, and exact. There was so much more to my father than the way he died. Why is there a journal in a nursery with his information? I flip through a couple of other pages, realizing everyone in here must have perished due to the curse. It's all been confined to one single journal. Lumped together as if that is all each person is worth, what the curse did to them. My throat clenches, flipping back to my father's page. Claire only knew my father for a few short years; she didn't get to know him as she should have. Anger spreads through my body, rising with disbelief and confusion.

"Clem," Jasmin speaks in a clear voice. "You shouldn't be in here."

She has some gall to tell me that now. She has a robe wrapped around her. The color has returned to her cheeks. Her hair is twisted and knotted, but she looks more like herself. I grab the journal, holding it out to her.

"My father." She nods but doesn't reach to take the book. She stays in the doorway, watching me hesitantly.

"I know." Her voice is softer now but not quite comforting. "You should leave." Anger fills my veins. My eyes roll over her body, back to the top. I huff in disbelief at her command. No explanation, no reasons, not even offering to explain later. I toss the journal back on the shelf and turn to leave before it hits. Her eyes go wide as the journal thuds into the vase behind me. She screams, running toward it. I grab the vase before it falls from the shelf, but the flower slips out. It lands on the floor just as Jasmin slides in beside it. One of the petals falls off the flower, landing softly on the ground. She lifts the flower, still in good condition minus the single petal. She looks up at me, glaring with hatred and disgust in her eyes.

"Get out." She says between gritted teeth, cradling the flower in her hands. Unsure how to process any of the last few days, I leave without saying anything. I didn't intend to knock the flower over, but the hurt of finding my father's name in the journal is overwhelming. Jasmin offers no information or explanation for the journal, just kicks me out again. She seems to be fond of pushing me away when things get difficult. That's fine. I need to clear my head anyway.

Chapter 26

JASMIN

The nursery has always been private. It's a relic from before the curse at this point. It was never meant to be that. I should have dismantled the nursery long ago. I couldn't be bothered after the curse began, and soon, I needed a place to be in misery. This room has provided the quiet safety to relive past traumas that may never heal. Should I die before the curse is lifted, this is the room that will house my decaying body. This is where I deserve to rot.

I return the flower gently to the vase. Clem has no idea of the meaning behind it. He was never meant to. Emmeline and Sunette are the only people allowed in the room. After my safety, this is the room the guards are here to protect. This isn't a space for other people. I never wanted any of the bachelors, true love or not, to find this room. If I had found my true love, I would move into the king suite with them, locking this room away, never to be touched again.

I blow out the three candles, their time having been served fully. Traditionally, I would spend more time in the nursery, reflecting, rereading the words I've written so many times. Traditionally though, I don't suffer as much as I have the past few days. I settle for a bath, then finding Clem. I don't know what to say to him, but I need to talk to him. Maybe I'll explain the importance of the nursery. Maybe I'll just apologize and hope it's enough. Whatever I say to him, an apology and thanks are required. No one other than Sunette and Emmeline has ever insisted on caring for me the way he did. I audibly sigh; he deserves an explanation.

I take my time bathing, brushing my hair, and making myself presentable. I dress, noticing the absence of Emmeline and Sunette. I wonder if they heard my interaction with Clem. I also wonder what he said to convince them to let him into my room the past couple of days. Part of me is angry over their decision to let him in. Despite him ending up in the nursery, I am not entirely mad at them for bringing him in. He did provide comfort in a way I haven't experienced. The pain was still excruciating, but a certain relief was fostered through him.

The halls of the castle are much cooler than my room. I pull my sweater tighter around my body, trying to block the chill. In the bachelors' wing, Clem's door is shut. I knock softly, waiting for a response. I don't hear one and decide to enter anyway. He came into my room without my permission. That works both ways, right? I open the door, saying his name softly. His room is empty but tidy. All of his clothes are put away. There are no papers anywhere; books are stacked neatly on his table. The only thing that seems out of order is a stack of papers on his desk. I step closer to look at them. It's a letter from his mother. I leave them alone, not really wanting to snoop.

A sudden thought flashes in my mind. I would rather be with someone neat like Clem than messy like Kian. As much as I enjoy my time with Kian, the mess in his room was overwhelming. That could be a problem if we were together. Clem really has everything I need in a partner. He has a great duality in sex that appeals to me more than I expected. He is organized, hardworking, thoughtful. I can overlook jealousy, especially when it is because of me. I...I love him. I grunt a laugh as the thought settles throughout me. Of course, I realize this while sneaking around in his room, unsure where he is after I have been terrible to him.

I really have been terrible to Clem. I deceived him, ignored him, and pushed him away. Sure, I can blame my history, the curse, and my own fear. But I still actively chose to do all of those things. I rub the sleeves of one of his shirts between my fingers. My chest aches at the acknowledgment of my feelings. It's been this way for a long time, but I refused to see it. I lift the material to my nose, breathing deeply. I have to go find Clem. I need him.

I leave the room undisturbed, closing the door on my way out. In the hallway, Kian is leaving his room, too. He has a knowing twinkle in his eyes. A grin spreads across his face. Kian would be the kind of partner that would not only encourage having trysts with other people but would want to join in too.

"Late night, Princess?" His voice is playfully suggestive.

"No. I'm looking for Clem. He's not in his room. Have you seen him?"

"I have not," he shakes his head. "Try the library."

I nod; that had been my next spot to check. I can usually count on finding Clem there. I go back through the castle, finding Tomas in the foyer. He looks a bit worried, like he is unsure what to do about something. He is fidgeting with his fingers when he spots me.

"Oh, Princess," he rushes over to me but stops. He looks back out the windows near the front door. A blizzard is whipping snow across the grounds harshly.

"What's the matter, Tomas? I was just looking for Clem, but I can help you." His eyes go wide with fear. "Tomas, what is it?" He chews on his lip, fiddling with the hem of his shirt more. "Tomas." There is a hint of warning in my tone, my fear, and concern growing exponentially.

"Well, it's Clem." Again, he looks back to the front door but doesn't say anything else. I grab his shoulders, trying to draw his attention. His eyes meet mine, fear and sadness mixed together.

"He came through here a while ago. He said he was going for a walk to clear his head. I tried to warn him about the storm, but he went out as if he didn't hear me. He hasn't returned."

My heart drops. I look to the main door, worry encasing my entire body. Is Clem still out there? Did he come in a different door?

"He hasn't returned," I say slowly, trying to process what this means. "Have you checked other places? Maybe he used a different door."

"Maybe, but I just came from the kitchen and library." My eyes focus on Tomas. I can hear his words, but it sounds like he is underwater. My whole world is being swallowed. All I can see is Clem caught in the blizzard, getting lost in the thick, whipping snow. I rush to the front door, ripping it open. I can hear someone saying I need to go save him. I have to find him, but I don't realize those words are coming from me. The frigid air blasts me in the face, snow pounding into my fragile skin. I suck in a breath as arms wrap around my body, pulling me back.

Erik and Kian are here, dragging me back into the warmth. I scream, clawing and fighting to get outside. Erik wraps his arms around mine, effectively seizing my flailing body. He pulls me away from the door while Kian secures it closed. I am still screaming, voice hoarse. Tears are streaking down my face; I only feel them because of the cold air in the foyer. Tomas is by my side, trying to console me, but it isn't working. Erik holds me tightly for several minutes as I fight against him. I soon realize I can't escape his grip and settle against him. He doesn't loosen his hold.

Kian steps up to me once I am calmer. "Princess, Clem goes on these walks regularly. I am sure he is smart enough to find a safe place to stay during the storm." His words are soft, ringing some truth in my mind. "If we haven't found him when the storm passes, we will all help you look." Kian strokes the tears away from my face as I relax into his touch. I want to go look for Clem now, storm be damned. "Erik is going to let you down now. We'll go recheck the library and his room, okay?" He is using a soft tone with me. I give a gentle nod but have no intentions of going to the library.

Erik releases me slowly. As soon as his arms are away from my body, I run for the front door. Kian and Erik curse loudly, but Tomas is the one to catch me. I scream again, frustrated they won't just let me leave. Erik grabs me from Tomas again, being stronger and larger and better able to contain me. I wail loudly, dropping my head against his shoulder in defeat. They discuss what to do, but I can't hear the words. Their voices are full of concern and unwillingness to let me go outside to look for Clem. He is in danger, and they are preventing me from helping.

They agree on something, and Erik carries me down the hall. I let him hold me, not kicking and screaming at this point. When he turns to go up the stairs, I grab onto the wall. Up is the opposite way from where I need to go. I need to go out.

I'm fighting as hard as I can to get away from Erik. He is strong, but I think... I almost... can... get away.

"Jasmin!" Kian's hand is on my face, forcing me to look at him. His strong voice and hand cause me to gasp in response, going quiet as he speaks. His voice is hushed but angry. "It is too dangerous for you to go out after Clem. You could get hurt, lost, or die. We will not let that happen." My body settles, realizing he may have a valid point. "We are taking you to Clem's room. You can see most of the courtyard from his window. When he comes back, you will likely see him. Or we will see when the storm lessens, and we can go together." His words are firm, offering me stability in a time when I have none. I nod against his fingers on my chin. His grip relaxes as he strokes my cheek. When he releases my face, Erik continues to carry me up the stairs.

"I can walk now." I offer softly.

"Sorry, Princess. I'm not taking that chance again." I huff, knowing he is making the right choice. While I wouldn't run now, he has no reason to trust me. We arrive in Clem's room, Tomas and Kian walking in behind Erik. Tomas stands in front of the door, blocking the way. As Erik places me on the ground, Kian steps behind me. I have nowhere to go unless one of them moves.

"He will be fine." I nod to Kian, sniffling, not realizing my nose has started running from the crying. Kian pulls out a handkerchief, rubbing my face. When he steps back, I collapse on the bed, exhausted from everything that has happened. Kian steps toward the window, looking out. Nothing can be seen; I can tell from here. The blizzard has turned everything white. I doubt he can even see the gardens below. Erik sits on the bed behind me; it shifts as he settles on the mattress. I curl at the foot of the bed, pulling my legs tight against my chest.

After several moments, someone drapes something across my body. I see Kian wrapping one of Clem's sweaters over my shoulders. I snuggle under it, rubbing the wool against my cheek. It's not the softest material, but it fits Clem well. Unwittingly, I doze off into a fitful sleep. There are hushed voices. The door opens and closes. My mind drifts into darkness again.

"Princess," Erik says softly, shaking my shoulders. I jerk up. "Is he back?"

"No, but the storm has stopped. Vesper and Shena are prepped for us to take out. You and I can go look for Clem." I jump off the bed, rushing to the door. Kian is already there, holding a thick coat, gloves, and a scarf for me. He helps me into them, then kisses my cheek. He tells me to be safe. Erik leads the way to the front. He has also added a few extra layers to his outfit. Sabeko is in the front with the two horses, both bundled up and carrying extra blankets. He tells us not to stay out too long, or all of us will be in danger. We promise and head off toward the woods. There are no tracks in the fresh snow. Everything is white and glistening.

"Tomas said he usually takes the trail headed to Arkaley, then turns back toward the royal fields." I nod, leading Vesper in that direction. Clem couldn't have gotten far before the storm became too strong to be in. It may have already been snowing when he went outside. A sinking feeling pulls at my gut. We ride silently, eyes on the area around us until we reach the tree line. I begin calling his name, unsure if he can respond but needing to do something more than just look. Erik yells a time or two also. We ride for several minutes with no luck.

"Princess, we need to turn back toward the grounds. The trail will be dangerous from here on out, and the horses won't be able to pass. Clem would know not to go any further than here." I sigh, looking out in front of us. Erik is right; the trail is already difficult on the horses and will only get worse from here. I yell out for Clem again, wishing he would answer. I stare for several minutes with no response.

Just as I am about to turn Vesper to follow Erik, I hear a rustling ahead in the distance. I halt, searching the area for any signs of movement. "Did you hear that, Erik?" He is searching now too. I yell again and hear a faint moan in response. I jump down from Vesper, running clumsily through the snow. Erik is yelling at me to wait, but I don't stop. There is a lump near the base of one of the thicker trees. It is shifting slightly but not making any significant movements. I rush over to it, recognizing a spot of thick blonde hair. A loud sob escapes my mouth as I tell Erik I found him.

I drop to my knees at the bundle, grabbing at the material, trying to expose Clem. I finally pull the coat back, finding his face buried inside the coat. His nose and cheeks are chapped and red, looking painful. He is crumpled into a ball as small as he can get. It's getting harder to see through the tears that are filling my eyes. I wrap my arms around him, crying against his frozen jacket. Relief washes over me as his body shivers violently underneath me. His teeth chatter loudly when Erik finally arrives next to me. He touches my back gently, trying to coax me back from Clem. I nod, sniffling and wiping tears off my cheeks as I move away.

Erik lifts Clem awkwardly as he is stiff with the cold. He carries his shivering body over to Vesper and instructs me to mount him. Once I'm up, he assists Clem in mounting behind me. It isn't a smooth process, but Clem gets on, and I pull him against my back. He wraps his arms around my waist, but his fingers are too cold to hold on well. Erik throws a blanket over Clem, and we ride back to the castle. We don't go very fast, not as fast as I would like. It's safer that way, but I'm still worried about how cold Clem is.

At the castle, Sabeko and Tomas meet us to take the horses. Erik dismounts first, moving over to help Clem. Clem tries to dismount but winds up just dropping. Erik isn't prepared for the full weight of Clem and drops his legs, only managing to hold up his chest. Erik curses several times but lifts Clem up and follows me inside. I ask him to bring him to my room since it is still warm from the fire I have going. He agrees, following me through the castle. Clem's teeth chatter the whole time; I'm sure he's shaking violently in Erik's arms. Clem doesn't even fight about being carried in this manner.

In my room, Erik puts him down in a chair and turns like he will leave. Emmeline and Sunette aren't here, but I need help getting Clem out of his clothes. They are freezing and only going to make him worse. I mention this to Erik. He looks uncomfortable but agrees to help. We strip off his jacket, sweater, and shirt. He pulls off his boots and socks but hesitates as I undo Clem's trousers. I stop, leaving Clem in the chair in front of the fire. I wrap my arms around Erik's shoulders.

"Thank you so much for your help. I know this hasn't been easy, but I dearly appreciate you." Erik returns the hug, wishing Clem and me well before leaving. I ask him to send Sunette or Emmeline up if he sees them, and he agrees. Once he is out, I grab several blankets, wrapping them over Clem. I leave his pants on for now. I remove my coat and outer layers and sit beside Clem. I pull him against my chest, draping my arms across his shoulders. His skin is so cold. He is still shivering violently.

I rise, grabbing his arms and tugging him down to the floor. I do my best to support him, but I'm not used to lifting another person. I manage to lower him to the floor closer to the fire. Once he is on the floor, I remove his pants, momentarily leaving him exposed in front of the fire. I remove the rest of my clothes and grab several blankets. I toss them over Clem, then slide in beside him, wrapping as much of my body over his. Body heat will help warm him. It occurs to me this is the first time we have been completely naked together. It's terrible conditions, but at least we are both still alive. The past few days have been a whirlwind of unusual physical ailments.

His shivering slows; teeth chattering lessens, too. His body feels warmer now, but his extremities are still cold. He turns his head so his cheek presses against my forehead. His cheek is warmer, but his nose is frozen. I lift my face to him, pressing my lips gently against the frozen tip of his nose. He wraps his arms around my back, but I jump when his fingers touch my skin.

"S-sorry," he mumbles, closing his eyes slowly. I sit up, grabbing his hands with mine. I rub them gently, trying to warm them. His fingers are frozen and red. He winces when I grab them. I stop trying to rub them and just hold them for now, letting the warmth from my hands warm his. A soft knock sounds on the door, and Emmeline asks if she can come in. I reach over and grab a shirt, pulling it over my head. I call out that she can come in, tucking the blankets around Clem tighter. His eyes are still closed, but the shivering has stopped, except for a random chill. As she walks in, I realize I grabbed Clem's shirt. The collar is too loose and is doing little to cover me. I try to tie it together, but Emmeline won't mind.

"I heard what happened. How is he?" She is speaking quietly to me. Clem doesn't react to her being in the room. I chew on my lip, concerned about how he is actually doing. He's stopped shivering for the most part, and his teeth aren't chatting, but his skin is still chilled. I finally shrug in response.

"I don't know. He's stopped shivering." Emmeline nods, giving an assessing look to the pile on the floor. She turns and asks how I am. There's a question with a loaded answer if I ever heard one. I fiddle with the strings hanging from the collar as tears build in my eyes. Emmeline gives a soft, cooing interjection as she hugs me. The tears fall down my cheek again. Honestly, I'm surprised I still have any at this point. She releases me, stating she's bringing food up and that we should both rest in the meantime.

I make my way back over to Clem. He's fallen asleep, breathing deeply. An occasional chill runs through his body, but he's mostly peaceful in his rest. I stroke the hair back from his face. He left it down or took it down to help fight against the cold. I feel like such an idiot over how I treated him. I'm also mad and angry and hurt and sad over his decision to go for a walk during a blizzard. Most of all, I'm just relieved he's still alive. I kiss his forehead gently as Emmeline knocks again, bringing in a cart with lots of food. She brings up an extra kettle in case we want warm water later. She leaves just as quickly as she arrives. I eat some food, watching him sleep on the floor in front of the fire. My heart is overwhelmed by all the emotions I am feeling at the moment, though. The one feeling I am absolutely sure of is my love for him. I don't know if he is my true love, but I certainly love him deeply.

The night passes slowly. He wakes at one point, and I force him to eat some food. He takes it begrudgingly, complaining his throat hurts. I refrain from calling him names as I make him take more food. His fingers are still bothering him; his grip is weakened by how affected they are. I help when they shake too much. We decide to settle in the bed instead of the floor. It's not as close to the fire as I would like, but we bring all the blankets, leaving a few more by the fire for later. I snuggle into him, holding him tight as we lie in bed. Neither of us speaks about what happened. We also don't comment on our nudeness, just resting in each other's arms.

Chapter 27

CLEM

I wake with Jasmin wrapped around me. My body aches from the cold I was exposed to. My mind didn't process how bad the storm was when I walked outside. It wasn't until I was too far from the castle that I realized the danger I was in. Instead of turning back and possibly getting lost, I hunkered down and waited. It took longer for the storm to pass than I anticipated. If Jasmin hadn't come for me...

I don't finish that thought as her arms tighten around me. Her warmth surrounds me, almost to the point of being too hot. I shift to relieve a sore spot on my leg, bumping against Jasmin's body. I'm not wearing any clothes. I manage to open my eyes to find her sleeping in my shirt. I vaguely remember her lying with me by the fire, then force-feeding me in the bed. My memory is choppy, and I am unsure of what is real and what isn't. I try to get out of bed but groan at the soreness lancing through my muscles.

"What? What is it? What do you need?" Jasmin shoots up, rubbing her eyes, but her voice is still groggy. Her eyes finally open, finding me next to her. I give up on moving for the moment, letting my muscles adjust to being awake. She grabs my hands, then rubs my arm, shoulders, and chest, searching for injuries.

"I'm just sore." I croak, realizing my throat is also sore. She relaxes the smallest fraction possible, clearly worried about my health. She spins her hand around so her fingers are in my palm and instructs me to squeeze. I do, but my fingers are still weak. They aren't shaking, just not as strong as expected. She seems satisfied with my squeeze, though, probably better than last night.

"Okay. I'll go track down some food for us. I think Emmeline brought clothes for you if you want to get dressed. There is a wash area through there." She points across the room but looks back at me before moving. She looks like she wants to say more but doesn't. She climbs out of bed, turning back to me. "I'm glad you're okay, Clem."

Before I can respond, she's moving through the room, grabbing her clothes, and disappearing in the hall without actually dressing. I sigh, turning slowly to get out of bed. We need to talk about everything; too much is floating between us. The last several days have been a whirlwind. Has it been a week? I've lost track of time now. I splash water on my face, rubbing the soreness from my cheeks. They are stained red with dry, cracked skin. Maybe Jasmin will have something I can put over them to soothe them.

When she returns, I sit on the couch, staring into the dying fire. I added another log but didn't stoke it well. The handle was too hard to manipulate enough to really get it going. She brings over a tray of food, placing it next to me on the couch. She sits on the other side of the tray instead of beside me. The distance isn't welcome, but it is understood.

"I tried to pick foods you could eat with sore hands. I didn't think oats would be good, so you get meat and bread instead. Oh," she slides off the couch to grab a kettle and place it near the fire. "I did get tea to make. I thought a warm mug might help your fingers. And the tea will soothe your throat." She kneels next to the fireplace, trying to position the kettle so it will warm. After spending the night in bed with her, I don't want her so far away. Many, many things are left unsaid right now, but she doesn't need so much literal space between us.

"Jasmin," I whisper in a hoarse voice. She turns to look at me but doesn't try to get closer.

"Clem," she holds her hands up to stop me. "There are a lot of things I need to say to you. So many." She shakes her head, looking down at her hands now in her lap. "I am going to say them all. Today. But right now, I need you to eat, build your strength, and be healthy again." Her cheeks flush as if she might cry. Unsure what else to do, I nod, taking a sausage from the tray and taking a bite. She offers a small smile as she turns back to the kettle. We remain silent while we eat. She was correct; the tea did soothe my fingers and my throat.

When we finish eating, she stacks all the items on the tray, putting them on a table near the door. She glances between me and the hallway, looking nervous.

"Do you feel like walking?" Her question is sheepish. I rise in response, walking over to her. I take her hand as she leads me down the hall. She ambles, looking me over as I move. I don't walk as smoothly as I normally do, but my gait isn't terrible. Nothing another day or two of recovery won't help. I'm surprised when she leads me into the nursery. She pulls me over to the rocking chair, motioning for me to sit down. She hands me a small pillow, fussing over me to ensure I'm comfortable. When she's convinced I am, she begins to speak.

"I'm going to tell you my story. My whole story. It's long, but I want you to know." Standing next to the crib, she sighs and traces her fingers along the edge. "Sunette and Emmeline don't know everything, though I'm sure they can fill in the parts they don't know. I had hoped I wouldn't need to share this with any of the bachelors. Maybe not even my true love, at least not for a while. But I believe you deserve to know. And I want you to know." She walks over and kneels at my feet, not touching, just beyond my arm's reach. She takes a deep breath before she starts speaking.

"On my sixteenth birthday, my parents bought Vesper for me. I didn't know then that they also bought Sabeko's family. Sabeko and Sunette had a daughter the same age as me, Dahlia. We were instant friends. We got along well, enjoyed the same activities, loved all the same things, and had similar temperaments, much to our parent's chagrin. My father fostered the relationship at first, thinking it would be good publicity for the kingdom to see the princess with a dark-skinned friend.

I didn't understand the full scope of his reasoning at the time. I was young and naive.

"The days bled into months, and soon Dahlia and I were inseparable. We created mischief, wreaked havoc, just being regular sixteen-year-old girls. My mother was annoyed with our behavior, but my father overlooked it for a while. As winter settled in, we became more bored. One afternoon, in one of the rooms in the castle, she kissed me. I was shocked at first, but something felt so right about it. I had heard rumors that two women would do things like that, but they had always been rumors. Someone's long lost aunt had a neighbor whose brother lived next to a couple, something like that." She shrugs, pausing momentarily. Her fingers trace her lips, remembering the kiss she shared with her friend. I try to quell the ache, knowing this isn't about me.

"After that first kiss, it took no time for us to take things further. We snuck around rooms and closets, hiding in the library or the throne room when no one was around. Any way to steal a few minutes alone. It was exciting and wrong and blissful. I fell in love with Dahlia. I swore she was my soul mate." She looks down at her hands, fiddling with some bit of fuzz. It hurts hearing her words, but the sadness in her voice feels worse than knowing she loved someone else. Her eyes find mine again, sorrow and longing present.

"Shortly after spring began, we started taking rides, stealing away to the forest to be together under the open sky. I learned how to slip away from my guards. She learned how to throw Sunette off the scent. Though, looking back, I don't think she was ever as successful as she thought." She chuckles at the thought, a weak smile spreads on my face. No, Sunette surely would have known what they were doing. Parents know far more than they let on, and Sunette seems to know more than most.

"We grew more careless over the summer. Hiding in the shrubbery of the garden, not locking doors, slipping into each other's rooms in the middle of the day. We were foolish and in love. So deliriously happy together. We believed we were invincible. We slipped into a room on the lower level one day, forgetting to lock the door. I had her pressed back on a table, skirt hiked up as I kneeled in front of her, savoring her taste. There was no denying what I was doing to her. When my mother walked in, she lost it. She began screaming about how horrible I was, calling me names. Then she started on my 'filthy friend' and how she ruined me. I tried to take the blame, but Mother just had guards escort me to my room. Dahlia was taken back to her family's rooms in the stables." I have been in the stables a few times, and no decent living conditions exist. It strikes me that they were living there as slaves. Sweet Briar is definitely not free of dark secrets.

"Mother ignored me for several days, sending my father to speak to me. She also had several priests come to wash away my demons." Jasmin gives a heavy eye roll. "No one answered when I asked about Dahlia. Emmeline finally whispered that she was okay but confined to her quarters. Mother barred me from seeing her again. I begged Father to let me, but he refused, not willing to stand up to Mother or risk word spreading of my deviancy. For months, I didn't get to see Dahlia. I knew where she was. She was within shouting distance, but I never saw her. Whatever Mother threatened her family with worked." Her voice breaks several times as she speaks. The emotions are still raw for her, spilling out in every word.

"My seventeenth birthday came around. My parents learned not to buy animals for me. Instead, they just stuck with the people. They insisted I start courting men to find a suitable husband. After all, I was to rule the kingdom one day. The courting process was miserable. I only wanted Dahlia. I wanted her to rule with me. I wanted her to be my Queen. I didn't care what others thought. But droves of men were forced upon me. We had ball after ball of men coming and going. They were all terrible. Many make Oscar look like Prince Charming." She shudders at the thought. I remember the stories of the balls that were occurring. Ma always pushed me to go, but I never wanted any of that. Even after my proclamation of marrying the princess, I wasn't willing to go to a ball for it.

"One was worse than all. I would rather create a harem of four Oscars and all of his cronies than ever have to look that man in the face again. So naturally, that was who Mother wanted me to marry. She forced me to spend time with him despite my pleas. My father was no help. No one listened to my claims that he was dangerous. No one cared. They wanted me married and quiet. They believed

Jackson would be a suitable King when the time came, and that was all that really mattered." Jackson? I wonder if it is the same Jackson from Arkaley. No, it couldn't be.

"They forced me to spend more time with him, lessening the supervision with every visit. He was brash, pushing me against walls, kissing me, holding, touching me all the time. At first, I didn't think the supervision was even effective because of how forceful he was, but I was wrong. I was so wrong." She drops her head, sniffling. I can't stand the distance anymore. I lean forward and take her hand, pulling it to my lap. She slides closer, pressing her body against my leg. I hold her hand with one of mine as the other hand strokes her arm soothingly. This story isn't easy for her to tell, and I want to make this process as easy as I can for her.

"The first time we were left alone, he shoved his hand under my dress. The next time he forced his cock in my mouth. I sometimes question why I didn't bite it off then. I wasn't in a good place. I knew I would have been blamed for that situation, and it didn't feel worth it. After that point, I stopped fighting, but he kept pushing. It went on for a couple of months. I didn't tell anyone. No one listened when I complained about the kissing; why would they care about anything else?" I squeeze her hand, angry for her. How could no one notice what he was doing? Why did her torment go on for so long?

"After one dreadful night with him, I tried to tell Mother. I wanted her to understand how horrible he was. She told me it was normal. Once I popped out an heir, he could get a concubine, and everything would be fine for me. As if that was all that I was good for. They just needed me to further the royal line, and beyond that, I was useless." Tears are streaking down her face now. The pain of her story is palpable in the room. My own chest aches for her.

"That morning was the first time I saw Dahlia again. I was so broken that when I saw her, I burst into tears and ran. I didn't want her to see me. I didn't want her to see the darkness in me, what my life had been diminished to. She followed me, though. When she caught me, she demanded I tell her everything. I did, and she wanted to kill him. She tried to storm from the room right then to find him. I stopped her, not wanting to endanger her or worsen the situation.

She put up quite a fight to get at Jackson. Imagine Sunette as a love-scorned seventeen-year-old." She huffs a laugh empty of humor, wiping tears from her cheeks. I feel my own emotions going numb over her words. I don't know what to feel anymore. Dahlia clearly felt strongly for Jasmin, something I can relate to. A moment of sadness passes through at the thought that I won't get to meet her.

"I convinced Dahlia to find a way to meet with me again. If I was to be reduced to a broodmare while the king got a concubine, I was going to claim Dahlia. We devised a plan to see each other in secret. It worked at first. Jackson continued his forcefulness when we were alone, but I found solace in spending time with Dahlia. Eventually, she was released from her confinement to her living quarters. We weren't allowed to be together, but I got to see her daily in passing, in addition to our frequent secret visits.

"The seasons faded again, winter solstice coming and going. Things were not good, but I was surviving. Dahlia still had her mind set on Jackson's death, but I held her off. Not wanting to spend my limited time with her discussing the worst part of my life. One morning, I woke, realizing I hadn't had my monthly cycle lately. I began counting dates, realizing how late I actually was. I had never been late before. There was only one reason it could be happening. My mother walked in as I was counting the clean cloths. She realized right away what had happened. Instead of showing terror and anger over me being forcefully impregnated out of wedlock, she was ecstatic. She said we would plan a spring wedding, we could have a large dress to hide my stomach if I started showing early, not that many would care. There would be a new heir in the kingdom." I don't remember hearing about any of this. It would have been huge news, even out of wedlock. My hands still against her skin as I rack my brain for any memory of these announcements.

"Mother placed her hands on my stomach and claimed I was having a girl. I still don't know what possessed her to say that, but that was what she believed. She instantly got to work making plans. I was devastated. Dahlia was the first person I told. She was livid. I almost didn't stop her from going on a murderous rampage. It would undoubtedly be her end if she went after the Queen. I couldn't let that happen. I told her I couldn't go through with the wedding or the pregnancy. That

I needed them to go away. Dahlia informed me that was something she could actually do. She asked for a few days and disappeared.

"In that time, Mother began working on the nursery." Jasmin waves her hand around the room. The pink lace and flowers make sense now. This was her mother's doing. I hate it. I despise being in this room and have a deep urge to burn it down. "I walked in one morning to find the room exactly like this. I have never seen my mother so excited about anything. She put together an entire room in three days. My heart shattered into a million pieces. Dahlia scooped me off the floor later that evening. She snuck through the back passages into my room, bringing supplies with her. We sat in the middle of the floor while she mashed some herbs and chanted for several minutes. When she was done, she gave me a small glass with liquid and herbs, instructing me to drink it all. I didn't even question her. I drank the mixture in one gulp."

My chest tightens as I realize what she is saying. This woman that I love and have grown so close to in the past few months has such a dark history. While I have my own experiences with dark moments, I can't even compare to what Jasmin went through. I wish her words would stop there, and that would be the end of the story, but I know this story isn't over. She is stronger than I ever realized.

"I eventually fell asleep on the floor, waking the next morning to the most intense pain of my life. I yelled out, and Mother came running. When she saw me, she became hysterical. My dress was soaked in blood. The floor was stained; I could barely focus through the pain. Mother cursed the heavens, trying to order servants to clean me up and get me to my room. At some point during the chaos, she found the cup Dahlia had mixed for me. She stormed into my room, yelling for everyone else to leave. Emmeline tried to argue that I needed help, but Mother grabbed her and shoved her out of the room. Once we were alone, Mother threw the glass, shattering it against the wall. She reared her hand back and slapped me. Her nails were always sharp, but I never realized how sharp they were." She runs her fingers along the edges of the scars on her cheeks. It's unfathomable that a mother could do such damage to her only child. I reach up and slide my fingers across her scars with her. Her eyes close as my fingers lightly trace the scars. I want to take her pain away from her. She doesn't deserve this.

"She brought in shears and began removing chunks of my hair. She told me if I couldn't behave like a woman, I wouldn't be allowed to look like one." Her fingers pull the ends of her hair, now longer than when I first arrived at the castle. I had assumed she kept it short as a way to rebel against beauty standards. Her mother had such a significant impact on her life. I can only imagine how painful the Queen's words must have been.

"I was limited to my room for several days. When I finally came out, my father insisted on a family meeting. He didn't apologize or offer any sympathy for what I had just gone through. Not Jackson, the pregnancy, or the subsequent ending. Nothing. The most I got from him was a hurt look as he took in my hair and scarred face. Father informed me Jackson had been sent back to Arkaley to remain and would not be allowed at the castle again. Relief washed through me despite the cold delivery. Unfortunately, the news didn't stop there. Over the past few days, Dahlia had tried to run away. But she fell, injuring her foot. Due to the winter conditions, starved animals found her, and she didn't survive the attack." Jasmin sniffles again, lowering her face as she takes several slow breaths. A sinking pit forms in my stomach as the realization settles that I ran off in brutal winter conditions, too.

"Without giving me a moment to process what he said, he continued by telling me both he and Mother would be traveling to Hollyhock in search of a more suitable man for me. They wanted to find a prince to foster better relations. I didn't say anything as they packed up and left. I didn't even say goodbye. I didn't speak to anyone for a week. I had to fill in on some of the royal duties, but I did so as an empty shell. I wasn't really present at any of the meetings.

"On the first night I was finally coming to terms with everything, thunder began to boom outside. The brightest, most colorful lightning I had ever seen flashed across the sky." I know the night she is speaking of. I saw and heard the same storm. "A haggard old woman in rumpled clothes stormed into the castle, demanding to speak to me. I met her in the foyer, where she recited the curse.

I don't actually remember most of the words. I did catch punishment, whore, suffering, true love, and responsibility."

She pauses her story, collecting her thoughts. The storm looked fascinating from the house. It was another hour or so before we learned what the storm actually was. I still remember the chaos of those first few weeks after the barrier fell. Ma kept us all at home, not letting us leave the house. My hands return to her hand and arm, stroking her gently as she talks. Jasmin takes a shuddering breath, then continues with her story.

"The hag said the King and Queen had died outside of the kingdom. She brought their carriage and items with her, leaving them outside the front door. She left as quickly as she came, turning my entire world upside down from its already sideways position. Things devolved into chaos. I tried to do what I could, but I was still processing so many other incidents I might as well have been a ghost.

"Just before the curse's first anniversary, I had no luck breaking it. We had all tried. The Lords brought dozens of men through the castle. I physically recoiled at most, unable to be around men I didn't know for fear of events repeating. That was when I started the journal. I needed to focus on why I had to be around men. I needed to remind myself who I was doing this for. I had to remember the real people in my kingdom." She reaches back, grabs the journal, flipping through the pages. It lands open on my father's name. "This is actually the second journal I've written. The first one was worn out from flipping through the pages." She holds the journal up for me. I take it from her, tracing my fingers over my father's name. The ink is worn on his name as if she has run her fingers over it more often than any other page.

"Every year, the day before the anniversary, I come in here, light candles, and read through the list to remind myself." She sighs, fiddling with a string, not meeting my eyes. I listen patiently, sensing there is more to her story. "The first year came with an extra surprise. I had lost track of my monthly cycles, distracted by everything else. On the first anniversary, the bleeding started. It was as intense and painful as the night I drank the liquid. I knew it wasn't another pregnancy, but I didn't understand why it was so intense. We summoned a healer, but as soon as he lifted my shirt, he began screaming and ran from the room. The markings had shown up with the first bleed. It was another part of the curse, though easier to hide and manage than the rest. I remained covered around everyone, including Sunette and Emmeline, though they knew about the markings. We ensured no meetings were planned around the anniversary so I could hide away while the bleeding lasted. There haven't been any problems until this year." She finally looks up at me. Her cheeks are streaked with tear stains.

"You are the first person to see me like that. The first person to hear any of this." She squeezes my hand in hers. She swallows, looking back up at me. "I tell you all of this, Clem, not to justify my actions but to help you understand." Tears are falling from her eyes again. "I am sorry for the way I have treated you. I know it was wrong, deceiving you when we first met, pushing you away every time you got close. Not being honest with you about what was happening to me. I am so sorry, Clem." Her voice breaks as she drops her face against my hands. Unable to stand the distance any longer, I grab her, pulling her into my lap. I wrap her tightly in my arms, holding her close.

The journal is still in my hand, wrapped around her back. My heart is breaking over her story. There isn't anything I can say. Nothing will add to this situation. Instead, I just hold her firmly against my body. Her arms wrap around mine. I can't fix the damage that has been done. I can't even hurt the people involved in creating this situation, even though I would very much like to. I realize there is one thing I can do, one thing I can say. It won't fix the problem. It may not even make it better. But it is still something I can give to her at this moment.

Chapter 28

JASMIN

"**I** love you, Jas."

A gasp escapes from me as I sit up to look at him. I stare into his eyes, searching for any signs this isn't real. He's proven his feelings are strong. He's shown me time and time again how much he cares, and I am still surprised by his confession. No, not surprised. I'm not surprised he loves me. I'm caught off guard, unprepared for that confession. I just told him my deepest, darkest secrets. I didn't expect his response to be that he loves me.

"I don't care about the curse. I don't care if I'm not your true love. I'm not scared of your past. I know that I love you, and I just want you to know that."

Tears build in my eyes; my throat constricts, making it hard for me to respond. I love you, too. That's all I need to say. Why am I still so scared? What if I tell him and he's not my true love? Will I be forced to pretend to be happy with another person again? A stuttering breath shakes my body, forcing me to lean against his chest. I close my eyes, trying to stop the tears from falling. So many tears have already spilled in the past week. I can't cry anymore. His arms press me tightly to his chest as a realization hits. Even if I am forced to pretend to be with someone else to break the curse, Clem is still here. He's still with me now. I vow to soak up every minute that I have with him.

"I love you, too, Clem," I whisper against his chest. His arms squeeze tighter; the only sign I get that he heard me. After a moment, Clem tosses the journal I didn't realize he was still holding onto the shelf. He stands with me in his arms. He feels a bit shaky, though. I wiggle in his arms, trying to get down.

"No, you can't carry me now." He can't hold me as I fight against him. He isn't as well as I want him to be now. My feet hit the floor, and I look up at his face. He is hurt that I won't let him carry me, but I'm not risking his health for something so trivial. We walk hand in hand back into my room, leaving the nursery behind us. I guide him to the couch, letting him settle, then climb against his chest, needing time to realign before we do anything else. His breathing is steady and sure, providing me comfort in his stability.

"How are you feeling, Clem?" My words are softer than I want them to be, but I don't want to be too loud now, either. He takes a deep breath, considering my answer.

"My body is still sore, but I don't feel sick. Just tired." His arm tightens around my body. "How are you?" I puff out an empty laugh.

"I'm exhausted and spent." His lips press against my head. I close my eyes, trying to commit the feeling to my long-term memory. No matter what happens, I want to remember how this feels forever. My fingers toy with his hair, finding tangles, unable to stroke through the strands. I lean back, looking at him. He still seems worn out. His cheeks are wind-chapped, despite the rest of his skin looking better.

"You're hair is tangled. Would you like a bath? It would probably help with your sore muscles, too." He considers for a moment, as if being away from me for the length of a bath is too much, but soon nods. His eyes are starting to glaze over; he is more exhausted than he lets on. I probably shouldn't have told him that story today. It was too soon; he wasn't well enough. I drag him into the bathroom, showing him how everything works. My bathroom is an impressive display of wealth and privilege, but he doesn't seem to register any of it. Before I even leave the room, he has stripped out of his clothes and sunk down into the deep, heated pool.

I wait outside, running a comb through my own tangled hair. After several minutes, I hear him call my name. I stand outside the door, considering that we haven't consensually been naked in front of each other. The times we were without clothes were out of necessity. I crack the door open, asking what he needs.

"Um, I need help."

Inside, bubbles are in the water, and the bar of soap is on the floor. "I can't hold it well." He shows me his hands, indicating they are still weak. Of course, they are. They were so cold when he came back inside. I take a cloth and rub the soap on it, preparing to wash his body for him. He doesn't say anything as I clean him, just shifts so I can reach him better. It's such a peaceful, intimate moment. Once his body is clean, I wash his hair and finger comb most of the tangles. It isn't perfect, but it's better. I help him dress after he gets out, then lead him to my bed.

"You need more rest."

He doesn't even argue. He practically collapses onto the bed, unable to hold his body up any longer. Despite his apparent exhaustion, a smirk grows on his face.

"Read to me?" His voice is soft and playful, repeating the words I have said to him so many times. I smile back at him, grab a book from my shelf, and climb into bed with him. He rests his head on my lap, wrapping his arms around my waist and thighs. I read to him for a long time until he drifts off. I slide down next to him, snuggling into his chest. The past few weeks have been emotional torment for both of us. I don't know what all of this means for us, for the other bachelors, for the curse. In this moment, though, I know I want to be with him.

We wake several hours later to Emmeline bringing in food for both of us. She doesn't say much, only asking if we need any specific herbs. She asks if we plan to go to breakfast tomorrow or if she should bring it up. I'm more than willing to let her bring it up, but Clem mentions the others will want to see us. We settle on going down on our own. Emmeline leaves, stating she will see us in the morning. After eating, I clear our tray and stand next to the bed.

He pulls me down on the bed, hovering over me. I expect him to say something, but he covers my jawline in tiny, quick kisses. He scrapes his teeth gently across my ear lobe, causing me to squirm at the wetness building between my legs. This man seriously has the magic touch when it comes to my arousal. It may not be a magic fun ball like Kian has, but Clem doesn't need other devices to get me going.

He plants slow, lingering kisses along my neck. I moan his name in response, soaking up every little touch he gives me. My fingers twist through his hair. I try to run them through, but he still has many tangles from the past few days. Instead, I just play with small chunks, twisting and twirling it in my fingers. I call his name, but he shushes me, continuing on his journey of planting kisses along my body. When he reaches my collar, he grabs the hem of my shirt and sweater, lifting it up to remove it. I lean forward, assisting him in removing the clothing.

I lie back, bared in front of him in a sexual manner. We didn't mention our nudeness over the past several days while we were sick. It wasn't meant to be sexual or arousing. There were other reasons for our lack of clothing. This, though. This is intentional. He takes in my chest, stomach, down to my waist, where my leggings are secured. Instead of removing the leggings, he kisses across my collarbone, to my shoulder, then down my arm. His work is slow and methodical; he is savoring his time with my body. He kisses each of my fingertips before moving back up my arm, over my shoulder, across my collarbone, and to the other side. His lips are warm and firm against my skin. It takes all of my effort not to rub my thighs against him.

He finally returns to my torso. His eyes meet mine, but instead of kissing across my chest, he lowers to his side, using his hand to caress my ribs. His fingers stroke just under my collarbone, gliding across ever so slightly lower until he floats just above the top of my breast. I moan again, desperate for him to touch more, take more, claim more.

"If you keep making noises, I will gag you."

My eyes go wide in shock, both at being told what to do and being threatened. I don't typically receive such concise rules with actual consequences. At this moment, I'm divided. I could do what he says and see what he will do. But I also want to know if he would actually gag me, following through with his threat. An additional voice in the back of my head wants to be gagged. Seriously, I need to spend some time considering the implications of my sexual preferences.

His fingers are slowly stroking lower across my chest. He is just skimming the top of my breasts, dropping his fingers between them, then massaging the other one. Back and forth, side to side. It's the purest form of torture. My pussy is throbbing, aching with desire, wanting him to move faster, go lower, touch more. He skims the edge of my areola; my nipples already budded with pleasure.

"Clem, please," I beg. I don't even care that it's begging. I need him to do more, but as soon as the words are out of my mouth, he rises from the bed. I groan at his loss, both the warmth of his body and the touch of his fingers. He walks to my closet, digging through various items until he finds what he is looking for. When he returns, he has several sashes in his hands. I watch with curiosity as he moves onto the bed, kneeling next to me.

"I told you to be quiet." He whispers against my cheek, his breath warm against my skin. "Since you can't behave, I'm going to make you."

He pulls one of the sashes free, placing it in my mouth. He gently lifts my head, tying the sash behind my head without any issues. His strength must have returned to his hands. Once secured, he lowers my head to the pillow. I watch as he tries to memorize how I look right now. His fingers caress my cheek, just above the sash. A touch so tender, I melt beneath it. I close my own eyes, enjoying the feel of his fingers against my cheek. I open them as he pulls away to find he is pulling out another scarf. He drapes it over my eyes as my breath catches. I've never been blindfolded like this before. It's one thing to close my eyes willingly during intimate times; it's another to lose control of that. Clem senses my uncertainty. He lifts my head again, but this time his lips press against my ear.

"You're safe, Jasmin. You are in control. You won't be hurt again, unless you want it."

Oh fuck. Why is the first thought in my head that I want it? I want him to hurt me as he did last time. I want him to fuck me so hard I feel it for days. My legs rub together, aching for any sort of sensation they can get. I stifle a moan, biting down on the already-soaked silk material in my mouth. Clem is excellently teasing me, drawing out every last bit of patience and pleasure from my body. He finally ties the sash, lowering my head again as he moves away. He pulled the material over my nose, so I can't see anything at all. The bed shifts as he rises from it.

"If you want me to stop, clap your hands together."

I nod, but I likely won't stop. He hasn't done anything to make me feel unsafe or uncomfortable before. I just want him to touch me again. He is agonizingly slow about this process, and my core is throbbing with intense need. His hands wrap around my foot to remove my slippers. I take a deep breath, trying to settle some of the ache. His fingers drag across my skin, tracing my heel, ankle, and calf. He slips his fingers under the hem of my leggings and starts tugging. They slide slowly, having much more tension when pulled from the bottom. He tugs in just the right manner to slide them all off. They thud against the floor as he tosses them across the room.

I am laid bare in front of him. Intentionally exposed for his pleasure, for his eyes to enjoy. My knees squeeze together, nervous about him seeing me. Which is a ridiculous thought since he has seen me before. He grabs my ankles, pulling them down, spreading them apart. My head turns to the side, trying to hide my face despite the sashes wrapped around me. He lifts one leg, bringing it to his lips to press a kiss on the inside of my heel. I moan at the touch, unable to stop the noise. The cool air of the room caresses my soaking cunt. I need more; I'm going to burst with desire.

He leaves a slow trail of kisses from the inside of my ankle, up my calf, over my knee, then on top of my thigh instead of staying on the inside. His fingertips dance along my inner thigh. My breathing is choppy as my core clenches around nothing. Unable to withstand the ache any longer, my fingers slide down quickly, trying to rub my clit on my own. He grabs my wrist before I actually touch anything and chuckles.

"I am going to worship you the way you deserve, and you are going to let me."

His voice is so deep and saturated with lust. I nearly orgasm from the rich timbre of his voice. If his body is any closer to mine when he speaks, I probably will. He raises my hands above my head, holding them with one hand. I wiggle, trying to get more contact with his body that is now hovering over mine. Another sash wraps around my wrists, twisting around and between as he secures my hands together. When he's done, he secures the sash onto part of the headboard, suspending my hands above my head.

"If you want me to stop, snap your fingers. Do it for me now." I obey, snapping my fingers twice.

"Good girl." He breathes against my ear. My eyes roll back in my head in pleasure. My chest arches toward him, trying to get more sensation. He laughs but shifts on the bed. Then his mouth is on my nipple, licking, sucking, biting. I groan loudly behind my gag. His body settles between my legs. As soon as he is there, I wrap my legs around his back. He has removed his shirt and is bare against my skin. I rub my clit against his stomach, searching for release. I don't find that, but I get some pleasure from rubbing against him.

He slides back, breaking free from my legs. He pulls his body away from mine, sinking down further past the apex of my thighs. Nothing happens for several moments. Nothing aside from me wriggling and whining. The lightest touch I have ever felt skims my aching pussy. He is licking me in a slow, teasing manner. Months ago, when the bachelors first arrived, and I thought I would die from lack of release? I was wrong. This is the moment I will die. He is torture-pleasuring me to death, and I fucking love it. His tongue caresses my wet lips, circling my clit with pressure slightly harder than a breath. I thrust my hips at him, but he is faster, jerking away before I make contact. He places a hand on top of my pelvis, holding me in place. I groan as he chuckles again.

"So impatient, little flower. I'm trying to savor you."

I groan in protest, thrusting my hips near his face. My fingers stretch, then link together, staying in a position that cannot be confused with a snap. I want release; I don't want this to end before that. Without any warning, Clem's mouth is on my clit, sucking hard. My entire body is on fire. Every nerve in my body lights up as his tongue swirls. He slips a finger inside me, making circles around my inner walls. His lips pop off my clit as his tongue enters my core. His finger brushes my clit, pressing against it. His tongue laps at my center, thrusting in and out. I twist with growing pleasure, so very close to an orgasm. He increases the speed against my clit while his tongue is relentless. Then my body explodes harder than I ever have before. My legs shake against his body. I can't take in a breath, my chest frozen in its position. Stars are bursting in my vision as every muscle in my body seizes. He is still tonguing my core as it repeatedly clenches around him. My body jolts several times until finally relaxing against the bed. My breathing is fast, and I cannot catch my breath after that orgasm.

Clem climbs over me, resting his body against mine. His shirt is gone, but his pants are still on. I can feel his erect cock pressing against my leg. He pulls the gag down from my mouth, his lips meeting mine in a passionate kiss. I can taste my orgasm all over his face. His lips, cheeks, and nose are soaked in moisture from my core. His tongue thrusts into my mouth, swirling with my own, leaving my taste in my mouth. My hands tug against their binding, instinctually wanting to grab his back. He rubs his hard penis against me, searching for his own release.

He pulls away from me, emptiness creeping in quickly. The rustling of his pants reaches my ears moments before I hear them land on the floor. The bed shifts under his weight as he climbs back on, hovering over my body. He slides between my legs, fingers dancing against the sensitive skin inside my thighs. I jerk as his fingers rub over my opening, tapping the bundle of nerves at the top. He drags his cock across my slit, coating it in my moisture. The sensation of him against me is overwhelming. He leans over, taking my nipple in his mouth again while slowly stroking his cock along my entrance. My hands jerk to touch him.

"Clem, please remove these sashes. I want to touch you. I need to see you." I'm not even ashamed of my begging. The bondage was fun while we were doing things we have done before, but he is not about to enter me for the first time when I can't see or touch him.

His lips pop off my nipple as he looks up at me. "Yes, Your Majesty." His whispers cause my core to contract, ready for him despite the powerful orgasm I just had. He repositions his body and then slides the sash off my eyes. I blink them a couple of times, adjusting to the light. His face is soft, with a warm smile.

It doesn't match the harshness he has just given me, but it's part of the reason I love him so much. The duality between hard and soft is one of my favorite things about him. He gently kisses my cheek as he unties the sash around my hands. Once they are free, my arms wrap around his shoulders, fingers tangling in his hair.

His body settles against mine as he notches the tip of his cock at my entrance. My breathing slows down in nervous anticipation. No one has fucked me like this in nearly a decade. Thoughts start racing through my mind about the meaning and implications of doing this with him. Just as I begin to question whether this is a good idea, his lips press against mine as he slowly slides inside. Instantly, my brain is shut off. The worries and fear stop. All I can feel is Clem.

His lips are against mine in a delicate kiss. His hands are on my body, one on my shoulder as his arm supports his weight. The other is on my waist, holding me in place. His cock presses slowly, so slowly, inside me. Deeper and deeper until he reaches the hilt. He holds there for a moment, both of us adjusting to this new sensation. It feels like heaven. It feels like nirvana. It feels like this is where I belong; this is everything I want. It's quiet here, just him and me. His body is warm, filling, soft, and hard. He's perfect. He breaks the kiss, leaning back just a couple of inches to take in my face. With his cock buried deep, unmoving, he presses several kisses along my cheek, then the other.

His hips slowly pull back, dragging his cock out of me. My breath catches at the movement, an ache and emptiness taking over simultaneously. He pulls back, leaving only the tip inside, then presses into the hilt again at the same agonizingly slow pace. The first time, this speed was welcome. Now he's back to his torture bullshit, and I need it to stop.

"Clem, please." He chuckles but continues his excruciatingly slow pace.

"Yes, Jas?" The humor in his voice is not funny to me. I wiggle beneath him, trying to drive him further inside me. Instead, he stops moving, holding his hips away with his penis barely nocked inside me.

"Fuck, Clem. Please. Please, just fuck me. You're going to kill me with this torture!" I cry out, scratching my nails along his back, thrusting my hips at him, anything to get him to move.

"Am I going too slow?" He teases as he sinks in at a snail's pace.

"YES!" I scream at him, whimpering at the need building deep in my body. His hips land flush with mine again. At least when he is fully seated, the emptiness isn't as prevalent. It does nothing for the need to be fucked building inside me.

"Anything for my little flower."

He pulls back and slams inside me. My head rolls back with pleasure. He starts up a near-brutal pace, and I love it. He is pounding into the spot so deep inside that has been aching since he first showed up. My arms wrap around his back, holding him tight as he thrusts vigorously. His hair dangles over my face, dancing against my skin. We begin to sweat with desire and effort. I push his hair back, watching his beautiful face as he rams deep inside my pussy. My body tenses with pleasure, another strong orgasm building. He shifts his weight, bringing his hand to my clit. He finds the perfect angle, circling my already sensitive nerves as he slams into my core. My hips shift, causing him to hit a new position deep inside me.

"OH! That's it. Please don't stop." I cry out, breathing fast as my vision blurs with pleasure.

"Come for me, Jas. I want to feel you squeezing my dick."

His words, his voice, it sends me over the edge. A gush of fluid squirts from my body while his relentless pounding continues. My eyes close tight as bright explosions burst behind my eyelids. I think I am yelling. I think I am falling. Whatever my body is doing, it's the most intense pleasure I have ever experienced. It usually is with Clem. As my body settles, he jerks out quickly, lifting his cock over me. I look down in time to see jets of his own release falling over my stomach. Warm, white bits of semen fall on my dark, bruised skin. It's a stark contrast between his release and my damaged skin. It sends tingles over my sensitized body to see him release on me. I did that to him.

As the last bit jolts out, he collapses by my side, staring down at the mess he made. For several moments, we lie quietly, catching our breath. Letting our bodies return from their states of bliss. He kisses my cheek softly, and I snuggle into his side more. His fingers trace around the edges of my marked skin. His face is serious, contemplating something heavy.

"I love you, Jasmin." His voice is soft, just above a whisper. "I may not be your true love, but I will support you with whoever it is. And if it's someone terrible, I'll kill them after you break the curse." His words squeeze at my chest. I kiss his lips gently, unable to find the voice to respond to him. Several moments later, he shifts away, only to return with a wet cloth. He wipes the mess he left on my skin, making a pass over my core too. It's such a tender, intimate moment. I have never experienced something so gentle and meaningful. He puts the rag to the side and then crawls back in bed with me. He tugs the quilt over us, snuggling close without saying anything else. I quickly drift off, falling into a deep sleep. At some point during the night, Finn finds his way into bed. He spreads out against my back. I can feel the smile on my face as I sleep, squished between Finn and Clem.

Chapter 29

Jasmin

Sunshine is creeping through the window. I stroke my hand down the body next to me, thinking Clem is much hairier than I remember. I crack my eyes open, finding Finn squished between Clem and me. Of course, he just has to be at the center of everything. I chuckle, sitting up to look around the room. Emmeline must have been in here at some point. Our clothes have been picked up; there is a new pile of clean clothes for us and a fresh jug of water for us to drink. Clem is already awake, still lying on the bed, just watching me.

He sits up, leaning over Finn to give me a gentle kiss. Finn whines with our movement, trying to stretch out further between us. We both chuckle, rubbing his back. His tail wags, crashing against our legs.

"We should probably go down for breakfast."

It seems like such a long time since I have seen the other men. I only spent a few hours with them when Clem was missing, and even that was several days ago. I nod, stretching before trying to get up. My fingers run through my hair, realizing it is heavily tangled from being in bed for so long.

"I need to bathe first."

Clem nods, his hair in a similar state. His hair is longer, but mine is catching up quickly. I am so pleased my hair is growing back. It had fallen most of the way down my back when Mother cut it. It could still take several years to get back to that, but at least it is growing again.

"I need to also. Want to bathe together?" He gives me a smirk with a playful glint in his eyes.

"Together?" I question, surprised by his suggestion. He nods in response. I shrug, leading the way to the bathroom attached to my room. The bath is large enough for us both to be in. Witches spelled it a long time ago when the castle was first built. The water is always warm, something I realize is more of a luxury than most ever experience. As I lead Clem in, his eyes widen, taking in the luxurious space now that he is well. While I have never been to his home, I have toured several like his in the villages. Many have outdoor bathing areas in the summer, with barely heated rooms for winter. I never understood why they didn't have witches come into our villages to help them. Maybe the witches didn't want to. I should ask Kian about it.

I walk over to the bath, stepping in while Clem continues to take in the room. It is lavish, with large fluffy towels on a shelf, several soaps, and oils near the vast pool. Small sconces on the wall are lit, though unnecessary, with the light streaming through the large windows opening toward the gardens. Thick, dark curtains are tied back on either side of the window. It has been a luxury in and of itself to bathe in the sunlight with fewer people on the grounds. Clem seems entirely swept up in the lavishness of the room, so I flick some water at him, wanting him to join me. He jumps as the water splashes his chest, but a smile spreads across his face. He climbs into the tub opposite me.

"It's warm."

"It's magic," I offer as an explanation.

"You're lucky."

"I am," I speak softly as I slide through the water and climb into his lap. His arms wrap around my back as I lean against his body. He's been spoiling me so much lately, taking care of my needs first. I kiss his cheek, working my way down to his neck. I nip and suck at his neck as he moans under my touch. My hand slides between us, wrapping around his already half-hard penis. I stroke the shaft slowly, kissing around his neck to the other side. My lips brush against his soft skin, savoring his taste, the way his unshaved skin scratches my smooth face. He whispers my name, something between a prayer and a plea.

"No, Clem. It's my turn." My soft voice isn't nearly as powerful as his. I can't imagine my words having the same effect on him as his do on me. I'm not much of a talker, but I don't need to be either. His cock is already hard, standing erect between our bodies. I lift my hips, positioning myself over him as I slowly lower, taking him in deeply. I don't have his patience, though. Once he is entirely inside me, I settle my arms on his shoulders, using them for balance and support as I rise and sink on his dick. The warm water creates an entirely new sensation, different from being in bed. His hands grab my waist, trying to guide me faster. I manage to set my own pace, slower than the one he is trying to force me into. I give him a devilish grin before kissing him tenderly. Soon, my speed becomes too slow, needing him deeper and faster. He realizes my needs, using his hands to guide me at a quicker pace. As I slide up and down, I rock, letting my clit rub against his stomach. I moan, arching back, my breasts pressing forward into his face. His arms wrap around my back as he buries his face between my breasts, kissing, biting, breathing them in. I wrap my arms around his head, holding tightly as I ride him through our building ecstasy. Water sloshes around us, sending tiny droplets spraying onto our bodies.

I drop my arms to his shoulder, grabbing his hair and pulling it down tightly. He gasps as he is forced to look up. I latch onto his neck, savoring the taste of his skin. The slight change in our positions increases the pressure on my clit. I'm about to climax as he stutters through a similar statement.

"I'm going to come, Jas." My core clenches around him as he says my shortened name.

"Do it," I whisper against his skin, bouncing harder against him. He leans back, thrusting to match my pace. He only does that twice before I burst around him, moaning his name as my body soars through pleasure. He slams into me, his hand grabbing my hips and holding me in place as he empties deep inside me. My muscles clench and release several times as he releases inside my cunt. I settle against his chest as he leans back against the tub's edge. We sit for several minutes, wrapped in each other's arms, as the water calms to rest around us.

"Are you on the tea to prevent pregnancy?" He asks softly.

"No," I start slowly. It's not a topic I have considered much in the past decade. "I'm pretty sure I'm infertile, though. With the scar and irregular cycles, I don't think I can have any more pregnancies." I sit up, looking at him, realizing this is the first time I've explained that to him. "Is that a problem for you?"

He shakes his head quickly. "No. I got to experience Claire as a baby. As much as I love her, I have no desire to have my own. I would rather just have you." I smile, relaxing against him. I never really got the chance to experience parenthood, but it's not something I particularly want. It's expected of me, to the point of being forced on me. But it isn't something I actually want. I climb off him, grabbing the brush.

"Turn around and let me brush your hair."

He does as instructed, sinking down and resting against me so I can reach his hair better. He moans as I stroke the brush through his tangly hair. He tells me he hasn't had anyone else brush his hair like this. I kiss his cheek, working out a knot of hair as gently as possible before moving on to others.

"I know Jackson." He speaks softly. I hesitate at the name, unsure where he is going with this. "He is a horrible man. The wife he married has several kids, but he is rarely home. Instead, he warms the bed of all the other girls he can get to." He pauses, and I resume brushing his hair. I have been keeping tabs on Jackson, insisting on regular updates. We know what he is doing. "Though, now I wonder how willing they are." His words are spoken softly but filled with so much hate. I kiss his shoulder, working through another mess of tangles in his hair.

"I broke his nose a couple of years ago." I chuckle at his confession. Jackson has always been prone to fighting, but I didn't always know who did it. "He started talking shit about Bea at one point." I squeeze his shoulder as I finish brushing his hair. "He had many terrible things to say about you. I thought he was jealous or just making up rumors. He has a tendency to do that." He turns to face me, taking the brush from my hand. He looks like he will say something, but I don't want him to say anything else. I don't want to tarnish our time together with that conversation. I kiss him gently, spinning around so he can brush my hair. I decide to change the subject.

"Did you brush Claire's hair a lot?" He accepts the turn in the conversation. We chat about his sisters and his role with them as we finish bathing. We climb out of the tub, clean and in better spirits. We speak while we get dressed, helping each other with our hair. I can't help but marvel at how natural this all feels. There aren't awkward lulls in conversation. We work together seamlessly, knowing what each other will need next. Emmeline is back at it as we dress, matching our clothes. I have dark leggings and a cream sweater with large, twisted sections running from top to bottom. Clem has on beige-colored trousers with a dark sweater on top. I roll my eyes at her choice of clothing. He extends his hand to me.

"Ready?"

The smile on his face is contagious. This feels like a big moment for us, but it isn't really. We're just going to breakfast after being holed up in my room. Fucking, sharing secrets, and taking care of each other for days. Perhaps it is more significant than I am giving it credit for. Will others recognize it as the same? Will they know the depths Clem and I have been through? I search his face, trying to identify anything that might give that away. He does look different to me, but I can't pinpoint why. It's probably just my own feelings for him tinting his appearance. He bids good morning to the guards standing post outside my hallway. I pause, turning to them.

"Clem should be given access to my rooms anytime, and he does not need an escort to enter. Please let the others know also."

"Yes, ma'am," they say in unison.

"Add Kian and Erik to that list also. Thank you."

I nod thanks as we return to walk toward the dining hall. Clem is tense now, still holding my hand, not saying anything, but noticeably tense. We've been in such a secluded bubble for so long, barely mentioning anyone else, certainly not discussing our changing roles. As we near the dining hall, my own nerves ramp up. At the last minute, I duck into an alcove, pulling Clem in with me. We aren't in privacy but hidden from the view of the dining hall. We should have stayed in the room and sent for food. My breathing is quick, and my appetite has disappeared. Clem looks me up and down, pulling me into a hug. I can smell my soap on his skin, blending with his own smell from his clothes. It's so comforting to just be in his arms. I haven't thought much about how I behave with all the men, or at least multiple at the same time. I've always done what I felt like doing. Having changed the type of relationship with Clem, though, I'm not sure what I am supposed to do with the others now. Touching Clem the way I want will probably upset them. Touching them the way I usually would will definitely upset Clem. I'm going to be so awkward; if someone questions me, I'll have to tell them I fucked Clem in the bath this morning. Okay, I don't have to, but I probably definitely will.

Clem leans back to say something, but Finn comes sniffing around before he can. He barks excitedly when he finds us hiding. I try to shush him, wave him away, and step out of the alcove to silence him.

"Jasmin!" Kian calls out my name from opposite the door to the dining hall. It's just my luck that now is the time he enters. "There you are! We've been wondering if you were okay! Emmeline has been really tight-lipped about your activities the past few days." I step out of the alcove completely, rubbing Finn's ears as Kian walks toward me. I'm glad Emmeline hasn't said anything, but this situation is less than ideal for me.

"Oh, yes. Well, I'm here for breakfast now."

I smile at him, rubbing my arm. This past week has really done a number on my ability to socialize. I have always been able to handle social interactions with grace and dignity. I wonder if the sex, confessing my secrets, or love destroyed my ability to think clearly. Whatever it is fades to the background as Clem steps up behind me, wrapping his arm around my waist. It's such a possessive move. None of them have really been possessive. Even to this point, only Clem has shown signs of jealousy. I don't react to Clem's assertiveness. Kian glances at his hand on my hip, then my eyes.

"Hey, Clem." Kian looks to him in greeting, ignoring Clem's movement. "How are you feeling?"

"Much better. Thank you."

I didn't tell Clem how involved everyone else was in his rescue. I also didn't exactly tell him how I reacted when I learned where he was. As much talking as we did, we missed some crucial subjects. I take a deep breath, trying to regain my composure.

"Are the others already in there? I'm starving." Kian looks like he might say something devious, but I push past him, pulling away from Clem and entering the dining hall before he can. Erik spots me and waves, calling me over to him. I leave Clem and Kian behind, not wanting to deal with whatever bullshit they are thinking about starting. Erik pulls me into a tight hug. My lungs constrict as the tight embrace stirs emotions I haven't adequately dealt with. After he releases me, he hands me a mug of tea. He asks how I'm doing, but I respond with a short quick answer. We go to the tables of food, grabbing things we want. My appetite is gone, but I grab bread and some jam, hoping I'll remember how hungry I am once I start eating.

We sit at the table where Tomas and Zander are already together. I love seeing them side by side. They look wonderfully happy with each other, and it warms me to think of them being content, knowing they deserve it. Kian and Clem join us just after we sit down, each sitting on my side, with Clem noticeably closer this morning.

"Clem, I trust you and Jasmin have made a full recovery?" Erik questions as he bites into his sausage. Clem looks confused over his question.

"Um, yes. We're both well now." He looks at me, confused. No one knew about the previous bleeding episode. I lean closer to Clem and use a softer voice, but not so quiet the others can't hear.

"Tomas told me you were out in the blizzard, and I didn't react so well." Erik guffaws, slapping his leg. He nudges Tomas's side and says, "'Didn't react so well.' Did you hear that? Funniest thing I've heard all year!" He wipes tears of laughter away from his eyes. Tomas, Kian, and Zander are chuckling along. I smile softly, fiddling with my bread, not wanting to look at anyone else. I can feel Clem's eyes staring at me.

"She tried to run into the blizzard. Twice," Erik explains. "We had to carry her, kicking and screaming, and lock her in your room until the storm passed. She even bit me."

"I did not!" I gasp in astonishment at his claim, eyes going wide. He just nods matter-of-factly, popping a piece of sausage in his mouth. I look to Kian and Tomas, who are both nodding. Erik adjusts his shirt, pulling the collar over to expose a fading set of bite marks above his collarbone.

"Holy gods, Erik. I am so sorry! I don't even remember doing that!" He waves away my concern, but now I feel terrible. My reaction was unorthodox, but I didn't realize how horrible it was. My appetite was fading before, but it is completely gone now. Any food would sit heavy on my stomach. Just before I push my plate away, Clem wraps his arm around my shoulders, bringing me close to him. He whispers so only I can hear, "I'm here now."

"Did you hear the thunder last night?" Kian can always be counted on for a quick subject change. Clem releases me, eating his own food. I'm sure he's trying to persuade me to eat something through his actions, but I can't right now. Maybe later.

"Thunder? Last night?" I question. I don't remember hearing thunder.

"Yes. It was crazy and shook the building."

"How do we have so much thunder in the winter? We never get thunder throughout the winter."

"It could be the curse lifting," Kian suggests far too casually for what he is implying. "The barrier was set with a huge storm." I tense, fiddling with the chunk of bread. He has a point, but that doesn't exactly clarify things.

"True, but that doesn't really help. It could be any one of you. And Oscar is still here. What if it's Oscar?" I wail dramatically, snickering over my own theatrics.

"Have you identified any object that could be linked to the curse?" Kian questions. He had been hunting on his own at one point. I shake my head.

"No. I haven't come across anything that would make sense." Clem shifts uncomfortably next to me. I glance at him, but he is lost in thought.

"It could be losing some of its magic now if the curse is lifting," Kian suggests. I scan through objects I have previously considered linked to the curse to see if any of them have changed lately.

"Wait, if the object could be changing, does that mean the barrier could be too?" Kian nods his head. I look to Erik. "Has anyone checked the barrier lately? If it's crumbling or weakening, we must be prepared for what could be on the other side." He gives an affirmative motion.

"I'll speak with Henry about searching it and preparing for anything." He shoves the last bit of his food in his mouth before rising to leave. He pauses, swallowing his food, and adds, "Glad you are both back now." He smiles sweetly as he turns to leave. Tomas and Zander both announce they are going to tend to the horses. I suspect that isn't what they plan to do, not immediately, anyway.

Once it is just Kian, Clem, and I left at the table, I try to eat a few bites of my now cold bread. It's not as good as freshly toasted, but it's still sustenance. Clem slides closer to me, the entire length of our thighs pressed against each other. The warmth of his body is comforting.

"Oh, Kian," I say, turning to him but not pulling away from Clem. "I had you added to the list of people that can access my rooms, should you need in there for anything. Clem and Erik have access, too. I keep it limited as a personal preference." I don't tell him about the nursery, but I will probably lock the room for now.

"Jasmin," Clem says softly, drawing my attention. "You never explained the flower to me." It takes me a minute to remember what flower he is speaking of. When I remember, I consider what to say in front of Kian. He is usually good about not prying, though.

"Right. The flower is a dahlia. It was given to me before the curse." Despite him not prying, Kian interjects a question.

"Wait, you have a flower from before the curse? Is it dried?"

"No," I shake my head. "My friend that gave it to me dabbled in witchcraft. I assume she had some sort of protection spell on it."

"What coven did she practice with?"

"She didn't. She lived here at the castle." I pause, debating how much to tell him. "It was Zander's sister."

"Have you had anyone look at the flower to see if it is linked to the curse?" My breath hitches as I grab Clem's knee. Could this be the piece I have been missing? Has it really been there the whole time? Of course, it has.

"No," I grab his hand. "Will you come to look at it?"

"Yes."

We clear our plates quickly, both men following me back to my room. Finn runs in the opposite direction to go outside to play. I'm sure someone will find him and let him out. The flower is still in the nursery. I do not want to take Kian into that room. It's not something I can emotionally handle right now. I turn past the guards and ask Clem and Kian to go to my room while I grab the flower. They agree and walk that way.

In the nursery, I find the flower resting on the shelf with the single petal that fell off when Clem first found it. Of course, this is the object the curse has been tied to. I'm not surprised I missed that, but I'm angry at myself for overlooking something so obvious. I hold the flower momentarily, letting the reality that this could answer many questions sink in. I press it to my nose. It hasn't released a smell since I first got it. I thought it was her protection spell, but it had a scent prior to the curse. The more powerful magic must have subdued that part of the flower. I take a deep breath, stealing myself for what may happen.

The two men are in my room, standing anxiously in the sitting area next to the fire. I stand between them and hold the flower out to Kian in both hands. He doesn't immediately take it, staring at it instead. Clem is standing by my side, silent but strong. Kian runs his hand just above the flower, leaving it in my hand. He looks at me, leaving the choice to continue to me. I press my hands closer, indicating he should take it. Slowly, he places his hand on the stem. He doesn't lift it, just touches the flower. His eyes glaze over, staring at some spot behind my head. His eyes dart back and forth, unfocused on anything in the room. He jerks his hand back after a minute, uncertainty written on his face.

"This is the object." His voice is flat. I don't know what he saw. He rubs his hands together, shifting his eyes between me and the flower. "An old spell was used. It's powerful and functions differently than the spells we use now." I wait to learn what he means.

"This flower, this magical object," he looks nervous; I'm not used to seeing Kian so nervous. "This tells your story. Why you were cursed. I assume there may be some clues in there about who did it. There should also be at least clues about who your true love is." Hope rises at his claim. "But it means I need to see your story to learn more."

"See?" I question, nervous about what that means.

"Yes. It plays out as images, similar to the story I showed at the winter solstice, but with more detail. Almost like an old memory."

I close my hands around the flower, pulling it to my chest. It's one thing to tell someone my story; it's another for them to see it as if walking through my memories. I look to Clem, needing some guidance on how to handle this. I need to learn more about the curse, but I don't want him to see my past.

"Could I see it with you?" Clem's suggestion stings. That is not the response I wanted from him.

"No," I sob, but Kian shrugs.

"Possibly." They both look at me, waiting for me to agree to this.

"Clem, no. You know what happens. It...It isn't something I want you to see." I turn to Kian. "It's a terrible story." He nods sympathetically. Clem steps in front of me, putting his hands on my arms. He leans in, kissing my cheek gently, taking care not to crush the flower between us.

"I want to see, Jasmin. I need to see it." I shake my head, not wanting them to have visuals of everything that happened. Clem has already seen so much. He knows so much. Tears build in my eyes as the two men watch me. One of them is likely my true love. One of them already loves me, regardless of the curse. I can't let them see the visions. But I need more answers about the curse. It's been excruciating not knowing. I sniffle, holding the flower out.

"Kian, I don't know what all you will see through this. I was not innocent in the years before the curse. I..." I struggle to find the words to prepare him for what he may see. He squeezes my shoulder.

"I can handle it. If it makes you feel better, it starts with a dark-skinned girl you kiss." I smile softly at him. I hold the flower out for him.

"I wish that was the worst part of it. That was two years prior to the curse. That was Dahlia, Sunette's daughter." I square my shoulders, ready for the two men I care about most to watch the darkest, most devastating part of my life. Clem steps to Kian's side, across from me. Kian tells Clem how to hold the flower and how he's going to touch it so they can both see. They leave it in my hand while they touch. Once they make contact, their eyes glaze over, darting back and forth, watching whatever scene is playing out for them. Both smile for a moment. They must be seeing me with Dahlia. Then Clem flinches as Kian's face drops. A few moments pass before Clem's body tenses. His free hand balls into a fist, eyebrows knitting together in anger. That would be Jackson. He would recognize him and know what's coming. The next moment, Kian flinches like he will pull away, but Clem grabs his shoulder, not letting Kian stop.

Kian's eyes are wide, fear and nervousness showing on his face. I almost jerk the flower away from them at that moment. Clem looks determined to see this through. Kian begins to physically recoil, trying to step away from this situation. Clem puts his arm on Kian's back, keeping him in place. At first, Clem's touch refuses to let Kian move, but it quickly changes to a more comforting touch. Tears are falling down my cheeks, guessing which part they are seeing. Kian still looks terrified. Clem looks hurt and angry, tears building in his own eyes.

Their eyes are glazed over for several more moments as they watch the vision occurring off in the distance. Clem's tears have started falling down his cheek silently. Kian looks less terrified but still unsettled and hurt. Clem closes his eyes, dropping his head down. His hand is still on the flower. Kian's eyes stop shifting but are still glazed over. After another minute, he pulls his hand back from the flower, stepping backward until he hits a chair and drops into it. His head falls into his hands. Clem looks at me, eyes wet with tears. I leave the flower in his hand, walking over to Kian. I kneel in front of him, wrapping my arms around his shoulders. He hugs me in return and begins breathing deeply.. His face is buried against my neck, arms tight around my back.

"I'm sorry," I whisper softly to Kian, feeling terrible that he had to see all of that. He laughs callously, sitting back with an astonished look on his face.

"You're sorry?" he asks incredulously. "After everything I just saw, you are apologizing?" He shakes his head, wiping his face. "You have nothing to apologize for." He sits back in the chair, looking over at Clem. I turn around, looking at him. His elbows are on his knees, head bent, looking down at the flower in his hand. He looks broken now. It tears my chest apart, especially knowing how hard he and I have worked in the past few days to not be so broken.

"That was..." Kian speaks softly, looking up to the ceiling like he just can't support his own body anymore. "I have never seen a cursed object play out like that. I'm not certain who cursed you. I don't think it was the hag, but I think she had something to do with implementing the curse. It was obvious who your true love is." He brings his head to a normal position to look at Clem, who lifts his head at Kian's words. It takes me a moment to realize he is implying it's Clem. Clem catches on faster than I do, looking stunned.

"You saw that?"

"Didn't you? Your essence was embedded in every single image. And before you ask," he holds his hand out to stop either of us from interrupting. "I thought maybe it was because you were touching the flower. But Jasmin was too, and I didn't get the same presence from her. The image shook when you touched me like you were able to alter it."

I sit quietly for a minute, processing what he has said. Clem is also quiet, staring at the flower still in his hands. I finally look up at Kian to find him staring down at me. My heartbreaks realizing my relationship with him is about to change. While I have relief in knowing who my true love is, there is still pain over who it isn't. There are still strong feelings between Kian and me. Those won't just go away overnight. I take his hand in mine, pressing a small kiss to the top of his hand. I don't know exactly what to say in this situation. What should one say to a lover that just told you someone else is your true love?

He leans forward, taking my face in his hands. I stare into his eyes. They shift from hurt and longing to resolve and kindness. "Go to him," he nods to Clem. "I'll see you around soon." He kisses my forehead, rising from his seat to leave.

"Are you staying at the castle?"

He gives me a soft, warm smile. "Of course. True love or not, you are and always will be my Queen." I wrap my arms around him in a tight hug, trying not to cry over his words. He returns the embrace, an air of finality settling around us. I watch him leave my room, feeling a vast swarm of emotions.

Chapter 30

JASMIN

Kian leaves the room quietly, but I stay on the floor in front of his chair. I'm not entirely ready to face Clem. I just need another minute or two or ten. Maybe another year or so of just sitting on the floor, feeling everything and nothing. I stare at the intricate design on the upholstered chair. The gold and green swirls in the blue background with flowers spread throughout. I take a deep breath, rising and turning to Clem.

His head is lowered, elbows on his knees, hands meeting in between with the flower between his fingers. His thick blonde hair creates a curtain around his face, blocking him from my view. I take soft, quiet steps until I reach him, kneeling next to him. My fingers gently rest on his arm as he finally looks up at me. He doesn't speak, but he doesn't need to, either. I pull the flower from his hand, resting it on the low table in front of him. I push him back and climb into his lap, resting my head against his shoulders. His arms circle around my body, holding me tightly. We sit like that for several minutes, needing the closeness and comfort of touch.

About the time I think he has fallen asleep, he begins to speak. "When you first got Vesper, you went on a tour of all the villages. Do you remember that?" I nod in response, unsure where he is going with this.

"I was 17 at the time. Several of my friends and I went to watch the proceedings. You looked ethereal when you rode by. Your hair was long down your back, in contrast to the cream-colored dress you were wearing and Vesper's solid white fur." I'm surprised he remembers what I was wearing. I don't even remember that much detail. "I felt like I was under a spell. I couldn't take my eyes off you. I accidentally announced out loud that I would marry you one day. My friends regularly gave me hell until the day I left Arkaley about that comment." He huffs a laugh, shaking his head at the situation. "I never thought there was any weight behind that comment. And now here I am, your true love." We both giggle now. I bury my face against his neck as the laughter grows. We devolve into hysterics, wiping our eyes as tears fall from laughing. We need laughter to keep from crying.

"Some part of you always knew." I sigh dreamily. Despite knowing I had a true love, it never really seemed genuine. I didn't spend much time thinking about what that would look like. "What now?" I ask, shifting so I can look up at him,

"We could plan your coronation." I grimace at his suggestion. "We could talk about our relationship." I scoff, rolling my eyes at that. I've had enough talking for now. Clem briefly considers, then his face lights up with an idea. "Do you trust me?"

I shrug. "Guess it would be pretty weird if I didn't at this point."

He puts me on the floor, rushing to my wardrobe, digging around in the drawer for more sashes. He has several in his hands when he walks up to me. He grabs my hand, pulling me through the room to my desk.

"Take off your clothes and kneel here." He points to the floor near his feet. I give him a questioning look, but he just motions for me to do it. I start removing my clothes and tossing them onto the bed. He pulls things from my desk, securing them in different places around the room. I ask what he is doing, but he presses his fingers against my lips and threatens to gag me again. When I am fully naked, I drop to my knees, watching him pull the desk away from the wall. I wasn't aware rearranging my room was part of this. When he's happy with where the desk should be, he turns to me, a sadistic look on his face.

He circles me slowly, letting his fingers brush against my exposed skin. Chills run down my body at the light touch, anxious about what his plans are now. He stops in front of me, dragging his finger along my neck, lifting my chin to meet his gaze.

"My princess," he starts, staring down with lust in his eyes. I've never spent time kneeling before someone before. I wouldn't consider doing this for anyone else. Something about being on my knees for Clem sends electric pulses through my body. "Doesn't want to do her duties. Doesn't want to accept her responsibilities." He tuts, shaking his head at me. "This is unacceptable. Rise." I stand smoothly in front of him. "Take off my shirt, Princess." His commands are loaded with power and lust, a combination I haven't quite seen in him. But I love it. He could command me to do anything at this point, and I probably would without question.

I grab the hem of his shirt, lifting it over his head. I lick my lips, leaning in to kiss his chest. His fingers grab my cheeks roughly before I get close enough. "No." The word is so charged I freeze, unwilling to push my luck right now. He steps back from me, keeping me at arm's length. He circles around me, releasing my face. He drapes one of the sashes he picked up over my skin. I close my eyes, the sensation tingling in every part of my body. He stops behind me, pressing his chest to my back.

"You want to avoid being a princess?" I incline my head, bumping into his chest.

"Then we'll find something for you to do." His hand cups my ass, and I press back into it. "On the table on your stomach." His hand pulls away from my ass, only to return in a quick smack. I gasp at the sudden pain lancing through while my pussy clenches at the touch. I look back at him but do as he says, lying on my stomach. The lacquer on the wood is cool against my exposed breasts. The table is hard and smooth, a sensation I am not used to feeling on my stomach. This desk is short and ends under my hips, allowing my legs to fall straight to the floor. He rubs his hand over my stinging ass, gently massaging my reddening cheek. He walks to the front where my head is, kneeling at the end of the table. He holds his hand out for me without speaking. I place my hand in his, then he kisses the back of my hand gently. He surprises me by using the sash to tie my hand to the leg of the table, then doing the same to the other.

"No talking or I'll gag you again." He winks, rising to walk behind me. He stops to press a kiss on my shoulder before moving behind me. He pushes my feet wide, exposing my core and ass to him. It feels odd to be on display like this, but it sends a thrill through me like I have never known. Clem drops to his knees behind me, but I can no longer see what he is doing. I try to look over my shoulder, but lifting my head that high hurts my neck. So I rest against the table, waiting to find out what he will do next.

A finger lands softly in the hair above my core. He strokes across my clit, through my soaking wet opening, then continues up, running his finger over my ass. When his finger leaves, his tongue starts on the same path, stopping at my back entrance to press against it.

"Oh gods, no." I breathe, completely forgetting the instructions he gave me. He stops, removing his tongue from my ass. "No, please don't stop." He chuckles, flattening his hands over my ass cheeks and squeezing.

"We need something for you to say other than no. Pick a different word. If you want me to stop, use that word. Then, I'll ignore your no's. Sound good?" I nod.

"Does that mean I can talk?" I question, unsure how far I can push him before he gags me.

"Do you want to?" His hands slide to my thigh as his lips find the cheek he slapped earlier, pressing several kisses against it. I nod, knowing he can see my movement from his angle.

"Ok, pick a word to use instead of no." I think for a moment before the perfect word pops into my mind.

"Flower." He chuckles, kissing my other cheek now. He bites lightly, causing me to squeak. He kisses the bite, then returns to what he was doing before. He licks me from one entrance to the other, swirling circles around my ass. His finger enters my aching core, only going knuckle deep. He slides around my wet walls, but it doesn't bring me much pleasure. I want him deeper and faster and harder.

After a moment, he removes his fingers, getting a grunt from me. His lips are against my cheek again, but I can feel his smile against my skin. Then his finger is pressing at my tight hole. He circles it several times before pressing in, barely spreading it apart.

I gasp at the new sensation. He calmly instructs me to relax as he leaves his finger pressed against me. I try to take several deep breaths, not really sure what to think of this new protrusion. As my body relaxes, he pushes his finger in further until he is knuckle deep in my ass. It feels wrong and wonderful; it stings and feels so pleasurable. His tongue licks my pussy, slowly stroking up and down. Between the two differing pressures, I'm pretty sure I'll explode. I'm whimpering, moaning his name, begging for more, imploring him not to stop. His tongue moves faster and deeper into my core, adding to the wetness. His finger in my ass begins to wiggle, sliding in and out in short strokes. Within moments, ecstasy courses through my body as I scream out with my orgasm. He continues to work both holes through the waves of pleasure. By the time my body has settled, Clem is standing, removing his pants. He presses against me, coating his dick with juices from my pussy. His thumbs run between my ass, spreading me wide for him. One thumb circles the opening, pressing in slightly.

I look back, wanting to see how he looks. His face is fierce and focused, with only one thing on his mind at this moment, and that's me. I love the way he looks at me when we are together like this. I am the thing in his world. I am the only thing he wants. Nothing could take him away from me in these moments. He is so intense, his eyes trained on exactly what he wants. His face always tells precisely what he wants. I am what he wants.

He doesn't realize I am watching him. His jaw shifts then he spits into my exposed ass. Something about that sight, about his warm spit landing in my ass, causes my core to ache. I need him now. My ass rises to his as his thumb smears the saliva around, then presses inside, deeper than his finger was. My back arches, causing my ass to rise toward him. His thumb stills inside me, allowing me to adjust to him being deeper and having me spread wider. I cry out his name, needing more from him. His free hand releases my cheek, notching his dick at my empty, throbbing pussy. He slowly slides in, thumb still in my ass, filling me in a way I have never known before. I feel so full, so used, so stuffed. I groan at the pleasure, enjoying every bit of the stinging fullness. He thrusts his cock in and out of me slowly, but I need him to go faster.

I beg him, my hips rising off the table. My hands are pulling against the sashes, restraining me to the table. His speed increases, then he shoves his thumb at the same pace. My moans increase, relentlessly begging him not to stop. He pulls this thumb out of my back entrance, and I grunt at the removal. His hands spread me open again. I swear I almost like that sensation as much as having his fingers inside me. Being on display for him is far more arousing than I ever thought possible. As quickly as he removed his thumb, his index finger enters my hole. This elicits a sigh of pleasure and relief. His cock is pounding into my core at a fast pace. My ass is being stretched again as he adds another finger into my tight hole. I never thought I could be stretched this far.

I yell out, a string of curses, prayers, and pleas exploding from my mouth. His fingers move slowly, stretching and twisting in my ass. My core is clenching; my whole body is clenching, close to release. With two fingers inside me, he begins thrusting harder, slamming me against the table, sure to leave bruises on my hips.

"There's my Queen. Taking her true love in both her holes like a good girl." My eyes roll back in my head at his words. I arch my back, creating a new angle for him to pound against. He notices my shift, his free hand grabbing my hips as he drives into me relentlessly. "Is that what my dirty slut likes?" He slams into me, fingers and dick beating against my most sensitive parts. "Come apart on me, Jas." I lose all sense of control. I cry out as wave after wave crash through my body. I am writhing under his touch as he pounds into me from behind. I moan, both of my holes tightening and releasing around him. He yells with his own release, spilling his seed deep inside me. My body spasms beneath him several times.

He slowly pulls his fingers from my ass. I gasp at the emptiness and burn they leave behind. He massages my cheeks as his dick softens inside me. When he finally pulls out of my body, he wets a cloth from my wash basin. He returns, wiping both my holes, ensuring I am clean before tossing the material aside. He walks to the front of the table, kneeling to untie my hands. He presses his lips against my forehead, both of us drenched in sweat. Once they are untied, he helps me stand from the table. It is covered in my sweat, desperately needing to be cleaned.

Clem scoops me up, carrying me over to the bed. I mention that we need to clean the table, and he assures me we will do it later. I snuggle against his body as he wraps a blanket around us. I sigh, closing my eyes and listening to his steady heartbeat in his chest. I'm not sure how I got so lucky with him, but I make a note to pray to every god known that could have possibly had a hand in this.

"At some point," he speaks softly, "you will have to fulfill your responsibilities. Like planning your coronation and discussing our future." I groan, rolling my head and eyes at him.

"I would rather do this."

"If we keep this up, I'll have to stick my dick in your ass at some point." I gasp in surprise at his comment. That wasn't something I had ever considered before. I had never considered anything in my ass, but after just his finger, I don't know if I could stretch wide enough to take his dick. A devious grin spreads across his face. "Guess we'll have to work up to that." I giggle at his comment, flushing with excitement at the thought.

"You are such a dirty girl." He mumbles, pressing kisses to my neck and ear. I giggle more, settling back on the bed and pulling him on top of me. I would much rather work up to having his cock in my ass than try to do anything else.

Chapter 31

CLEM

We leave Jasmin's room precisely four times over the next week. We have dinner twice with the other men, once we take Finn outside, and another time we go to my room to gather some of my things to bring back. Emmeline has been bringing us food and drinks. Kian stopped by once in a prearranged meeting to avoid interrupting any activities. Everyone in the castle knows what we are up to. It's no secret at this point. Even if we wanted to keep it a secret, Jasmin isn't very good at being quiet.

We have to leave the room today. The roads have cleared enough for some of the Lords to travel in. We are getting updates from them and making plans for the coronation. Jasmin insists I be there, despite my arguments that I don't need to be. She doesn't even discuss the matter with me, so now I am getting dressed for another meeting I don't want to attend.

Jasmin is actually wearing a dress today. It's a simple dress, floor length, with a pleated bust. That is her preferred style when she wears dresses. This particular dress is a deep purple that makes her skin appear silky. Emmeline is styling her hair while I sit on the couch reading some notes Mikhail sent me about the upcoming harvest. I need to meet with him soon about my official duties, but I haven't made that a priority so far. My only priority is Jasmin, specifically her body, exposed and in my mouth.

I shift in my seat, adjusting my pants and my train of thought. I do not want to walk out of this room with tented trousers. When she is ready, she walks over to stand next to me. I grab her hips, pull her in front of me, and press my face against her stomach. She drapes her arms over my shoulders as I lift to bury my face between her breasts. I just want to be here, tented pants and all. A cloth smacks against my back.

"You two are leaving this room today!" Emmeline practically shouts at us as we laugh at her. Jasmin and I have not put any effort into actually leaving. The few times we did were more out of necessity than choice. While a change of scenery will be nice, I'd still rather stay here. I haven't worked up to put my dick in her ass yet. That still needs to happen. The cloth hits me again, harder this time.

"Alright." I laugh, standing next to Jasmin. Emmeline pushes us out of the room, not letting us linger any longer. We all know where that will go. She demands we go straight to the meeting room, swearing if she has to come find us, but she doesn't finish the statement. We all know she is jesting, though I worry there may be a hint of truth under her playful tone.

I walk beside Jasmin, holding her hand. I've known at some point, we would have to get back to reality. We've been pretty secluded for weeks now. It has been so peaceful and necessary. I feel like a new man, better than I have in ages. The castle looks brighter; everything feels warmer and not so desolate. Finn catches up to us, nudging between our legs to get in front and lead the way. He turns to go outside while we head in the opposite direction to the meeting room.

We stop outside the door to the meeting room. She takes both my hands, squeezing them tightly. She leans up to press a kiss on my cheek. She has been making this a bigger deal than it needs to be. We've been doing these meetings for months. They are always pretty dull and uninteresting. I'm not sure why she is so worried about this one. She opens the doors, walking in by my side instead of behind me like I expected.

Simultaneously, everyone in the room rises, then bows. I tense, not entirely sure how to react. Jasmin grabs my elbows, leading me over to our seats. Her chair is the same one she used for the rest of the meetings, but a new one has been brought in beside hers. They are a matching pair, one slightly smaller but still as ornate and intricately designed. I glance around the room, noticing it is the only chair unoccupied. It dawns on me that this chair has been brought in for me. Unease spreads through my body about the special treatment. I hadn't realized being her true love would change how I am treated. She tells everyone to rise, then she sits as everyone else follows.

"Thank you all for coming. I trust your journey went smoothly and everyone is settling in." Jasmin has such a presence about her. She hasn't addressed anyone in an official capacity in a long time. Probably since Oscar was punished before the winter solstice. I had almost forgotten how serious she could be in a different setting. Looking around the room, Erik, Henry, Tomas, and Sabeko sit together. Kian and Mikhail are beside them. Lord Gustavo from Tilrade and Lord Thurston from Vadried complete the circle, sitting between Mikhail and me. Lord Gustavo's dark skin looks dry and cracked from the weather. Lord Thurston has more grey hair than he did when he left. Things must be difficult for him in Vadried this winter.

"We are here to discuss my coronation and other changes I plan to make within the kingdom." Jasmin looks so serious. It's hard to concentrate on what she is saying when all I want to do is take her back to her bedroom and replace that serious look with moans. She asks Henry for an update on the border. He informs us that it appears to be weakening but is still solid. He has set up regular patrols to watch the other side for any signs of danger. Shortly after the barrier fell into place, some friends and I went to see the closest point. It almost isn't noticeable until you touch it. It has a rippling effect that can be seen. In certain lights, there is a shimmer on it, but for the most part, it's nearly invisible.

They discuss changes to the guard, increasing the number of guards, patrols, training, everything, and anything else they can think of. All the dry stuff that doesn't really affect me. No one knows for sure when the barrier will come down.

Jasmin and I have some theories, but that's all it is. We haven't put too much thought into what it will take to bring it down.

"Before the coronation, Clem's family should be brought to the castle. Clem would like to travel to Arkaley as soon as it is possible and bring them here. He will need a guard detail for the journey." What? I'm trying to shake my mind from the haze of daydreaming to understand what she just said.

"No, I don't need a guard. I've made the trip before. I can make it again." She gives me a dubious look.

"Clem, you're part of the royal family now, officially or not. You cannot travel alone anymore." She turns her attention to Lord Thurston. "To that point, can we have the court protocol advisors return to the castle? We have a short time to prepare Clem for his role. He did not attend many of the meetings we held last autumn and will need to be educated on as much as possible." What? What is she talking about? The confusion is written across my face. My role as Master of Gardens requires court protocol? What does she expect me to do? Before I can even ask, Jasmin continues with the meeting topics.

"I plan to have the coronation on spring solstice. Kian will be performing the ceremonies. I want to open the castle for everyone to attend. I expect full cooperation from everyone. Emmeline and Sunette are working on the details of the day and will have notices to send out to the villages before you leave." She motions to the Lords, but I'm still hung up on my roles and court training. Why do I need an escort to travel home? I have taken that path several times. It's perfectly safe in the right weather. Obviously, that wouldn't be a blizzard, but I won't make that mistake twice.

"Kian will be traveling to the covens to invite them personally. I would like him to have an escort as well." Kian and Henry both nod. Erik writes out something on the parchment paper he has. My mouth is firing faster than my brain at this point.

"He only needs an escort, but I need a full detail?" My tone is incredulous, but I manage to stop myself from asking if she believes me weak. Her eyes meet mine, full of disbelief. I don't understand why she is in disbelief when she just implied I can't be trusted to travel to my own home alone. Instead of responding to me, she turns back and speaks with the Lords about further plans for the coronation. I huff, leaning back in my seat. I keep my hands on the arms of my chair, not wanting to be entirely childish by crossing them over my chest, as my instincts would demand. In the corner of my eye, Kian calls over one of the servers, whispering to him. Kian may have more finesse than I do, but I'm sure I could handle myself as well as him on a simple journey home.

A moment later, the server Kian whispered to arrives between Jasmin and me with two glasses of wine. He places one in front of me and the other in front of her. She offers a quick thanks, staying focused on the discussion. I look toward Kian, still feeling angry. He motions for me to drink. I don't want to do as I'm told, but I see the benefit in the wine. I offer a slight nod of thanks, taking the wine. I take several large gulps, trying to focus on what Jasmin is saying. I can question her about my escort later.

"I would like to go ahead and set that date too. I want it to be after the coronation. Not too far out, as I don't want to delay any longer, but not too close, so the wedding eclipses the coronation." I choke on the wine I was drinking. Did she say wedding? We have mentioned it once or twice, but not to the point of selecting a date. Tiny droplets of wine spew from my lips as I swallow what I can. Jasmin shrieks my name, jumping up to wave over someone with a cloth. Beside me, Lord Gustavo looks uncomfortable. Just as I regain my ability to inhale air, I hear Erik loudly whisper to Kian.

"He's already on track to be a good husband, hasn't listened to a word she's said." Half the table bursts out in laughter while the Lords look ill at ease. Jasmin is rolling her eyes at his comment. The movement is so familiar it brings me some comfort. The server finishes wiping the wine I just spewed everywhere. I apologize and thank him for his assistance. Jasmin slides her chair back to the table, a bit more irritated than before. I grab her hand, leaning over to whisper to her.

"I'm sorry for that. I didn't realize we were to the point of selecting a date already." I sit back, waiting to hear her response. She is searching my eyes, intent on finding something I'm not sure is there. In the momentary lull, Kian elects to add one of his ever-helpful comments.

"What have you been doing with him in your room for the past week, Princess? I would think he would be better prepared to be King with all the time you two have spent together." I can feel every drop of blood drain from my face. He said King. He thinks I will be King. That is a terrifying, utterly untrue claim. Marrying Jasmin wouldn't make me...holy gods.

"Oh, for fuck's sake." Jasmin sighs, standing from her seat. "If you would all please excuse us. We will adjourn this meeting for now. Please, enjoy lunch and your afternoon, and we will meet again after dinner. Thank you." The others rise, chuckling and commenting on my current state. I don't register what they say. She walks around to Kian, admonishing him as she walks with him to the door. They laugh as he leaves, then she closes the doors once everyone is out.

"Clem," she sighs, sounding exacerbated. She walks over, climbing into my lap. Her head lands on my shoulder, placing her arm over my chest. The weight of her body is calming, bringing a sense of security to my shaken existence. "How did you not realize you would be King? We've been talking about my coronation for weeks now." I shrug my shoulders, draping my arms over her body.

"I never really considered what I would be to the kingdom. I know who I am to you, but I...I haven't thought beyond that." She presses a kiss to my jaw, rubbing circles over my chest. She doesn't say anything for several moments. My racing mind calms down, realizing how ridiculous I have been. The fact that I overlooked my place within the kingdom is embarrassing enough, but when I consider my actions today, it is almost excruciating to think about.

"Now, do you understand why you need a full detail to travel to Arkaley while Kian only needs a single escort?" She looks up at me as she questions me. Of course, no king would ever travel alone. Even lower-ranking members of royalty rarely travel alone. "I'm sorry for bringing it up the way I did. I thought you understood what being my true love would entail." I huff at her comment.

"I thought true love would mean fucking you senseless. I didn't think there would be much else." She laughs, adjusting in my arms to raise her head next to mine.

"You were meant to fuck *me* senseless. Not you." We laugh as I tickle her side. She squirms in my lap, trying to get away from my fingers.

"I can do both." I tease.

"You certainly have."

We settle down, holding each other for another moment. I am terrified of being King. I absolutely will not be good in that position. I'm going to ruin something important like I just did with this meeting. The only good thing is that I get Jasmin. She settles me in a way I've never known before. Her touch comforts all of my doubts and fears. I hope I can do the same thing for her. With each other, we can make it through this.

"Holy gods, Ma is going to have a heart attack."

Jasmine huffs a laugh, "What will Bea think?"

I laugh, looking up at the sky mural on the ceiling. "I don't even know." I hesitate. "I can't be King, Jas. That's not a role I can fill."

She turns in my lap so she is straddling me. Her hands adjust her dress over my legs, then rest against my shoulder. She has a serious look in her eye, but there is a hint of something else, something devious.

"It'll be a while before I give you any real tasks. You'll basically be the beauty in this relationship." She kisses my cheek. I hate that she feels like she isn't beautiful. I've heard what some people say about her, with the scars and the choppy hair she had for years. She is beautiful. "You'll have time," she continues, "to practice ruling people with your Master of Gardens position. It'll start small and grow." She kisses down my jaw to my neck, heat rising in my core. My cock is already waking. "It's always good to start small when ruling people. Best to start with..." she accentuates her words with small bites along my neck, "just...one...person. Tell them... what to do... in a setting you are comfortable with." Her lips travel to the other side of my neck, grinding her hips against mine. My rigid member is now pressing against her core, aching to be inside her again. "The good thing about being in power," she whispers, while her hands trail down my body, "is you get to adjourn meetings to fuck whomever you want."

I slide my hands up her thighs under her dress. She is sucking on my neck in the spot that drives me fucking wild. I thrust my hips under her, desperate to be inside her. Her touch is driving me crazy, and I need more.

"Fuck me in this chair, Queen," I say with a smirk. She bites onto my neck, causing me to yelp in pain. She immediately kisses the spot, easing some of the ache. I don't like pain the same way she does, but it isn't a deal breaker for me. She occasionally enjoys being sadistic, and as much as she lets me play with pain, I don't have a problem allowing her to explore too. Her hands slip down to my waist, unlacing my trousers. My dick finally springs free as she instantly moves over it, lining it up and sliding down my cock with a moan. I grab her shoulders, holding her tight against me as we adjust to being united. It's been less than half a day, but that is too long for me. She groans, arching her back, then begins bouncing in my lap.

I pull the string holding her pleated top together. Her breasts spring free once it is loosened enough. Her tits rise and fall with her pace on my lap. I slide both hands to cup her breasts, then capture her nipples between my thumb and index finger and squeeze them tightly, giving a slight twist. She arches back further, grinding her hips into mine while shuddering at the sensation. Her pussy clenches around my cock, already close to orgasm. I bury my face between her breasts, squishing them beside my cheeks. They hold her scent so well. The fragrances from her body oils mix with her scent, which is probably my favorite smell. She resumes her bouncing as I suck a nipple into my mouth. I look up at her face, loving the way she has her eyes closed, head tilted back, just enjoying the pleasure of being together. If being King means canceling meetings to fuck her, I will gladly take that title.

My fingers slip beneath her dress, finding the spot where we meet. I press my thumb against her clit, causing her to moan deeply. She lands hard several times, her pace becoming frantic and irregular.

"Hold on to the chair." She plants her hands behind my head, doing precisely as told without any questions. Her obedience sends a thrill of pleasure through my body. Being able to command her like this is my favorite form of intoxication. I grab her hips, adjust my position, then start pounding into her. She cries out my name, her throbbing core on the verge of orgasm.

"That's a good girl. Come on my dick in the meeting room. Show me what a queen does for her king." I growl at her. Her orgasm hits her hard, her body collapsing against mine as I continue to thrust inside her, feeling my own balls tightening. Her cunt clenches, releases, then clenches again around my cock, sending me into ecstasy. I growl against her neck as I empty deep inside her. We both relax into the chair, breathing heavily. She shudders through the last waves of her orgasm. I kiss her head several times, holding her tightly against my chest. Her arms finally wrap around me.

"See? You're good at giving commands." She coos into my chest. I chuckle, stroking her back and sides gently with my hands.

"Anything for my Queen," I whisper against her forehead. I'm not comfortable with the thought of being King, but a few more of these practice sessions should get me there.

Chapter 32

CLEM

Vesper is being prepared for me to ride along with the detail to accompany me to my family's home. It still seems excessive that I need so many people to go with me, but I didn't try to argue about it. Having extra men to help my family pack and assist my younger sister along the ride will be nice. I haven't sent a message to Ma. I don't know how much gossip is spreading about this situation, but it wasn't something I wanted to tell her in a letter. I'll stay in Arkaley for a few days to chat with some of the farmers, meet with Lord David, and give my family time to pack. I'm not looking forward to being away from Jasmin for that long, but we'll survive. It should make for some phenomenal sex when I do get back.

I wait in the foyer with Kian since he is leaving at the same time as me. We haven't had a chance to speak one on one in a while. I've been relatively preoccupied, but he has also avoided being alone with Jasmin or me, only once visiting us together. I walk over to him, scanning the area to be sure no one else is nearby.

"I want to thank you for what you showed me with Jasmin. I know that wasn't easy for you to see, and I'm glad you shared that with me." He nods, but I continue before he can speak. "I hope there are no hard feelings for how things turned out between us." Kian chuckles, holding his hands up.

"No hard feelings. I suspected it was you for a long time. I had hoped it was me and needed time to process the realization that I love a woman that isn't mine. But some part of me always knew it was you." I give a confused look.

"You knew?"

"No. It was intuition. There was always something between you two." He sees my unconvinced look and huffs a laugh. "At the autumn equinox celebration, you pulled her away from Oscar. You were the one that noticed how she was feeling. You," he emphasizes the words, "were so in touch with her already that you saw something no one else did." I consider his words. I don't particularly remember what made me pull her away from Oscar. I just remember knowing she needed someone else to intervene. Now knowing her past with Jackson, I understand what she was feeling. I didn't at the time. I have doubted myself the entire time, but it was always there. I am meant for her. Kian steps closer to me, leaning so his mouth is next to my ear.

"I didn't say anything before, but she is infertile." He steps back, a sad look on his face. I nod to him.

"She already suspected that. The curse has affected her, and she believes it will continue." Kian shakes his head, scanning the area before speaking in a hushed voice, leaning close again.

"The tea she drank that made her lose her pregnancy is meant to cause permanent infertility. Some use it to end pregnancies, but it always has long-term effects." There had been a small strand of hope that maybe the curse would reverse the issues with her cycle, and her fertility would return. Kian confirming that isn't the case stings a bit, but it isn't devastating. I meant what I said when I said I am satisfied only being with her. I don't need children of my own.

Jasmin walks up, wrapping her arms around my waist. "What are you two whispering about over here?" She looks up at me, tucked under my arm with her chin against my chest. I will never grow tired of seeing her in my arms. I kiss her forehead, squeezing her shoulders.

"You," I say softly before planting a gentle kiss against her lips. I debate whether to tell her what Kian just told me. It seems terrible to drop on her before leaving for several days, but I also don't want her to hear from anyone but us. I keep my voice soft, ensuring the words stay between the three of us. "Kian believes the tea you drank is the reason for your fertility issues, not the curse." She looks shocked, looking at him in question.

"The blend Dahlia mixed used several herbs to end a pregnancy," his eyes scan the area as he keeps his voice low. It's better to be careful when discussing this subject, even nearly a decade later. I hold her tight, not wanting to let her go right now. "When mixed in that way, and in such high concentrations, they cause infertility." Jasmin looks shocked.

"She said they would help, not that they would permanently affect me." She bites her lip, looking down at the ground, considering what we have just told her.

"You said she was practicing without any guidance. She may not have realized the harm in blending everything the way she did. She might have thought she was just covering all her bases. It's a common issue with new witches. It's one of the reasons they stay in training for so long." Jasmin looks to Kian, nodding softly. She doesn't seem devastated but isn't happy either. There must be some pain in learning the person you loved and trusted hurt you in such a severe way. Jasmin looks up at me, regret shining in her eyes. I press a soft kiss on her forehead.

"I meant what I said. I don't care about having children." My lips find the tip of her nose as her arms tighten around me. After a moment, she looks back to Kian.

"Thank you for telling me." Erik walks in at that moment, informing us everyone is ready to go. We all walk outside together. Kian walks to his horse, and Jasmin follows. She says a few words to him, gives him a long hug, then steps aside as he mounts his sizeable brown horse. I'm surprised I don't feel as jealous of him as I once did. Kian and the guard traveling with him take off along the path to Greynon. They will return in a couple of weeks, arriving just before the coronation. He has his work cut out for him, but I'm sure he will enjoy some time with his family.

Jasmin walks up to me, standing next to Vesper. No matter how many times I remind myself this is only for a few days, I still don't want to go. I want to see my family and pack up my belongings to come here but leaving Jasmin alone for several days is the last thing I want to do. She nudges my arm, shoving me playfully.

"It's three days, Clem. You'll forget all about me once you see your family." I pull her into a tight hug, breathing in the scent of her hair. All the different things I could say to her run through my mind now, but nothing comes out of my mouth. She pushes back just far enough to kiss me. I kiss her back deeply, savoring the feel of her lips, her body, her warmth. It's only three days. Vesper huffs behind me, growing impatient with my stalling. Jasmin laughs, rubbing his back, as I sigh, rolling my eyes at the large white beast.

"Fine, Vesper. Let's go." I groan, walking over to mount him. Jasmin heads back to the castle's steps, pulling her shawl tighter over her shoulders to fight off the chill still in the air. Finn joins her, sitting by her side. He will take care of her and entertain her while I'm gone. She offers a small wave as my detail, two guards on horses and one with a cart, leads the way to the path to Arkaley. A messenger was sent to Lord David a few days ago, so we know the road is safe for us to travel. Despite my disbelief in needing the detail, they are armed and ready for any situation we may come across on the trek.

We travel at a much slower pace than I am used to. With the horse and cart, it's slower than I had planned on traveling. Vesper can make this journey in just a couple of hours if we ride hard, but there really isn't much rush at this point. No one is in danger or in need of saving. We don't need to risk the horses' health to get there quickly. As we ride, we make idle chat about the upcoming coronation. I quickly forget my role within the kingdom, creating a bit of awkwardness in the conversation. I still make comments that a future King shouldn't be saying. It will take some time to get used to how people treat me now. I have had a couple of lessons with the court protocol advisor. The classes are easily the most boring thing I have ever done in my entire life. They are worse than the regular meetings with the Lords. I do not feel bad about skipping out on them previously to help with the harvest at the castle. I would gladly do that again, but since I am the only person receiving the training, I can't exactly skip without someone noticing.

When we reach my home, I see Ma sitting outside while Claire plays in the yard with some goats. They look up at the commotion on their street. It takes them a few moments to realize it is me. They all jump up and run toward us. I am overwhelmed with the emotions of seeing them. I'm happy, excited, relieved to finally be here, but also nervous to tell them about the recent developments. We pull the horses up and tie them onto the fence, ensuring the cart is out of the way.

"What is all of this, Clem?" Ma questions while wrapping me in a tight hug. Claire wraps herself around my body, hugging me tightly. A tightness clenches my chest over seeing them again. After Ma releases me, I rub my sister's back, happiness releasing some of the tightness, but not all.

"Let's go inside, and I'll tell you." As she leads the way, she informs me Bea is at Ferd's farm, helping him deliver some goats, and will be home later if all goes well. Ma offers tea and biscuits to all of us. It's mid-afternoon, too early for dinner but too far from lunch to keep us from being hungry. We all accept willingly. The guards sit in the kitchen at the table while I go to the living room with my family. We all settle in the small room. Being in the castle for several months has made me realize how small this space is. There are closets bigger than this room. My favorite alcove in the library is the same size as my living room but doesn't hold as much furniture. As I am taking in the small size of the living room, Ma draws my attention.

"So, tell me, son. Why have you come home with royal guards and a cart?" I offer a soft smile.

"The Princess is being crowned soon." I don't know how to properly tell her everything without sounding weird. Making it awkward and dragging it out sounds much more feasible. Ma nods in response.

"Yes. I heard that."

I bite my lip, trying to figure out how to word it. I finally just blurt it out poorly. "I'm her true love. We're getting married a couple of weeks after the coronation, and I'll be King." Ma doesn't react. She sits frozen, staring at me with unseeing eyes. Claire sits quietly, shocked, looking between Ma and me, unsure what to do in this situation.

"You're..." Ma starts. "You..." She's opening and closing her mouth, still staring off into space. I take her hand, rubbing it gently to bring her back to reality. She laughs once, then twice, then falls into a total fit of laughter. My younger sister and I sit awkwardly, unsure whether to laugh or be concerned. I send Claire off to get a bottle of wine from the kitchen and to offer one to the guards. Ma doesn't drink often, but she always keeps a couple of bottles around for guests. Claire returns after a couple of minutes with the bottle and a glass, but Ma is still laughing hysterically. She is wiping tears from her eyes, taking deep gulps of breath between fits of laughter. Once I open the bottle, she begins to settle down. I offer her a glass, and she takes it appreciably.

"You're going to be King?" she questions in disbelief.

"Yes, Ma. And I would appreciate it if you treated me as such." I use a stern voice, but it's still a tease. She begins laughing again, nearly spilling her wine. Claire comes over to sit beside me, and I wrap my arm around her shoulders.

"Does this mean I will be a Princess?" Before I can answer, Ma speaks up.

"No, sweetie. That's not how royalty works." Claire looks sad, so I add my thoughts.

"I think Ma is right. But I'm sure you can convince Jasmin to give you a crown. Probably even a fancy title." Claire beams at me, super excited. After a moment, her face grows sad.

"Does this mean you won't be coming back here?" That shatters my heart. I pull her around to sit on my leg, a little surprised she still lets me. At eleven years old, she usually's too old to sit close to me like this. I squeeze my arms around her petite body.

"Yes, it does. But you can come to the castle to visit any time you want. You're coming to stay with me now." Ma looks shocked, but I roll my eyes at her. "That's why there's a cart. I want you all at the castle until the wedding. We can bring in tutors for her. Rooms are being prepared for you all now." Ma looks giddy, leaning back on the couch as she sips her wine. I hold Claire tight for a few more minutes, then the door bursts open.

"Why in the holy gods are there so many horses in the front yard?" Bea cries out as she storms inside. "Clem!!" She shrieks in surprise when she sees me. Claire stands up, letting me turn toward Bea. Before I can say anything, Ma blurts out her thoughts.

"He's marrying her! He's going to be King! I told you he loved her!" If Bea's eyebrows go any higher, she wouldn't have a forehead anymore.

"You serious?" She demands of me. I nod to her, a smirk spreading across my face. She rushes over and pulls me into a hug. I knew they would be excited, but I didn't expect this reaction from them. I tell them I am here for three days before we all travel back to the castle. Ma sets about rearranging the bedrooms. She will share with Claire while I stay with Bea again, leaving the third room open for the guards. We help her get everything squared away, then she heads into the kitchen to prepare dinner. Bea and I join her, helping out. I share more of what happened in the castle since Bea was last there. I skip over the gritty details of what led to the discovery of me being Jasmin's true love, but I am sure to include details about Erik. Despite Bea refusing to directly ask about him, I can see the joy in her eyes when I share stories with Erik.

After a large dinner of stew and bread, we all retire to our rooms, settling in for the night. I lie in bed, exhausted, happy, but also a little lonely. I haven't slept without Jasmin in several weeks, and it feels wrong now. I toss and turn for a while before Bea smacks me with her pillow. She swears I won't live to be King if I don't settle down and stop moving so much. I chuckle, threatening to find Erik a new girlfriend when I return to the castle. She doesn't respond, and I start to doze off. I'm awoken by a sharp pain lancing through my arm. Bea punched me with all her might to wake me up. I had forgotten entirely how vicious she could be.

Bea heads out after breakfast to make arrangements with Ferd to be away for several weeks. It's a tough time for her to be away, with the planting just gearing up, but I'm not leaving her here. I have no issue pulling rank to get her to the castle now, either. I don't even know if I can officially pull rank yet, but that won't stop me from trying.

I walk into town to speak with the local Head of Gardens. I have a pretty good idea of how Arkaley operates, but I look forward to hearing more from him. He is a frail old man, which surprises me. While Mikhail isn't young, he's far from frail. Mikhail is built for being in this field. The man that sits before looks like he is ready to wither away. He tells me what I already knew about Arkaley's planting process. I offer a few tips I picked up from Mikhail. The old man seems intrigued, though I won't know this year if he makes any changes. He informs me that Arkaley saw an increase in production last season. We haven't been told about that, only hearing about the castle's increase. He says it wasn't significant, but still notable. I consider whether it may be related to me or just a coincidence.

After meeting with him, I meet Lord David in the town center. He is cordial and also surprised at the situation. He admits he never suspected it would be me. He only agreed to let me go because I was closer to the Princess's age and thought she might be more comfortable with some older men. I thank him for allowing me to go, even if he had no faith in me. We both laugh over the situation, knowing I was entirely unlikely. We chat for several hours, him giving me tips and tricks for my upcoming position. He tries to fill me in on as much as possible, but it feels daunting. The information is overwhelming, and my brain is swimming by the time I leave. He informs me he'll be at the castle in a week and will set time aside to assist me further. I thank him and leave, heading back home. Ma's home. It's not really mine anymore at this point.

Just outside the town center, a feminine body crashes into mine as I walk along the street.

"Thank you, thank you, thank you!" She cheers. I manage to pull her far enough away to recognize Ingrid. Her chubby arms and nearly orange hair make her easy to identify. I hug her back, knowing she is excited to make more jewelry for the Princess. Jasmin commissioned her to make more, but I didn't get the details on everything she wanted or how much she spent. I laugh, pulling Ingrid back.

"You're welcome. How are you doing?" Her face lights up as she looks up at me. She's a couple of years younger but kind and outgoing. She married one of my friend's younger brothers but hasn't had any children yet. I know her well enough to know she is talented and make small talk but not well enough to ask personal questions.

"Oh, Clem. I'm so good right now. You have to come see what I am making for the Princess." She grabs my arm, pulling me toward her house. She makes all the pieces out of her home, not having a storefront or other building to work in. As we near her porch, I realize the way this situation looks. I dig my heels in, knowing I can't enter her home.

"Ingrid, wait." I pull my arm away from her, stalling her long enough to explain. "I can't go inside with you. Why don't you bring one of the pieces out to me?" At first, she looks at me like I am crazy. Then she looks up and down the street. She notices the guard that has been tailing me all day. He's tried to stay out of sight but has still been visible. Realization shines on her face. She nods, motioning for me to wait as she runs inside. She returns a few moments later with a crown in her hands.

The crown is made of silver metal. It has long stems, several inches in height. Chains link between the limbs, matching the style of the necklace I had made for her. Instead of the emblems, there are five panels of gems across the front of the crown. The panels of gems are all the same color, representing each village. There are a few other gems dispersed throughout the crown. It is a breathtaking piece that will look amazing on Jasmin. It matches the necklace perfectly, should she choose to wear them together. The crown is a stunning display of talent and skill. I tell Ingrid how unique the piece is.

"I'm glad you like it. The Princess has asked me to make several pieces. I didn't think she would like the necklace as much as she did. Thank you so much for letting me make it and giving me credit."

"Of course, Ingrid. You deserve it. I'm glad it worked out." I lift the crown to the sunlight, watching the light glint through the gems. Just like the necklace, colors shine around the area as the light is refracted through the gems. Ingrid tells me more about the piece and how she makes it, but her words barely register as I imagine Jasmin wearing the crown at her coronation. My mind quickly shifts to her wearing nothing but the crown, light glinting off her body. I end the conversation with Ingrid, continuing on my way home, worried about having tented pants for the rest of the journey. I try to distract myself as I walk to my childhood home.

I stroll through the streets, watching people move through their yards and houses. A sense of déjà vu takes over as I walk the path I have walked hundreds of times. The bright spring sun is setting, casting my favorite golden hue over the village. People look more magical, happier, and moving with a sense of purpose. Despite the sunny disposition, I begin to feel melancholy. This place is no longer my home. This isn't where I belong. I watch the people sweep their porches, chase their animals, and get ready for the evening. Nothing has changed for them in the months I have been gone. Their life has carried on like normal while mine has been turned upside down. There is some relief in knowing where I belong, but it still feels strange in this moment, not belonging to the place I grew up.

My younger sister is in the yard, playing, screaming joyfully. I smile softly, finding Ma sitting on the porch. I settle on the floor next to her chair, needing to be close to someone. I've grown accustomed to being physically close to Jasmin and feel her absence now. Ma begins to stroke my hair as we sit and watch my sister play. She squeals and screams, darting back and forth across the yard. She is chasing some chickens around the yard, yelling at them to obey her. A slow ache builds in my chest, realizing I will never get to share this with Jasmin. At this moment, I am sad about the loss of having children of my own one day. I allow myself to be forlorn while watching her, knowing this feeling isn't real and only occurring because I am so far away from Jasmin.

The next morning, Ma and Bea finish packing while I entertain Claire outside in the yard. One of the guards comes over, showing her some of his weapons. She is thrilled to see them up close, even more so when he lets her hold them. I put a limit on that since I'm not interested in anyone losing limbs today. Soon we are all packed and loaded up, heading toward the castle. Anticipation eats at me, knowing how soon I will see Jasmin.

The journey back to the castle is even longer than the trip away. We have to stop more frequently because of Claire. Even Ma needs a break from riding in the wagon. Claire takes turns riding with me on Vesper. Due to the slow pace, I allow Vesper to gallop ahead, then back to everyone. I do it once with Claire, then again by myself. After the second time, the ranking guard reminds me I need to remain with them. I grimace, apologizing for my misstep. It will definitely take time to adjust to this new role.

Chapter 33

JASMIN

Being without Clem and Kian in the castle has been a complete bore. I cannot remember what I did before the bachelors showed up. Thankfully, Emmeline keeps me busy with details for the coronation and wedding. Clem should be involved with the wedding details, so we don't settle much of that. The coronation planning is essentially complete. We need to wait for Kian to return to finalize a few pieces of his role, but everything else is settled.

The castle has been a flurry of activity. Guards are training and preparing for crowds. Servants are cleaning and ensuring rooms are ready to be occupied. The cooks have been preparing more food, when possible, to accommodate extra people. Sometimes, I have simply sat back and watched people scurry from one location to another. I learned long ago that they will not let me help, no matter how much I try.

Clem's party is due to arrive any time now. I have already taken Finn for a walk. Now we sit on the front steps, awaiting his arrival. Most of the snow has melted, but patches are still scattered around the grounds. Finn is currently trying to dig in one of these piles, looking for something only he is aware of. I smile as I watch him, feeling a deep love for my silly dog. Suddenly, Finn perks up, looking toward the road to Arkaley. He turns, dashing down the trail after the noise he hears. I stand, searching for any signs of Clem and Vesper. It's several minutes more before I finally see them. I step inside the foyer, calling the butler to let them know they are arriving. Several others join me on the front steps as they all ride in.

Clem charges ahead of the group, coming to a halt directly in front of the steps. He lowers a blonde-haired girl, his sister Claire, from Vesper, then dismounts quickly, barely staying on his feet. He rushes toward me, engulfing me in a tight hug. I hug him back, but he quickly starts kissing my neck and face. I give him one brief kiss, then capture his face between my hands, forcing him to look at me. He looks sad that I won't return his affection.

"Remember how you'll be King soon, and that comes with certain rules?" His face is crestfallen as I speak. "Now would be a good time to practice them." I slide one hand down his neck, moving my lips to his ear. I whisper gently to him. "I missed you too, but we have to have some decorum. Save the rest for the bedroom." His chest vibrates against mine in a chuckle, nearly breaking my control. He steps back, kisses my cheek, then bows before me. I roll my eyes at him, walking past him to greet his family. His sister and mother are waiting on the steps for us. She curtsies as I approach.

"Ada," I say softly, taking her hand, "it's so nice to see you again."

"Again?" Clem interjects, and I turn to him with a scowl. He has to stop interrupting me like that.

"Clematis Byrne," his mother scolds as his cheeks redden, "I did not raise you to interrupt like that, especially not the Princess." Oh, I'm going to like spending time with her. Clem apologizes, looking bashful and so young. I can't help the smile spreading across my face.

"Yes, Clem. Again." I explain. "I met with all the families that suffered losses due to the curse. It has been many years since I last met with them. You were one of the few family members I didn't meet." His eyes dart between his mother and me.

"I told you I was meeting about your father. You were always too angry to attend." Realization spreads across his face as he pieces this new information together. I reach back, grab his hand, and lace our fingers together. I give a gentle squeeze, reassuring him. His younger sister, Claire, whom I only met as a toddler, walks up to me.

"Will I get to be a princess, too?" She skips all pleasantries, going straight for the hard questions. Her mother scolds her, but I chuckle.

"Officially, no. But I think we may have some other spots open for you." I add a wink, having already considered this. Clem was positive she would ask about that within the first day. He drags her to his other side, wrapping her in his arm. She is only a few inches shorter than me. She has on a pink dress with long blonde hair. From what I know of her, she will enjoy her time at the castle. I greet Bea next, offering her a hug. Finn is sitting next to her, wagging his tail with a look that tells me Bea has been giving him treats.

Some servants have unloaded the cart, carrying their belongings into their rooms. Clem requested that we put them in the bachelors' old rooms. He specifically requested that his mother be allowed in his old room so she could overlook the gardens. We lead them through the castle; Clem shares details he knows they will enjoy as I let him lead. He is so comfortable around his family. A minor hurt twinges through my chest, longing to have my own family. Mine was never as cohesive as he is, nor as comfortable. But I would still like to have them back some days.

In his mother's new room, he shows her the view, pointing out the gardens that are just starting to show signs of life.

"It's smaller than I thought." She observes quietly. I nod to her, even though she looks out the window, not at me.

"After the curse, we decreased the size due to reduced staff. We've mentioned expanding again. Possibly in a few years. In the morning, I can have Sunette, our head planter, show you around the royal gardens."

She tells me she would like that. We show Claire to her room, then show Bea to hers across the hall. She has been looking around for something but hasn't outright asked. Clem clearly knows and, based on the smirk he tries to hide behind her back, avoids saying anything to her. I lean close to her and whisper that Erik has moved into the guards' quarters but will be at dinner later tonight. Bea tries to hide a blush but is unsuccessful.

We leave them to settle in and rest briefly before dinner. Clem and I make a beeline for our room. It has been too long since we have been together. Based on his reaction when he first saw me, he feels the same way I do. Once inside our room, his lips are on mine instantly. He pulls me close to his body, pressing me tightly against him. I moan, grabbing his back, bunching his shirt in my hands. His tongue pushes into my mouth, desperate and assertive. I love his typical assertiveness in the bedroom, but this feels different. He walks me back, crashing me into the wall while he grinds his hips into mine. His cock is already hard against my hips. His lips are demanding against mine.

I try to pull back from the kiss to ask him to slow down, but he follows me. My head hits the wall as he presses his hips against me harder. I feel like I can't breathe, like I'm trapped. He finally breaks the kiss, only to pepper my cheeks and neck with kisses and bites. I try to calm myself down, knowing I am safe with him. My brain won't listen to reason despite my efforts.

"Clem," I whisper his name, unable to use my regular voice.

"Fuck, I've missed you." He kisses my neck and collarbone, but my body isn't reacting as it should. This doesn't feel right.

"Wait," I whisper.

"I need you now." He grabs the top of my dress, ripping the material, exposing my breasts. I gasp, my body reacting finally. I cover my chest, trying to turn away from him, but I have nowhere to go.

"Flower," I sob, "Flower." He freezes, then looks down between us and steps back quickly with his hands in the air.

"Shit." He drags his hands through his hair as I try to pull my dress back over my chest. He meets my eyes but quickly turns away. He goes to the closet, grabs my robe, and brings it out to me. He holds it open for me, allowing me to pull it around my body. He stays at arm's length while my body calms down. I walk over to the bed, sitting on the edge, not wanting to stand anymore. He stays where he is, not following me.

"Clem," I start.

"I don't know what got into me." He finally walks up to me, dropping to his knees far enough away that I can't comfortably reach him. I'm not entirely sure what to say now. A small part of me wants to say something to make this better, but a bigger part knows this isn't my responsibility to fix. His hands are in his lap, his gaze fixed on his fingers. He finally looks up at me, misery and regret filling his eyes.

"I'm so sorry, Jas." I reach out, placing my palm on his cheek. He turns his face into my hand. "What can I do to make this better?" I hesitate, realizing no one has ever offered to repair an offense like that. His hands wrap around my forearm as he kisses my palm. I grab his cheek, pulling him toward me. I bend, pressing a soft, light kiss against his lips. Unsure what to say now, I guide him up as I slide back on the bed. I pull Clem with me, shifting to lie in his arms on the bed. I settle against his side, but he asks if he can wrap his arms around me before he does so. The question settles the raging emotions in my gut. I nod against him, wanting him to hold me now.

We lie together for several minutes before I find the words I want to tell him.

"I don't like being trapped or restrained without being told about it first." His fingers are stroking my arms, offering a small comfort. "I enjoy being tied up when you tell me what you are doing first. Moving that fast and forcefully brings up unwanted memories for me." He whispers an apology, kissing the top of my head several times. I grip his ribs, holding him close. He had no ill intent in his actions. My past experiences caused my body to react the way it did. I'll be forever grateful that Clem established the alternate word to 'no' and stopped when I used it. While that moment was intense, the relief when he stopped is something I'll never forget. I drift off in his arms, feeling safe and secure again.

The heat is stifling as I wake and return to reality. My mind is foggy from the warmth surrounding me. My body squirms, trying to get away from the heat. There is a robe covering my dress. No wonder I am so hot. I rip it off my body, cool air hitting my breast. I look down, realizing they are exposed, then everything comes crashing back to me. Clem is leaning against the headboard, watching me with tired eyes. I shrug the robe off, pulling the torn material of the dress over, not to hide from Clem but to protect the exposed skin from the chill in the room. His hands drop to his sides, trying to refrain from touching me. Sadness weaves through my chest about this situation. I slide back to sit next to him and curl into his side, resting my head on his shoulder. I clear my throat, feeling dry from the harsh nap.

"Thank you for stopping earlier." My voice is just above a whisper. "That means so much to me." I place my hand on his chest, looking up at his face. He has a soft smile but still looks upset. We've always been fairly rough in the bedroom, but this time wasn't the same. His lips press against my temple firmly; I close my eyes, savoring the touch.

"Dinner will begin soon. We should get you changed. I'll find a way to repair the dress for you." He points at the torn fabric on my chest but keeps his hands away, avoiding touching me. I sigh, shuffling off the bed.

"Emmeline will be able to fix it. Or do something with it. Don't worry about that." I offer my hand to him, helping him climb to the edge of the bed. He stands, staying next to my side, not too close. I step into him, wrapping my arms around him. He may be nervous, but I won't stand for the distance. He sighs, relaxing against my body. His arms wrap around my back as our bodies collide. He buries his face in my neck, apologizing again. This time I chuckle.

"You don't need to apologize. Just help me change." I start to release him, but his grip stays firm. I return the hug, realizing he probably just needs the connection at this point. After three days apart, this isn't the way things should start. He soon releases me, leading me to my closet. We select a dress that matches the sweater he is wearing. I've never cared for matching anyone else, but I have to admit, I like doing it with Clem. Once my clothing is squared away, he catches my wrists before I can leave the closet.

"Are you sure you're ok?"

I pull one hand from his grip to stroke his cheek. A small voice responds with a yes before I gently kiss his lips. He seems satisfied with my response, so we leave for dinner. We discussed having a more formal dinner but decided to stick with the dining hall tonight. It seems less difficult after everyone has been traveling. The cooks still outdid themselves with the spread of food. There is roasted rabbit, a variety of root vegetables, loaves of bread, and a few fruit pies. Clem and I grab food and wine, joining others since we are the last to arrive. Ada and Claire sit in the middle of the table, with Bea and Erik at the end. They both look so uncomfortable I can't help but smile. I nudge Clem's side, pointing out how uncomfortable they look. He presses his head against mine, trying to disguise his laugh as a kiss. At least that justifies my goofy grin. I sit across from his mother, asking how she is settling in.

"Honestly, it's a bit overwhelming. I never thought I would get the chance to visit. Let alone have my son marry the Princess." She looks between us, disbelief written across her face. I can't relate to her feelings, but I can sympathize with her. We chat about her work in the village while we eat. Claire is particularly talkative, discussing everything from her schooling to what she thinks about the curse. I engage in her discussions, enjoying hearing the perspective of an eleven-year-old.

Most people leave to tend to other things within the castle. We stay late into the evening, talking and getting to know each other better. When I spent time with survivors' families, it wasn't very long, usually only an hour at most. I didn't know Ada well, just basic details and a few random tidbits she told me. She is a wonderful woman; I can see so much of her in Clem. She has had a powerful impact on who he is. Soon, Claire is resting against Ada, fighting off sleep. Ada excuses herself, saying she needs to take Claire to bed. Clem walks over, grabs Claire, and lifts her against his chest. Despite Claire's size, she still settles against Clem, falling asleep before we reach her room.

I walk with Ada and Bea, listening to them chat. They have such a close, comfortable relationship. Clem leads the way with his sleeping sister in his arms. Sadness swims through my mind at seeing how good he is with his younger sister. He would make a wonderful father. He said he doesn't mind not having kids, but will he always feel that way? Can I be the reason he doesn't get to have his own children?

Ada and I watch as Clem tucks in Claire, kissing her forehead lightly as he pulls the blanket around her chest. Ada leans against the door with a warm smile on her face.

"He'll make a great father one day." She says softly, smiling at me as he finally nears us. I maintain a stoic face. He hasn't told her I can't have children. Why didn't he tell her? I may look calm on the outside, but my emotions are roiling. As he nears, I bid Ada good night, turning to leave. Clem grabs my hand, stopping me. I don't turn back as I hear him bid good night to his mother, kissing her cheek. Tears are threatening to spill down my cheeks over these thoughts and fears. Finding true love is supposed to be easy. That's how all the books make it seem. Why is there so much doubt and hurt involved in mine?

Ada touches my shoulder, "Good night, Princess." I turn my head just slightly. "Yes, good night. Sleep well." She turns to leave, and Clem is by my side. I don't look up at his eyes. I can't meet his gaze now, not when I'm struggling with my own doubts and worries. We walk to our room silently, bidding a quick good night to the guards outside my room.

Once in the room, Clem grabs me, pulling me into a tight hug. A sob escapes at the sudden embrace. I cling to his back, needing his comfort. His arms engulf me, wrapping me in a protective cocoon of his warmth. A few tears stream down my face while I take deep breaths, trying to settle my mind before I speak to him. I breathe deeply against his chest, inhaling his scent, so familiar that it feels like I've always known it.

"Why didn't you tell her I can't have children?" I mumble against his chest. I can't fathom looking at him yet or trying to speak clearly. Something rumbles through his chest, not quite a growl, but not words either.

"I didn't know how." He speaks calmly but is still holding me tight. "Also, we haven't really discussed who we are telling." I finally look up at him. His eyes are full of concern and love. His hand drifts to my cheek, stroking over the scars along my face. "Did she say something?"

I shake my face in his hand. "No. Well, she said you would be a great father. I was already thinking that after seeing you with Claire. It didn't help that she is not only thinking the same thing but expecting it." He presses a soft kiss to my lips.

"She will be sad, but it won't be a big deal. I promise." I kiss him again, glad he has calmed some of my concerns. I still feel terrible about this situation, but there isn't much I can do about it now. I can worry about those things at some other point. He helps me out of my dress slowly, wrapping my thin robe around me in preparation for bed. I am more exhausted than I realized. I help him undress completely. He has taken to sleeping in the nude since he moved into my room, and I love it. His body is amazing. His chest is defined with strong muscles. His shoulders are broad and still sporting a slightly darker shade of skin from working in the fields without a shirt. His legs are powerful and thick. His cock is accentuated by a tuft of blonde hair; even soft, it hangs in perfect proportion to his body, large and beautiful.

He leads me to bed, ensuring I climb in, then I hold the quilts back for him to join me. Once he is next to me, I curl into his side, resting my head on his shoulder. His body is warm and hard against mine. His hands are on my arm, being careful not to arouse me. He is still concerned about my reaction from earlier. I'm not, and finally seeing him naked after three long days is enough to send warm pulses through my core. I try to settle against him, but I really just want him inside me. I wrap my leg over him, doing my best not to hump his thigh, even though that's all I want right now. I adjust my position, moving closer to suck and kiss his neck. He whispers my name, both hesitantly and desperately.

My breasts press against his ribs, getting just enough sensation from being against his skin that my pleasure increases. Clem rubs one hand from my arm down my back to rest on my ass. He squeezes several times, causing an ache in cunt. I'm ready to be filled by him. My hand glides down his chest, wrapping around his growing cock. I stroke slowly, enjoying the feel of his silky skin in my fingers. He's always in charge when we fuck. Maybe it's my turn. Before he gets the chance to move, I shift my position, so I am straddling him. His eyes go wide in surprise, pupils blown with lust. With my hands on his chest, I lean down to kiss him. His hands grab my ass cheeks as my tongue slides into his mouth. I swirl mine around his, savoring his taste, his warmth.

I withdraw my tongue from his mouth, catching his lip between my teeth as I pull away. He groans at the motion. I lean back, letting my robe teasingly slip over my shoulders, falling to a pile on the bed. I raise my hips, positioning his cock at my entrance. His hands wrap around my hips, holding me tight as I lower myself on him. I drop slowly until I am sitting on him, his dick buried deep inside me. My eyes spin as I swirl my hips in small circles. My hands grab onto his wrists, readying myself to move. I slide up, enjoying his cock against my tight walls. I lift until he is nearly out, then drop down on him, moaning at the sensation. I impale myself on him several more times before finding a rhythm. His hands slide up to my breasts, cupping them and squeezing my nipples between his fingers. I moan, loving the tight sensation.

"You're so perfect."

My eyes meet his as one of his hands drops to my hips, guiding me to sway in a circle around him instead of just up and down. He squeezes my hip, eliciting another moan as my head tips back toward the ceiling. His hands are on my hips now, directing my movements over his dick.

"You are such a good girl. Taking my dick like it was made for you."

His words turn my insides to mush. I feel warm and gooey, like I'll probably melt. Then he places one hand on my hip bone. His hand spreads across my abdomen as his thumb circles against my clit. Heat zings through my body, sending surges into every small spot. My skin is on fire, and my orgasm growing ever closer.

"Let me watch your orgasm, Jas. Come on me, like the good girl you are."

I fall forward, my hands landing on his chest, unable to hold myself back anymore. My hips keep up his pace, brutal and quick but oh so satisfying. His thumb shifts from a circular motion to flick against my clit. My body tenses, and I cry out, almost to the point of release. He slams into me, thrusting inside me since my movements become irregular and jerky.

"That's my girl. You're so beautiful."

The deep growl in his voice sends me over the edge. I cry out, breath catching as my body spasms with the orgasm crashing through my body. He holds my hip with one hand and my clit in the other and pounds into me. My body soars as I gasp for breath. As I open my eyes, Clem climaxes, face twisting in pleasure. His thumb flicks against my clit again, sending another wave of pleasure through me. I fight to keep my eyes open, wanting to watch him ride the torrent of his own orgasm. I lose the fight and collapse against his chest, both of us heaving with exertion. His arms wrap around me, stroking my arms and back in a calming manner. I close my eyes, enjoying the feeling of being against his chest. We're both sweaty from fucking, but it's so comforting to be in his arms.

"I love you, Clem," I whisper against his skin, closing my eyes as I try to relax. He wiggles his hips, letting his penis slip out of me. I giggle at the sensation but don't move away. Unintentionally, I begin to drift off. I wanted to stay awake to talk with him alone, but I am too exhausted from everything. He readjusts the quilts over us as I sink into slumber, content with how the day ended.

Chapter 34

CLEM

Claire hasn't stopped talking since we brought them to the castle. She has always been chatty since she first found her voice as an infant, but she's eleven. When does she run out of things to say? How does she possibly have this many topics to discuss as the sun is just beginning to rise.

Jasmin and I joined everyone for breakfast today. Finn is stationed under the table, begging for scraps of food. Claire is tearing her food into small bites, something she has never done. She pulls two small pieces, putting one in her mouth after making some statement, holding the other in her hand. In an attempt to be sneaky, that hand drops under the table, only to rise a few minutes later with the food surprisingly gone. Finn is going to get so fat from them being here. I make a mental note to tell her not to feed Finn later.

"Clem!" Claire cries with a sudden gusto that can only be managed by a child at this time of day. "Did you hear the thunder last night? It was so loud! There has been so much thunder this winter. I don't remember ever hearing thunder before. Arthur, do you remember him? He is Ferd's grandson. He said the sound wasn't thunder but actually ogres crashing into the barrier trying to break into our kingdom. I told him he's dense and should quit schooling and work in the fields. That's all he's destined for. No point in wasting the tutor's time." She pauses here to take a drink of her juice. Jasmin is snickering beside me, trying to hide behind her hand, but is not even remotely inconspicuous. Ma isn't listening to Claire at all; she has a tendency to block her out now. I had that ability at one point, but my time away has made it hard to tune her out.

"Claire," I sigh, rubbing more forehead. "You can't go around telling kids they are dense! Besides, both of you're siblings work on farms. Do you think we are dense?"

"But he is, Clem!" she argues. "He believes in ogres and thinks he can build a swing high enough he can touch the sun." She rolls her eyes heavily, a motion I have grown fond of on Jasmin but is just exasperating on Claire.

"The thunder," Jasmin starts kindly, "is actually the barrier breaking down, but not by ogres." She pats my shoulder, pressing a small kiss to my cheek before returning to her food. Ma perks up at that comment.

"Really? You have heard the thunder here, too?" Jasmin nods to my mother, chewing her food.

"We were actually able to trace the storms back to some significant moments for us," I say, trying not to elaborate beyond that. Ma does not need the intimate details of my relationship. She nods her head, understanding what I mean.

"What moments?" Ah, I forgot about Claire for the single moment she was silent. How do I explain to an eleven-year-old that the first time I fucked the Princess created a storm of thunder?

"Do you remember the thunder on the winter solstice?" Jasmin questions. That would be a better moment to share with my young sister. My mind is not in the right place. Claire nods, stuffing more pastries in her mouth while someone else speaks. "That was the moment Clem realized he loved me." Claire goes all doe-y-eyed, practically cooing at Jasmin.

"Did you already love him?" Claire asks. I physically cringe. This isn't a line of questioning I want to answer. Not for my younger sister. Or my mother, or anyone really.

"Well, no. Not exactly. It was a little later before I realized I loved him too." Claire nods matter-of-factly as if this makes perfect sense to her.

"He isn't who I would pick to love either."

"Claire," I groan. Ma scolds her as Jasmin bursts into laughter.

"Would you like to go for a walk to see the gardens?" Jasmin asks, changing the conversation at just the right time. They agree, and we clear the plates and go outside the castle.

The air outside is warm in the sunshine but still brisk in the shade. As we walk through the garden paths, Claire runs ahead with Finn, laughing and chasing each other, working off most of the food they just shared. Hopefully, she'll burn off some of her chattiness and quit asking so many questions. Doubtful, but one can hope. Jasmin holds my hand as we walk, telling my mother about different aspects of the garden. She explains what her mother had done, what she wants, and what Sunette has planned for the future. She and my mother get along well. I had always assumed whomever I married Ma would be friendly with, but they genuinely seem to enjoy each other's company.

We spend the day wandering the grounds. Sometimes we tell stories about the castle; sometimes, we talk about life in general; sometimes, we just walk quietly together. The peace of this situation is so comforting. Part of me wishes I had met Jasmin sooner, but I doubt things would have worked out the same. While we are meant to be together, maybe things wouldn't have been so natural before now.

The day wears on and turns to night; after dinner, we show them the library then settle into a large sitting room. We spend the evening relaxing, reading, talking, and laughing. We soon head to bed, tired but content. I couldn't have asked for a better day, even with Claire's questions and the constant sneaking of food to Finn. I sleep better than I have in days.

Jasmin and Emmeline are going through her wardrobe, planning outfits for the coronation. I am lying in bed, reading a book. Pretending to read, really, I'm watching Jasmin try on a multitude of dresses. They are all beautiful, and she looks fantastic in every single one, but none have been sufficient for her.

"I'm so tired of fucking dresses. Can I please put my pants back on?" Jasmin whines, staring in the mirror at an oversized, extravagant dress with puffy layers and a hoop skirt underneath. Emmeline sighs, shuffling through the discarded dresses Jasmin has deemed unacceptable.

"You have to wear a dress to the coronation, Princess. We also need to decide what you will wear for the tour. Kian will be returning in just a few days. The coronation is just over a week away. We are running out of time." I feel bad for Emmeline. Jasmin is normally more pliable, but I imagine Emmeline has seen her in far worse moods than she is now. Jasmin shuffles out the dress, tossing it unceremoniously to the ground. She begins to work on the ties holding the farthingale up. Emmeline is trying to collect the crumpled dress. The whole scene is both endearing and painful.

I make my way over, tossing my book aside, and help Jasmin out of the skirt. She huffs, looking forlorn and exhausted. I kiss her cheek, hoping to bring her some comfort.

"Why can't you wear pants at the coronation?"

Emmeline is the one to respond. "Because she is a woman. She will be Queen, and queens do not wear pants." Jasmin looks at me, deep in thought, considering my comment.

"Why, though?" Emmeline looks at me, exasperated and uninterested in this line of conversation.

"Because women wear dresses. We are proper, and that is what the kingdom expects. They need their ruling monarch to set the tone. And a woman wearing pants is not one they will appreciate."

"Many women wear pants now, especially the field workers. What if she compromised and wore pants with a long train or something." Jasmin's eyes light up at my suggestion. She rushes over to her desk, her shift half undone from her attempt to remove it. She shuffles things around, finding a parchment and pen. She begins scribbling furiously on the page. I gather the remnants of the skirt, handing them to Emmeline as she tries to organize the dresses. Jasmin finally whips around.

"Yes!" she exclaims, excited over her sudden inspiration. "Look." She holds the parchment out toward us, revealing a dress she has drawn. "The dress could split in the middle." She points to a roughly drawn line between the skirt. "I could wear the pants beneath the skirt and a bum roll to make it look fuller." She is lost in thought. "Oh!" she exclaims, still focused on the drawing. "And we could make several. This would be perfect for the tour. I wouldn't need a side saddle, which you know I fucking hate." Emmeline sighs but still listens to Jasmin. "I would look like I'm wearing a stupid dress," the amount of sass spewing from the future Queen is comical, "but would actually be comfortable in my pants. Yes. This will work." She quickly turns to Emmeline. "Please go fetch the seamster. We need to get to work quickly!" Emmeline leaves the room, looking unimpressed but still following orders. Jasmin and I finish clearing the dresses, returning them to her closet.

When the seamster arrives with Emmeline, I leave the room, wanting to spend time with Ma and Bea. Bea has been suspiciously preoccupied since she arrived here. I set my mind on finding her first. I check in the stables, but Zander hasn't seen her. Tomas, who works closely with Zander, suggests I check the training area. He saw her there yesterday afternoon, chatting with Erik. It's not a bad idea. They were friendly the last time she was here and have been close since her return. I don't want to acknowledge the implications of that situation, though. Instead, I check the other animal coop. They tell me she checked in this morning but quickly disappeared. I sigh, resigning myself to go to the training area.

Just outside the door leading to the training ring, I hear moaning from one of the rooms nearby. A smirk spreads across my face. Even though I know others in the castle also have intimate relationships, I haven't encountered any. I need to start exploring other rooms with Jasmin soon. Seems a shame to have an entire castle and only use a couple of the rooms for fucking. I continue walking toward the training area, trying to ignore the couple, when I hear a distinct voice moan a name.

"Erik."

I freeze. I would recognize Bea's voice anywhere. You don't share a room with someone for 27 years without learning the unique tones of their voice. My rational brain is screaming to just keep walking. Unfortunately, my rational brain isn't loud enough. I jerk the door open, finding Bea against the wall; Erik pressed against her, hand under her shirt. His shirt is missing. She gasps at the sudden intrusion. Her face is flushed, hair mussed from his hands. His face matches hers, but his hair is too short to show any differences. He jumps back, dropping his hands to his crotch, but not before I notice the bulge in his trousers.

"Clem," Bea says but doesn't add anything else. Erik turns away from me, looking for his shirt. My rational brain finally catches up to my caveman brain. I should not have opened the door. I knew what was happening. I didn't need to see it. Now the image of a shirtless Erik with tented pants is seared into my mind. Thank the gods, Bea was still decent. I don't think I could have recovered from that. A chuckle escapes my lips, alerting me that I'm on the verge of a hysterical, uncontrollable reaction.

"Um," I look to Erik, then back to Bea. "Just don't get pregnant, okay?"

I shut the door and run back to my room, holding in the laughter. Tears are building in my eyes from the hysterics of the situation. Once I get through the door, I collapse to the ground, laughing hysterically. Not that I find Erik and Bea together funny, but the fact that I opened the door. I caught them. They seriously should have chosen a better room. A new surge of laughs courses through my body at the thought of them fucking in that room. I can feel Jasmin, Emmeline, and the seamster staring at me. I laugh again, taking deep, gulping breaths. I lift my face to them, wanting to explain.

"I said," I gasp between laughs, "I said." I drop my head, clenching my side that has started burning from the laughter. "Don't get pregnant." I drop my head to the floor, unable to support myself through the fit any longer.

"What the fuck, Clem?" Jasmin asks but instructs the seamster to continue working. My brain slowly calms back down, the laughing fit finally ending. Emmeline walks over, handing me a handkerchief and a glass of water. I shift my position, sitting back against the door. I take the items and offer a quick thank you. The reality of finding my sister with a man I consider a friend settles in. Erik and Bea would actually be good together. Both are hard-working and serious but able to relax when needed. They would match each other seamlessly, assuming I didn't ruin things between them. I suddenly feel like an ass, which I am. I'll need to apologize as soon as I can stop giggling at the thought of finding them together. That time is not now.

Jasmin soon walks over to the door, escorting the seamster out of her room. He promises to have one of the pieces done in a few days. He gives me a judgmental look as he leaves the room. Jasmin squats down next to me, stroking my cheek softly.

"My dearest Clem," she coos in a sweet voice. "What the actual fuck, love?" I laugh at the softness in her harsh words. "Don't start laughing again." She jerks her hands back from me, not wanting to send me into another fit. Emmeline is shuffling around the room, tidying materials, pretending she isn't listening, but I know she is.

"I found Bea," I tell Jasmin, taking a deep breath to settle the last of the laughter in my chest.

"Yes, Clem," she nods her head condescendingly. "Bea is here in the castle." She pats my shoulder in a childlike manner. "You'll find she will be around a lot." Emmeline snorts from across the room. I shoot her an angry glare, then turn to give Jasmin the same look. I knock Jasmin's hand off my shoulder, rising to stand. I help Jasmin stand also.

"No, I found her in a room with Erik."

"Obviously. They are close. There are lots of rooms. Why is that so funny?" The real question is, why doesn't Jasmin understand what I'm saying? Emmeline has given up looking busy and is just waiting for me to respond now. An exasperated sigh escapes my lips.

"They were fucking, Jas." Her and Emmeline's gasps perfectly match, and I have to fight off another round of giggles at the sound. "I walked into the room, and he was shirtless, and they were both flushed. Now I have this image of a shirtless Erik with raging arousal seared into my brain."

"Oh, he does look great without a shirt." Jasmin sighs with a dreamy look on her face. Is she kidding me right now?

"Jasmin!" I nearly yell at her, but the loud response is enough to snap her out of whatever images she was thinking. She looks guilty, glancing at Emmeline and then back at me.

"Oh, sorry. You are the only beautiful man in this castle, Clem." She teases, wrapping her arms around me. She turns her head towards Emmeline. I'm pretty sure she means to mouth her statement but actually whispers, "But Erik is fucking handsome." Emmeline nods to her, then sees my face and scurries out of the room, claiming she needs to tend to Finn's laundry. Jasmin snickers in my arms, finally letting me go. She presses a kiss on my cheek. I try to tamp my jealousy down. Even knowing Erik has no claim on her, I still don't particularly like hearing she finds his nude torso arousing.

"So you walked in on them accidentally?" She questions as she walks through the room to get water for herself.

"Well, not accidentally." She turns, eyeing me suspiciously.

"Clem, what did you do?" I groan, telling her how I knew it was them but couldn't stop myself. She laughs at me, collapsing on the sofa, pulling me with her. We spend the rest of the afternoon relaxing and cuddling. She tells me about the meeting with the seamster and how he will attempt her design. Emmeline and Finn join us for a while. My favorite parts of the day are when we can just relax, being ourselves without the social demands of ruling a kingdom weighing us down. Emmeline and Jasmin are entirely different people behind closed doors.

Before dinner, I leave ahead of Jasmin to seek out Erik and Bea, preferably separately, because I have already had enough awkwardness for one day. I need to apologize and ensure I didn't ruin things between them. I may not be close to Erik, but he means a lot to Jasmin and will play an essential role in my life as a guard. Plus, I would consider him a friend. I could probably ignore the situation with Bea altogether, but I won't do that. We're adults now; we can apologize.

I find Erik in the hallway, calling out to him. He looks terrified when he sees me but walks toward me. "Clem, I'm not going to do anything with Bea. It was rude of me to put her in that position, and I won't do that again." His response throws me off. I didn't expect him to say that.

"No, Erik. You don't have to do that. I actually came to apologize to you. I shouldn't have barged in on you two like that." He looks uncertain of my response. "I want you two to be happy. You two would be good together." He is unconvinced, staring at me like I have two heads. "If you want, I am giving you permission to pursue my sister in a romantic relationship."

"You're not mad?" He asks incredulously.

"No." The reality of what he said first hits me. "Is Bea mad?"

"She's upset. I told her we couldn't continue, and she left in a storm."

"Shit." I sigh. I hadn't considered their reactions to being caught. Bea is going to kill me. I excuse myself, heading to her room to make this right without being murdered. I find her in her room, seething still.

"Bea, I'm so sorry." She glares at me but doesn't approach me. I scan the room, not spotting any visible weapons, but I can't put it past her to have some hidden away. Bea is always prepared for any situation, and of course, she is now courting a guard. I need to increase my own guard detail.

"Look, I talked to Erik. You can keep fucking him if you want." This is the wrong thing to say because she charges me, slamming me into the wall. Bea and I typically fight with words, and we haven't fought physically as adults, not counting an occasional jab. Despite her large size and the fact that she works with animals, I always underestimate her strength. As I struggle to breathe from the impact of the wall, she rears her hand back, slamming her fist into my face. I crumple to the floor, raising my hands over my head in defense. My face is burning from the impact. Instead of continuing her assault, she steps back away from me. I peek through my arms, looking to see what she is doing. She is cradling her fingers against her hand, facing away from me.

"I have no intentions of just fucking him, Clem." One hand massages the ache on the side of my head as I lower my other hand. I have thoroughly insulted her, probably twice now, with my earlier comment. I try to stand, staying close to the wall, though, not entirely sure she won't hit me again.

"I know. That's not what I meant. I spoke poorly, Bea." She doesn't move or acknowledge my words. "I want you to be happy. I know he makes you happy, and I don't want to stand in the way of that." She finally turns to look at me. She assesses my face, which is likely already bruising.

"I suppose that makes us even, right?" She inclines her head at my face. I chuckle, hoping to release some of the tension between us.

"Yes. I'll find a way to explain it to Jasmin. She's not going to be happy." Bea lets out a loud, cawing laugh.

"No, you just tell her exactly what you just said to me. I'm sure you'll be lucky to walk away without another black eye." Damn. Bea is right. Jasmin wouldn't hit me, and it certainly wouldn't be as powerful as Bea's. However, Jasmin will absolutely tell me I deserve it.

"If it makes you feel better, I want to see you with Erik. You two would make a handsome couple." She eyes me warily again. I tense, worrying I've said the wrong thing. She is still cradling her hand, so I nod to it, changing the subject quickly. "Did you break anything?" She flexes her hand.

"No, but we should probably get to the kitchens to treat these." She motions at my face, and I nod. Maybe they will have something to hide the bruise on my face. Jasmin is not going to take this well. I just hope it clears before her coronation.

Chapter 35

CLEM

"Where's Kian?" Jasmin yells, pacing around her room. The coronation is in a couple of hours, and she is losing her mind. Emmeline and I have been caught in a perpetual state of helping and avoiding her all morning. She's understandably nervous, but knowing how to help her is hard. I can't make time speed up.

The seamster made a stunning outfit for her. The dress is a deep navy color, bordering on black. The collar just covers her shoulders, scooping from one side to the other across her chest but still covering her breasts. The bodice has intricate silver details, swirls, and flowers that aren't overly feminine. The design looks more magical than flowery. The waist flares over the bum roll she wears under the skirt. It is long and pleated, resembling a standard gown, but it isn't that. This particular piece has a small gap below her navel, just wide enough that someone could tell it's there. She wears black leggings underneath and will have raised heels on her feet. The seamster made several outfits similarly, some with wider gaps at the legs and some with overlapping layers. All were made for wearing pants underneath. Jasmin squealed with delight when she got them.

I received several pieces that match in color and details. Mine are all trousers and tunics, though. I didn't ask for more clothes, but these are nicer and will coordinate with Jasmin's better, especially when we tour the villages together. I have my trousers and a long shirt on, saving the tunic for later so as not to ruin it before the ceremony. Jasmin has her pants on but just a shift on top, keeping the dress to put on later. Kian walks into the room, already dressed for the ceremony. His tunic has the emblem of his coven stitched into the chest. It's hunter green with gold stitches.

"You called for me, Princess?" Jasmin turns to look at him, relief flushing her face.

"Yes. Can you fix his face?" She motions at me, referring to my eye that Bea punched. Jasmin was beyond livid when she saw. We treated it as best we knew how, but Bea did some real damage to my skin. Despite the week since she hit me, my face is still bruised, primarily yellow and green. It's not as bad as when it was purple, but it is still noticeable.

"I'm sorry, Princess. I can't fix facial features. Clem was just born uglier than the rest of us." I sneer at his teasing, but Jasmin isn't impressed. She puts her hands on her hips, staring at Kian.

"You know good and damn well Clem is fucking beautiful."

"Aww, thanks, Jas."

"But he doesn't know when to shut his fucking mouth, and I can't have the future King looking like a fucking gladiator." I chuckle at her comment, focusing on the humor instead of her insults. She's just stressed, but she isn't entirely wrong either. I've never held back my comments from Bea and have always paid that price.

"Nothing I can do will change the bruising. At best, it would look the same. There's the risk of making it worse. Bruises aren't something we focus our magic on as it normally isn't worth it. I'm sorry." She sighs, staring at the bruising on my face. "I do have something else for you, though." He instructs her to sit next to me. He kneels before her, touching either side of her forehead. He chants softly as her eyes close, and she relaxes against me. I ask what he did, and he just shrugs.

"I just put her to sleep. She'll wake in an hour or so, rested and in time to get ready." Emmeline and I both sigh in relief. I carry her to the bed, letting her rest while ensuring everything is in place. The castle is packed with people who have come for the coronation. I still have anonymity since very few people know my face. Everyone knows she has found her true love, as news of the wedding spread faster than the coronation. I wander through the castle, checking in with a few people. Jasmin will appreciate the update when she wakes. Everything is going smoothly. The few issues that have come up are being dealt with quickly and properly. With this being the first major event the castle has hosted in nearly a decade, I am almost surprised everything functions as it should. I expected more issues to arise.

Jasmin finally wakes up, more relaxed and less hostile than before. Kian is a miracle worker. We should probably be paying him more than whatever he receives. Emmeline helps Jasmin get ready, applying powders and lip color to her face. I love Jasmin with a bare face, but she looks fierce with Emmeline's styling. I slip into my tunic as she dresses, ensuring I look presentable, minus my face. Once she is ready, I hold my arm out to her, escorting her to the throne room. Emmeline hurries past us, taking a side route I will follow in a minute to put us in the front without walking down the center. That privilege is reserved for Jasmin.

I hold her hands while she takes several deep breaths. I offer affirmations and reminders that she can do this. I kiss her forehead, careful not to affect the powder or her hair. I meet her eyes, telling her how much I love her before I walk away, leaving her to wait with the guards for her cue. I make my way down the side hall, entering the side of the dais. The room is packed. Several rows of benches are filled with the noblemen and their families. Several high-ranking witches sit beside the noblemen, who look nervous and excited. Behind them, everything is standing room only, and it is packed. Nearly everyone that could travel came to the castle. So many people are here to see their Queen appointed.

Kian stands on the stage, watching the crowd. He doesn't show any signs of being nervous. I don't even know if he is. I would be, but I've never spoken in front of a large crowd. This crowd is ten times the size of the group he told his story to during winter solstice. People are still crowding at the doors and in the halls, unable to squeeze into the main room. When I get to my seat, he glances at me, and I nod, the signal for him to start the ceremony. He uses magic to cast his voice around the room. Even if he yelled, he still wouldn't be heard by everyone. Jasmin made an excellent decision in asking him to officiate the coronation.

Kian draws everyone's attention, greeting them and giving a brief introduction. Then he signals for Jasmin to enter. The doors at the back of the room swing open slowly as the whole room shifts to see her. Light from the hallway floods into the room. She begins to walk down the center aisle, everyone bowing to her. She keeps her eyes trained on Kian; her only goal is to make it to the dais. She looks exquisite in her gown, wearing the necklace I gave her. The windows to her right allow the late afternoon sun to shine through. Her necklace shimmers under the sunlight, causing the crowd to murmur and whisper. Joy shines through her eyes, but her face remains stoic. Her eyes meet mine briefly just before she passes. I give her a warm smile and bow deeply as she walks by. Once she reaches the dais, we all find our seats, and Kian begins the ceremony.

He talks about a girl who has faced unfathomable challenges only to persevere and lead her kingdom to prosperity. He doesn't seem to follow a script, but his words detail her strength, compassion, and fight for justice. After his speech, he begins to ask her the questions she must answer for the coronation. He asks if she dedicates her life to serving the kingdom, her people taking precedence above all. This moment is one she was most concerned about. She didn't want to sound weak when she answered. When she speaks, her voice is loud, firm, and powerful. She sounds like a Queen. Internally, I am jumping for joy over her response. Outwardly, I watch calmly as Kian asks the four other questions, similar in nature, to finish the ceremony.

The five Lords approach the dais as she turns to face the crowd. She makes vows to each Lord, swearing to protect their villages and make decisions based on the people of each community. Each Lord accepts her new role, bowing deeply. After all five have accepted her, she turns back to Kian, then kneels in front of him. He takes the crown Ingrid made for her from a table by his side. He places the crown on her head, grabbing a sword with several gems in the handle. He holds this out for her. She accepts the sword as she rises, then turns toward the crowd.

"Sweet Briar, I present to you, Queen Jasmin, ruler of your kingdom."

She stabs the sword into the ground next to her as the crowd cheers enthusiastically. As if on cue, clouds part in the sky, allowing light to fall on Jasmin. The sun hits the crown, scattering colored light across the opposite side of the room. The crowd gasps as the colors dance over the walls, ceiling, and people as she walks. Cheers grow even wilder as Jasmin walks down the dais, taking the center aisle back. She pauses next to me; I bow, doubling in half. Her fingers graze my chin. I lift my head as she guides me up. I kiss her cheek.

"You are amazing, my Queen," I growl at her. She gives a knowing smile before continuing along the aisle without me. As she passes, the crowd bows deeply, respecting her new position. Once she leaves the room, Kian announces the celebration will continue outside near the royal gardens.

Emmeline, Kian, and I sneak out of the side hall, avoiding the crowd, to reunite with Jasmin. Unlike the prior celebrations we have been to, tonight, she will stay close to the throne that has been placed outside for her. Citizens will be allowed to congratulate her, give gifts, and say whatever they feel so inclined to say. I will be by her side most of the night but will have more freedom to leave if needed. I thank Kian for his effort, commending him on his work. I take my place by Jasmin's side, squeezing her hand briefly. I was repeatedly warned not to show my affection for her. It's not proper for a crowned queen to look sappy and in love at her coronation.

The rest of the night is another challenge Jasmin has been worried about. She has to stay on her throne, listening to people congratulate her without looking bored or uninterested. She has to stay focused on the hundreds of people who will speak to her tonight without being overwhelmed. She cannot have any food or drink during this period, as her goal is to focus on the people. The line in front of her is long, but she is strong; she can handle this.

I occasionally squeeze her hand, reminding her I am here and giving her something to focus on. She maintains the persona of Queen throughout the whole night. Her smiles are regal, her posture strong, her words kind but firm. She has been trained for this role her entire life, and despite the last nine years of the curse, she is still perfect at it. The hours wear on as person after person stops to speak with her. I leave her side twice. Once to get a drink for myself when I feel myself losing my persona, and again to relieve myself from the drink I consumed. While Jasmin never seems to struggle with chatting with people coming to her, I grapple with my attention and the emotions showing on my face.

After many long hours, the final guests reach Jasmin, wishing her luck as our future Queen. Erik arrives behind the last guest, letting Jasmin know she can leave now. I nearly crumple with relief, but remember I can't do that yet. Together, we walk through the crowd, heading back into the castle. My anonymity is ending, as everyone will know who I am now. Once inside the castle, we take her secret passage to her room, not wanting anyone to follow us. The crowd will be allowed to continue the celebration outside through the night.

We pause outside her door, celebrating that we both made it through the evening. I kiss her deeply, no longer worried about the lip stain she wears. I push the doors open, dragging her in with our lips still melded together.

"Huzzah!"

The cheer startles us apart. We realize several of our close friends have gathered in our room to celebrate with us. That wasn't what I had planned, but I can still adapt at this point. Another few minutes, and they would have been getting a full show. My family, Emmeline, Mikhail, Kian, Erik, Tomas, and Sunette's family, along with Finn, are all in the room, holding goblets of wine. They hand us goblets, informing us they want to make a quick toast and then will be out of our room. I pull Jasmin into my side, tired of her being so far away from me. She sighs, giving me a contented look. I kiss her forehead as Mikhail starts the toast.

Mikhail vows to serve her in fields and in life for the rest of his life.

Emmeline vows to always be her voice of reason.

Kian promises to help her repair relations with the witches, creating unity within her kingdom.

Erik swears to lay down his life to protect us.

Tomas pledges to serve her however she sees fit.

Zander and Sabeko swear to care for her and the stables as their own.

Sunette promises Jasmin will always be treated as her own daughter, even if she is Queen.

My mother promises the same thing, assuring her she will always have a home to visit should the castle be too overwhelming.

Claire vows to serve Jasmin as best she can.

With only me left, having not said anything, I raise my glass higher. I wasn't told about this little celebration and didn't have any prepared. I could say so many things to her, but most are inappropriate in mixed company. Instead, I stick with a simple salute.

"To Queen Jasmin." Everyone repeats my toast, and we all drink. After the toast, they each hug Jasmin, leaving the room with their full goblets. I'm relieved they don't plan to stay any longer. I'm somewhat exhausted but ready to have the Queen to myself. Once everyone is out of the room, she collapses on the couch. I kneel in front of her, sliding my hands over her body.

"You did it," I whisper against her torso. Her fingers slide through my hair. I press my lips against her body, over her chest, beneath her necklace. She grabs the crown, placing it on the table. I watch the motion, making a note of where she sets it. I will need that again in a few minutes.

"How does it feel, Queen?" My voice is deep and gravelly, the one she likes so much.

"So good." A wide smile spreads across her face as she lowers her head back on the sofa. I peel away from her body, reaching down to remove her shoes. I rub her feet briefly before standing in front of her.

"Can I have time to worship the queen now?" Her eyes meet mine, desire pulsing through her gaze. I give her a wicked grin, holding my hand out for her. She takes it, standing in front of me. I turn her around, undoing the back of the dress to remove it from her. We get her out of that and the bum roll, then I peel her pants off her. I pull my tunic off, tossing it aside. My gaze stays fixed on her body; red marks across her waist from the pants and dress closures fade slowly. I adjust my cock in my trousers. I have a plan for her, and that doesn't involve my cock yet. I need to wait for my turn.

I guide her over to the bed, standing behind her while she faces the foot of the bed. My arms wrap around her waist as my lips find her neck. She places one hand over my arms and the other circles around my neck. I remove my hands from her waist, grabbing her wrists with my arms. I knew she wouldn't be able to keep her hands from exploring, and this isn't her turn to touch.

"This is my time to worship you." She gives a small grunt of displeasure. "To ensure you don't spoil my plan, I'm going to tie you to the bed." Her eyes open wide, turning her head to look at me. I stretch one arm out to a sash she hasn't noticed on the top railing of the bed. I pull the material down, tying it around her wrist loosely so it doesn't cut off circulation. It's secure enough that she can't get out of it. I slowly guide her other hand above her head on the other side, allowing time for her to stop me. She doesn't; she is pliant for me.

Once her hands are secured in the top corners of the uncovered bed posts, I step back to the table where she left her crown. I grab it and saunter back to the bed. I climb on the mattress, making my way in front of her. She realizes what I am doing and angles her head down for me to place the crown on the top of her head. I ensure it is on her head well, knowing I'll need to remove it soon so she doesn't send it flying across the room. Now, she stands in front of me, exposed, only wearing her crown and necklace. I stare at her for a moment, willing my throbbing dick to wait its turn. Her breathing is shallow, her chest rising quickly. The necklace rests against her smooth skin. The contrast between the bruise on her abdomen, the silver necklace against her exposed breast, combined with the darkness of her hair under the silver crown is exquisite. It's an image I try to burn into my memory. She is absolutely stunning, standing stretched out and ready for me.

I shift closer to her, placing my legs on either side of her body as I suck one of her nipples into my mouth. She moans, rocking her hips in the space between us. My arms wrap around her back, caressing her body. I take the other nipple in my mouth, swirling my tongue around the bud, nipping it with my teeth. I pop it out, leaving the bed to stand behind her. I wrap around her delicate body again, holding her tightly as I kiss her neck repeatedly. She holds her head awkwardly, unable to roll it back because of the crown. I step back, admiring her backside. Unable to help myself, I smack her ass, squeezing the reddening cheek. She groans, pressing her ass toward me. I kiss her cheek, pulling the crown off her head.

"You may be my Queen, but you don't need this here."

She moans, tipping her head back once the weight has been removed from her head. I place it on the table, pocketing the item she dubbed 'magic fun ball' Kian gave her and a small bottle of oil. I use them occasionally but haven't in a while. I stroll back to her, practically prowling around the room. She's so beautiful and so ready for me. I want to give her everything, but I also want to hear her beg. She is my Queen, and I plan to treat her as such.

I drop to my knees behind her, pressing several small kisses across her lower back. She groans, pushing her ass back against me. My hands cup her ass cheeks, massaging my fingers into her supple skin. I circle her cheeks, then drag one knuckle lightly between them, following the line through her pussy. A breathy moan sounds from her chest as her head drops to the front. I lightly tap her clit several times, teasing her. I drop my hand, using both to tap the inside of her ankles, forcing her to stand wider. Once satisfied with her new position, I turn to sit underneath her, my mouth finding her core. My eyes meet her as my tongue licks through her opening. Her taste is my favorite, every bit of her essence on my tongue. My tongue plunges deep inside her as my hands grab her hips, bringing her closer to me. Our eyes stay connected as I devour her like a starving man.

My nose presses into her clit while my tongue flits through her opening. The muscles in her arms tense several times as she tries to pull her hands down to touch. I knew she wouldn't keep her hands off me if they weren't restrained. This moment is about her, not me. My cock aches painfully in my pants, but it will stay there until I am ready for her. Her cunt clenches around my tongue as I drive deeper inside her. I shift my face, bringing my hand down to pinch her clit with my fingers. She falls apart with the first touch, screaming my name as her orgasm barrels through her body. I watch her twist and tighten as ecstasy overcomes her. As she begins to settle, I slip my tongue out of her cunt, kissing her core. She groans, but I just slide out from under her.

I remove my clothes, almost to the point my dick will finally get some action. I drag a small table over, placing the oil and cylinder on it. I want it accessible without her seeing them. I press my body against her back, rubbing my aching cock against her butt. Unable to control how hard I am, the tip leaks a small drop of liquid against her ass.

"How does it feel? Being Queen?" I hold her tight against my chest as it rumbles with my voice. She mentioned once how much she loves it, so I always try to oblige her if I am speaking this way. She doesn't even reply, unable to form words at this point. That's fine. I don't need her to speak.

"My Queen is speechless," I chuckle, releasing one hand from her body to grab the oil. I pop the cork out with my finger, tipping the jar over into my hand. I smear the oil around in my hand, using my cock to spread it where I need it.

"That's okay, Jas. You don't need to speak for me. You just need to accept me." I press my fingers against her ass, slowly sliding two fingers in as deep as I can. She moans, chest heaving with the sudden intrusion. I grab her breast with my free hand, squeezing and caressing as I wait for her to relax against me. I nibble on her ear, peppering her neck with kisses. When she finally settles, I begin sliding my fingers in and out gently. She begins to rock into my hand, seeking her own pleasure. My free hand caresses from breast to breast, playing with both. My fingers swirl in her ass as she continues to grind against me. I kiss her shoulder and collarbone over the necklace still around her.

I press a third finger deep inside, pausing to let her adjust to the new sensation. A thin sheen of sweat builds across her skin as her body temperature rises from arousal. I rub my fingers as a unit inside of her, twisting and sliding in and out. She drops her head forward, pressing her ass closer to my hand.

"You're such a good girl," I whisper in her ear. "You should see how beautiful you look with my fingers buried deep in your ass." I continue to fuck her ass with my hand for a few more moments as she pants against my body, head still bowed. My cock is jerking with inaction. I passed the point of pain a while ago but have suffered through it for this moment. I slowly pull my fingers from, eliciting a long, needy groan.

"Don't worry, Queen. I'm not done with you yet."

I pour more oil over my cock, then press the tip against her hole. She gasps as she realizes my intentions.

"You have given nearly every bit of yourself to your kingdom. Now, I'm going to claim this as mine." I press inside her ass slowly, letting her adjust to the larger size. She pants, moaning in pleasure and pain. Her hands pull against the sashes tethering her to the bed. I press my forehead against the back of her head, willing my cock to hold out a few minutes longer. The tightness and warmth of her ass are nearly overwhelming. I certainly won't last long this time. My balls are already tightened, readying for release. Once I am flush inside her, I kiss the scars on her cheek. I keep one hand on her hip, the other wrapping around her stomach, holding her tightly.

"You are mine," I growl viciously, causing her to moan and roll her head back onto my shoulder. I slide out of her ass, then press back in. The tight ring around my cock creates such a glorious sensation I moan, my chest vibrating against her back. I quickly reach back for the magic fun ball, tapping it to start the vibrations. I place it against her clit as I increase my thrusting. She cries out, body writhing in pleasure. I lift her thigh, resting her foot against the bed, hitting a different spot inside her. Her pants come out as animalistic cries now. Occasionally crying out my name. Her breasts jostle under my arm as I thrust deep inside her ass. My orgasm hovers on the brim, almost spilling over.

For the first time in my life, no words are in my mind, only Jasmin. Her body, her ass, her clit, her breasts, her. I cannot say anything to her. I tap the fun ball, increasing the speed as my orgasm crashes through my body. My eyes roll back in my head as my teeth clamp down on her on the base of her neck. She screams as her orgasm barrels through her. Her ass tightens around my cock, making moving nearly impossible. We sway together as our bodies soar in ecstasy. Her cunt clenches as I keep the vibrating cylinder against her clit. Her body continues to spasm as she struggles to breathe. The last of my release spurts deep inside her as she still shakes. She gasps for breath as I finally pull the magic fun ball away from her clit. I tap it off, tossing it back on the table, not looking to see where it lands.

I wait for her body to stop convulsing. I kiss her gently, rubbing my fingers over her body to calm her. She finally relaxes, my arms supporting most of her weight. Without pulling out of her, I release one hand from the sashes. She drops her arm, sagging in my hold. I reach up to remove the other one. Once her hand is free, her body collapses against the bed. She slips out of my grip, ripping her body away from my cock. We both groan at the sudden removal.

I lift her up, carrying her over to the side of the bed. Her eyes are barely open, entirely unable to support her own weight. I grab a wet cloth, clean her, then myself. I remove the necklace from her, realizing I left a bite mark on the front of her neck. She won't be able to wear a shirt without a high collar for a few days at least. I cringe, knowing she won't be happy about that. Maybe she'll be glad about the experience. I put the necklace away, then crawl into bed with her. She is already asleep, snoring lightly. I tuck her into my side, quickly falling asleep with her in my arms. As I fall asleep, the thunderstorm crashes and booms outside.

Chapter 36

CLEM

Jasmin groans, twisting in my arms as she wakes up. The curtains are yanked open, and light pours into the room. I nuzzle my face into her neck, trying to hide the light from my eyes, wanting to sleep longer. Jasmin winces, grunting in pain.

"Why does that hurt?" she mumbles, voice thick with sleep.

"I don't know what you two did last night after we left, but I am not touching that table over there." I lift my head to see Emmeline shuffling around the room, pointing at the table with the oil and the rounded cylinder. I chuckle, letting her know I'll clean it shortly. Jasmin sits, stretching her arms over her head. She winces again, dropping her arms and turning to the side. My arms slide around her waist, trying to keep her close. Emmeline smacks me with a rag, her favorite method of reprimanding me.

"No, you have to get up. You two are due to breakfast in...Oh my gods, are those bite marks?" Emmeline nearly shrieks the last part. Jasmin looks alarmed, shifting her gaze between Emmeline and me. I offer an apologetic shrug with an awkward smile. Jasmin wiggles awkwardly off the bed toward the mirror in the room. It takes a moment for her eyes to find the teeth marks on her neck. Her fingers rub over the spot gently, but she winces again.

"Fuck, Clem!" I climb out of the covers and walk toward her. I forget that I am also undressed. Emmeline is comfortable with Jasmin being nude since she helps her dress and bathe. She is not comfortable with me being naked, though.

"Clem!" She shrieks, turning away, covering her eyes.

"Shit, sorry." I quickly locate my trousers from last night, slipping them on. I step behind Jasmin, wrapping my hands around her as I look at her in the mirror.

"He's got pants on, Emmeline." She says, meeting my gaze in the mirror. "What the fuck, Clem?" She whispers to me. I kiss her cheek.

"I got a little carried away last night. I'm sorry." She sighs but settles back against my body.

"We need to change my wardrobe again." Her voice is exasperated, but she gives me a wicked grin. She enjoyed what we did last night. Emmeline wanders off to her closet, searching for options to hide the bite, muttering under her breath. I grab the items from the table, return them to their original places, and clean them. Jasmin and I walk into the washroom, needing to bathe before we can leave the room.

"If you two start fucking in there, I will come in and beat you off each other!" Emmeline yells from the other side of the door.

"Promise?" I yell back. Jasmin laughs, smacking my chest before getting in the tub. Emmeline grunts outside, walking away to take care of other things. I slide in to join Jasmin in the deep tub, and she holds her hand up, stopping me.

"Emmeline is right. We don't have time for you to be crazy today." I give her a shocked look.

"It's not just me who is crazy here." She laughs, closing the space between us and draping her arms over my shoulders.

"I am sorry about the bite mark." I nuzzle against her cheek as her wet fingers run through my hair.

"No, you're not." I shrug, closing my eyes to savor the touch of her fingers against my scalp. Emmeline bangs on the door.

"No sex!"

"Just a quick one!" I shout back. Jasmin smiles, caressing my scalp as she straddles my lap. If she keeps that up, there will be a quick one happening. I moan her name, tightening my hands on her back.

"I don't hear you washing!" Emmeline yells again. That poor woman has put up with so much from us in the past few weeks. Jasmin rolls her hips, spurring my cock to life. Her lips are on my neck as my cock hardens beneath her. Before I say anything else, she slides down on my penis. I groan loudly as she reaches the hilt.

"Don't make me come in there!" Emmeline shouts through the door.

"You'll get a show if you do!" Jasmin shouts before she starts bouncing in my lap. My lips find hers, kissing her deeply. My fingers slide up her back, grabbing her hair and pulling it down. She breaks the kiss, face turning toward the sky. Her breasts lift above the water, and I bury my face against them. Her pace isn't as brutal as the one I set last night, but it is so satisfying. I nibble against her breasts as they bounce in my face, splashing water between us. This is absolute heaven.

"Come with me, Clem." She whispers as her pussy begins to tighten around me. I flip us around, pressing her back against the edge of the tub. I start thrusting into her, driving me to the point of release.

"Come now, Queen," I growl at her. Her eyes widen as she shivers, then rolls her head back in pleasure. My orgasm rolls through my body, releasing deep inside her cunt. I drop my head against her shoulder, relaxing as my body settles. We take deep breaths, returning to normal.

"Why don't we give Emmeline the next two weeks off?" I suggest, pulling out of her slowly.

"What? Why?" She looks stunned as I grab the soap to wash her body.

"She deserves it, for one. And I'm pretty sure you and I can manage to get you dressed for a few days. Your riding outfits will be easy enough." I shrug, rubbing the soap over her body. She's quiet, considering my suggestion.

"I swear to the holy gods, you two better be almost done in there." Jasmin chuckles as I give her an acknowledging nod toward the door.

"Okay, maybe you have a point. I'll ask if she wants to do that when we're done." We quickly finish up, not wanting to annoy her anymore. Jasmin leaves the room first, bringing my clothes back so I can get ready before I walk out.

When I leave the bathroom, Emmeline runs to wrap her arms around my neck. "Thank you. I would love a break. I love you two, but you are so exhausting. So if you embarrass each other, it's on you." She laughs, going back to help Jasmin get ready. I step up, taking over for her. I instruct her to get breakfast, and we'll be down shortly. She glances at Jasmin, who nods at her. She scurries out of the room. Jasmin sits at the vanity, so I follow her to style her hair. Since it's still wet, we agree to do a simple updo. That's something I can manage. I've helped Claire enough with that. When I finish, I rest my hands on her shoulders. Her small fingers wrap around my wrist. I stare at us in the mirror, loving our reflection. We look good together, like we belong, and our clothes don't even match today.

"Oh, we should get you a scarf or something." I run my finger over the spot on her neck, realizing there are tiny scabs in some places. I didn't know I broke skin when I bit her. She sighs, not wanting to wear a scarf. "Unless you want to wear a sweater." She groans, telling me to find a scarf. We find one that doesn't look too suspicious and style it around her neck.

We make our way to the dining area. It is more crowded than usual. People bow and curtsey as we walk by, everyone excited to greet their Queen. I forgot about so many people being in the castle. We get our food and find Emmeline waving us over. She is at a table with Kian, Erik, and my family, with two spots reserved for us. There had been talk about establishing a specific table for us, but Jasmin didn't want to do that. She would rather have all of them open for anyone to use. Thankfully, we have many friends willing to save us spots.

"Clem," Claire calls before we are even in our seats. "What did you do last night? The thunder was so loud, and there was so much of it." Gods damn her. All the blood rushes to my face, embarrassed over explaining what I did last night to my family. Jasmin doesn't acknowledge the question, settling into her chair to begin eating. Her eyes catch mine, though, and I know she heard the question. "Clem?" Claire sings out, trying to force me to address her.

"Um, well. I…" What am I supposed to say now? "We celebrated her becoming Queen." My mother is ignoring the conversation, but the others nod in approval of my answer.

"Yeah, but so did everyone else. What did you do?" She emphasizes every word in her question, demanding specifics of my evening. My face burns deeper now, being put on the spot. I will not under any circumstance tell anyone I fucked Jasmin in the ass, let alone tell my younger sister.

"Well…"

"Claire, you can't ask people questions like that. It's not your business what he did." Ma speaks to Claire, saving me from further embarrassment. I look at Ma, then realize how awkward this whole situation is. So I just shove food in my mouth, staring down at my plate.

"But Ma," Claire whines, "this is a real-life true love story. I need all the details. History needs to know what he did!" Jasmin, Kian, and Erik chuckle at her response. I just shove more food in my mouth. It's hard to chew right now.

"No one needs to know what he did," Emmeline mumbles to Kian beside her, but it's still loud enough for several of us to hear. I cough, spewing bits of food behind my lips. Jasmin rubs my back, trying to calm me.

"That's enough, Claire. They are in love, and that's all history needs to know." If I weren't struggling with the food in my mouth, I would thank Ma for saving me. Claire gives a dramatic, exasperated sigh.

"Jasmin, are you ready for your tour of the villages?" Ma asks. They begin chatting about our upcoming journey as I calm down. Erik leans across the table toward Kian and Emmeline. He whispers softly but still loud enough that I can hear him on the other side of Jasmin.

"Okay, but what did he do to her?" Emmeline sighs heavily while Kian snickers. My cheeks are still warm, embarrassment still coursing through my body. Bea reaches up and pinches Erik's arm. He jerks away and rubs his arm tenderly, and I'm suddenly glad I'm not the only one receiving that kind of treatment from Bea. The idle chatter continues through breakfast. Contentment settles deep inside me, realizing not only is Jasmin mine, but the others are people I would consider family, too. I came to the castle to escape Arkaley and found my home.

The carts are loaded, and the horses are prepped. We stand outside the front door, ready to get on the horses and begin our tour. We will ride through the villages, starting with Tilrade and traveling west in a circle until we end in Vadried. I am excited to go on this tour because I have only been to Obele and Arkaley. Ma and Pa used to take Bea and me to Obele once a month to see performers when we were children before Claire. Once she came, traveling became more difficult. We haven't left Arkaley at all since the curse began. Jasmin is excited but nervous. She hasn't been through the villages in many years and worries about her reception. Based on the turnout for the coronation, I doubt she will have any issues.

Ma and Claire are leaving to go back to Arkaley. I tried to convince them to stay at the castle, but Ma wanted my sister to return to her regular tutors. We didn't put up much of a fight over the topic. They will all return to the castle before the wedding. Bea is staying at the castle, helping with the extra animals on the grounds. There are more goats, chickens, pigs, and rabbits than in years; they need extra hands now. I was surprised to hear she is staying since Erik is traveling with us. They spend a lot of time together now. Emmeline is staying back, taking care of Finn. She swears the tradeoff isn't worth it, but at least she gets to sleep in her own bed. Bea offered to help with Finn, but he has already been banned from other animals because he kept chasing them.

The weather is sunny and warm today, spring finally melting all the snow and making way for summer. As much as I enjoy the winter, I prefer warmth. We mount our horses, getting in the line before we head out. Jasmin wanted to ride on her horse instead of a carriage, claiming she wanted to be more visible. We take off with a few guards in the front, followed by Kian, Lord Gustavo of Tilrade, Erik, Tomas, several servants, and more guards behind us. The Lords of each village will meet us at their town to escort us through. The others have already left, but Gustavo decided to ride with us instead of traveling ahead. It will take a few hours to reach Tilrade today. There will be a small parade as we make our way through the town. Each village visit will occur the same way. We will walk through in the evening and spend the night in the inn with limited access from locals. The next day will be for villagers to visit. The third day will allow time for Jasmin to tour the village, then we will ride out either that night or the next morning, depending on how far we need to travel. The only exception is Arkaley; Ma will host dinner for Jasmin, Kian, Erik, and me.

The leading guards finally take off down the road, lessening my nerves from waiting so much. We ride down the service road as the trees thicken around us. After a couple of minutes, I get Jasmin's attention, pointing to the flower on the side of the road. It is the one she used as a marker for the pond. It is blooming amongst the green grass, just like in the fall. She smiles, looking past me to where the pond is. We can't see it from here, but we both know it's there. The ride is long and quiet. A few people chat with each other, but Jasmin and I are silent. It has been a while since we have been on horseback together.

The ride is uneventful, stopping for breaks a few times, mostly just pressing on steadily. We finally reach the outskirts of Tilrade. The town is built into a coast, thriving on fishing and boating. The sea beyond the village glistens in the lowering sun. The town spreads wide over the cove it was built around. The city center is close to the shoreline but set back a safe distance to avoid storms. As we near the edge of town, Lord Gustavo falls back to ride next to Jasmin, forcing me behind her. I scowl but let him take the spot. He starts telling her all the changes he has approved in the past few years, pointing to different landmarks. As we ride closer to the city center, people are lining the streets, hoping to get a glance at Jasmin. She waves at a few, but Vesper starts hesitating, jerking around. He brays loudly at one exceptionally crowded intersection, trying to turn back. I ride next to her, encouraging Vesper to keep moving. Past the intersection, there are fewer people, and Jasmin dismounts quickly, walking around to stroke Vesper's face.

"I don't think you should be down, Jasmin," I tell her, looking around for the guards. They are watching the situation, keeping an eye on villagers nearby. I motion for Erik to ride over. He asks what the problem is when he gets to the other side of Vesper, blocking Jasmin between us.

"I think he is wary of the crowds. He hasn't been around crowds in years. He's been pretty lax recently." Jasmin is stroking his face, trying to calm him down. Erik rides off to Tomas, returning a few minutes later.

"There are extra blinders, but they are packed away for now. Why don't Clem and I ride on either side of you to keep Vesper away from the crowds for now?" She nods, stepping back to mount him again.

"Isn't there a narrow bridge at the city center, though?"

Erik thinks for a moment, staring off as he considers the question. I am unfamiliar with the route and cannot answer that question.

"Yes, but it's a single-person lane. There won't be any people on it. We stop on the other side of the bridge. I'll send a rider ahead to be sure the other side is clear." Jasmin thanks him as he rides to the guards in front. One of the men gallops away as Erik returns to us. We settle into a smooth trot with Vesper and Jasmin between us. I haven't been overly concerned about Jasmin's safety, trusting her guard. However, I do feel better with her between Erik and me. Erik is an excellent guardsman, and I trust him with my life and Jasmin's.

The crowd thickens the closer we get to the town center. People are squished beside buildings and houses, hoping to glimpse their Queen. Jasmin waves at all of them, giving a kind, warm greeting. I try to match the sentiment, but few know who I am. I don't recognize any faces from the coronation, and they don't seem to care about me at all. Vesper is still uncertain but walks smoothly between Shena and Acer. At the bridge, I cross first, with Erik following Jasmin in case Vesper reacts poorly. He doesn't, and we soon arrive at the inn we will be staying at tonight.

Jasmin ensures Tomas will personally see to Vesper during the evening. She keeps telling him how to care for the horse as if Tomas hasn't been in the stables more than her in the past few months. Granted, Tomas wasn't exactly there to see Vesper, but he was still in the stables frequently. I finally manage to drag her away and into the inn. Dinner is already prepared for us. Everyone rises and bows as she enters, and she finally switches from worrying over her horse to playing the role of monarch. She roams from table to table, greeting people as I follow her. I say very little, mostly just following along like a lost puppy. I don't mind, though; being here isn't about me.

We finally get to our table and take a seat. We are seated at the back of the room, facing out, so we see everyone. This is the standard placement for royalty. I've never been to a dinner party like this, but being on this side of the table feels bizarre. Jasmin doesn't share my grievances, having grown up on this side of the table. Even Erik and Kian seem comfortable in their positions on our side. I try to hide my discomfort, but I am not entirely successful. Food and wine are brought to us, and the servant places the food on the table. I take small bites of my food, trying to remember the protocol for eating as royalty. Most of that information did not stick. I accidentally finish my wine too quickly and want more. Jasmin is speaking with Erik on her other side, so I rise to get more wine for myself. Her hand lands on my wrist, holding me in place. I look at her, but she doesn't stop talking to Erik. I just want more wine; surely, she can wait a moment for me to get some. I settle in my seat, waiting for her to finish with Erik, her hand on mine the whole time. She finally turns toward me with a smile, leaning over to whisper in my ear.

"We don't rise to get our own food and drink. You should motion for someone to bring you more." That lesson crashes back into my mind, bringing heat to my cheeks. I offer a small apology as she motions for someone to bring more wine. She squeezes my hand while my goblet is refilled. Her touch is reassuring, but I still feel overwhelmed by everything.

Dinner ends, but the chatter continues. Jasmin doesn't let go of my hand often, keeping me grounded and not worrying about my actions as much. Once the conversation dies down and the servers have stopped serving dinner, Jasmin bids good night to everyone, both of us heading to our room. A couple of guards stand outside of our room, protecting us from any threat that may arise. I help Jasmin out of her riding clothes, a dress made similar to the one she wore at her coronation but in more comfortable materials. We ready for bed, settling into each other's arms, falling asleep quickly, exhausted from the day of riding.

The next day is filled with meeting villagers, receiving gifts, hearing stories, being congratulated, and just talking with people visiting. We sit together in the large room in the town center. This room functions as a throne room, courtroom, and general event room for weddings or other celebrations. It isn't nearly as large as the castle but still has room for hundreds of people to proceed through during the day. It is another long exhausting day. On our final day, we are escorted through the village in a carriage. Neither Jasmin nor I mind being in the open-top carriage. It is more comfortable than being on the horses all day and allows us to view the city without other distractions. Lord Gustavo rides with us, telling us about different parts of the town he is so proud of. I appreciate his enthusiasm, but at the end of the day, Tilrade isn't overly special.

In the afternoon, we mount our horses, forming the line we rode in again. Obele is only an hour or two from here, so we leave later in the afternoon. While Tilrade has a booming market with unique items from being a coastal village, Obele has many artists. There are performers, painters, quilters, and smiths; anything a person can create can usually be found in Obele. The previous royal jewelers were all from Obele. It's part of the reason Ingrid was so excited to earn that title. She always wanted to go to Obele for opportunities but could never relocate.

Tomas already has the blinders on Vesper, who seems more relaxed today. He just needed time to adjust to the return of his duties. We ride along the coast for a while before turning inland to reach Obele. Parts of Obele are near the coast, but most of the city is inland. I've never looked into the history to know why they settled inland instead of staying on the shore like those in Tilrade. As we arrive on the edge of town, Lord Erland meets us and drops in line in front of Jasmin. He doesn't strive for power the same way Lord Gustavo does. Despite this, I'm still not as fond of Lord Erland as some of the others. He is very old, usually hunched over, appearing to have one foot in his grave already. But he continues with his duties and seems to be fair. I don't particularly have any complaints about him, just don't want to spend time with him unless necessary.

As the streets become more populated, we realize Obele took a different approach to greet Jasmin than Tilrade did. The streets are lined with lanterns instead of people. People are watching from the buildings, waving down at us. Colorful lanterns are hanging from ropes between the buildings. The streets look magical, with lanterns hanging, providing fresh pops of color against the brown and white buildings. I want to walk through after dark to see them all lit up. We soon arrive at the inn, this one more ornate than the fisherman's inn we stayed at in Tilrade. The walls have been painted with detailed images, and even the ceiling, with a large chandelier in the middle, has a design on it. Candles and sconces are lit around the room, creating a dim, romantic feeling.

The dinner is more subdued here, being calm and peaceful. I remember my manners this time, staying in my seat and asking for more when needed. I chat with Jasmin about our previous trips to Obele. She tells me these decorations are standard when they come through. I explain that I have never seen them but am highly impressed. She laughs at me, pressing a kiss on my cheek. The dinner passes uneventfully, and we soon retire for the evening.

In our room, Jasmin walks to the vanity to undress, but I catch her around the waist, stopping her.

"Let's go walk under the lanterns." She gives me a curious look but then agrees. We inform the guards where we are going. One of them follows us, getting another two guards to go with us and walk ahead of us. It feels like overkill, but I don't let it bother me.

We walk down the street together, holding hands as we stare at the lanterns. The dark skies make the lanterns stand out more. The colorful covers cast dim shades of colored light over the streets. With everyone in their own homes, the streets are mostly empty, allowing us some sense of privacy, despite the guards still nearby. We approach an area where all the building lights are off, only the lanterns lighting the way. I stop walking, pulling Jasmin into my arms and holding her against my chest. I have her hand as if we were dancing, placing my other hand gently on her back. She rests her cheek against my chest, and we softly sway. The only sounds are crickets chirping and the distant sounds of people going about everyday life. We rock back and forth slowly, enjoying the quiet, magical atmosphere created for us. I kiss her gently, enthralled with this evening.

We return to our room, not wanting to keep the guards out too late. There are only a few on a rotating schedule. Our walk forced one of them to come off his break to escort us. Even our room has a magical mood, with colorful shades around the sconces and intricate paintings on the wall.

We spend the next day in one of the theaters, allowing villagers to visit us. While the experience of being on stage is novel, it quickly fades to become redundant. The day is long, just as it was in Tilrade. I manage to not look terribly bored, but my ability isn't as refined as Jasmin's. By the end of the day, I am just ready to go to bed. The next day, we tour the merchant district on foot. I tell Jasmin I would like to return in the summer when the weather is warmer, and we can spend a few days exploring every booth and vendor. We each buy a couple of small trinkets, but it is soon time to mount our horses and ride to Arkaley. Excitement and nervousness course through my body. The day I spent in Arkaley previously, I wasn't on display the way I will be this time. Word has spread through the village of my new position by now. I am anxious to see how everyone reacts.

Chapter 37

JASMIN

Watching Clem during this tour has been more fascinating than I expected it to be. He is impressed with everything, so easily swept away with novelty, then so quickly dropped into boredom. He is trying so hard, though. I love him even more for his efforts. I have never been out after dark under the lanterns in Obele. They always have the lanterns out when we visit, but I have never been allowed to leave my room once the lights are out. I'm so glad Clem suggested it. It was enchanting.

We are riding into Arkaley now. I am most nervous about this trip. I haven't been to the city center since before the curse. After things with Jackson went sour, I stayed on the outskirts of the town, meeting families and courtiers there instead of traveling in. My guards were always alerted to keep Jackson away, but I never knew for sure that he wouldn't show up. All of the guards have been told he is not allowed to visit, but there isn't a great way to ensure that with the sheer number of people in the town. My guards don't know who Jackson is or what he looks like. He has connections within Arkaley that could get him close to me if he wanted. I don't know if he wants to, and can only hope he has no interest in seeing me after all of these years.

The ride between Obele and Arkaley is flat. Plains stretch between the two cities. Some of the land is farmed, some is left in its natural state due to unusable terrain for farming. During the summer, the grass grows tall, with flowers popping up in random bunches. This early in the spring, though, the grass is short, just beginning to grow in patches. We spot a few deer frolicking through the fields, but for the most part, the ride is unassuming.

We stop just outside of the city, taking a short break before we enter for the procession. Lord David is waiting for us there. He walks over to me and Clem, who is stretching beside me. David greets us, discussing some of the preparations within the city.

"I have informed Jackson he is not allowed to visit tomorrow...." David begins.

"Jackson?" Clem's response is startled.

"...But I am concerned he will try to come in. He was friends with Clem before the edict."

"Friend is a strong word. Even acquaintance is strong for what he was to me. I'll kill him if he shows up." He speaks so casually; I almost miss his threat. I gasp, dragging him away from Lord David.

"I know how you feel about Jackson; trust me, I feel the same way." Clem seethes as he says his name. "But you can't make threats like that now. You have some privilege as a fated partner, but we are not married, and I can only do so much to keep the Lords from condemning you to the dungeons. In theory, you can still break the curse from there." He huffs, closing his arms over his chest.

"I won't stand by quietly if he comes in." I sigh, nodding in defeat. I can only do so much to stop Clem when he sets his mind on something. Erik calls out a five-minute warning before we are to ride again. I leave Clem, walking over to chat with Erik.

"You are aware of the Jackson situation? Correct?" He nods yes. "Okay, Clem is particularly sensitive about this subject, only learning about it recently. Can you stay with us tomorrow in case Jackson does show up? I'm afraid Clem will do something stupid."

"Of course, my Queen." Erik places his hand on his chest, nodding in respect. I thank him, but before I walk away, he asks, "What did Jackson do? We were only told there is a situation." I sigh, not wanting to tell him everything, not wanting to relive any of it, not having the time to tell him the story.

"He hurt me a long time ago. A lot of what he did is linked to the curse, and Clem knows about it." I pause, considering whether to explain how Clem saw it but decide against it. That is too much to explain. I shake my head to clear it, offering a small smile to Erik instead. He nods, accepting my short response. We walk our separate ways to mount our horses and ride on them. Before I climb on Vesper, I find Clem wrapping my arms around him. I need his comfort to settle my memories of the past. I kiss him deeply, letting his taste wash away the discomfort of that situation.

"Hey, love birds!" Erik yells at us. "Time to move!"

We both chuckle as we mount our horses and fall in line. No one has said anything about activities in the bedroom. The guards never would, being sworn to secrecy. Kian usually makes a couple of comments, and Tomas has been known to say things, but no one has on this trip. I am glad we let Emmeline remain at the castle. While we have managed to mostly be on time without her, it has been nice to not have anyone yell at us while we are fucking.

Arkaley is situated in the foothills of a small mountain range. The city itself was built on the land in front of the foothills. Flat farmland stretches far on the southwestern side of the town. Across the north and to the east of Arkaley is the Beinn Mountains. The backdrop of the mountains is stunning. For as plain as the flat road is between Obele and Arkaley, the city is absolutely breathtaking. As we near it, I tell Clem this is one of my favorite views in the kingdom. The stark rise of the snowcapped mountains against the flat expanse of plains, with the small village resting in between, is something I have always loved seeing.

He smiles, watching the mountains grow taller as we enter the city. The roads here have been lined with flowers in pots on the sides of the street. It's beautiful to see all of the colorful flowers in bloom. This is also an effective crowd control technique, as people are made to stand behind them. We both wave to the crowd,

Clem recognizing more people in his home village. We ride through the city center, arriving at a quaint inn. While it is quiet, like the inn we stayed at in Obele, it is more casual, like the fisherman's inn from Tilrade. The cream-colored walls are accented with dark wood beams for decoration and structural support. Inside the inn, we find Ada and Claire waiting for us, along with several prominent families from the village. Thankfully, despite the appearance of his parents and other siblings, Jackson is not present.

We sit at the head of the table, like the other times. This time, Ada and Claire sit beside Clem while Kian and Erik are on my side. The dinner is warm and smells so inviting. Arkaley has never been particularly extravagant, usually maintaining a lower-class feel. This trip feels different, though. It isn't lavish, but it feels homely. It feels like we are family instead of royalty. Maybe that is because Clem's actual family is here. Typically there are other families near us, but today, I have people that I can consider family that live here. Butterflies flutter through my stomach as the feeling of being loved spreads through my body. Clem is speaking with his mother, who is actively ignoring Claire, who is asking decidedly inappropriate questions. Tears sting my eyes as I'm overwhelmed with a sense of belonging. I grab Clem's hand, squeezing it to calm my rising emotions. He places his other hand over mine as he finishes his sentence to his mother. He turns to look at me, and I offer a warm smile. He seems confused, noticing my flushed cheeks and teary eyes. I lean over to him, whispering as he moves closer.

"I love you."

He kisses my cheek, "I love you, too."

The night passes quickly, unlike in the previous villages, and we soon retire to our room. He steps into the small wash closet to clean up before we go to bed. He is telling me about something Claire had to say while he was in there. I quickly strip out of my clothes and lay back on the bed, waiting for him. He stops speaking mid-sentence when he sees me spread for him. A devilish grin spreads on his face as he rushes toward me, diving between my legs. His arms hook around my thighs as his tongue dives deep into my needy cunt. I tip my head back, putting my weight back on my arms.

"Yes, Clem. Taste me. Claim me. Love me."

His tongue works in a vicious pattern, thrusting, licking, and sucking my clit. I was already desperate for him, so I won't last long under his ministrations. He slides two fingers inside me, searching and caressing the spot that always sets me off. I cry out, not being able to contain my voice tonight. Knowing these inns aren't as thoroughly constructed as the castle, I try to control my volume so as not to alert everyone to what we are doing. I have no such restraint tonight as my first orgasm tears through my body.

Before my body calms, Clem quickly strips his clothes off. Then he slams deep inside my still throbbing pussy. I grab his shoulders, digging my nails into his flesh as he pounds deep inside me.

"Yes, tell all of Arkaley how you come for me." His words twist my insides.

"Let them hear how much of a slut their Queen is." I cry out again, pulling his chest against mine. His brutal pace and harsh words slash through the warm, loving feeling I had from earlier, exposing a euphoric gush of satisfaction. His lips are on my jaw, kissing, nipping, sucking. I need more pain; I need to peel back more of the warmth to expose my aching core of lust.

"Bite me," I tell him.

He leans back, still thrusting deep inside me, searching my face. He only considers for a moment before his teeth sink into my neck, near the almost invisible prior teeth marks. The pain lances through my body, ripping the final piece away as my body shivers in orgasm. Explosions burst through my vision. I can feel myself screaming, but my ears feel like they are covered with water. Clem jerks erratically, releasing deep in my tightening pussy. He supports most of his body weight on his elbows, but enough presses on me to send calming waves through my writhing muscles. We both breathe heavily, trying to return to a regular pattern. He finally slides off me, pulling out as his seed follows, dripping on my thighs. He stretches one arm behind his head while I curl into his side, his other arm wrapping around me. I snuggle in, ready to drift off to sleep, when I feel his voice rumbling in his chest.

"So, you did like the biting?" He teases, and I playfully smack his chest, but I did like it. So much.

The next morning at breakfast, Ada isn't there, so Erik and Kian return to their regular spots on either side. After we sit, Erik leans toward me, whispering loudly enough that we can hear, but other guests in the room won't be able to.

"Clem," he says, drawing all of our attention. "The thunder usually sounds on its own. You don't need to make Jasmin create it herself." I gasp, smacking his arm. Kian snickers on the other side of Clem, but Clem has a devious look in his eyes. I know he's about to say something crude, but I can't stop him now.

"Where's the fun in that?" That wasn't as terrible as it could have been. "I'm not going to deny the Queen what she asks for." Ah, there it is. My cheeks burn with embarrassment as I sigh, knowing there isn't much I can do to improve this situation. The three men around me laugh as I slather jam on my toasted bread.

"Keep laughing, and I'll lock you both in the stocks for the day." Clem leans over, kissing my ear, wrapping his arm around me in a side hug.

"Promise?" He whispers playfully before returning to his food. I don't feel bad for being as loud as I was last night. I thoroughly enjoyed the experience and would definitely do it again.

We soon make our way to the courtroom in the city center, taking our standard spots so people can visit. The day occurs like every other day. Congratulations, well wishes, and gifts. Clem knows more people and addresses some, though we don't have time to chat with anyone. He promises to plan an extended visit soon to reconnect with several people. He introduces some of his friends to me, hugging several throughout the day.

In the late afternoon, an odd lull in people coming through occurs. We are normally informed when the last guests enter, but we haven't been told anything, and it is too early in the afternoon for the end of the line. Two men burst through the doors with gusto, appearing to be the same age as us. I don't know the men but recognize them from previous visits. They hold positions in the city, some menial roles in the town duties. They step to the side, standing in front of the guards. The doors open again as Jackson struts into the room. Clem and I both rise from our seats. The guards step forward but are met with small weapons brandished by the men. I look to Erik, motioning for him to stand down for the moment. Is it too much to hope that this evening can pass without bloodshed?

"It's true, then? The whore princess is marrying the pauper." He stops a few feet away from us, chest puffed out. Erik's voice booms from his place by Clem's side.

"You are in the presence of the Queen. Your words are unacceptable and will be treated as treason if you continue." Jackson sizes Erik up, calculating his chances of winning against him. Despite what Jackson believes, he could never beat Erik in battle. The problem is, if we want to avoid bloodshed, Jackson has the upper hand at the moment. I can't promise I will avoid bloodshed for long, though.

"What do you want, Jackson? You were told not to show up." I remain firm, despite the rising anxiety in my chest.

"I had to see for myself that you chose someone like him over me."

"Of course, I chose someone like him, Jackson. Aside from your menial position that you don't do well, you offer nothing." His gaze focuses on mine, hatred coursing through his features. Clem takes a small step, trying to position himself in front of me. Jackson notices, eying Clem as he grabs my arm, trying to pull me behind him. I stay by his side, wanting to keep my sight on Jackson. Clem would block him entirely from my view with his broad shoulders.

"What does Clem offer that I don't? He's a field hand. He doesn't even have his own land." Jackson spits his last words. Clem's hand tightens around my arm. Every muscle in his body is tense. Every little detail of Clem crashes into my mind at once, everything that makes him better than Jackson. His beauty, his intelligence, his love of books, reading, and learning, his eagerness to please. Most importantly, his cock and sexual skills. I could say all of that, but Jackson would continue arguing. That isn't anything I want.

"You can leave now, Jackson. You have seen what you wanted." He considers his options, meeting the eyes of both men he came in with him.

"You're right. You two aren't married yet. There is still time for me." He jumps as if to grab me. I scream, dropping back near the chairs. I close my eyes, covering my head. Swords are drawn and start clashing. A fist crunching someone's face forces me to press my hands against my ears tighter. Hands grab my shoulders, dragging me backward. I scream, starting to kick, unsure who is grabbing me. I hear a voice that I recognize but can't make out the words. I open my eyes to see one of my guards pulling me. My feet find ground under me as I scrambled to escape Jackson. I glance back quickly, seeing the two men on the ground, bleeding from large gaping wounds. Jackson and Clem are in a fistfight as Erik comes up behind Jackson with his sword raised. The guard with me wraps his body around mine, blocking my view. A bloodcurdling scream rings out in the next moment as something lands hard on the ground. I am ushered into a small room off to the side of the room we were just in. Several other guards arrive, two taking a post by my side while the others rush to secure Clem and the rest of the building.

Within a few moments, Clem enters the room, and I run into his arms. He is covered with blood. My mind is frantic, trying to find the source of the blood.

"It's not mine, Jas." He whispers as I collapse into him, sobbing. He holds me tightly as several guards dart in and out of the room. Erik enters soon, telling me the building is secured and everyone else has been sent home. I take several deep breaths before I can respond. The mask of Queen slowly settles over me, and I ask where Jackson is and where Lord David is. Erik informs us Jackson has been apprehended and is being taken to the medical building. They found Lord David subdued in a broom closet near his position. I ask about the other two men and am informed they are now deceased. Realization dawns and I ask why Jackson needs medical attention. Erik smirks slightly, telling me Jackson no longer has a left arm. I nod, the words not fully sinking in. I look back over Clem, still covered in blood, face bruising.

"You bruise so easily." I sigh, running my finger lightly across his jawline. He chuckles, shaking his head at me. He looks to Erik.

"Can we go to the inn to bathe? Are we still allowed to visit my family tonight?" Something like relief settles inside as I realize he takes this role seriously. Erik nods, guiding us out of the room. We make it to the inn safely, stripping out of our clothes to bathe as soon as we are in the room. This room doesn't have a heated tub like my castle. We have to use buckets to get clean. I help Clem clean the blood away, finding he also has a bruised rib. I insist on having a healer come look at him. He tries to argue that it is just bruised but doesn't fight when I send for the healer. I slip into my leggings, pulling one of his long shirts over. I only packed the dresses with the split skirt, and now I regret not packing my own tops to wear. The healer comes in, thankfully ignoring my clothing choices. He informs that Clem's rib is just bruised and will take a few days to heal.

Clem offers to let me wear one of his vests to his mother's home. While it's tempting, I can't be seen in public like that. I put on a clean dress reluctantly as we finally leave. More guards are traveling with us, though I suspect we won't have any further problems. Erik and Kian join us. I ask Erik how he is doing, and he assures me he is fine. He asks about Clem, who tells him about the bruised rib in addition to the bruise blooming on his face.

We all arrive at Clem's home. The guards check the outside of the house, one taking a post at each door. One enters before us, checking the home for any potential threat. He soon informs us we can enter. Erik tells them he will stay by my side tonight, so the other guards can stay outside, offering some privacy to Clem's family. When we finally enter, his mother is shaken, unfamiliar with this process. I have been through this before, but not in a long time. Then Ada sees Clem's face, shrieking at him. He calms her down, guiding her into the kitchen to explain everything. Claire follows, and no one stops her. I sit in the living room with Kian and Erik, none of us talking. Soon, Clem and his mother return to the living room. Ada is pale as she serves drinks to everyone. I try to get her to sit, but she continues fretting around. Clem sits next to me, pulling me closer.

"She gets like this when she's nervous. It's best to just let her be for a bit." I relax back against him, not sure what else to do. Eventually, Ada settles down with us. We recount the story again, assuring her our guards are handling the situation. She questions how it could happen. I tell her of the pull Jackson has within the community. She suddenly remembers she was preparing dinner and rushes back into the kitchen. We all go with her, assisting in the final preparations. Once we all sit down to eat, we relax, and the evening is enjoyable. Ada and Claire question

Kian about his magic. Clem stays by my side, constantly touching me, both of us needing reassurance from the other.

The following day, our plans are adjusted. We decide to stay for the trial of Jackson. Aside from Oscar, there haven't been many severe cases of crimes in the past few years. Kian rides ahead to alert Lord Alwyn and his grandmother of the changes and sends riders to Vadried and the castle to notify them too. I send one of my guards with him, glad to spare one for his safety.

The courtroom is filled with people from the city. They have already determined Jackson worked with the other two men and no others. They found notes in his home. When the guards entered his home, his wife packed her bags and took her children to leave the village. She was originally from Tilrade and is returning to her parents. I'm glad she won't be here today.

The trial is quick. Lord David oversees the court this time since it is his district. I sit to the side with Clem, watching the process. Jackson is accused of treason, conspiracy, and solicitation of crimes. He doesn't respond when asked if he is guilty. That is accepted as a guilty plea. He is sentenced to death on the gallows. The laws in our kingdom have always been clear on the punishment for treason. I don't take death as a punishment lightly, but I haven't put forth the effort to change them either. No one in Sweet Briar has been accused of treason in my lifetime.

I sigh a breath of relief when it is over. Knowing I won't need to worry about Jackson anymore is comforting. The hanging is scheduled for sunset tomorrow night, but I plan to be long gone. I don't want to watch that; there has been enough violence at his hand for my taste. I refuse to give Jackson any more of me. He has already taken so much, and I won't stay to see his end. He can face that alone.

We set out the next day for Greynon. It will be a longer trip, requiring us to cross the mountains. The ride is long and hard, and many are subdued after the past few days' events. A large fire is built when we set up camp for the night. Rabbits are cooked over a spit for dinner. A cask of ale has been sent with us, though no one has more than two drinks. Someone starts playing a flute while another sings along. Erik stays close to Clem and me as we snuggle by the downed tree we sit on. Spirits rise slightly with the music, sending everyone to bed in a better mood. I maintain contact with Clem throughout the evening, not wanting to be away from him.

The long journey continues the next morning, not arriving in Greynon until almost dusk. Kian meets us at the edge of town, guiding us through. Lord Alwyn and his grandmother are meeting us at the inn. The roads through town have been lit with torches, and all other lights have been put out. It doesn't feel as magical as the lanterns in Obele because the torches are so bright. It does have a serene feel. The inn is built into the side of a mountain, windows poking through the stone, hidden behind green pine trees. It would be easy to overlook during the day. I haven't stayed at this particular inn before and wonder if it belongs to the witches.

Lord Alwyn stands beside Maud, Kian's grandmother, the leader of the second-largest coven of witches, when we reach the front of the inn. Alwyn steps like he will greet us first, but Maud moves faster, extending her arms out toward me. Several of my guards reach for their swords, taking a defensive stance. Kian winces behind his grandmother as she withdraws quickly. I motion the guards to settle and take a step toward her.

"Matron Maud, please excuse my guards. I trust Kian has informed you of the events in Arkaley. We are all a bit on edge after our visit with them." She nods in understanding, apologizing for her error. I wave my hand, dismissing her apology. She leads us inside, explaining this is the common ground between all the witches. They wanted me to feel as welcome as I made them feel when they visited the castle. She informs me the witches have never been allowed to sit so close during a coronation, let alone have one of their own perform the ceremonies. We chat for several minutes about the witches' status within the kingdom as she guides us into the dining area. Lord Alwyn walks defeatedly behind me. Clem walks next to him, looking fit for his role as King, in stark contrast to Lord Alwyn.

They have made several of their preferred dishes for dinner, unlike traditional dishes cooked within the kingdom. Several are made with magic, creating entirely different flavors and textures. Kian savors these, obviously missing them in the months he has been away. Other dishes are made in more traditional methods but use different spices common among the witches in their terrain. We spend the evening discussing their magic but don't go into any diplomatic changes. That will come later.

We spend the next morning meeting many of the heads of the covens. Unfortunately, we don't have time to meet them all. I wish there was more time, but we promise to return soon to visit for longer. At this rate, we will return to the castle for the wedding, only to leave again to visit more places within the kingdom. I feel some regret over remaining in the castle these past nine years instead of visiting these places. I could have been establishing my own relations with them. I can't change that now.

In the afternoon, we travel to the valley beneath the mountains, the non-magical areas of Greynon, to visit with those families. I try to question Lord Alwyn about why they are so segregated, but he never gives me a straight answer, deflecting or ignoring my comments altogether. The afternoon passes slowly but uneventfully. On our last morning in Greynon, the witches perform for us. Kian tells me it is a chant of good wishes, not the same as the curse or a spell. They are beseeching their gods and magic to follow and protect me. I tear up during the spell, feeling so loved and cared for by these people that have been treated so poorly by my predecessors.

After the performance, we mount our horses again, setting out for Vadried, our final stop before returning to the kingdom. With Kian back with us again, the trip is more enjoyable than the stretch into Greynon. He entertains us with stories of spells gone wrong and some of their folklore. At the base of the mountains, we camp again for the night. The next day we ride into Vadried. Lord Thurston meets us at the edge, assuring us our visit will be as uneventful.

The road through Vadried is lined with ropes containing stained glass pieces. The light fragments through, sending color dancing along us and the streets. I watch in quiet wander as color glitters around our view. People stand behind the ropes, bowing or curtseying as we pass by, unlike previous villages where they cheered and clapped. At first, I enjoy the silence, but I soon realize I prefer the applause.

Our inn is lavish, made from stone with intricate carvings and designs. The dinner is uneventful, and I struggle to maintain my character. We retire to our rooms a bit earlier than expected, unable to stay awake any longer. Clem wakes me the following day by treating himself to my pussy. That boosts my spirits, only for them to be crushed again by spending an entire day visiting people. I don't know how my parents managed this as often as they did. I'm also very thankful there are only five villages in my kingdom. I could not handle another one.

We tour Vadried the next day. Despite Lord Thurston's attempts to show us how wonderful it is, Clem and I are ready to return to the castle. Vadried is a beautiful city with lovely architecture. I love visiting when I can roam and explore everything they offer. However, I am ready to return home, bathe in my giant heated tub, and sleep for four days.

We finally get back on the road to the castle. It takes everything not to rush through the group and gallop all the way home. When the castle is finally in sight, Erik, Clem, and I race our horses down, pushing them at full speed until we reach the stables. The horses seem to appreciate the extra push, huffing, and trotting around the stables when we dismount.

I check in with Erik, ensuring we can be alone now. When he gives me a knowing grin, I grab Clem, pulling him toward my room. Emmeline has it cleaned, with Finn somewhere else. As I walk through the room, I strip out of my clothes, leaving them scattered everywhere. I enter the washroom, climb into the tub, and sink to my chin. I sigh heavily as Clem walks in behind me, stacking the clothes he picked up on a table. He leans against the door frame, watching me as I relax in the warm water.

"Aren't you coming to join me?"

"Of course."

He shrugs his clothes off, enters the bath, and glides to me. He presses several kisses to my cheek, then whispers against my ear.

"Do you realize we will be married in four days?"

Chapter 38

CLEM

Emmeline told me I can't stay with Jasmin tonight. Apparently, we will have a better marriage if we spend the last night before the ceremony apart. I tried to argue that we are fated and our marriage would be fine, but she isn't listening to reason. Worse, she convinced Jasmin of the same thing, and Jasmin is going along with it. So tonight, I am bunking with Bea because now all the rooms in the castle are full. Emmeline doesn't trust me to stay in any rooms down Jasmin's hall, which is fair. Accepting defeat, I told Emmeline to disappear until lunch. She didn't ask questions and hasn't shown up this morning.

Jasmin is still sleeping soundly next to me. My mind rolls through all the things I can do to her body. I've been forbidden from biting her where it can be seen. I can't leave any other marks on her arms or back either. I swear to all holy gods out there, she won't leave this room for a week after the wedding and will need a full-body suit when she finally does. For now, I need something that will relax her for the next day until I can get to her body again. My eyes scan her, mostly covered by the sheet, unable to decide what to do first. An idea strikes, and I leave the bed, grabbing the things I'll need.

I bring my items back, carefully pulling the sheets off the bed entirely. I don't want her to wake up just yet. I tie each wrist to the corner posts lightly. Then each foot to the opposite corners. She is spread out for me, her taut skin so beautiful. I settle on the bed beside her, sucking her nipple into my mouth. I swirl the bud in my lips, letting it pop out of my mouth before reaching the other breast. A soft moan escapes her lips as her head rolls, waking up. Her hands jerk against the restraints, eyes popping open to capture the scene. I give her a devious grin.

"If you're kicking me out for the next day, I'm gonna make you pay," I growl at her. She grins, closing her eyes, savoring my breath against her breast. I kiss her breasts, then up and down each arm, peppering light kisses across her skin, blowing warm air over sensitive areas. Tiny bumps appear on her flesh, reacting to the delicate sensation. My lips find her neck, then I leave a trail of kisses straight down her chest, across her stomach, stopping at the apex of her thighs. I nuzzle my nose in the brown hair between her hips. I blow against her sensitive core, teasing her lightly. She groans, wiggling her hips, trying to get closer to my face. I give her what she wants, licking her slit before circling the bundle of nerves. She moans louder as I slide a finger inside her, fucking her gently while sucking on her clit. I add another as she writhes under me. Her arms jerk on the bed frame. She loves running her fingers through my hair when I'm tonguing her. Preventing her from doing that always makes her more frustrated, but it also makes for more intense orgasms. Her breathing quickens as her cunt begins to clench around me. She's on the cusp of her orgasm. So I pull my fingers out of her and sit up, leaving her unsated. She looks at me in disbelief, so hurt and sad. My wicked smirk returns.

"I told you you're going to pay."

Her eyes go wide as her body calms down. I lean over her, pressing my lips against hers, forcing my tongue into her mouth. She accepts me, juices from her covering my lips. My fingers enter her again, thrusting at a more unforgiving pace. I rub the heel of my palm against her clit, driving her right to the edge again. Then I slowly remove my fingers and bring them to my lips. She watches, biting her lip, as I savor the taste of her on my fingers. Her hips jerk with need. My thumb tugs her lip out of her mouth.

"We can't be leaving any marks on you, Queen."

I drag my finger over the top of her core. I don't slip inside or rub her clit; I just slide my finger across her. She cries out, letting me know she is exactly where I want her. She's desperate, needy, and frustrated. I grab the other items I brought, oil and the magic fun ball. I have other sashes in case she needs to be blindfolded or gagged, but I don't think she'll need those this morning. I modified the magic fun ball without telling her. I checked with Kian to be sure it would still work because I didn't want to ruin the item. I put a hole in the middle using a small chisel and tied a strong, thin rope through it. This will allow me to put the rounded cylinder inside her without worrying about losing it.

I loosen the straps on the foot of the bed, allowing her to lift her legs just enough. Then I crawl between her, settling on my stomach, face in her cunt. I press a quick kiss to her pussy, causing her to flinch with desire. She lifts her head, watching me. I probably should have given her a pillow, but I won't be down here for too long. I adjust her heels, propping her knees over my shoulder. I grab her ass cheeks, pulling them apart to access the hole I want. I swirl my tongue in her cunt, then slide down and circle her other hole. She moans, jerking her hands again. I love the sound of restraints pulling on the bed frame. I rotate my tongue around her tight opening several times before pulling back to get the oil out.

I rub oil over the rounded cylinder, tapping it to turn it on. Then I press it against her ass. She gasps, clenching, then relaxing her hole. I slide my thumb to her clit, circling it around as I slowly press the item inside her, then pull it back. I push it in a bit deeper, swirling it around. Her orgasm is growing again, her core clenching, desperate for something to fill it. I press a kiss to her before removing my thumb from her clit. I leave the toy in place as she begins to cry out.

"No, no, no. Oh gods, please."

"Look at this dirty slut, begging to be fucked." I chuckle, blowing into her cunt.

"Yes, please. Fuck me, Clem, please." I hum, considering her request.

"No," I say, tapping the item to increase the speed, then pressing it all the way inside her. I leave the knotted rope hanging out of her to access later. She whines, hips undulating, as the magic fun ball vibrates inside her ass. I slide to the end of the bed, tightening the sashes around her ankles. Her legs stretch flat, changing the position of the vibration inside her. This is apparent by how her eyes suddenly go wide then roll back in her head. I debate whether I have teased her enough yet, but my cock jerks, hard and leaking, ready to be buried inside her. Unable to help myself, I stroke my dick slowly, watching her writhe on the bed, ready for an orgasm. Ready for me to fuck her. I'm ready for that too.

I climb back on the bed, crawling to notch my cock in her soaking pussy. She cries out hopelessly, worried I'll deny her again. I place kisses across her chest.

"Please, Clem. I can't wait. I need you." My cock tries to jump inside her at her words.

"Is that so, Queen? Tell me what you need."

"I need you to fuck me." She whines, trying to push her hips over my cock, but I lean back, only letting the tip press against her entrance.

"You want my dick inside you, Jas? Where do you want it?" She groans, pressing her breasts against my face, seeking any pleasure she can.

"I want your dick in my pussy, Clematis! I need you to let me have an orgasm. Please!" She sobs several times. Hearing my full name on her lips sends a wave of uncontrollable pleasure through my own body. I shove my dick inside her, sinking down to the hilt. She groans, rubbing her body against mine now that I am inside her.

"Fuck," I moan against her neck, feeling the item in her ass vibrating against the sensitive underside of my cock. I begin to pound inside her, setting an unforgiving pace. With only a few thrusts, her orgasm rips through her body, causing her pussy to clench tightly. It's nearly enough to send me over the edge, but I'm not going that easily. I continue pounding in her as she rides wave after wave of endless orgasms. As soon as one ends, she begins panting with another. I slip my hand between our bodies, circling her clit with the tip of my fingers. A gush of fluid coats my dick, dripping onto the bed from her core. I continue pounding inside her, her walls clenching and releasing constantly.

"No, no. Move your hand. It hurts." She gasps, twisting her head from side to side. I grin, doing as she asks.

"One more orgasm, Jasmin. Come with me." She groans as I slam into her. I kiss her neck, nibbling but resisting the urge to bite her as the familiar tingling runs down my spine, tightening my balls.

"Bite me, please." She begs. That's all it takes. My willpower is gone as my teeth clamp down over her neck. My cock releases angry spurts of my fluids deep inside her. Her body flexes against mine, and I growl at the sensation. She draws a long, stuttering breath before she finally relaxes. I release her neck, breathing heavily as my cock softens in her, the vibrating item still going inside.

"Turn it off, please."

Reluctantly, I climb off her, releasing the ankle sashes. I press her legs up, carefully removing and tapping the item to stop it. I leave it on the bed, moving to undo her wrists. I grab a blanket, pulling it over us as I lie down next to her, wrapping her in my arms. My hands rub down her sides, soothing her. Her face is pressed against my chest, hands tucked between our chests. I kiss her forehead, looking down at her to realize she is crying. That isn't the right reaction.

"Jas, what's wrong?"

I don't want to let her go, but I don't know what to do either.

"Did I hurt you?"

She shakes her head against my chest, using her fingers to swipe away some tears.

"Why are you crying?"

She chuckles against me, shrugging on her shoulder.

"I don't really know. That was amazing." She sniffles, scooting up to press her lips against mine. I tighten my arms around her, holding her close as she sniffles. I hold her for several minutes, afraid to let her go. "I don't know how you're going to top our wedding night." Her voice is soft and warm against my chest.

"Me? How are you going to top that on our wedding night?" I tease. She laughs in my arms. We stay wrapped together for another hour before Emmeline starts banging on the door. At least I got that time with her.

It's finally time for the wedding. Despite my nervousness, I have never been more optimistic about anything. I never expected to come out here and fall in love with Jasmin, let alone marry her. We have been through a lot together in several months, but I wouldn't change any of it. It got us to this point, and this is where I am meant to be.

The throne room has been decorated for the wedding. Bouquets of white flowers are hung on all the walls with light blue material draped between each one. A white carpet has been laid down in the center of the room for Jasmin to walk down. The early afternoon sun shines through the windows, casting a bright glow over everyone in the room. All the villagers are wearing their finest clothing. A quartet plays music in the corner of the room. The whole room feels enchanted, glowing, and bright.

The back doors open as Claire walks in. She is wearing a light blue floor-length gown that matches the drapery. She carries a woven basket containing flower petals and small ribbons. Sunette spent all night plucking petals from the flowers she has grown. It almost seemed wasteful, but seeing Claire spread them across the floor before Jasmin walks through feels surreal. The witches contributed the bits of ribbon. Each one contains a wish: long life, happiness, wealth, and prosperity. Every piece is individually blessed by a witch then added to the basket with the petals. The ribbons and petals glow under the magic and sunlight, creating a path of shimmering light down the center.

Kian is officiating this ceremony also. I didn't want to ask him initially since he also loved her. Jasmin swore that wouldn't be an issue, and she wanted it to be him. We asked him together, and he was excited to be given the opportunity. He stands behind me now in black pants and a black tunic. Over his head is the emblem of the kingdom on a banner. His dark hair is pressed back, giving him a godlike appearance. Claire reaches the dais, dropping the last few petals and ribbons at my feet. I bend down, kissing her cheek, then she walks over to sit with our mother. Ma is already wiping tears from her eyes. She was given a new dress for this ceremony but chose a simple style, not wanting to accept anything 'too fancy.'

The seamster made a suit for me in the style of what previous princes of the kingdom have worn. I have light-colored trousers with a blue panel on the side. My tunic is long and fits perfectly across my shoulders and chest. The kingdom's emblem is stitched into the chest above my heart. My hair is loose, despite several people wanting it pulled back. Jasmin prefers when I leave it loose, and she will get what she wants.

Claire sits between Ma and Bea, with Erik sitting next to Bea. They are trying to be inconspicuous, but I can tell from here he has his hand wrapped around hers. Beside them are Sunette and her family. Tomas sitting next to Zander, though they aren't touching. The Lords and prominent families are in their spots, along with the witches. The rest of the hall is also crowded. As many people attend the wedding as they did for the coronation. There are now more guards in preparation for the curse to end and the barrier to disappear.

The doors open once more as the quartet plays the processional song for Jasmin. Everyone in the crowd rises, growing silent as Jasmin enters the doorway. The afternoon sun shines through doors. At first, the side of Jasmin is basked in sunlight, but when she steps into the room, the sunlight behind her makes it impossible to see her. She slowly begins to walk down the aisle. She is dark because of the sunlight behind her, and I cannot see her face or dress yet. Small flashing lights begin to flicker around the entire room, drawing my attention briefly. I look back to Kian, wondering if it's his magic. He stands with his hands folded together at his waist. He notices my look and gives a faint shake of his head, pointing one of his fingers at me. These shimmers of light are the curse lifting. This is much better than the thunder we have been receiving.

I turn my attention back to Jasmin as the doors close behind her. I can finally see her. She wears a long cream-colored dress with a full skirt. The bodice is fitted with long trumpet sleeves hanging in front of her. The dress was originally cut low, meant to display the necklace I bought for her. With our recent activities, they had to add a high collar to the dress to cover her neck. The necklace lies on top of it. She wears a smaller crown, similar to the one she wore for the coronation, but more functional, her hair curled and falling softly against her shoulders. The darkness of her hair clashes brilliantly with the light color of her dress. As she moves closer, I realize she has a bouquet of white jasmine with green leaves from the greenhouse.

She is easily the most beautiful person I have ever seen. She once referred to me as beautiful, but I am nothing compared to her. She carries herself with grace and confidence. I can't tear my eyes away from her as she approaches me, not that I want to anyway. She stops in front of me, and I am unable to breathe. This is the part where I take her hand to escort her up the stairs to where Kian waits, but I can't move. I can't think. I want to touch her. I want to hold her. But my body is frozen with inaction. A smile spreads across her face as my body slowly begins to function again. My hands reach for her arms, grasping both slowly. I lean down, needing to kiss her. Her smile deepens as she realizes my intent.

"We're not to that part yet."

Her voice is so soft and so quiet it almost doesn't register. My brain catches up just before I reach her lips, and I turn to the side, kissing her cheek with the scar. My eyes close, savoring the warmth of her cheek under my skin.

"I love you," I whisper against her as I pull back, body returning to reality. Her eyes are still on me, so filled with love and joy. We finally turn, climbing the few glittering steps. We stop in front of Kian, turning to face him for the ceremony. He has something like adoration shining in his eyes as he looks between us. It also takes him a moment to remember his own role. A huge grin spreads across my face, a quiet chuckle escaping, realizing I am not the only one swept away by the powerful presence of Jasmin.

Kian welcomes everyone to the union of Jasmin and me. He talks for a minute about true love, then shares his intuition that we were made for each other. Instead of telling the painful story of Oscar at the autumn solstice or the funny story of how she fooled me into believing she wasn't the Princess for a week, he tells about the first time the thunder occurred. He explains the winter solstice celebration, where everyone was in this room waiting for Jasmin to walk in. I had been lucky enough to be the one to escort her in. As soon as the doors opened, everyone was looking at Jasmin, but he noticed the way I looked at her. Kian said that was the moment he realized what she meant to me.

I glance over at Jasmin, a small tear streaks down her face. I reach out and grab her hand, squeezing her fingers in mine. Kian pauses, noticing the intimate moment between us and letting it shine through the ceremony. More of the small bursting lights explode throughout the room, garnishing a wave of awestruck noises from the crowd. Kian begins speaking again, continuing on with the ceremony. We soon turn toward each other. Emmeline sneaks up, grabbing the bouquet from Jasmin. We take each other's hands as Kian prepares to read our vows.

Before he can start, the doors at the end of the room bang open. Several gasps and shrieks sound at the sudden noise. Light fills the hallway, blocking whoever just bursts through the doors. A person with a dark halo around her head rushes through the room, the guards not quick enough to catch her. She stops at the end of the rows of seats, close enough to see her. A hush falls over the entire room, everyone anxious over this interruption. She is a dark-skinned woman with dark kinky hair standing straight out from her head, creating a halo effect. She wears only a thin, white shift., her dark skin nearly visible beneath it. Her eyes are wild but glued on Jasmin. In the corner of my vision, I notice Sunette and Zander jump from their seats.

In the woman's hand, she holds the dark flower from Jasmin's nursery. It has a brighter glow around it than I have ever seen. Light shimmers and flickers between Jasmin, me, and where this woman is standing. She is panting, but her gaze is focused solely on Jasmin. Jasmin takes a single step toward her as the woman speaks.

"I'm still here." She cries. "I'm still here."

"Dahlia."

To find out what happens next, follow this link

aprilgaisford.com

to get Fate and Lightning.

Also by

SWEET BRIAR SERIES

A completed why choose fairy tale series about a cursed princess who must find her true love. Spicy, queer, and magical.

Curses and Thunder

Fate and Lightning

HIDDEN GODS SERIES

A series of dark romance ranging from sapphic mafia, FFM motorcycle club, MMF mafia, and more.

Corrupt Goddess

Hidden God

Secret God (coming 2025)

ROOMMATES

A queer why choose romance about a guy down on his lucktaken in by three roommates.

About the author

APRIL GAISFORD

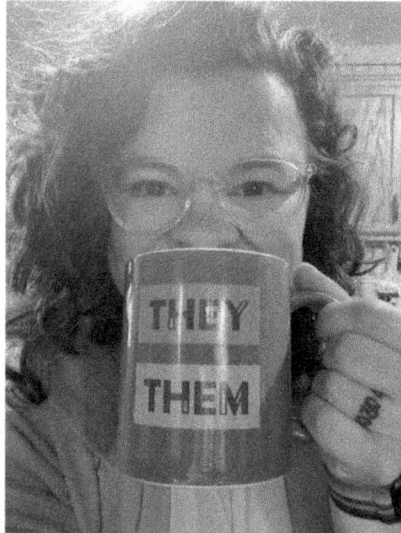

April is a non-binary parent living in Minnesota. They are an avid reader, with a special interest in smut. They love collecting random things, such as coffee mugs, posters, graphic tees, scrunchies, and more. They love long romantic trips around Target and buying new books to add to their emotional support pile.

Acknowledgements

A huge thank you goes out to my readers! Everyone that has left reviews, comments, made posts, or told their friends, I owe it all to you! You give me the courage to keep going!

I have given so much to Sweet Briar Series. I could not have done it without my partner in crime. For reading my first draft (we don't talk about the three person hug) to hearing all my crazy ass ideas and putting up with the endless hours of tapping and clicking. I love you so much and hope this book will suffice as your birthday present this year. Because it's all I've been working on.

To my sisters from different misters. Even though you are turds and haven't read Curses, I still greatly value your opinions on all my random ass questions, graphics, and videos I have sent. I love you bunches.

And I can't forget my beta readers: Caitlin, Kandace, Nicole and Stella. I appreciate your reading and offering feedback to help get the best version of Curses out to the world. Your opinions are invaluable!